GW00493707

Palgrave Studies in the History of Subcultures and Popular Music

From 1940s zoot-suiters and hepcats through 1950s rock 'n' rollers, beatniks and Teddy boys; 1960s surfers, rude boys, mods, hippies and bikers; 1970s skinheads, soul boys, rastas, glam rockers, funksters and punks; on to the heavy metal, hip-hop, casual, goth, rave and clubber styles of the 1980s, 90s, noughties and beyond, distinctive blends of fashion and music have become a defining feature of the cultural landscape. The Subcultures Network series is international in scope and designed to explore the social and political implications of subcultural forms. Youth and subcultures will be located in their historical, socio-economic and cultural context; the motivations and meanings applied to the aesthetics, actions and manifestations of youth and subculture will be assessed. The objective is to facilitate a genuinely cross-disciplinary and transnational outlet for a burgeoning area of academic study.

More information about this series at
http://www.springer.com/series/14579

Ryan Shaffer

Music, Youth and International Links in Post-War British Fascism

The Transformation of Extremism

palgrave
macmillan

Ryan Shaffer
Washington
DC, USA

Palgrave Studies in the History of Subcultures and Popular Music
ISBN 978-3-319-59667-9 ISBN 978-3-319-59668-6 (eBook)
DOI 10.1007/978-3-319-59668-6

Library of Congress Control Number: 2017944093

Printed on acid-free paper

This Palgrave Macmillan imprint is published by Springer Nature
The registered company is Springer International Publishing AG
The registered company address is: Gewerbestrasse 11, 6330 Cham, Switzerland

Acknowledgements

This book has taken many different twists since I conducted my initial research. Initially, I planned to write a study about inter-war fascism and empire, but the project evolved to focus on early post-war fascism and eventually included contemporary British politics. I discovered that when studying the National Front (NF), it was necessary to discuss the British National Party and its more recent developments. This research was helped through that process by many scholars, including Kathleen Wilson, Michael Barnhart, Nigel Copsey, Geoff Eley, Cora Granata, Young-Sun Hong, Jeffrey Kaplan, Robert McLain, Graham Macklin, Joel Rosenthal, Wolf Schäfer, Pete Simi, Laichen Sun and Nancy Tomes. Additionally, my friends and family provided encouragement and help with editing, especially my parents and wife. My peers in the Department of History at Stony Brook University and the School of Criticism and Theory at Cornell University also offered advice and ideas that shaped the research, especially Adam Charboneau and Cristobal Espinoza-Zuñiga. Numerous librarians and archivists have provided valuable help in response to my inquiries, particularly Lizzie Richmond and Donna Sammis. I am also grateful to editors Emily Russell, Carmel Kennedy and Matthew Worley, as well as the manuscript reviewers, for their interest and help in the book's development.

All books are shaped by access to sources. Writing about political parties that are widely criticized, have little electoral success and have activists who are weary of outsiders posed unique problems. I am thankful to all the former NF and British National Party activists as well as their opponents who allowed me to interview them. They spoke at length, giving me insight into their experiences and views. I am grateful to all the people from across the political spectrum who answered my questions and provided details never published before. I thank Phil Andrews, George Ashcroft, Keith Axon, Bart (who did not want his last name published), Bill Baillie, John Bean, Carl Booth, Andrew Brons, George Burdi, Garry Bushell, Eddy Butler, Mark Cotterill, Richard Edmonds, Robert Edwards, Cheryl Glass, Warren Glass, Nick Griffin, Peter Hain, Patrick Harrington, David Hoffman, Tom Holmes, Gareth Hurley, Alistair Lewis, Andy McBride, Trevor Maxfield, Tom Metzger, Arno Michaels, Eddy Morrison, Joseph Pearce, Christian Picciolini, Nick Price, Peter Rushton, Simon Sheppard, Peter Swillen, Nick Toczek, Colin Todd, Keith Thompson, Tim Turner, Martin Webster and many more anonymous people who wished not to be publicly named. Some allowed me to interview them about their politics, while others provided documents, publications, music, recordings, photographs or tips about locating further sources. In some cases, it was the first time these people had been interviewed and opened their personal archives to a historian.

Contents

Abbreviations

AENM	Alliance of European Nationalist Movements
AFBNP	American Friends of the British National Party
AGM	Annual General Meeting
ANL	Anti-Nazi League
APF	Alliance for Peace and Freedom
B&H	Blood & Honour
BNP	British National Party
BUF	British Union of Fascists
C18	Combat 18
EEC	European Economic Community
EGM	Extraordinary General Meeting
EU	European Union
GLC	Greater London Council
GWR	Great White Records
ITP	International Third Position
LEL	League of Empire Loyalists
MEP	Member of European Parliament
MP	Member of Parliament
NAR	Nuclei Armati Rivoluzionari (Armed Revolutionary Nuclei)
NDF	National Democratic Front
NF	National Front
NFSG	National Front Support Group
NFTUA	National Front Trade Unionists Association
NPD	National Democratic Party of Germany
NSM	National Socialist Movement
NUJ	National Union of Journalists

NUR	National Union of Railwaymen
RAC	Rock Against Communism
RAR	Rock Against Racism
ROR	Rock-O-Rama Records
SHARP	Skinheads Against Racism and Prejudice
SWP	Socialist Workers Party
UKIP	United Kingdom Independence Party
UM	Union Movement
WAR	White Aryan Resistance
WNC	White Noise Club
YNF	Young National Front

CHAPTER 1

Introduction

British fascism transformed following the Second World War. With the defeat of Nazi Germany and Fascist Italy, fascists in the Allied countries attempted several new outreach methods to recruit supporters, revive their ideas and win broader backing. Though post-war British fascists failed to gain significant electoral support, they garnered headlines with their associations with violence, rebellious youth, radical proposals and international connections. The changes in fascist outreach followed a search for new ideas to inject energy into the movement. Music proved to be a successful fascist tool that generated revenue for political campaigns, attracted youth who joined the movement and developed communication with like-minded supporters in foreign countries. While the fascists mostly failed at the ballot box, skinhead music transformed the marginal fascist scene and gained an international audience willing to buy records and gather in the hundreds for concerts.

This book examines how fascism in Great Britain developed after the Second World War by focusing on the two largest fascist political parties, the National Front (NF) and the British National Party (BNP). It explains how important music was to finance and sustain membership, and how international links boosted morale during key moments. Specifically, this book argues that post-war fascism in Britain became increasingly transnational through communication and ideological exchanges with foreign radicals. It shows how one of the key mechanisms for the initial international connections between the extremists was youth culture and music. While fascism and youth culture are not

R. Shaffer, *Music, Youth and International Links in Post-War British Fascism*, Palgrave Studies in the History of Subcultures and Popular Music, DOI 10.1007/978-3-319-59668-6_1

new subjects, as evidenced by Nazi Germany's well-known Hitler Youth, British fascists successfully developed a brand of music that became synonymous with neo-Nazi music and became an international movement. Though it failed to turn this interest into sustained electoral victories, British neo-Nazi skinhead music communicated slogans, ideas and emotions to a worldwide audience in ways that it could not with political publications, broadcasts and campaigns.

Since the 1980s, radical teenagers throughout the world have associated with British fascist outreach by listening to a genre of music that was developed in England. From the racial violence on the streets of Dallas to Berlin marches, youth recited lyrics and themes that originated in London. This book explores how and why that happened by tracing the transnational aspects of British fascism and the radicals' search for new philosophies and outreach methods. Though skinheads and European fascists regularly cross borders now, this happened with far less frequency and with less uniformity prior to the injection of youth culture into fascist politics. The regular contact between foreign fascists has impacted international fascism by introducing new influences, such as Third Way ideas from Muammar Gaddafi, and helped forge common themes between people in disparate countries. Additionally, the British outreach developed closer transatlantic bonds between American and British radicals.

This book draws from interviews with extremists, rare publications and video recordings to explore the youth experience and international evolution of extremism. Over the course of several years, every effort was made to contact and speak with people who had leadership positions in fascist groups or were active in the organizations at some point. Ultimately, several dozen agreed to meet in person, with only a handful preferring to talk over the phone. For many of the interviewees, it was their first time speaking on the record. Former NF Directorate member Colin Todd, for example, was asked who had interviewed him before and replied that the police wanted to, "but I've always told them to piss off."[1] In other cases, people provided magazines and internal party documents, which are illegal to possess in European nations as they are classified as inciting hatred, contain banned fascist symbols or deny the Holocaust. In certain instances, while several fascists declined interview requests, some supplied papers and recordings. Other material was obtained from archives, such as the Modern Records Centre, the British Library, The National Archives and large private collections of people who amassed this material and provided it to be analyzed for the first time. Some of these collectors sympathized with extremism, others were just interested in the history, but a few acquired the material for their own research in order to criticize the groups.

This research offers new insight into the impact youth and music had in fostering links with foreign radicals and transforming fascism. The last major books about the National Front, such as Stan Taylor's and Nigel Fielding's works, were published in the early 1980s and failed to mention youth as one element of the party or mostly ignored the phenomenon. Taylor's work, published in 1982, was completed prior to the founding of the NF's record label and development of international groups.[2] Similarly, Fielding's 1981 sociological study examined the political beliefs of party members to understand what drives the organization and its members' "personal standards."[3] More recent scholarship on British fascism, however, has centered around the political history of the BNP and mostly looked at the history of the NF in light of the founding of the BNP. Nigel Copsey's research on the BNP probed the role of its founder, John Tyndall, in leading the NF to its peak electoral popularity and the BNP's quest for electoral legitimacy.[4] Roger Griffin's analysis of the NF and BNP argued that the reason "there is no public pressure for a British *Front National*, or for the introduction of the proportional representation necessary for it to win seats in parliament, is because it is tacitly understood that the instinct of most died-in-the-wool Tories once in government is to do everything in their power to stop immigration and impede the social advance of ethnic minorities."[5] Matthew Goodwin's study, which includes mostly anonymous interviews along with quantitative data, examined more recent developments of the BNP and also drew upon the NF's history to discuss the BNP's roots.[6] Similarly, there has been recent interest in looking at the BNP and violent Islamism to probe the meaning of "extremism" as well as threats to modern society.[7] This includes understanding the evolution of British fascism and the changing age of its members, wherein "support for the extreme right in contemporary Britain is concentrated among older respondents," which is the opposite of the NF's experience in the 1970s.[8]

These scholars are not the only ones to have examined the NF and BNP, as several academic dissertations and a number of journalistic accounts have appeared on this topic. Daniel Trilling, for instance, wrote a narrative about the BNP, drawing from several key figures involved in the party's transition from a hardline fascist group to a more populist anti-immigrant party.[9] In addition, Graham Macklin explored Oswald

Mosley's post-war political activism to show his failure to "recalibrate" British fascism by internationalizing it.[10] There have been many studies of inter-war British fascism, but Stephen Dorril examined Mosley's inter-war and post-war political projects, including financing received from Benito Mussolini and fractured fascist "internationals."[11] Furthermore, Jeffrey Kaplan and Leonard Weinberg have traced transatlantic fascist ties with attention to the Aryan Nations and National Socialist Liberation Front, but they do not explore the skinhead movement as a significant player in transnational fascism, linking figures and organizations together.[12] Indeed, missing from the scholarship are named interviewees and documentation from leading NF and British National Party activists that not only highlight youth and internationalism, but explain how instrumental young post-war radicals were in infusing new ideas and music into extremism at a time when politics was eclipsed by the New Right.

Building from the extensive scholarship, this book shows how music breathed new life into post-war British fascism, attracting youth and developing new connections. However, the NF lacked a coherent strategy and its older leadership even attempted to sideline the youth in the 1970s. The image of neo-Nazi skinheads harmed the local electoral efforts of the NF and the British National Party to the point where the people involved in the early music outreach efforts tried to completely divorce themselves from the image by the 1990s. Moreover, the British National Party's efforts to recruit youth proved highly unsuccessful in modern multicultural Britain because society had changed and the original appeal of the NF's 1970s demands for repatriation, for example, were even less feasible or appealing in the 2000s. That is, while society and politics had changed, British fascist political parties and their core principles did little to actually embrace wider contemporary issues that mattered to the average voter. Likewise, skinhead music from the 1980s no longer had the marginal appeal it once did, and British fascism's main audience consisted of older people who reflected on how different society was and saw the British National Party as offering the antidote to those changes. Nonetheless, the transnational links British fascism developed during the 1980s continued to play an important role, as they served as a key network where British extremists could find like-minded people.

Sources

This research is drawn from primary sources obtained from activists involved in the fascist movement. The sources for this research include author interviews with leading NF and British National Party activists. Hundreds of people, including fascists, anti-fascists and collectors of extremist material, were contacted. Dozens of people were interviewed in Europe and North America during multi-hour discussions about their experiences and ideas. In several cases, the interviews lasted as long as eight hours and covered a range of topics. Moreover, often the subjects provided rare documents, magazines or books not available anywhere else. The key people interviewed include Phil Andrews, Keith Axon, Andrew Brons, George Burdi, Garry Bushell, Eddy Butler, Mark Cotterill, Richard Edmonds, Nick Griffin, Peter Hain, Patrick Harrington, Andy McBride, Tom Metzger, Joe Pearce, Peter Rushton, Keith Thompson, Colin Todd and Martin Webster. These people all had key roles in extremist politics and some provided documentation to support their statements. Many other people declined interview requests, were deceased at the time this research began or died before being interviewed, such as Ian Anderson. Nevertheless, the dozens of interviews and records provided a solid basis to document the transformation of British fascism.

Many rare publications came from a range of collections in North America and Europe. These include music and fascist magazines from the British Library in London, the Bodleian Library in Oxford, Cambridge University in Cambridge, the Modern Records Centre in Coventry, and the National Archives in Kew. Court records and documents were also obtained through filing information requests with law enforcement agencies, including the London Metropolitan Police Service and the Federal Bureau of Investigation. Several private collections of fascist material also provided details about internal party developments. Additionally, many documents and music albums that are illegal to possess due to race relations laws in Western Europe were obtained through contacts who wish to remain anonymous in Australia, Belgium, Canada, Denmark, France, Germany, Poland, Spain, Sweden, the United Kingdom and the United States. Audio and video sources obtained from collectors, businesses and political parties also provided powerful insights about political events and campaigns. These recordings range from the

BNP's monthly DVDs for activists to cassette audio tapes of editor decisions about raising money for NF campaigns in party publications.[13]

The variety and location of the sources demonstrate the truly transnational character of post-war fascism. Indeed, exploring the British extremists' visit to Tripoli as guests of the Libyan government required tracking down publications produced in Australia, while documents about joint British and Danish fascist music production were located in the United States. In some instances this required investigation into business records or court histories, and in other cases individuals provided tips about certain documents. Often the United States proved to be a significant location for the dissemination of racist material due to the country's First Amendment, which allows web-hosting for foreign extremists and distribution of racist material. However, in other cases the distribution of European-produced publications indicated addresses in the United States and Republic of Ireland merely as a "smoke screen" to hide the actual locations of its authors in Britain.

Definitions

Fascism has evolved in several ways since the Second World War by adapting to the social and political climate. Notably, post-war fascist rhetoric is often toned down, incorporating more nuanced notions of race and adapting to "illiberal" notions of democracy. Yet the fascists have remained committed to the core principles of inter-war fascist movements, including the British Union of Fascists, Fascist Italy and Nazi Germany. Indeed, post-war fascists seeking to emulate inter-war fascist leaders have adopted their style, ideology and methods, but have also adapted to some demands of contemporary society, including issues of immigration, employment and European integration. As a result, fascism has evolved both superficially and ideologically, but remains true to its ideological basis of anti-democracy and xenophobia. Roger Griffin described fascism in his classical work as "a genus of political ideology whose mythic core in its various permutations is a palingenetic form of populist ultra-nationalism."[14] He explained that the core of fascism is rooted in opposition to liberalism, conservativism and rationalism mixed with charismatic politics, elements of totalitarianism and racism.[15]

This book explores the history of the NF and the British National Party, which have been labeled "fascist" parties by scholars, journalists, opponents and party members. However, some members and leaders of the parties have consciously tried to shed the fascist brand due to its negative connotations, which impact its electoral appeal. Nick Griffin, former leader of both the National Front and the British National Party, has denied ever being a fascist and in turn replied that the true fascists are the London and Washington DC political establishment.[16] Griffin was intimately involved in the use of music to recruit young extremists to the National Front and worked to rebrand the British National Party as a patriotic family party. In contrast, Eddy Butler, the national elections officer who ran several general election campaigns for the BNP, described the BNP as a former "Nazi book club" whose ideology was "more interested" in Germany than Britain.[17] The common self-description used by supporters is "nationalist" rather than "fascist." In some contexts this refers to "white nationalist," implying a person seeking a "whites only country," or in certain cases "nationalist" is used to mean "white patriot." Yet in other instances "nationalist" is used synonymously with "fascist" by activists, such as in 2002 when Griffin, as leader of the BNP, compared his party to the British Union of Fascists by saying, "we took the highest ever vote for any nationalist organization in British history and that includes the 1930s when Oswald Mosley was there before the Second World War when all the kind of things he was doing were thoroughly discredited."[18]

Both mainstream literature and academic publications have a long history of describing the NF and British National Party as fascist. In terms of popular outreach and journalism starting in the 1970s, coverage of the Anti-Nazi League and Rock Against Racism has documented the fascist principles and neo-Nazi associations of the parties. Anti-fascist publications, such as *Searchlight*, have also exposed the parties' fascist leanings by using informants and documenting party activities.[19] Scholars have categorized the NF and British National Party as "fascist" because of the direct genealogy the parties have in the inter-war British fascist movement, self-description from the parties and the members' own words, goals and overt political leanings. Indeed, the NF was founded by A.K. Chesterton, a significant figure in the British Union of Fascists in the 1930s, and the party was later led by John Tyndall, a former member of the National Socialist Movement during the 1960s. Tyndall went on to start the British National Party in 1982 after leaving the National Front, and Griffin, a former National Front chair, replaced him as BNP leader in 1999.

The literature produced by fascists and even former fascists who have left these parties and movements have described their beliefs as directly or indirectly fascist. In 1964, John Tyndall and Martin Webster started *Spearhead*, a monthly magazine published until Tyndall's death in 2005, which described itself in the first issue as "an organ of National Socialist opinion in Britain" to replace their previous periodical, *The National Socialist*.[20] Indeed, Tyndall later reflected how reading Adolf Hitler's *Mein Kampf* "was a revelation," written by "a highly intelligent and observant man who clearly loved his country with a passion."[21] The NF was started by Chesterton in 1967 as a unity party of several extremist organizations with the objectives of protecting "civilization in lands threatened with a reversion of barbarism" and to "preserve our British native stock."[22] As former NF national activities organizer Webster explained, Chesterton was a fascist in the "broadest sense," and when Tyndall became chair of the party in 1972, Tyndall "was still a national socialist, but had to mind his P's and Q's."[23] Indeed, under his seven-year leadership until 1979, the NF's *Statement of Policy* declared it was "a party of democracy," but politicians were "impotent to tackle national problems with national solutions."[24] Parliament was described as a location where "a vast complexity of anti-national interests and pressure groups exert a malignant influence on British life."[25] Likewise, rights of "non-white" citizens were not part of the NF's or BNP's platform, as "coloured immigrants" would be repatriated while "Commonwealth citizens of European descent should be allowed unrestricted access into Britain."[26] Despite nearly identical ideologies, the internal organization and decision-making processes of the NF and the BNP differed greatly, with the BNP having a more authoritarian internal system compared with the NF.[27] While the BNP was founded out of John Tyndall's belief that a political party needed "strong" leadership, the NF's directorate structure, with twenty members voting in each "decision," led to factionalism and weakness.[28]

Though race was a constant theme for fascists, it is notable that concepts of "whiteness" and "blackness" are not defined according to biology or genetics.[29] Rather, they are socially constructed by geography, politics and changing cultural descriptions. Consequently, "white" has varied meanings for different organizations and individuals. Historically, some groups did not consider the Irish people "white," while particular extremists discussed in this book believed they had more in common with Muammar Gaddafi or the Nation of Islam than with their own relatives who had opposing political views. Likewise, some people whose politics focuses on race and being "white" have friendships with "non-whites." Mark Cotterill, for instance, was a former NF and BNP activist who was chair of the England First Party and won a local council seat along with Michael Johnson in May 2006, when the party campaigned for "voluntary repatriation" and opposition to "the multi-racial experiment."[30] After the election, it was revealed that Johnson was a quarter African and when Cotterill was asked about his friendship with Johnson, he responded that he has no issue with "individuals" but objects to "populations" and "numbers."[31]

Structure

This book documents the youth and international impact British fascism had after the Second World War. While British fascists failed to seize national power at the ballot box, the post-war fascists made more electoral gains than the fascists in the 1930s and found their ideas being read and listened to in homes throughout North America and Europe. Tracing the development of fascism in the largest post-war organizations, the NF and the British National Party, the book highlights key themes about the political parties' outreach, internal issues and transformations. In doing so, it shows the successes, failures and changes that have made fascism an evolving political ideology even as it has remained true to its ethno-nationalist, anti-democratic nature.

Chapter 2 examines how the search for a new fascist platform began even before the end of the Second World War. With the creation of the League of Empire Loyalists, A.K. Chesterton focused on "preserving" the Empire by pressuring politicians to focus on global supremacy and the safeguarding of race. Failing to achieve any meaningful political change, Chesterton's group merged with several other marginal extremist parties and became the NF in 1967. Harnessing public disenchantment about immigration and racial strife, the NF made gains in local London elections. However, its leadership faced several challenges, which saw John Tyndall, a military veteran and fascist leader, become chair of the party. Moving away from the tactics of the elderly Chesterton, Tyndall focused on recruiting the white working class, but this never turned into any meaningful political power. Indeed, the true attention and mobilization came from street activity and violence.

In Chapter 3, youth emerge as a dominant force in the NF. The party started harnessing the energy and interest of teenagers and created its own youth section. At the same time, these young party members were interested in a new, aggressive music style that served as both an expression of anger and a magnet to attract teenagers to the burgeoning movement. Following the failure of the NF to have its candidates elected during the 1979 general election, internal party disputes caused Tyndall to resign from the leadership. Andrew Brons, deputy chair of the Front, was elected party leader, but due to his management style and his distance away from the NF's headquarters and activities in London, youthful activists, such as Nick Griffin, Patrick Harrington, Derek Holland and Joe Pearce, took on important roles directing the political movement. Notably, these young radicals developed Rock Against Communism in reaction to Rock Against Racism so that white youth could have their own music subculture and to attract like-minded youth to the Front.

Chapter 4 builds on this by examining the domestic and international developments of British fascism. With the NF's creation of White Noise Records and *White Noise* magazine, audiences in North America and Europe were introduced to ideas that originated in London. Groups in the United States, such as the American Front and the National Democratic Front, were started to mirror the NF's political methods and music, which developed transatlantic bonds. Yet the actual number of members was small and there were no significant political consequences of the international bonds between marginal groups. The true international impact was felt from the NF's role in producing and distributing music through its own international network and keeping the party alive through music sales. In the face of splits and internal fights, demand for the music helped push the movement to innovate. In 1987, Blood and Honour was founded by Ian Stuart Donaldson, vocalist for the skinhead band Skrewdriver, to disseminate the Rock Against Communism genre, organize concerts, report music news and distribute music without a particular political party agenda.

Expanding on international contacts, the Chapter 5 explores the emergence of a truly transnational network when the NF disbanded. Following a change in party structure and ideology and its decision not to contest the 1987 general election, the NF suffered a decline in membership. By the late 1980s, skinhead music was spreading at a rapid rate throughout the world as the NF dissolved. This demonstrated the change in fortunes for the NF as it was eclipsed by the subculture it nurtured. In late 1989, the party decided to no longer continue, but in its place the Third Way and the International Third Position were founded by former members. The goal was to continue promoting the ideology developed by the NF internationally, but it moved away from electoral campaigns. However, the British National Party emerged as the recipient of not just British fascists interested in street marches and political campaigns, but also the young skinheads involved in violence. In 1993, at the same time the BNP had its first candidate elected to office, Ian Stuart Donaldson died in a car accident. Yet his music became more popular and his fame only increased. Meanwhile, violent youth made headlines for associations with racist assaults, including murder, which hurt the BNP's image as it hoped to continue winning elections.

Chapter 6 looks at the rebranding of the fascist label after the British National Party became the largest British fascist party in the 1990s. Skinheads associated with the party were identified by the media as violent racist thugs involved in numerous racial clashes. The party leadership attempted to distance themselves from this, but a series of racist bombings in 1999 only seemed to confirm this association. That same year Griffin, who once led the NF, was elected chair of the British National Party and set out to change it. His new plans emphasized building local support as it used music to deliver its message and developed meaningful international associations and organizations. The party started Great White Records and hosted family festivals to promote folk music with fascist themes, but also distanced itself from violent and offensive skinhead music. Moreover, the BNP established a branch in the United States, called the American Friends of the British National Party, to fundraise and campaign for the party in North America.

Chapter 7 highlights how the British National Party successfully reached out to local communities and won dozens of local elections. This, in turn, propelled Griffin and Andrew Brons into the European Parliament, where the leadership increasingly focused on transnational politics. Yet this came at the cost of alienating the party rank and file which, in addition to party disputes over power and money, led to an implosion that forced Griffin from the BNP. This did not slow Griffin's transnational networking, however. Indeed, Griffin had already established international contacts, including making visits to Syria, and ultimately turned his focus away from local issues and toward large geopolitical causes.

Chapter 8 concludes that post-war fascism was centered on youth and international links. Though the British fascists had limited appeal in their own country, they found a passionate population of rebellious youth who enjoyed music that mirrored their emotions in heavy, aggressive, anger-driven rock. Yet the shaven-headed and thuggish-looking young males scared off the bulk of the population, even some sympathetic to fascism. While the domestic audience was limited, teenagers in other parts of Europe and North America were also drawn to the music sold and promoted by the NF. With a series of political missteps and its association with skinheads, the appeal of the already marginal British fascist parties declined further. By the 1990s, the British National Party had honed its local election skills and refocused its political campaigns and youth outreach. The party achieved several dozen local electoral victories as well as two seats in the European Parliament by 2009. Yet within a few years the power of the Internet and the changing geopolitical landscape saw the British National Party's music outreach fail. Moreover, internal party disputes and the rise of Euroskepticism competition from the United Kingdom Independence Party (UKIP) caused fewer political victories and a hemorrhaging of party members. In the 2000s, youth have not been a major faction in British fascism, but the transnational focus and international links have remained vital to the movement.

Conclusion

This book offers insight into how British fascists spread their message and made international connections. It takes an empirical, rather than theoretical, approach through the documentation of developments in extremist politics. It does not dwell on definitions or categories. While some works explore distinctions between the extreme right, fascism and neo-Nazism, interviews with the people involved in the NF and British National Party reveal elements of all those beliefs. Clear and simple definitions are not connected to the reality of the people who joined these movements for a range of psychological, sociological and ideological reasons. Indeed, some youth with affection for neo-Nazism or British fascism also had an affinity for hardline Conservatives, while other figures concerned about Muslim immigration and Islamist politics were former Labour Party members. The objective of the research was to understand and trace the history of British extremism instead of focusing simply on individual or group beliefs, which were sometimes contradictory. In addition, while other scholars have focused on neo-Nazi or fascist youth in order to prevent or de-radicalize youth, this work aims to document history and does not offer policy or political recommendations.

At all times during its history, British fascism remained marginal in the political realm and among society at large. It is important not to overstate its role in Britain, but marginality does not equate with insignificance. Marginal political groups can sometimes have a greater impact than their vote counts show. The NF and British National Party made marks on the world by developing an international fascist movement with racist skinhead music and a transnational outlook. The ideas in the music were sometimes put into action with racial violence and murder, but more often were the soundtrack to the lives of people with extremist beliefs. Later on, the extremists learned from the negative impact of their violent associations and focused their efforts on creating a new image that was softer and family-friendly. In both cases, the themes were picked up by radicals in other countries who hosted visits of foreign extremists and promoted their ideas in local settings, which spread British fascism throughout the world.

Notes

1. Colin Todd, interviewed by Ryan Shaffer, audio recording, 3 October 2014.
2. Stan Taylor, *The National Front in English Politics* (London: Macmillan, 1982).
3. Nigel Fielding, *The National Front* (London: Routledge, 1981).
4. Nigel Copsey, *Contemporary British Fascism: The British National Party and the Quest for Legitimacy* (Basingstoke: Palgrave Macmillan, 2008), 20.
5. Roger Griffin, "No Racism, Thanks, We're British," in *A Fascist Century: Essays by Roger Griffin* ed. Matthew Feldman (New York: Palgrave Macmillan, 2008), 125.
6. Matthew J. Goodwin, *New British Fascism: Rise of the British National Party* (New York: Routledge, 2011), 37.
7. Roger Eatwell and Matthew J. Goodwin (eds.), *The New Extremism in 21st Century Britain* (New York: Routledge, 2010), 2.
8. Matthew J. Goodwin, Robert Ford, Bobby Duffy and Rea Robey, "Who Votes Extreme Right in Twenty-First-Century Britain?: The Social Bases of Support for the National Front and British National Party," in *The New Extremism in 21st Century Britain* eds. Roger Eatwell and Matthew J. Goodwin (New York: Routledge, 2010), 199.

9. Daniel Trilling, *Bloody Nasty People: The Rise of Britain's Far Right* (London: Verso, 2012).
10. Graham Macklin, *Very Deeply Dyed in Black: Sir Oswald Mosley and the Resurrection of British Fascism After 1945* (New York: I.B. Tauris, 2007), 140.
11. Stephen Dorril, *Blackshirt: Sir Oswald Mosley and British Fascism* (New York: Penguin, 2007), 269, 600.
12. Skinheads and Blood & Honour are only briefly mentioned on two pages. Jeffrey Kaplan and Leonard Weinberg, *The Emergence of a Euro-American Radical Right* (New Brunswick: Rutgers University Press, 1998), 19, 89.
13. In one recording an unknown speaker said, "David Tate… photocopied the latest copies of *Attack*, which is our members' bulletin, we're also going to a weird copy of this one. The whole of the front will be the same how it is on the copy of I sent you, but under the next side under 'action' we'll mention of all of it except, we'll it will say, a little change, 'these actions permit us to distribute our material to thousands of homes even in hostile areas. This campaign cannot be properly fought without adequate funds. Do you want the NF to make an impact this year? If so, please send donations to the Ulster Fund by recorded delivery.'" This recording was discovered on a cassette recording of radio news broadcasts about the National Front and British National Party obtained from an activist. Untitled (n.p.: unknown, n.d., circa late 1980s) (Cassette Recording).
14. Roger Griffin, *The Nature of Fascism* (New York: Routledge, 1993), 26.
15. Roger Griffin, *Fascism* (Oxford: Oxford University Press, 1995), 4–9.
16. Nick Griffin, interviewed by Ryan Shaffer, audio recording, 8 October 2014.
17. Eddy Butler, interviewed by Ryan Shaffer, audio recording, 16 September 2011.
18. Nick Griffin said, "we took the highest ever vote for any nationalist organization in British history and that includes the 1930s when Oswald Mosley was there before the Second World War when all the kind of things he was doing were thoroughly discredited. An incredibly charismatic figure, a millionaire in his own right getting £50,000, that's $80,000 a year in those days, from Mussolini to help to finance his party and he never came anywhere near what we just got." Nick Griffin, *Nationalist Movements and the Crisis of the Liberal Elite* (Marietta: American Renaissance, 2002) (DVD Recording).
19. For further details, see: Nick Lowles (ed.), *From Cable Street to Oldham: 70 Years of Community Resistance* (Ilford: Searchlight, 2007); Nick Lowles, *Hope: The Story of the Campaign that Helped Defeat the BNP* (London: Hope Not Hate, 2014).
20. "Editorial," *Spearhead* no. 1 (August–September 1964): 2.

21. John Tyndall, *The Eleventh Hour: A Call for British Rebirth* (London: Albion Press, 1988), 100. Tyndall noted that one particular issue in the book that he drew parallels with was "the workings of certain Jewish forces in Germany."
22. "Forward with the National Front," *Candour* XVIII, no. 462 (March 1967): 24.
23. Martin Webster, interviewed by Ryan Shaffer, audio recording, 3 June 2010.
24. *Statement of Policy* (Croydon: National Front, 1979).
25. Ibid.
26. Ibid.
27. For instance, the NF's constitution under Tyndall's leadership in the 1970s explained that the National Directorate was the governing body led by the chairman, with each of the twenty Directorate members voting on issues, and was elected each year. *The Constitution of the National Front* (n.p.: National Front, 1973). In contrast, the BNP chair had "full power" on "all the affairs of the party," including power to decide party literature and proscribe individuals. *Constitution of the British National Party* (Waltham Cross: British National Party, 2005).
28. John Tyndall, "Resignation: A Personal Statement," *Spearhead* no. 135 (January 1980): 18.
29. "From a scientific point of view, the concept of race has failed to obtain any consensus; none is likely given the gradual variation in existence." L. Luca Cavalli-Sforz, Paolo Menozzi and Alberto Piazza, *The History and Geography of Human Genes* (Princeton: Princeton University Press, 1994), 19.
30. "On-Line Manifesto—National," England First Party, 7 May 2006; available online at http://web.archive.org/web/20060507074710/http://www.efp.org.uk/_pages/localman.html; accessed 1 July 2016.
31. Journalist Ben Turner spoke with Johnson's mother, who confirmed his grandfather was from Cameroon. Ben Turner, "African grandad of 'racist' party councillor," *Lancashire Telegraph*, 9 May 2006; available online at http://www.lancashiretelegraph.co.uk/news/755106.African_grandad_of____racist____party_councillor/; accessed 1 July 2016; Mark Cotterill, interviewed by Ryan Shaffer, audio recording, 14 October 2014. (Abbreviated as "Interview with Cotterill 2.")

CHAPTER 2

The Fascist Tradition, 1967–1977

Enoch Powell's warning of racial strife was a landmark event for post-war fascists in Great Britain. As a Conservative Member of Parliament (MP), he said "we must be mad, literally mad, as a nation to be permitting the annual inflow of some 50,000 dependants" and "I am filled with foreboding; like the Roman, I seem to see 'the River Tiber foaming with much blood.'"[1] These words echoed on television and in newspapers throughout the country in April 1968. For many, the "Rivers of Blood" speech played to the worst fears of the population about multicultural Britain and stoked tension in diverse urban cities. Yet for others it reflected a common sentiment among a disenchanted portion of the white population. The fascists immediately praised him and stated that not only did it reflect their long-held beliefs, but Powell's condemnation by the political establishment was proof that the mainstream parties deliberately ignored important issues such as race and immigration. The marginal fascist parties quickly set out to harness the attention and gain members by appealing to those who shared Powell's views. The National Front (NF) began marches and demonstrations supporting Powell, and called for the forced repatriation of all "non-whites" from the country. A media frenzy ensued that brought the NF attention and a surge of new members. This event proved to be a watershed moment for the fascists that gave them a bridge to escape political marginality.

This chapter examines the origins of British fascism and how the fascists adapted to issues that arose after the Second World War. It traces the path from inter-war fascism to the early post-war movement by showing

R. Shaffer, *Music, Youth and International Links in Post-War British Fascism*, Palgrave Studies in the History of Subcultures and Popular Music, DOI 10.1007/978-3-319-59668-6_2

how the organizations harnessed the concerns of the population that supported the Allied war effort against Nazi Germany and Fascist Italy. Not only were several key leaders interned by the authorities and demoralized by the situation during the Second World War, but the devastation wrought by the conflict and the Holocaust meant that fascism's anti-democratic and racial ideas were discredited in the eyes of the public. For British fascism to survive, it needed to modify its message and focus on the contemporary issues that the country faced. More than twenty years after the war, Powell's speech provided a platform for the NF to spread its racist policies and tap into popular discontent with the major parties. To fully harness the energy surrounding fears about race and immigration, the NF launched several initiatives to spread its message, gain supporters and win elections. This chapter explores those developments and most significant NF initiative, which was worker outreach through "white unions" that opposed multiculturalism and leftist politics.

Inter-War British Fascism

Contemporary British fascism's ideology and tactics are rooted in the social and political turmoil that followed the First World War. The devastation of the conflict challenged tradition and order throughout Europe, which paved the way for young war veterans to introduce new ideas and solutions. In continental Europe, Adolf Hitler made his rise to power with the National Socialist German Workers' Party, while Benito Mussolini led the National Fascist Party to political control in Italy. Likewise, politicians in Britain sought new ideas to address the unprecedented economic and social changes brought about by the war. In 1918, war veteran Oswald Mosley was elected in Harrow to the House of Commons with more than 80% of the vote, becoming the youngest Member of Parliament.[2] Mosley's election and party affiliation as a Coalition Conservative was shaped by the war experience and the destruction of pre-war political alliances. As David Howell explained, Mosley argued in his first election campaign that modernization would occur with full employment by growing wages from high productivity, but he also targeted "aliens," using anti-German, anti-Irish and anti-Semitic "stereotypes."[3] Yet by the next election Mosley had become an independent and successfully defeated the Conservative candidate.[4]

For the next decade, Mosley altered his political positions and affiliations. In 1924, he lost re-election, but won a by-election in Smethwick as a Labour candidate. In 1929, Mosley won re-election while his wife, Lady Cynthia Mosley, was elected for Stoke.[5] Mosley's arguments for reforming banking and his support of trade unionists and socialism made him a "hero" for Labour and "hated" by the Conservatives. In that election Ramsay MacDonald became Prime Minister and Mosley, hoping to gain a position in the government, became Chancellor of the Duchy of Lancaster. Yet his policies put him at odds with the Labour government and he became the first minister to resign his post. In May 1930, he gave a 70-minute speech in the House of Commons, described as the "pinnacle of his political career," where he argued for insulating the economy and offered specific employment, education and pension policies.[6] In search of a new political vehicle for his ideas, he started the New Party in 1931, but it proved ineffective due to internal party differences and it never established a clear political identity.[7] Mosley blamed the party's failure on an intentional campaign by the press and political establishment that kept "its policy and aims" from being "known or discussed by the public."[8]

During autumn 1931, Mosley continued exploring new political strategies and looked towards fascism in continental Europe as a social and political solution to the growing economic problems caused by the Depression in Britain. Scholar Martin Pugh wrote that in January 1932, Mosley traveled to Italy where he found himself "admiring fascist achievements," which spawned regular visits to Italy and even funding from Mussolini.[9] Though ideologically closer to fascist Italy, Mosley also built connections with Nazi Germany, including meeting Adolf Hitler in April 1935, and Mosley married his second wife, Diana Mitford, in October 1936 at Joseph Goebbels' Berlin home.[10] Despite foreign influences, Mosley's new movement hoped to draw patriotic supporters of the Conservative and Labour parties who were disappointed with the political response to the economic crisis.

In October 1932, Mosley started the British Union of Fascists (BUF) with a radical political platform that would replace British democracy with a dictatorship. Scholar Richard Thurlow's work focused on connecting inter-war fascism with post-war fascism by showing their ideological genealogy and the role key figures played in influencing groups. Thurlow specifically examined how Mosley "increasingly came to see himself as the political spokesman for the lost generation and the survivors of the First World War."[11] Indeed, Mosley's 1932 *The Greater Britain* offered his vision for the country and how the fascist party would rule the nation. Calling the political parties a "farce," his goal was to establish a "corporate state" that could reconcile "class interests" with a new political structure and a new economic system to address Britain's unique issues.[12] One year later, in a much shorter publication, Mosley wrote that "[f]ascism is dictatorship in the modern sense of the word, which implies government armed by the people with power to solve problems which the people are determined to overcome."[13] In 1936, Mosley expanded on his ideas in *Tomorrow We Live*, which highlighted the "Jewish question" by affirming "the right of every nation to deport any foreigner who has abused its hospitality, and we hold the aim of finding, together with other European nations, a final solution of this vexed question by the creation of a Jewish National State."[14]

When the British Union of Fascists was launched, it generated enthusiasm not only among traditional Labour supporters in industrial towns, but also among Conservative-minded businessmen. Mosley attracted devoted youth as well as fellow military veterans with an aversion to democratic rule. Notably, A.K. Chesterton, a South African-born British Army veteran, joined the BUF in November 1933. Scholar David Baker detailed Chesterton's attraction to Mosley's organization based on his desire to preserve the Empire, his opposition to liberal democracy and his interest in "achieving the 'god-like' in man."[15] A professional writer who specialized in William Shakespeare, Chesterton became editor of the BUF's newspaper *Blackshirt* and his articles were featured on its front page.[16] His writing focused on the "Christian ideal" being "increasingly undermined," the Empire "slipping adrift" and how National Socialism provides "work and bread."[17] In 1937, Chesterton went on to write an openly sympathetic biography titled *Oswald Mosley: Portrait of a Leader*, which was also serialized in BUF publications.[18] With chapters such as "Leader of Men," the book also attacked BUF opponents, including blaming "the Jews" for the violence at Mosley's Olympia rally in 1934 as well as Mosley's "discovery" that "the whole bunch of purely parasitical occupations were found to be Jew-ridden."[19] Chesterton's praise was not the only support Mosley received from writers and journalists. In fact, Lord Rothermere, who controlled a number of newspapers including the *Daily Mail*, *Sunday Dispatch* and *Evening News*, showed an interest in supporting Mosley in December 1931 and praised fascism throughout the early 1930s. Martin Pugh argued that the newspapers began a "campaign of promotion" for the BUF with regular sympathetic reports about the group, including the infamous *Daily Mail* article "Hurrah for the Blackshirts" in January 1934, until the violence at the Olympia rally caused Rothermere to withdraw support.[20] Yet despite support and even foreign funding, the BUF membership peaked in 1934 with an estimated 50,000 members and declined to about 20,000 members by 1939.[21]

Though Mosley popularized fascism in Britain and targeted BUF propaganda on issues involving xenophobia, fascism and racism were not new to British politics. Important elements of fascist ideas, such as social Darwinism and anti-Semitism, predate the advent of British fascist parties.[22] The first organized fascist party in Britain was the British Fascisti, established in 1923 by Rotha Lintorn Orman with financial support from her mother.[23] The party explained that it had adopted the term fascist "because of the success attained by Mussolini and his supporters."[24] An early issue of its publication, *The British Lion*, declared its policy as "upholding" the monarchy, Empire and Christianity as well as "improving" social conditions.[25] The organization developed a branch in Australia and described itself as an "anti-socialist" movement, which even started "clubs" for children in order to "remedy" communism in Sunday school.[26] The membership remained small, and revenue peaked with magazine subscription orders of £6848, dropping to less than £400, and the party went into bankruptcy in 1934 with an estimated 300 members.[27] Likewise, Arnold Leese, an active racist and anti-Semite, started the Imperial Fascist League in 1928 in opposition to socialism and was later found guilty of public mischief.[28] Though Leese's group had a much more marginal role than the BUF, his influence and legacy within British fascism grew decades later.

The British Union of Fascists' success was limited to two local elections in the country, and due to the combination of bad publicity regarding violent behavior and Britain's drift towards war with the fascist countries, domestic fascists came to be viewed suspiciously.[29] In May 1940, the British government arrested Mosley and Leese along with hundreds of leading fascists under Defence Regulation 18B, which allowed the government to detain people with associations with, or sympathizers of, foreign enemies. Mosley, who had been campaigning for peace with Nazi Germany and Fascist Italy, was released in 1943 and re-entered politics in 1948 with the Union Movement, which campaigned for the creation of Europe as "a nation."[30] The organization's publication announced that its objectives included a union between Europeans and resistance to communism.[31]

While Mosley was detained in Britain, Chesterton was in the British Army fighting against the Axis powers in Africa. By 1937 Chesterton had grown disillusioned with Mosley and resigned, complaining about Mosley's favoritism and ego as well as the failure to recognize actual problems in the movement.[32] Chesterton's military duty during the war was spent in Kenya and Somaliland, where he wrote the racist novel *Juma the Great*, until his health suffered in 1943 and he returned to Britain, writing about politics during 1944.[33] Mosley's and Chesterton's experiences profoundly shaped the post-war nature of British fascism. While Mosley continued his descent into obscurity and failed to regain his inter-war following, Chesterton developed political policies and became a significant fascist leader.

Early Post-War Fascism and the League of Empire Loyalists

During the Second World War, the British government kept a watchful eye on Chesterton even though he publicly disavowed associations with the British Union of Fascists. He divorced himself from the Mosleyites and denounced former BUF member William Joyce, who had fled to Nazi Germany, as a traitor despite their previous connections.[34] In November 1944, Chesterton and Colin Brooks, editor of *Truth*, started the NF with the stated goals of protecting British sovereignty, Empire and Christian traditions as well as finding an "honourable, just and lasting solution" to the "real Jewish problem."[35] The organization was quietly started as the After Victory Group and in turn became the NF, which was launched at the end of the war, to avoid opposition.[36] First led by Brooks and then by Chesterton, the NF considered changing its name to the Empire Front or the National Front Against Communism.[37] A Security Service file marked "secret" discussed the "importance" of the NF as a fascist party with the backing of "suitable men," but noted that by the summer of 1945 it was experiencing problems due to an "internal" fight over leaks to the rival British People's Party led by John Beckett, a former key BUF activist.[38] The NF quickly disintegrated and by 1953 Chesterton had become a "literary advisor" to Lord Beaverbrook, ghost-writing his publications.[39] Later that year Chesterton, using the pseudonym Philip Faulconbridge, launched his own periodical titled *Candour*, which caused Beaverbrook to terminate Chesterton's employment.[40]

Conscious of Empire due partly to his South African birth, Chesterton had long taken an interest in preserving British imperial power. With the decline of British influence and the increasingly loud rumblings from the colonies for independence following the war, Chesterton established the League of Empire Loyalists (LEL) in 1954 and *Candour* became its official periodical. The structure of the association included Chesterton as chair, with a council comprising J. Creagh Scott, G.S. Oddie, Austen Brooks (who became deputy chair), Lady Freeman, Alice Raven, M.C. Greene and N.A. Bonnar.[41] Rather than focus on elections, the LEL sought to pressure politicians and the public to maintain and strengthen the "bonds" between British subjects in the world.[42] In an October 1954 pamphlet promoting imperial loyalty and the LEL, Chesterton explained that his group "supports no political party, believing that all have helped to undermine the British present and betray the British future."[43] He went on to write that there is no difference between American capitalism and Soviet communism, and that the LEL "fights these enemies and their fifth columns in the Empire."[44] The group organized visits to Africa, but mostly served as a pressure group to get politicians to support strong imperial policies. According to former LEL member Bill Baillie, the group would "heckle" Conservative Party meetings and communist gatherings, which proved to be dangerous in many cases.[45]

Due to Chesterton's fame in fascist circles as well as his writings on Jewish conspiracy, the LEL drew people who later became leading postwar fascists, including John Tyndall, Martin Webster, Colin Jordan and John Bean. Indeed, the LEL served as an important training ground for these men. Tyndall wrote that "*Candour* brought me face-to-face for the first time with what is sometimes called the 'Conspiracy Theory', the idea that the great events of recent history and of the present were not chance occurrences," and he decided to "join the League of Empire Loyalists and help the spread of A.K. Chesterton's ideas."[46] Similarly, Webster said that he realized society and the world were changing, "but wasn't readily able to interpret the meaning of what I was noticing" until the League of Empire Loyalists "started" helping him.[47] John Bean joined the LEL in 1955, finding that Chesterton's thinking was in tune with the current issues, and rose to be the LEL's northern organizer, while Colin Jordan, a school teacher, was the Midlands organizer.[48] At the same time, *Candour* served as an outlet for some of the earliest publications by these future fascist leaders.[49] Webster explained that the group attracted "old fashioned Tories" as well as a "scattering of pre-war fascists" who would disrupt other political party meetings with heckling and ask politicians tough questions.[50]

While Chesterton's League of Empire Loyalists attracted attention from hardline radicals, Mosley launched his post-war Union Movement and maintained the support of a fringe minority, but suffered from poor election returns and mass protests.[51] Even some fascists avoided Mosley's movement because of his post-war objectives. Martin Webster, for example, was horrified by Mosley's proposals for Europe to become as a "nation," believing that such an idea was similar to the European Economic Community (EEC) and would dilute British nationality and sovereignty.[52] Moreover, another reason Webster had little interest in joining the Union Movement was because he considered it merely a fan club for Mosley's pre-war politics that attracted "seedy" people.[53] This sentiment was echoed by John Bean, a former member of the Union Movement before joining the LEL, when he described Mosley's post-war followers as containing "a higher percentage of degenerates and the socially dysfunctional" when compared with his inter-war movement.[54]

The League of Empire Loyalists not only drew on myths of the imperial past, but argued that Britain should maintain racial and global power. Indeed, *Candour*'s goal was to offer news with "distinctive British attitudes toward the phenomena of a changing world hostile to British power."[55] Chesterton argued that there was an urgent need to protect "Christian principles" from "internationalist" organizations, such as the United Nations, that would destroy the values and traditions of the country.[56] Despite its opposition to internationalism, the LEL had foreign chapters through Chesterton's connections in South Africa.[57] His conspiracies reached a global audience in 1965 with the publication of *The New Unhappy Lords* about "the new world power," communism and capitalism, that "subdue and govern, not the British nations alone, but all mankind."[58] The book was popular among extremists, with the first edition selling out in three months and copies sold in Australia, Britain, Canada, Rhodesia, South Africa and the United States.[59]

The League of Empire Loyalists had a global readership, but the bulk of its members lived in Britain and focused on local concerns. Despite its status as a non-electoral group, a few LEL members ran for election in the late 1950s and early 1960s, and their campaigns reflected the views shared by the LEL rank and file. Notably, Rosine de Bounevialle

(1916–1999) ran as an "independent" LEL candidate in the 1964 general election on a platform opposing the Americanization of Britain, the Conservative government's support for independence in Africa and joining the Common Market.[60] Bounevialle, a former member of the Conservative Party, began writing articles in *Candour* and became increasingly close to Chesterton. She served as a member of the Candour Advisory Council and continued publishing the periodical after his death in 1973 until her passing in 1999.[61] Immigration was also a key issue addressed in LEL election leaflets, which stated that "the immigration policy must at all costs be reversed," which "is one of the many reasons why the League of Empire Loyalists deserves your support."[62] Bounevialle's election campaign, as all of the LEL election contests, was unsuccessful outside of generating attention in local newspapers.

Some of the most adherent supporters grew frustrated with the League of Empire Loyalists' limited impact and started branching out with their own groups. In 1957, Chesterton described how the group's tactics attracted "world" attention with its "public demonstrations," but the "hardcore" membership remained "pitifully small."[63] That same year, John Bean grew increasing disappointed with the League's political goals and wrote to Chesterton describing the reason for his inactivity as rooted in the LEL's "limited future."[64] In April 1958, Bean, John Tyndall and several other Londoners left the organization and formed the National Labour Party, which lasted two years and attracted about five hundred members.[65] Bean, a self-described "radical," had been asked by Chesterton to take Tyndall "under his wing," and both wanted to form a party that appealed to the "working class" who "suffered from the effects of immigration."[66] Around the same time, Colin Jordan also left the League and established the White Defence League, which mirrored the LEL as a pressure group, not a political party.[67] In 1960, the National Labour Party and the White Defence League merged to become the British National Party (BNP), with Jordan as leader and Bean as deputy.[68] Tyndall remarked that this period was a useful learning experience and helped provide "good training for the speakers."[69] Despite being the leader, Jordan was expelled, along with Tyndall, by the BNP due to their support for a "self-defense" group on behalf of their political activities.[70]

In response, Jordan and Tyndall started their own party. Borrowing from Nazi Germany, they named it the National Socialist Movement and welcomed the involvement of many enthusiastic young radicals, such as Martin Webster and Andrew Brons. The organization had international links with American Nazi Party leader George Lincoln Rockwell, who stayed at Jordan's home as they worked to establish transnational alliances under the World Union of National Socialists, with Jordan being elected "world Führer" and Rockwell named "heir" in summer 1961.[71] Without their rivals in the BNP, Jordan and Tyndall's new group also launched a uniformed paramilitary organization called Spearhead. In 1962, Jordan, Tyndall, Denis Pirie and Roland Kerr-Ritchie were found guilty of violating the 1936 Public Order Act that prohibited creating a military force to promote politics; Jordan received a nine-month sentence and Tyndall received six months.[72] In 1964, the National Socialist Movement disintegrated over disagreements between the two men. Tyndall along with Martin Webster formed the Greater Britain Movement and launched *Spearhead*, a magazine in support of the party.[73] Like Tyndall's previous organization, the Greater Britain Movement was self-described as National Socialist, with its "official programme" explaining "to the British people the meaning of National Socialism and its programme for the Greater Britain of the future."[74] *Spearhead*'s first editorial announced that it was "an organ of National Socialist opinion in Britain" and would "fill the same basic role as our previous journal, *The National Socialist*."[75]

The National Front

As the groups that broke from the League of Empire Loyalists suffered from internal disputes and low membership, Chesterton began rethinking his political approach and seeking unity among the different parties. He missed many LEL meetings in 1965 due to his frequent visits to Africa and his poor health.[76] Following the March 1966 general election, the far-right and fascist organizations decided to pool their memberships and resources for greater social and political impact. The LEL would merge with the BNP, founded by John Bean and led by Andrew Fountaine, and the Racial Preservation Society (RPS) to become the NF, with Chesterton serving as the leader. Meanwhile, Mosley's election returns in the 1966 election, when he failed to receive even 5%, were embarrassing and he never campaigned again.[77] He did not associate with the National Front as a result of his fringe popularity among post-war fascists and, as Robert Skidelsky wrote, Mosley had "renounced" some of his pre-war views that appealed to the radical elements in Chesterton's organization and this European unity project was very different from NF objectives.[78]

Discussion began that year in the LEL's publication about "the unification of right-wing groups" that would "serve the patriotic cause and remedy the damage done by needless fragmentation."[79] At the LEL's October 1966 Annual General Meeting, the party supported a resolution "for a merger" with "like-minded groups."[80] On December 15, 1966 a "private" meeting was held at Caxton Hall to organize the integration of parties. Despite violent attacks, including milk bottles being thrown at the attendees, the meeting proved successful. John Bean told the audience that the NF was "a new party not of apologists but which believes Britain remains for the British."[81] By combining the parties' strengths, he explained, "we can grow faster."[82] The plan was for Chesterton to be appointed head of the NF, as he was an obvious choice for leader. As Austen Brooks said at the meeting, Chesterton "is the man who has done as much as anybody since the war to awaken the British people to the way in which their heritage is being destroyed."[83] Not only was he a well-known figure from the BUF and LEL, he also had resources that eclipsed those of others, including consistently publishing a periodical for more than a decade and having an office across the street from Parliament in Westminster and near the old Scotland Yard building at Palace Chambers, Bridge Street.[84] Indeed, the LEL's office was notorious among the radicals as its members would regularly drink at the nearby Red Lion pub alongside MPs and the police.[85]

On February 7, 1967 the NF was officially started with the signing of documents that merged the League of Empire Loyalists, the BNP and the Racial Preservation Society. The Caxton Hall gathering represented the culmination of negotiations on party policy between the LEL and the BNP, which agreed to limit membership to people of "natural British/European descent."[86] Robert Edwards, a member of Mosley's Union Movement, attended the inaugural meeting as a "spy" for the group and recalled that Chesterton appeared "inebriated" and "could hardly keep his head up" while Andrew Fountaine gave a "militaristic" speech about Empire.[87] Concerns about foreigners in the LEL caused an agreement to be worked out wherein the LEL remained an organization for those outside the United Kingdom.[88] Domestically, former members of the BNP were encouraged to join the NF by John Bean, who received a high-level position in appreciation of his efforts.[89] Aside from Chesterton as the leader, the party had a Directorate with "plenary powers," mandated by the constitution to be not "less than 20 not more than 40," which had the power to expel and suspend members.[90]

As a new political party the NF needed members, but not everyone who wanted to join was admitted. The NF sought political legitimacy and expected its critics to denounce the party as fascist. From the outset of its creation, the NF stated that it would exclude people involved in neo-Nazi parties.[91] Just one month after the NF's formal creation, the party chose three candidates, including Bean, to run in Ealing for the Greater London Council elections.[92] The official membership numbers were never published by the party, but occasionally party leaders did mention figures. According to journalist Martin Walker, the NF claimed to have 2500 members, but really had about 1500, with 300 from the LEL, nearly 1000 from the BNP and more than 100 from the RPS.[93]

The NF immediately began spreading their ideas through newspaper sales and leaflets across the streets of England. Among the more radical policies they publicized in order to win support was the "orderly repatriation of non-white immigrants (and their dependants) who have entered since the passing of the British Nationality Act, 1948."[94] However, the NF also proposed more innocuous policies, including the development of a "movement" for the "healthy mental and physical development of British youth" and building "the closest cooperation" with Australia, Canada, New Zealand, Rhodesia and South Africa.[95] Single-page handbills advertising the party included the words "stop immigration" in large, bold print, and described Britain as "overcrowded" and called for "repatriation" because "immigration is destroying our national unity."[96]

Despite radical demands for forced repatriation, youth with neo-Nazi associations were initially kept away. Yet this quickly changed, and they were not only allowed to join the NF but went on to have leading roles. Chesterton wrote that "we must never run away from the word 'extremist,'" and that the NF is a "serious movement."[97] Tyndall joined the NF months later and recommended that more than one hundred Greater Britain Movement followers do the same, believing the NF "represented beyond any doubt the best hope in our section of the political field."[98] Many members did join, including Tyndall's friend and lieutenant, Martin Webster.[99] Tyndall proved to be a dedicated politician, working as a salesman with all his free time devoted to politics until the NF began paying him £6 per week in 1969.[100] The power started to shift in the NF, with Chesterton's long-time supporters, such as Rosine de

Bounevialle and Austen Brooks, beginning to miss more meetings. As the composition of the meetings changed, so did the setting. The first Annual General Meeting of the NF was a marked contrast to previous LEL gatherings, including the presence of guards to protect members from opponents.[101]

After Tyndall joined the NF, he publicly toned down his radicalism, especially his neo-Nazism and anti-Semitism.[102] Besides his known incarceration for the Spearhead paramilitary and his membership in the National Socialist Movement, he hosted private Adolf Hitler birthday parties until 1966.[103] In addition, Tyndall was with Webster when he was arrested in July 1964 for assaulting Jomo Kenyatta, Prime Minister and later President of Kenya, in London.[104] Aside from newspaper coverage about the attack and arrest, they were paid by the press agency for providing a tip about a "demonstration" against Kenyatta, and those funds were used to publish the first issue of *Spearhead*.[105] Before joining the NF, Tyndall authored two tracts, *The Authoritarian State* (1962) and *Six Principles of British Nationalism* (1966), that also highlighted his extremism. *The Authoritarian State*, published by the National Socialist Movement, argued that "democracy has failed" and is connected to a Jewish and communist conspiracy.[106] *Six Principles of British Nationalism*, published a year before he joined the NF, laid out a racist and anti-democratic ideology, with policies such as racial separatism and goals for attracting "both sides of the present political spectrum."[107]

In addition to his personal friendships with other members of the National Socialist Movement, including Jordan, Webster and Andrew Brons, Tyndall was linked to other known fascists. Tyndall was romantically involved with Françoise Dior, a French neo-Nazi from the famed Dior family. She, however, went on to marry Colin Jordan in a public wedding in which they spilled their blood on an unread copy of Hitler's *Mein Kampf* in 1963.[108] A few years later, after becoming estranged from Jordan, she was found guilty of conspiracy to commit arson against Jewish synagogues and was sentenced to eighteen months in prison in 1968.[109] Meanwhile, in the same year Tyndall joined the NF, Jordan wrote *The Coloured Invasion*, denouncing "non-white" immigration as a "burden" to taxpayers that caused crime and the peddling of drugs and brought a "huge increase in disease to Britain."[110] The merging of these fringe parties into the NF successfully united people with a range of extremist beliefs, ranging from older imperialists and racists to neo-Nazis. Even without Colin Jordan ever joining the NF, the public did not have to examine the group closely to see its fascist leanings. For the NF to draw any support from beyond the fascist margin, the party needed a major issue to attract the broader public.

Rivers of Blood

When Conservative MP Enoch Powell made his "Rivers of Blood" speech in front of the West Midlands Area Conservative Political Centre in Birmingham, not only did he feed on racial fears, but he expressed ideas that were already part of the far-right and fascist fringe. Powell, whose 1968 speech coincidentally was given on Hitler's birthday, April 20, discussed a conversation with a constituent about race and immigration. Powell concluded his speech by supporting repatriation of "non-whites" and opposing anti-discrimination laws, but also worrying about the violence brought about by immigration. Three days later, the Race Relations Act of 1968 was passed following a heated debate in the House of Commons, prohibiting racial and religious discrimination in housing, employment and services.[111] Like the previous Race Relations Act of 1965 that banned public discrimination, public opposition was expressed by people who saw no difference between "non-whites" in Britain and those who wanted to migrate to the country.[112] Those who were opposed to immigration and who held racial prejudices praised Powell's blunt speech, but others denounced its racism and divisiveness.

The impact of Powell's "Rivers of Blood" on the NF was nearly instantaneous. Notably, *The Times*' headline "The Jordans and Mosleyites are Rejoicing" connected the speech with the far right and fascism, and included comments from Chesterton and Mosley.[113] The article explained how neo-Nazi Jordan and former BUF leader Mosley supported Powell, with Mosley saying, "Mr. Powell is saying nine years later what I have always said."[114] Indeed, Mosley ran his unsuccessful post-war campaigns with promises "to end coloured immigration" and "send all the coloured people back."[115] Meanwhile, Jordan told *The Times*: "What Enoch Powell said in his speech constitutes what I said in a pamphlet—for which I got 18 months under the Race Relations Act."[116] Yet the newspaper was most interested in the NF's members who were "rejoicing over the Powell furore at its one-room headquarters in an office opposite the Houses of Parliament."[117] Chesterton, described as head of the NF, said: "What Mr. Powell has said does not vary at all from our views," which was that "[i]t is impossible to assimilate people of such differing racial stocks."[118] In addition, John Tyndall's editorial in *Spearhead* was also quoted, claiming "we may as well start preparing ourselves for an era of racial strife that will make Little Rock and Sharpeville look like mild skirmishes after closing time."[119] The article not only highlighted the racism of the NF and like-minded groups, but also focused on repatriation. Internally, the NF saw Powell's words as an opportunity to break from the margins and harness support for repatriation and ethno-nationalism that seemingly came from a mainstream source.

For the NF, supporting Powell meant protests, marches and campaigning to ensure the proposals became realities. Following news about the speech, John Bean called Chesterton who agreed with the idea to apply for a permit to stage "a rally in support of Powell."[120] However, at the next NF meeting Andrew Fountaine as well as the majority of the Directorate opposed this out of concern they would be outnumbered by opponents and "slaughtered."[121] Internally, Chesterton told supporters, "it is better" that Powell spoke out now even if he did not previously, but "[h]e has done an immense service not so much in being heard himself—the problem was obvious enough—as in providing an occasion for the voice of the nation to be heard."[122] The NF's literature was reaching a large section of the population and about one hundred new members were joining weekly.[123] The NF, with Bean and Webster, participated in rallies with other groups, such as the Smithfield Meat Porters' pro-Enoch rally, but also attended protests against Powell to heckle critics, which turned violent.[124] According to Union Movement member Keith Thompson, Powell's words also helped Mosley's organization and combined the Union Movement and NF at the local level.[125] The head of the Smithfield Meat Porters was a Union Movement member, along with local dock workers' groups who led workers' anti-immigration marches.[126] Aside from regular discussions about party issues, the NF's bulletin encouraged members to join a march from Smithfield to Westminster to "protest" the government's "immigration policies."[127] The unity in support of Powell came at an important time as there was a "clumsy attempt to split the NF."[128] The activity gave the members a rallying point for solidarity and generated party enthusiasm. Indeed, NF marches in support of apartheid, complete with drummers, led about

150 supporters against an anti-apartheid demonstration, which gave members purpose and the opportunity for street action to make their voices heard.[129]

For nearly a year, Powell's speech gave the NF energy and a message with which to engage the broader population that shared its views on race but were not overtly sympathetic to its fascism. Journalist Martin Walker described how the NF derived political benefit from Powell's words, but also that the NF risked losing members to the Powell wing of the Conservative Party, while other NF activists were disappointed with recruits who were merely interested in anti-immigration and not the NF's other issues.[130] Nonetheless, the image of the NF was not directly associated with more extremist elements that would prevent recruitment. As Keith Thompson recalled, the NF was seen as less extreme because it lacked the decades of publicity that associated Mosley with fascism.[131] The membership grew at the time and drew in many people who became key fascist figures. Richard Edmonds, a future NF and BNP activist, later became involved in politics over immigration and cited Powell as speaking for millions.[132] In 1969, Webster became the NF's national activities organizer, which he described as "a euphemism for troublemaker," and led anti-immigration marches to generate publicity for the NF.[133] The public attention brought new members to the party, including former Conservatives sympathetic to the NF's stance. For example, two local Wandsworth councillors left the Tories and announced their affiliation with the NF.[134]

After a year of membership gains, the NF's growth slowed and during 1970 internal conflict broke out in the NF over strategy, ideology and Chesterton's regular trips abroad.[135] Chesterton, for example, doubted the NF's ability to run ten Parliamentary candidates in the June 1970 general election.[136] Chesterton was correct and the election returns were embarrassing, causing a split in the party's Directorate with Bean and Tyndall as well as former LEL members supporting Chesterton.[137] More than that, Chesterton had criticized Powell's economic policies to the disappointment of some NF members.[138] At the 1969 Annual General Meeting, Chesterton was sharply critical of Powell for allowing the Race Relations bills to "pass through Parliament without protest" and for not supporting members of the Racial Preservation Society against criminal charges.[139] Regarding his own opponents, Chesterton wrote that his NF critics were a mere ten out of thirty Directorate members.[140] These people, known collectively as the Action Committee, were behind a plot to force him out of the leadership, with a small group of people supporting Tyndall. The meetings turned into "shouting" matches wherein the Action Committee wanted Chesterton "deposed by constitutional means."[141]

Despite Tyndall's associations and radicalism, his energy and devotion earned him increased duties, allowing him to ascend to the leadership several years later. By 1968, John Bean's *Combat* was absorbed by Tyndall's *Spearhead* and began to promote the NF.[142] While Tyndall's support among the party did not reach critical mass, Chesterton resigned from the NF leadership in late 1970. Webster explained that Chesterton was opposed to adopting a democratic constitution that would prevent the chair from acting in an authoritarian manner, and rather than submit to this change Chesterton quit.[143] The party felt the loss of Chesterton's leadership and at the NF's Extraordinary General Meeting (EGM) in 1971, Tyndall praised Chesterton's "unique contribution to the NF" and denounced Chesterton's critics.[144] Tyndall, who had known Chesterton since 1956, wrote that Chesterton was "a model to all those who might follow him in single-minded dedication to a cause."[145]

Following Chesterton's resignation and a brief period during which a committee filled the leadership role, the NF's structure was changed. In 1971, John O'Brien, the NF office manager, became the party's chair and he attempted to "democratize" the party.[146] While the party's administration changed, O'Brien remained committed to radical policies such as repatriation.[147] Previously, the NF's leader held firm executive power, with the Directorate mostly serving as an advisory board, but this was changed under O'Brien, giving the chair, who would be elected by the party members, a single vote among the twenty-member committee.[148] Under this new system, according to O'Brien, the NF grew to include between 7000 and 10,000 members and 84 branches in 1971.[149] However, these numbers were undoubtedly an exaggeration. Webster described O'Brien as a good speaker but "incompetent" as an administrator, which harmed the party.[150] In 1972, further internal disputes caused O'Brien to be replaced by Tyndall, who had "reservations" about the new democratic governance of the NF.[151]

While race was a major issue for the NF, it also campaigned against European integration and the European Economic Community. Stan Taylor wrote "that the main thrust of the NF's 'exoteric' appeal was aimed at capitalizing upon racism" and described "other" issues as the NF's anti-EEC rhetoric.[152] However, not only was opposition to the

EEC a significant issue, it also led to the NF's most significant electoral campaign. Starting in the early 1960s, Britain sought Common Market membership, but French resistance prevented the country joining until the Heath government's negotiations in the early 1970s. The NF was vocally opposed to this, claiming it would destroy British character and independence. Even though Chesterton was no longer NF leader, his work in *Candour* continued to be read favorably by NF members and he wrote several new tracts that reflected the NF's views. His association with Rosine de Bounevialle grew closer and her residence, Forest House in Liss Forest, later became the address for Chesterton's publications. In 1971, Chesterton completed *Common Market Suicide*, which denounced the British government for committing "treason" by supporting the international "cabal" of the European Economic Community and American power.[153] When Chesterton died of pancreatic cancer in August 1973, he was writing a manuscript titled *Facing the Abyss*, which de Bounevialle published with the addition of two chapters based on his early drafts. It mirrored his previous conspiratorial writings but focused on liberalism, including university education, "hippies" and the "nexus" of capitalism and communism.[154] *Candour*, both under Chesterton and later under de Bounevialle, likewise wanted to "expose the Common Market conspiracy" and "Zionist finance capitalism's aims and methods."[155] Chesterton's *Spearhead* obituary, written by NF deputy chair Frank Clifford, celebrated his life by calling him a "great patriot" and praising his "truth and factual reporting."[156] Meanwhile, Tyndall wrote that Chesterton was "a great friend and counsellor" who educated "thousands" of people about "contemporary affairs" to improve the future of the country and civilization.[157]

Tyndall followed in the footsteps of Chesterton's anti-Common Market campaign. As editor of *Spearhead*, he ran cover stories such as "Why We Must Say No to Europe" and "Europe: The Fight to Get Out Begins." In 1971, *Spearhead* devoted a "special issue" to the Common Market, which denounced its "internationalism," wage losses, "bureaucratic dictatorship" and shift to a "United States of Europe."[158] Then in January 1973, the magazine reported on Heath signing the Treaty of Rome to enter the Common Market and declared that "getting out" was the "foremost task that faces the British people."[159] The NF's angst about Britain signing the Treaty of Rome was rooted in a conspiracy theory about a small group of wealthy bankers working against the nation and the people for their own personal benefit. Clare Macdonald's tract, published by the NF's Policy Committee, claimed that the "only" course to "save Western civilisation from moral and material bankruptcy," including the future control of a "Socialistic World Government," was reforming how capitalism functions by creating loans with interest-free credit.[160] Likewise, John Tyndall denounced the Common Market as "internationalist thinking," arguing for an "alternative" economic system that was against capitalism and focused on the domestic market.[161]

While NF opposition to the European Economic Community won the party support, attention-grabbing race issues attracted a stronger influx of membership. Playing on racist fears about immigration causing violence and disease, the party harnessed media attention by talking about asylum seekers and the associated social as well as economic costs. The religious NF members circulated biblical justifications for racism, claiming "a multi-racial society" has not worked and will not "work" because "God doesn't intend it to work, as race mixing in the sight of God is wrong."[162] In August 1972, President Idi Amin of Uganda sought to "Africanize" the country and ordered the Asians in his country to leave within three months, which prompted several countries to take in the stateless immigrants. Edward Heath's government offered "vouchers" for 3500 displaced Asians to enter Britain, which was met with displeasure from members of his own party. The NF, as with Powell's 1968 speech, saw its opposition to immigration and the media attention to the issue as a recruitment vehicle. Tyndall's *Spearhead* described the government's actions as "a campaign to flood our own country with alien migrants," which was "without exaggeration" a "conspiracy."[163] In a later issue, the magazine discussed the expansion that allowed tens of thousands of immigrants to enter Britain in an article about "the possibility of large scale racial conflict."[164] Meanwhile, Martin Webster linked race and disease in the "Asian immigrant disease menace," connecting it with the "sustained invasion of our country by coloured aliens" from East Africa.[165] The claim that immigration "threatened" Britain generated publicity that, in turn, was a boon to membership.

In the next few years, the NF declared "success" in local elections with increasing vote shares, even though they failed to win any elections. During 1972, the NF praised its candidates, who received hundreds of votes in local London elections.[166] The 1972 by-election in Uxbridge was described as a "great moral victory," with candidate John Clifton receiving about 3000 votes, or 8.2%, against former NF member Clare

Macdonald and a candidate from Mosley's Union Movement.[167] The public relations for the NF campaign was led by Martin Webster, whom the party credited with attracting press coverage by holding a large march that drew onlookers and led to the publication of photographs of NF slogans in the local newspaper.[168] Even though the attention did not result in a single electoral victory, the NF claimed that its membership doubled by 1973.[169] In fact, the NF reported that its Annual General Meeting that year was the largest in its history, attended by about four hundred people and raising a record £1245.[170]

The NF's electoral high point was Webster's 1973 by-election in West Bromwich, which was a Parliamentary seat long held by the Labour Party. The election returns showed a Labour victory with 15,907 votes, but Webster won 4789 and the Conservative candidate received 7582.[171] With only three weeks before the election, Webster was selected to be the NF candidate and led marches through the area to make the public aware of the party's anti-Common Market and anti-immigration platform.[172] The election was notable because it demonstrated the NF taking Conservative support, and Enoch Powell declined to speak for the Conservative candidate, who was in favor of the Common Market. Webster claimed Powell's action was an intentional snub.[173] Arthur Osman explained that the NF's appeal extended beyond issues of immigration as "the bulk of Mr. Webster's support came from right-wing Conservatives" who lived far apart from "Asian workers."[174] Likewise, George Hutchinson wrote that Webster's votes were due not only to immigration but to the "[d]iscontent over the rocketing cost of living widely associated with our membership of the EEC."[175] He continued that these Tories would "vote for the NF candidate, where there is one, or for Labour."[176] This was the first election since the Second World War in which a fascist candidate saved their deposit, winning enough votes to receive the money back.[177]

The NF's radical literature had limited appeal, but one of the NF's strengths was its ongoing activity on the streets, where its physical presence was greater than its electoral appeal. According to Richard Edmonds, the NF was built around two men: Tyndall being the intellectual leader and Webster being the "man on the street."[178] Indeed, the party membership put its political words into action on the streets of Britain, confronting and fighting opponents at marches, demonstrations and meetings. Consequently, it became associated with violence starting in the early 1970s, which was part of Webster's tactic to generate media attention.

Webster, who was the NF's activities organizer from 1969 to 1983 and editor of the *National Front News* from 1976, had a history of starting fights, not only against Kenyatta but also "insulted and provoked" an interracial couple during 1969 that led to physical confrontation.[179] The violence reflected his radicalism, as demonstrated in his 1962 article titled "Why I am a Nazi."[180] However, the violence was not just an expression of ideas, but a tactic that he described to reporter Christopher Farman when he said, "we had to kick our way into the headlines" (Webster disputed this and claimed to have said "crash" instead of "kick").[181] There were also reports of an even more sinister group. Internally, the NF reportedly had "The Meat Gang," described as a "commy [*sic*] and nigger bashing outfit" that would be "disowned" by the NF if uncovered by the police.[182]

The NF marches regularly drew hundreds and later thousands of people. An article by Tyndall about "propaganda" showed a picture of bagpipers standing in columns with Union Jacks from an "NF march" and had the caption: "a rousing propaganda weapon."[183] At a Remembrance Day march in 1971, *Spearhead* reported the "biggest ever march and meeting" with more than eight hundred at the Cenotaph in Whitehall and an ensuing "parade" that caused the police to close Whitehall to traffic.[184] In 1972 the NF protested against Irish Republican Army speakers at Polytechnic of North London, which resulted in a "bloody battle."[185] Then NF activists joined apartheid supporters at Rhodesia House in London, where police forced the group away from leftists to avoid violence.[186] That same year a march on Remembrance Day was attended by 1500 NF supporters and the 1973 memorial reportedly involved 4000 supporters, including Tyndall and Webster.[187] Whereas the "main" London summer rally in 1973 drew between 900 and 1000, an increase from 600 in the previous year, earning cheers from onlookers who welcomed the "forest of red, white and blue flags."[188] Yet the marches were not just about displaying opposition to the Common Market and "coloured immigration," but increasingly were about refusing "to be intimidated by the threat of mob action by communists and coloured immigrants."[189] The protests included heckling and throwing leaflets during a Greater London Council (GLC) meeting, shouting during anti-discrimination Christian sermons and attempting to stop apartheid protests.[190] Some members supported the confrontations, including provocative marches through immigrant areas, but the negative press caused other NF supporters to reconsider the tactics, believing it hurt its image as a legitimate political party.[191]

The NF hoped for a political breakthrough in the next national election with attention on race and the increased media attention since the previous 1970 election. Tyndall announced that the Front would "contest not less than 50 seats," exceeding its first general election contest in 1970 with ten candidates and allowing the party to air its first televised political broadcast.[192] The Front ran fifty-four candidates in the February 1974 general election and received a mere 76,429 votes, but the leadership claimed this was a relatively positive result when compared with 1970.[193] Tyndall described the election as representing a "miracle" because of the "growth, planning and fundraising" beyond "any political party of our type in Britain—ever."[194] The Front sent election literature into two million homes, and the NF's image during its first election broadcast included housewife Sheri Bothwell, who Tyndall wrote was "one of the pleasantest NF representatives in our election broadcast."[195]

The February election produced a hung Parliament with the Labour Party unable to gain a majority, and a second election was called for October. After months of planning, the NF contested ninety seats, allowing the party to air two political party broadcasts.[196] The Front increased its election total, receiving more than 113,000 votes.[197] The party, however, again lost all its election deposits, costing £13,500, but Webster described the election attention as "a giant advertising drive."[198] At that time, a faction in the NF began organizing against Tyndall. John Kingsley Read (1937–1985), a former Conservative and military veteran from Blackburn, replaced Tyndall shortly after the October election.[199] He was a candidate for Parliament in both the February and October elections, and his appointment as party leader was described "as a bit of cosmetic surgery to give the Front a more acceptable image."[200] Indeed, as a one-time Conservative, he did not have Tyndall's openly fascist past and had support from party members who wanted to broaden the NF's appeal by steering it away from violence and fascism into anti-immigrant populism.

Following the NF's failures in the two 1974 general elections, the street clashes and the internal struggles, the NF had a reputation for violence and political marginality. In June 1974, about 1500 NF activists marched from Westminster to Conway Hall, Red Lion Square. Led by Webster to protest Labour's immigration policies, the two sides clashed violently, leading to the death of NF opponent Kevin Gately.[201] Webster described the violence and mayhem at the march as one of the most memorable in the NF's history.[202] Long-time members, such as

John Bean, had taken a back seat to the new members and were less involved in NF activities in the early 1970s. By that time Bean had lost two teeth as a result of street violence and had turned away from politics to spend more time with his family, ultimately not renewing his membership sometime around 1976.[203] Decades later he was critical of the NF's tactics up to that period, describing the marches and violence as counter-productive and harmful to its political appeal to the broader public.[204]

Fascist Unions

The public demonstrations surrounding racial issues were not enough to sustain the revolving door in the NF membership or to propel any NF candidate to electoral victory. The NF began looking for new ways to attract like-minded people to its ranks. Under Tyndall between the 1974 elections, the NF leadership drafted plans to launch its own trade unions comprised of white workers who not only supported its racial policies, but also opposed the leftist politics usually associated with unions. The NF's literature played on the racist rhetoric that minority employment meant whites were being fired, but also went further in denouncing the ideological link between unions and leftist politics. Nigel Fielding briefly explored the NF efforts to support white workers as part of a strategy to attract publicity and keep the issue in the public sphere.[205] Yet NF members saw this not as a strategy, but as the reality of their support. As Richard Edmonds explained, many NF supporters were working-class, and the NF saw "trade unions as effectively abandoning their own British members and certainly the British working class in general."[206] As a result, "we wanted to set up trade unions" in order to represent British workers and the issues they cared about.[207]

In contrast with previous discussions, the Front's goal was not only to recruit, but to provide a voice for racist workers and break the power of the major labor unions. In July 1974, Martin Webster denounced the left-wing influence in trade unions and organized labor, and called for an "alternative" to translate into "actual power" by developing a National Front Trade Unionists Association (NFTUA).[208] He described how a "second generation" of people, who were "unionists recruits," were joining the NF.[209] Webster concluded that in the "coming months" the NF Directorate would formally develop the NFTUA, which would in turn "lead" the trade union movement by "defending" the working class.[210]

As a result, the NF claimed it wanted "stronger, not weaker, trade unions" to better represent workers' interests.[211]

In August 1974, Webster organized a protest in support of the "white workers" and employers at the Imperial Typewriter Company in Leicester who refused to support a strike by hundreds of Asian workers for equal pay and promotion.[212] The workers' union did not recognize the demands, claiming that "total support for either white local officials or the East African Asian strikers' group might easily lead to a split in the union."[213] In response, the Interracial Solidarity Campaign staged a counter-protest and the ensuing confrontation resulted in three arrests, with the NF blaming the clash on the "reds."[214] Edmonds, who attended the march, called it a demonstration against bringing in "cheap" foreign workers and said opponents had "attacked" the NF with bricks as police targeted only NF members for arrest.[215] Webster's strategy worked to generate political support in light of the strike, and the NF candidate knocked "Labour into second place" with 24.4% of the vote in the local elections.[216] Indeed, the NF declared "victory" in the dispute as not only did it successfully execute a protest for the white workers, but the counter-demonstration helped give the NF "good publicity."[217] That November the NF reported another large increase in the number of supporters at its Remembrance Day parade, which attracted 5000 people.[218]

The idea of creating a radical union founded on non-white repatriation and opposition to "race-mixing" was enthusiastically received. *Britain First*, later edited by Richard Lawson, was launched in 1974 as a broadsheet that was "easy-to-read, down-to-earth" to supplement the "more serious articles and commentaries of *Spearhead*."[219] The paper included articles about the Common Market's "wasteful farm policy" and called for an "end to the employment of coloured labour, and repatriate all coloured immigrants together with their dependents and descendants."[220] Philip Gannaway, an NF member, hoped the NFTUA would fight the "cancer" of "left-wing" influence in the labor movement.[221] Likewise, Neil Farnell, as secretary and publicity officer for the NF Industrial Section, wrote that "union leaders seem completely out of touch with the wishes of ordinary people."[222] Claiming that whites were fired so that non-whites could be employed for lower wages, he denounced the current status of trade unions.[223] With Farnell as leader for the NF's industrial matters, *Spearhead* began advertising how to join the NF union effort by contacting a local NF industry organizer.[224]

Aside from creating its own unions, the NF also wanted to participate in organized labor and reap its benefits. In 1975, the NF Directorate passed a resolution "that all NF members should join trades unions," which prompted Richard Lawson and David McCalden, both writers for the NF, to apply for National Union of Journalists (NUJ) membership.[225] Lawson's and McCalden's applications went before the board and were voted down, citing racism.[226] The NUJ's executive council told the board to reverse the decision because "political affiliation was not a bar to NUJ membership," and McCalden could only be refused membership to the union if "he was unwilling to comply with the rules of the union."[227] However, both Lawson and McCalden were ultimately turned down by the NUJ because they failed to file their appeals within the twenty-eight-day period, and the NF denounced the union as "cowards."[228] The following year the NUJ in Yorkshire told its reporters not to write about the Front's activities because the party had prevented a black reporter from attending the NF's meetings in Leeds.[229] McCalden remained active in British politics until moving to Los Angeles in 1979, where he helped start the Institute for Historical Review and edited its journal, *The Journal of Historical Review*, which became the global mouthpiece for Holocaust denial.[230] Holocaust denial had long been a component of the NF, including in *Spearhead* articles, and Richard Verrall, *Spearhead* editor and NF Directorate member, wrote the infamous Holocaust denial book *Did Six Million Really Die* (1974).[231] McCalden continued to write and edit books that denied the Holocaust until his death of AIDS-related complications in 1990.[232]

The NF claimed success in other union activity, but also met resistance from political opponents. In May 1975, left-wing demonstrators in Glasgow fought to stop an NF meeting, and local union leaders from the mining and transportation industries were arrested while protesting the NF.[233] In October 1975, the NF Trade Unionists attempted to march with union members of the Trades' Council, Shop Stewards Committee and Communist Party.[234] However, the group was "asked" by dozens of police officers "not to take part in the march."[235] Ernest Pendrous, a former Conservative, wrote that he was disappointed the Tories and unions did not support their right to join.[236] Moreover, at a Transport and General Workers' Union factory in Dagenham, NF member Ian Newport was selected shop steward, but opponents began efforts to remove him from the post.[237] According to *Spearhead*, the workers then "rallied to his support."[238] In addition, Tom Holmes, then the Great Yarmouth NF organizer and NF chair decades later, became a delegate for the local trades council.[239] Holmes explained that "orders" from his union headquarters "barred" him "from holding any position in the union" for the "sole reason" of being an NF member.[240] He criticized the "left-wing trade union leaders" for their actions and insisted he would win support among the workers, if not for the higher-level union leadership.

Under the new NF leadership, internal disputes continued between John Kingsley Read and Tyndall's supporters. Tyndall believed his removal was illegitimate and protested the NF Directorate structure, claiming that it "seriously undermined" the authority of the chair.[241] After fifteen months, in December 1975 a court ordered Tyndall to be restored as chair because he had been removed illegally, in violation of the NF's constitution.[242] In response, Kingsley Read as well as others, including Richard Lawson, David McCalden and Denis Pirie, split from the NF and created the National Party, and the NF set out to expel anyone who joined or associated with the new organization.[243] In existence for over a year, the National Party at first appeared to be a threat to the NF, but proved unable to attract sustainable numbers of new recruits. The newspaper *Britain First*, which became the National Party's official publication, was devoted to promoting the party's principles, such as free enterprise and having industry "serving" the community.[244] The bitter and contentious fight included "smear leaflets" and attempts to remove other Directorate members.[245] Yet in terms of elections the National Party succeeded where the NF failed, as Kingsley Read and another party member successfully won seats in the local Blackburn council for their position on immigration.[246] According to then NF member Richard Edmonds, Kingsley Read made "a deal with the local Tories in Blackburn, Lancashire where he would have two seats to himself, no Tory candidate standing."[247] The reasoning was that without a Conservative candidate, there would be no "splitting" of the "right-wing vote."[248]

The battle between the NF and National Party was also ideological, with one of the main differences being the Strasserite policies of the National Party. Derived from the ideas of Nazi Party brothers Gregor and Otto Strasser, Strasserism was a populist and anti-capitalist version of National Socialism in which workers would be organized by profession in "guilds" and given rights by the state to run their industry.[249] Nick Griffin, who joined as a fifteen-year-old in 1974, explained that the

Strasserism of Lawson, McCalden and Steve Brady was far more radical than the Labourite and socialist tradition of the working class, which was in "opposition" to "Tyndall's Hitlerite Nazism."[250] Griffin explained that Strasserism was attractive in part as an ideological alternative to the "barely concealed extreme Hitlerism," which was out of step in a country that had suffered at the hands of Nazi aggression decades earlier.[251] According to Joe Pearce, who joined in 1976, the Strasserites of the NF were more focused on socialism and anti-capitalism, and the youth who joined in the late 1970s would even hold annual Otto Strasser birthday parties.[252] This was in contrast to people like Tyndall who were more sympathetic to Hitler's version of National Socialism.[253]

The National Party's "principles" mirrored those of the NF, demanding the repatriation of "all coloured and other racially incompatible immigrants," but also sought changes in industry with "the introduction of profit sharing and workers' co-partnership."[254] Richard Verrall, a Tyndall loyalist and editor of *Spearhead* from 1976 to 1980, denounced the "leftist influence" in the NF, specifically criticizing *Britain First* for its focus on trade unionists and its "Marxist" influence.[255] Without mentioning Lawson by name, Verrall connected the same thinking to Lawson's publication, *Spark*, for NF students.[256] Yet the NF still saw the need to recruit workers and support racist unions. Neil Farnell, as head of the NF's industrial department, continued to focus on worker issues with an "Industrial Front" column in Tyndall's *Spearhead*, which discussed the "betrayal of the British worker" and how a "nationalist government" could end "unemployment for all time."[257] The NF then launched *National Front News* to replace *Britain First*, which supported the National Party after the split.[258] Within months the *National Front News*, edited by Webster from 1974 until 1983, was being circulated to tens of thousands, with 33,000 copies of its fourth issue published, far exceeding *Britain First*, which peaked at 17,000 copies.[259] Webster described how the newspaper was designed to have a tabloid appearance, with photographs and headlines that would "agitate" people on the streets and get NF commentary into the hands of the common person.[260]

That same year the NF continued its appeal to workers with the National Front Railwaymen's Association (NFRA).[261] Peter Floyd explained that the NFRA had been started and developed more than two years earlier by NF members who worked for British Rail with the goal "to eradicate the many ultra left-wingers that abound with the rail unions and ultimately the entire trade unions."[262] Believing that the transport unions did not reflect the "nationalist feeling" among workers, it established branches in London and the Midlands, with a national council of five men.[263] A membership form for joining the NF's Railwaymen's Association declared that the NFRA had been founded due to concerns about the "destruction of our industry" and had established branches at "large stations and depots."[264] Its policies included to unite "all right thinking railmen against the rise of Communism within the unions" and expose the "preferential treatment afforded to coloured immigrants in respect to British Rail discipline."[265] Specifically, it mentioned that "most white" rail workers "have personal knowledge of cases of coloured railmen breaking rules and regulations including being drunk on duty."[266] It protested union contributions to the Labour Party and argued that supporting the NF's union would "help us rebuild our [i]ndustry and [n]ation."[267]

Towards the end of the year, the leadership of the British Railways Board was discussing the NF's attempt to "infiltrate the railway" and considered responding to "their more unpleasant racist allegations."[268] The National Union of Railwaymen (NUR) general managers and managing directors told management that they "cannot condone open recruitment on railway premises, etc. or false statements."[269] Whereas, the Socialist Workers Party argued that the way to "defeat" the NF was "on the shop floor" and "then the ground will be cut from underneath the fascists."[270] In 1978, the NUR began to take "action" against the NF by working with the Amalgamated Union of Engineering Workers, who planned to distribute 10,000 anti-NF pamphlets.[271] Yet the Conservative NUR members tried to prevent this, opposing the "political action."[272] The NUR ultimately decided that NF supporters could join the union as long as they "respect" the rules.[273]

The NF continued gaining supporters through its media stunts and public demonstrations. In summer 1976, the NF received its largest number of votes in a parliamentary by-election in Thurrock that gave the party 6.6%.[274] Building from these gains, three more NF candidates contested parliamentary by-elections, including Andrew Brons and Charles Parker.[275] Brons, a former National Socialist Movement member who was first appointed to the Directorate as Education Officer in 1976, would continue his rise in extremist politics in later years, while Parker became closer to Tyndall when Parker's daughter and fellow NF member, Valerie, married Tyndall in November 1977.[276] Despite internal troubles with the National Party, local council elections showed "encouraging results."[277] The NF started a national effort to run in local elections in places such as Lancashire, Cheshire, East Anglia, Kent and Surrey, including an effort to contest all forty-eight seats in Leicestershire and twenty-two in Bradford.[278] By the end of 1976, the NF claimed it was "poised to replace Liberals" as the largest third party.[279] Despite the split in the NF, the party announced more than three hundred new members within nine months.[280] The NF also reported 4000 attendees at the Remembrance Day event in 1975, increasing to between 5000 and 6000 in 1976.[281]

Conclusion

After the Second World War, British fascism adapted to social issues and attempted to address broader public concerns. The NF was formed to pool radical resources together and united people on the political fringes with neo-Nazi and hardline Conservative backgrounds. Indeed, in its first ten years the NF went from being a cell of small fascist parties under an inter-war fascist figure to becoming a party associated with anti-immigration sentiment and opposition to the European Economic Community. Recognizing the support they received from white workers, the NF tried to capitalize on this. Indeed, the NF's worker initiatives sought to win wider support, but failed to materialize as an electoral breakthrough. While a few Conservatives on local councils joined the party, the NF did not win a single election despite running in hundreds of electoral races. Nevertheless, the media attention focused on its marches and meetings, as well as its extremist stances, earned it a growing membership and a larger but less active community of supporters. By 1977, the British political community was at a crossroads concerning the radicals. Until that time there had been no mass, coordinated response to the NF's gains or its street strategy. The next chapter examines the anti-racist response from mainstream and leftist parties as well as the NF's search for new membership beyond the racist and radical-right worker vote. Specifically, it explores the cultural forms of politics, with the creation of Rock Against Racism and the NF's establishment of their own racist music genre, Rock Against Communism, which improved morale and attracted financial and member support.

Notes

1. "Enoch Powell's 'Rivers of Blood' Speech," *The Telegraph*, 6 November 2007; available online at http://www.telegraph.co.uk/comment/3643823/Enoch-Powells-Rivers-of-Blood-speech.html; accessed 1 July 2016.
2. David Howell, *Mosley and British Politics 1918–32: Oswald's Odyssey* (Basingstoke: Palgrave Macmillan, 2014), 16.
3. Ibid., 15.
4. Ibid., 35.
5. Ibid., 98.
6. Ibid., 129.
7. Ibid., 173.
8. Oswald Mosley, *The Greater Britain* (London: British Union of Fascists, 1932), 148.
9. Martin Pugh, '*Hurrah for the Blackshirts*': *Fascists and Fascism in Britain Between the Wars* (New York: Random House, 2005), 126, 131.
10. Ibid., 131.
11. Richard Thurlow, *Fascism in Britain: A History, 1918–1985* (New York: Basil Blackwell, 1987), 29.
12. Mosley, *The Greater Britain*, 28.
13. Oswald Mosley, *Fascism in Britain* (London: British Union of Fascists, 1933), 8.
14. Oswald Mosley, *Tomorrow We Live* (London: British Union of Fascists, 1936), 60.
15. David Baker, *Ideology of Obsession: A.K. Chesterton and British Fascism* (New York: I.B. Tauris, 1996), 115.
16. A.K. Chesterton, *Blame Not My Lute* (Unpublished draft, n.d.), University of Bath Special Collections, B.3–B.7. A.K. Chesterton spent years working as a journalist and wrote a history of the Shakespeare memorial. He also edited *The Shakespeare Review*, which featured an article by his second cousin G.K. Chesterton in its inaugural issue. G.K. Chesterton, "Shakespeare and Shaw," *The Shakespeare Review* no. 1 (May 1928): 10–13. A.K. Chesterton, *Brave Enterprise: A History of the Shakespeare Memorial Theatre, Stratford-upon-Avon* (London: J. Miles & Co., 1934).
17. A.K. Chesterton, "Peace on Earth and Goodwill Towards Men," *Blackshirt* no. 87 (21 December 1934): 1; A.K. Chesterton, "Britain's Popular Front," *Blackshirt* no. 36 (24 October 1936): 11; A.K. Chesterton, "Death is on Thy Drums, Democracy," *Action* no. 58 (27 March 1937): 9.

18. For example: A.K. Chesterton, "Portrait of a Leader: I. Family Perspective," *Action* no. 55 (6 March 1937): 14; A.K. Chesterton, "Portrait of a Leader: II. Youth and Early Training," *Action* no. 56 (13 March 1937): 14.
19. A.K. Chesterton, *Oswald Mosley: Portrait of a Leader* (London: Action Press, 1937), 126.
20. Pugh, '*Hurrah for the Blackshirts*', 150.
21. Thurlow, *Fascism in Britain*, 122, 123.
22. Pugh,'*Hurrah for the Blackshirts*', 14.
23. Thurlow, *Fascism in Britain*, 53.
24. Cecil Battine, "Fascists in Italy and England," *The Fascist Bulletin*, 29 August 1925, 2.
25. "British Fascists Policy and Practice," *The British Lion* no. 1 (June 1926): 6. This publication was the successor to *The Fascist Bulletin.* "The New Official Organ," *The Fascist Bulletin*, 12 June 1926, 5.
26. "British Fascism in Australia," *The British Lion* no. 1 (June 1926): 4; "The Future of the British Fascists," *The British Lion* no. 21 (August 1927): 11; "Fascist Clubs for Children," *The Fascist Bulletin*, 7 November 1925, 5.
27. Thurlow, *Fascism in Britain*, 53, 56, 57.
28. Ibid., 75.
29. Copsey, *Contemporary British Fascism*, 124; Charmian Brinson and Richard Dove, *A Matter of Intelligence: MI5 and the Surveillance of Anti-Nazi Refugees, 1933–50* (Manchester: Manchester University Press, 2014), 44.
30. Robert Skidelsky, *Oswald Mosley* (London: Papermac, 1981), 448, 481.
31. "Objectives of Union Movement," *Union* no. 2 (21 February 1948): 3.
32. A.K. Chesterton, "Why I Left Mosley," The National Archives (TNA), Kew, United Kingdom, KV 2/1348 299084, "The Security Service: Personal (PF Series) Files: Arthur Kenneth Chesterton."
33. Skidelsky, *Oswald Mosley*, 194. A.K. Chesterton, *Juma the Great* (London: A.K. Chesterton Trust, 2012).
34. Baker, *Ideology of Obsession*, 189. Chesterton's *Why I Left Mosley* was published by Joyce's National Socialist League, but he condemned Joyce's pro-Nazi fascism and abandonment of Britain.
35. "Aims and Objects," The National Archives (TNA), Kew, United Kingdom, KV 2/1348 299084, "The Security Service: Personal (PF Series) Files: Arthur Kenneth Chesterton." This National Front should not be confused with one started by Chesterton in 1967 or the different entity founded by Andrew Fountaine.

36. "After Victory Group," The National Archives (TNA), Kew, United Kingdom, KV 2/1348 299084, "The Security Service: Personal (PF Series) Files: Arthur Kenneth Chesterton."
37. "No Action to be Taken Without Reference to F.3. Mr. Mitchell" and "Mr. Mitchell—F.3.," The National Archives (TNA), Kew, United Kingdom, KV 2/1348 299084, "The Security Service: Personal (PF Series) Files: Arthur Kenneth Chesterton."
38. "National Front," 1 November 1945, The National Archives (TNA), Kew, United Kingdom, KV 2/1348 299084, "The Security Service: Personal (PF Series) Files: Arthur Kenneth Chesterton." Beckett edited the BUF's newspaper *Action*. "Action," *Action* no. 36 (24 October 1936): 8.
39. For details, see: A.K. Chesterton, *Blame Not My Lute* (Unpublished draft, n.d.), University of Bath Special Collections, B.3–B.7
40. Baker, *Ideology of Obsession*, 197. "Sound the Alarm," *Candour* no. 1 (30 October 1953): 1; A.K. Chesterton, "The Devil's Agent," *Candour* XIII, no. 358 (2 September 1960): 73.
41. "Council," *Candour* III, no. 88 (1 July 1955): 8.
42. See Appendix 3 for the LEL Constitution in Hugh McNeile and Rob Black, *The History of the League of Empire Loyalists and Candour* (London: A.K. Chesterton Trust, 2014), 133.
43. A.K. Chesterton, *Stand by the Empire! A Warning to the British Nations* (Surrey: Candour Pub. Co., 1954).
44. Ibid.
45. Bill Baillie, interviewed by Ryan Shaffer, audio recording, 21 September 2011.
46. John Tyndall, *The Eleventh Hour: A Call for British Rebirth* (London: Albion Press, 1988), 50, 51.
47. Martin Webster, interviewed by Ryan Shaffer, audio recording, 3 June 2010.
48. John Bean, *The Many Shades of Black: Inside Britain's Far-Right*, 2nd ed. (Burlington: Ostara Publications, 2011), 100, 102. Previously, Jordan was a member of the British People's Party along with former Mosleyites. Colin Jordan, "Operation Post," *People's Post* 5, no. 8 (August 1948): 8.
49. For example, see: Colin Jordan, "Some Hope," *Candour* IV, no. 120 (10 February 1956): 52. John Bean, "India's Cry for Leadership," *Candour* VIII, no. 222 (24 January 1958): 29–30.
50. Interview with Webster.
51. Graham Macklin, *Very Deeply Dyed in Black: Sir Oswald Mosley and the Resurrection of British Fascism After 1945* (New York: I.B. Tauris, 2007), 57.

52. Interview with Webster.
53. Ibid.
54. Bean, *The Many Shades of Black*, 79.
55. "Between Ourselves," *Candour* no. 1 (30 October 1953): 4.
56. A.K. Chesterton, *Tomorrow: A Plan for the British Future* (Surrey: Candour Pub. Co., n.d., circa 1961), 2, 16.
57. "Rhodesian Loyalists," *Candour* XII, no. 347 (17 June 1960): 192; "S.A. Candour League's A.G.M," *Candour* XVIII, no. 443 (July 1965): 32.
58. A.K. Chesterton, *The New Unhappy Lords: An Exposure of Power Politics* (Hawthorne: Christian Book Club of America, 1967), 19.
59. "The New Unhappy Lords," *Candour* XVII, no. 458 (November 1966): 168; "You've Beaten Us To It," *Candour* XVIII, no. 461 (February 1967): 15.
60. "Empire Loyalist Enters Election Fray," *Hampshire Herald*, 3 September 1964.
61. See Rosine de Bounevialle, "Food for Darkest Britain," *Candour* X, no. 299 (17 July 1959): 224; "Candour Advisory Council," *Candour* XVII, no. 458 (November 1966): 168; Colin Todd, interviewed by Ryan Shaffer, audio recording, 3 October 2014.
62. *Vote Independent Loyalist* (Palace Chambers: League of Empire Loyalist, n.d., circa 1959). The typesetter and printer, Carlvenas Limited in Croydon, was the same as for Bounevialle's campaign material. *Petersfield-Parliament Election: Only Fifteen Years Ago* (n.p.: Rosine de Bounevialle, n.d.).
63. A.K. Chesterton, "Now is the Hour to Strike," *Candour* VI, no. 184 (3 May 1957): 142.
64. Bean, *The Many Shades of Black*, 117.
65. Ibid., 119; Tyndall, *The Eleventh Hour*, 182.
66. *John Bean: A True Nationalist* (Burnley: BNPTV, 2006) (DVD Recording). This is a video interview of Bean questioned by Nick Griffin.
67. Tyndall, *The Eleventh Hour*, 182.
68. Ibid., 182.
69. Ibid., 183.
70. Ibid., 185.
71. Martin Walker, *The National Front* (London: Fontana, 1978), 40, 41
72. Tyndall, *The Eleventh Hour*, 193.
73. Ibid., 199.
74. John Tyndall, *Official Progamme of the Greater Britain Movement* (London: Albion Press, n.d., circa 1964), 1.
75. "Editorial," *Spearhead* no. 1 (August/September 1964): 2.

76. "Tribute From Rhodesia," *Candour* XVII, no. 458 (November 1966): 168.
77. Skidelsky, *Oswald Mosley*, 516.
78. Ibid., 491.
79. "Right-Wing Patriots, Unite!," *Candour* XVII, no. 457 (October 1966): 156.
80. Ibid.
81. "Thugs Fail to Halt Merger Meeting," *Candour* XVIII, no. 460 (January 1967): 8.
82. Ibid.
83. Ibid.
84. According to LEL and NF publications, the address was 11 Palace Chambers, Bridge Street, London, SW1.
85. According to Bill Baillie, the pub was well known and had a bell to alert the Members of Parliament that there was a vote in Parliament. Interview with Baillie.
86. "National Front Formed," *Candour* XVIII, no. 461 (February 1967): 15.
87. Robert Edwards, interviewed by Ryan Shaffer, audio recording, 20 September 2011. Edwards later briefly joined the NF and served as chair of the Hammersmith Branch in the late 1970s, but became involved in writing and editing for the League of Saint George.
88. "Forward with the National Front," *Candour* XVIII, no. 462 (March 1967): 24.
89. Ibid.
90. *National Front Third Draft Constitution* (n.p.: unknown, n.d., circa 1967), unpaginated 1. Personal possession. This document was acquired from a collector and is an old typewritten copy with handwritten notes.
91. "Thugs Fail to Halt Merger Meeting," *Candour* XVIII, no. 460 (January 1967): 8.
92. "Forward with the National Front," 24.
93. Walker, *The National Front*, 67.
94. *The National Front Objectives* (London: National Front, 1967).
95. Ibid.
96. *Stop Immigration* (London: National Front, n.d., circa 1967).
97. A.K. Chesterton, "National Front as the Patriotic Elite," *Candour* XVIII, no. 465 (June 1967): 46.
98. John Tyndall, "Unity? Come Off it, Gentlemen!" *Spearhead* no. 22 (January/February 1969): 11.
99. Interview with Webster.
100. Walker, *The National Front*, 69.
101. Ibid., 85.

102. Aside from his public statements and associations, Tyndall was rumored to have a large private collection of Nazi material from the Second World War. Eddy Butler, interviewed by Ryan Shaffer, audio recording, 16 September 2011.
103. Walker, *The National Front*, 73.
104. Webster wrote that he "sent" Kenyatta "to where he belongs—the gutter" because the "national press" was "white-washing" his record "to create an image as a genial, worldly-wide, moderate elder statesman." Martin Webster, "I Attacked Kenyatta," *Spearhead* unnumbered (December 1964): 6.
105. The media representatives that were at the assault and spoke with Webster became witnesses. He later was sentenced to two months in prison and fined. TNA, Me Po 2/10633 299084, "Records of the Metropolitan Police Office: Correspondence and Papers: Martin Guy Webster." Interview with Webster.
106. John Tyndall, *The Authoritarian State* (London: National Socialist Movement, 1962), 5, 14.
107. John Tyndall, *Six Principles of British Nationalism* (London: Albion Press, n.d., circa 1966), 17, 27.
108. A photograph of the couple standing in front of Hitler's portrait at their wedding appeared in *A Well-Oiled Nazi Machine* (London: A. F. and R. Publication, n.d., circa 1978), 9.
109. She admitted to police discussing arson and going to a synagogue, but denied ever making a decision or encouraging anyone to burn it. "Françoise Jordan," TNA, CRIM 1/4749; "Mrs. Jordan, British Nazi, Is Sentenced to 18 Months," *New York Times* (18 January 1968).
110. Colin Jordan, *The Coloured Invasion* (London: Phoenix Press, 1967), 1.
111. Anthony Lester and Geoffrey Bindman, *Race and Law in Great Britain* (Cambridge: Harvard University Press, 1972), 135.
112. Kathleen Paul, *Whitewashing Britain: Race and Citizenship in the Postwar Era* (Ithaca: Cornell University Press, 1997), 176.
113. "The Jordans and Mosleyites are Rejoicing," *The Times*, 24 April 1968, 10.
114. Ibid.
115. *Mosley with the People, For the People* (London: Oswald Mosley, n.d., circa 1959). This is an election leaflet for Mosley's North Kensington Parliamentary election. Personal possession.
116. "The Jordans and Mosleyites are Rejoicing."
117. Ibid.
118. Ibid.
119. Ibid.
120. Bean, *The Many Shades of Black*, 206.

121. Ibid., 207.
122. A.K. Chesterton, "The Mystery of Enoch Powell," *Candour* XIX, no. 476 (May 1968): 49.
123. Bean, *The Many Shades of Black*, 207.
124. Ibid., 207.
125. Keith Thompson, interviewed by Ryan Shaffer, audio recording, 2 June 2010. (Abbreviated as "Interview with Thompson 1."). Thompson was briefly a member of the NF in 1976, but was expelled by Webster after organizing a visit to Diksmuide, Belgium.
126. Ibid.
127. "Immigration Control Association March," *National Front Member's Bulletin* (June 1968): 2. This bulletin was signed by "J. Bean, P. Maxwell, D. Pirie, G. Brown."
128. John Tyndall, "A Plot Fails," *Spearhead* no. 20 (September/October 1968): 12.
129. "Five Arrested After Apartheid Rally," *The Times* (27 May 1969). An undated "marching song" written by Harry Baxter included lyrics that denounced "all those who sold us" and called to "reunite or perish." Harry Baxter, "National Front Marching Song" (n.p.: unknown, n.d.), Modern Records Centre, MSS.412/HQ/4/2/8.
130. Walker, *The National Front*,116, 117.
131. Interview with Thompson 1.
132. Richard Edmonds, interviewed by Ryan Shaffer, audio recording, 15 September 2011.
133. Interview with Webster.
134. "Tories Switch to National Front," *The Times*, 12 November 1969.
135. Chesterton wrote that "every winter" he visits South Africa for health reasons and returns in England in the spring. A.K. Chesterton, "Forward the Extremists," *Candour* XXI, no. 496 (February 1970): 113; Interview with Webster.
136. Bean, *The Many Shades of Black*, 209.
137. Ibid., 210. Bean also noted that Chesterton was partly supported due to his access to wealthy contacts that could keep the NF operating. According to Chesterton, he received financial support from R.K. Jeffery, a Briton living in Chile. "Good News from Chile," *Candour* XIX, no. 477 (June 1968): 59.
138. Ibid., Bean; "National Front Denial," *The Times*, 8 September 1970.
139. A.K. Chesterton, "Our National Destiny," *Candour* XX, no. 492 (September 1969): 74.
140. "National Front Split Denied," *The Times*, 28 October 1970.

141. "Report on NF Sabotage to A.K.C From Several Sources," n.d., circa 1970. This is typed letter without a byline or signature sent to Chesterton about the rebellion. Personal possession.
142. "We Greet Combat Readers," *Spearhead* no. 20 (September/October 1968): 13.
143. Interview with Webster.
144. Letter from Marie Endean to A.K. Chesterton, 7 March 1971. Personal possession.
145. John Tyndall, "A.K. Chesterton: An Appreciation," *Spearhead* no. 39 (January 1971): 6.
146. Bean, *The Many Shades of Black*, 213.
147. John O'Brien, "Practical Considerations of Repatriation," *Spearhead* no. 39 (January 1971): 7.
148. Tyndall, *The Eleventh Hour*, 213.
149. Peter Scott, "Party Seeks Unity and Growth on Far Right," *The Times*, 16 March 1971. The numbers are undoubtedly inflated. In 1968, the NF told *The Times* it had about 10,000. If correct, a figure of 7000 in 1971 would mean a membership loss, or a figure of 10,000 equates with no growth after three years. "The Jordans and Mosleyites are Rejoicing."
150. Interview with Webster.
151. Tyndall, *The Eleventh Hour*, 215. Webster explained that O'Brien stole the NF's membership list to form his own party, but the police pressured him to return it. Interview with Webster.
152. Stan Taylor, *The National Front in English Politics* (London: Macmillan,1982), 98.
153. A.K. Chesterton, *Common Market Suicide* (Hampshire: Candour Publishing, 1971), 7.
154. A.K. Chesterton, *Facing the Abyss* (Hampshire: A.K. Chesterton Trust, 1976). The book was re-released by the A.K. Chesterton Trust in 2014.
155. A.K. Chesterton, "Fanfare for the British Rebirth," *Candour* XXIV, no. 539 (January 1973): 5; Rosine de Bounevialle, "We Carry the Torch," *Candour* XXV, no. 540 (January 1974): 1.
156. Frank Clifford, "Death of a Leader: A.K. Chesterton," *Spearhead* no. 69 (October 1973): 10–12.
157. Aidan Mackey, *Arthur Kenneth Chesterton, M.C.* (n.p.: Unknown, n.d., circa 1973), unpaginated 27.
158. "Britain: Free Nation or Province of Europe," *Spearhead* no. 45 (August 1971): 6, 7.
159. "Common Market: The Fight to Get Out Begins," *Spearhead* no. 60 (January 1973): 4.

160. Clare Macdonald, *The Money Manufacturers: An Exposure of the Root Cause of Financial and Economic Crises* (Croydon: National Front Policy Committee, n.d., circa 1971), 22.
161. John Tyndall, *The Case for Economic Nationalism* (Croydon: National Front Policy Committee, n.d., circa 1970s), 6, 10.
162. *God is Fed Up* (n.p.: National Front Christian Fellowship, n.d., circa 1970s).
163. "Why Keep Letting These Asians In?" *Spearhead* no. 53 (June 1972): 6.
164. "Government Prepares For Race War," *Spearhead* no. 61 (February 1973): 4.
165. Martin Webster, "Trouble Shooting," *Spearhead* no. 68 (September 1973): 17.
166. "London Local Election Successes," *Spearhead* no. 60 (January 1973): 19.
167. "Uxbridge: A Great Step Forward for the NF," *Spearhead* no. 60 (January 1973): 18.
168. Ibid.
169. "4000 at Cenotaph is Biggest Ever NF Turn Out," *Spearhead* no. 71 (December 1973): 18.
170. "NF Stages Best Ever Party Conference," *Spearhead* no. 70 (November 1973): 19, 20.
171. George Hutchinson, "The National Front's Growing Challenge to Mr. Heath," *The Times*, 31 May 1973.
172. Interview with Webster.
173. Ibid. Some commentators argued that Powell avoiding the Conservative candidate proved he distanced himself from the Conservatives. Simon Heffer explained this "did not take into account, though, that he had been willing to campaign in the Lincoln by-election during March, for Jonathan Guinness, but that Guinness had been told by Central Office to keep Powell away." Simon Heffer, *Like the Roman: The Life of Enoch Powell* (London: Weidenfeld & Nicolson, 1998), 667–668.
174. Arthur Osman, "National Front Poll Seen as Protest against Tories," *The Times*, 26 May 1973.
175. George Hutchinson, "The National Front's Growing Challenge to Mr. Heath," *The Times*, 31 May 1973.
176. Ibid.
177. Interview with Webster.
178. Interview with Edmonds.
179. "National Front's Man Insults Start Fight," *Kensington Post*, 10 October 1969. Reproduced in the Anti-Nazi League's *A Well-Oiled Nazi Machine*.
180. Taylor, *The National Front in English Politics*, 58.

181. Bean, *The Many Shades of Black*, 214.
182. "Report on NF Sabotage to A.K.C From Several Sources," n.d., circa 1970. Personal possession.
183. John Tyndall, "Some Reflections of Propaganda," *Spearhead* no. 87 (September 1975): 11.
184. "NF Holds Biggest Ever March and Meeting," *Spearhead* no. 48 (December 1971): 19.
185. "NF Men Protest Against IRA Speakers at College," *Spearhead* no. 50 (March 1972): 18.
186. "NF Demonstrates for Rhodesia," *Spearhead* no. 50 (March 1972): 18. Also see a previous protest, "Protesters Rained Off," *The Times*, 7 July 1969.
187. "4000 at Cenotaph is Biggest Ever NF Turn Out," *Spearhead* no. 71 (December 1973): 18.
188. "Great London Rally," *Spearhead* no. 67 (August 1973): 18.
189. "Hitchin March A Huge Success," *Spearhead* no. 42 (April 1971): 19.
190. "Stink Bomb dropped at GLC Meeting," *The Times*, 30 April 1969; "Sermon By Civil Liberties Leader Heckled," *The Times*, 8 November 1971; "Police Called to Keep Peace at Apartheid Protest," *The Times*, 19 January 1971.
191. Bean, *The Many Shades of Black*, 216.
192. John Tyndall, "The National Front and the General Election," *Spearhead* no. 72 (January 1974): 20.
193. "General Election Results," *Spearhead* no. 74 (April 1974): 20.
194. John Tyndall, "The National Front and the General Election: National Chairman's Assessment," *Spearhead* no. 74 (April 1974): 17.
195. Ibid., 18, 19.
196. Tyndall, *The Eleventh Hour*, 217.
197. "John Tyndall Elected NF Chairman," *Spearhead* no. 92 (March 1976): 18.
198. "Front Loses All Deposits," *The Times*, 12 October 1974.
199. "Kingsley Read Elected New Chairman of NF Directorate," *Britain First* no. 25 (December 1974): 4. The anti-fascist magazine *Searchlight* reported after John Kingsley Read's 1985 death that he had been supplying them with information. In 2002, *Spearhead* wrote, "now Nick Griffin claims that Read was not an enemy agent at all but a good nationalist! Just how does he therefore explain Gerry Gable's admission that Read was supplying *Searchlight* with information? Simple! The information, according to Mr. Griffin was 'false' information." "An Enemy Agent is 'Exonerated'," *Spearhead* no. 402 (August 2002): 11.
200. "John Kingsley Read" supplement in *A Well-Oiled Nazi Machine* (London: A. F. and R. Publication, n.d., circa 1978).

201. "What We Think," *Spearhead* no. 77 (July 1974): 2–3; "The Battle of Red Lion Square," *Britain First* no. 22 (July/August 1974): 2–3.
202. Interview with Webster.
203. *John Bean: A True Nationalist* (Burnley: BNPTV, 2006) (DVD Recording). During his interview with Nick Griffin, Bean said the NF gained 40,000 members, but the actual membership was likely one-fifth of that number.
204. Ibid.
205. Nigel Fielding, *The National Front*(London: Routledge, 1981), 159.
206. Interview with Edmonds.
207. Ibid.
208. Martin Webster, "An NF Trade Unionist Group Vitally Needed," *Spearhead* no. 77 (July 1974): 7.
209. Ibid.
210. Ibid.
211. "The Front Line," *Britain First* no. 17 (January/February 1974): 3.
212. Frances Gibb, "NUS Will March Against the Front," *The Higher Education Supplement*, 16 August 1974; "No Incidents in anti-Front March," *The Higher Education Supplement*, 30 August 1974.
213. David Leigh, "Asian Factor Complicates Unofficial Dispute at Leicester Factory," *The Times*, 2 July 1974.
214. "Reds Stir Asians to Violence," *Britain First* no. 21 (June/July 1974): 1.
215. Interview with Edmonds.
216. "Asian Factor Complicates Unofficial Dispute at Leicester Factory."
217. "The Victory of Leicester," *Britain First* no. 24 (October 1974): 3.
218. "5000 on NF Remembrance Day Parade," *Britain First* no. 25 (December 1974): 3.
219. "New Paper Launched," *Spearhead* no. 72 (January 1974): 19.
220. "Europe Farm Policy 'A Millstone'," *Britain First* no. 5 (3–16 April 1974): unpaginated 2; Richard Lawson, "Protect British Textiles Workers," *Britain First* no. 33 (October 1975): 1.
221. Philip Gannaway, "Trade Unions: Our Task," *Spearhead* no. 77 (July 1974): 20.
222. Neil Farnell, "Workers Against Immigration," *Spearhead* no. 81 (February 1975): 8.
223. Ibid.
224. "Work For the NF in Your Union," *Spearhead* no. 81 (February 1975): 19.
225. "NUJ Trotskyites Attack Britain First," *Britain First* no. 28 (May 1975): 3.
226. "Britain First Journalists Nujed Aside," *Britain First* no. 29 (June 1975): 2.

227. "Politics 'No Bar' to NUJ Membership," *The Times*, 24 March 1975.
228. "NUJ Turns Down Britain First Applicants," *Britain First* no. 31 (August 1975): 3.
229. "Journalists to Boycott the National Front," *The Times*, 16 June 1976.
230. Stephen E. Atkins, *Holocaust Denial as an International Movement* (New York: Praeger, 2009), 165; "David McCalden Interviews," *Race and Reason* (n.p.: White Aryan Resistance, 1984, 1985) (DVD Recordings).
231. "How the NF Lost World War II," *New Statesman*, 7 September 1979, 332.
232. Burt A. Folkart, "David McCalden; Failed to Disprove the Holocaust," *Los Angeles Times*, 25 October 1990. David Cole described him as "fascinating," noting that while he might have been racist, McCalden "had a non-white wife" and there were rumors he was gay. Cole further wrote, "the poor bastard had upped and died of AIDS after giving it to his wife as well." David Cole, *Republican Party Animal: The "Bad Boy of Holocaust History" Blows the Lid Off Hollywood's Secret Right-Wing Underground* (Port Townsend: Feral House, 2014), 24.
233. "65 Arrests After Protest Over National Front," *The Times*, 26 May 1975.
234. Ernest Pendrous, "National Front Unionists," *The Times*, 31 October 1975.
235. Ibid.
236. Ibid.
237. "Workers Back NF Trade Unionists," *Spearhead* no. 101 (January 1977): 18.
238. Ibid.
239. Ibid.
240. "Letters," *Spearhead* no. 104 (April 1977): 16.
241. John Tyndall, "NF Constitution: What Do You Think," *Spearhead* no. 84 (May 1975): 9, 10. He included a poll for readers to take about changing the constitution.
242. "National Front's New Chairman is Former Tory," *The Times*, 22 October 1974; "National Front leaders 'Must be Reinstated'," *The Times*, 20 December 1975; "Former National Front Leader Back in Power," *The Times*, 10 February 1976.
243. "Urgent Appeal: Stand By The National Front," *Spearhead* no. 90 (December 1975/January 1976): 4.
244. "National Party Statement on Principles," *Britain First* no. 36 (March 1976): 5; "Are You Pushing Britain First?" *Britain First* no. 36 (March 1976): 8.
245. "A History of Mr. Read's Big Gamble," *Spearhead* no. 90 (December 1975/January 1976): 7.

246. Robert Parker, "National Front to Field 318 Candidates in General Election," *The Times*, 2 July 1976.
247. Interview with Edmonds.
248. Ibid.
249. Douglas Reed, *Nemesis? The Story of Otto Strasser* (Boston: Houghton Mifflin Company, 1940), 261, 262.
250. Nick Griffin, interviewed by Ryan Shaffer, audio recording, 8 October 2014.
251. Ibid.
252. Joe Pearce, interviewed by Ryan Shaffer, audio recording, 9 November 2009.
253. Ibid.
254. *Build the National Party of the United Kingdom* (n.p.: National Party Constitution, n.d., circa 1976), unpaginated 4. The National Party even described itself as having "broadly" the "same" policies as the NF. "Support the National Party!" *Britain First* no. 35 (January/February 1976): 1.
255. Richard Verrall, "Left-Wing Shift in the National Front," *Spearhead* no. 90 (December 1975/January 1976): 10–11.
256. Ibid., 11.
257. Neil Farnell, "Industrial Front," *Spearhead* no. 90 (December 1975/ January 1976): 13. See also: Neil Farnell, "Industrial Front," *Spearhead* no. 91 (February 1976): 13.
258. "New National Front Newspaper," *Spearhead* no. 93 (April 1976): 19.
259. "Record Sales for NF Paper," *Spearhead* no. 98 (October 1976): 18.
260. Interview with Webster.
261. "Railwaymen," *Spearhead* no. 98 (October 1976): 19.
262. Peter J. Floyd, "A National Front Railwaymen's Association," *Spearhead* no. 101 (January 1977): 20.
263. Ibid., 20.
264. TNA, AN111/1089 299084, "National Front Railwaymen's Association."
265. Ibid.
266. Ibid.
267. Ibid.
268. TNA, AN111/1089 299084, Richard Faulkner to C.A. Rose, 2 November 1977.
269. TNA, AN111/1089 299084, R.H. Wilcox to Richard Faulkner, 10 November 1977.
270. *The Fight against the Racists* (London: Socialist Worker, 1977), 14.
271. "Tory Trade Unionists Attack NUR Policy on 'Front'," *The Times*, 5 April 1978.

272. Ibid.
273. Paul Routledge, "NUR Pledge on Front Members," *The Times*, 11 April 1978.
274. "NF Vote in Thurrock Shocks Old Parties," *Spearhead* no. 96 (August 1976): 19.
275. "NF to Fight Three By-Elections," *Spearhead* no. 98 (October 1976): 18.
276. "Training the Party," *Spearhead* no. 97 (September 1976): 18; "John Tyndall Weds NF Girl," *Spearhead* no. 111 (November 1977): 19. *Spearhead* reported that Valerie, daughter of Charles and Violet Parker from Brighton, was an NF activist for four years and "campaigned for her father when he stood as the National Front's Parliamentary candidate."
277. "Encouraging Results in Local Elections," *Spearhead* no. 98 (October 1976): 18.
278. "NF in Nationwide Local Election Campaign," *National Front News* no. 2 (May 1976): 4.
279. "Walsall Vote Proves It: NF Poised to Replace Liberals," *Spearhead* no. 100 (December 1976): 18.
280. "AGM Celebrates Year of Success," *Spearhead* no. 99 (November 1976): 18.
281. "Impressive NF Ceremony on the Day of Remembrance," *Spearhead* no. 90 (December 1975/January 1976): 19; "Thousands March on NF Remembrance Day Parade," *Spearhead* no. 100 (December 1976): 19.

CHAPTER 3

Youth Against Tradition, 1977–1983

The National Front (NF) failed to win any elections, but its marginal popularity surged after 1974, leading to an increase in street conflict and racial violence. The opponents of racism and fascism in Britain became increasingly concerned about the NF's popularity, no matter how limited. The Socialist Workers Party (SWP) along with several other groups launched the Anti-Nazi League (ANL) and helped host Rock Against Racism (RAR) events to confront the NF on the streets and in popular culture through music. At the same time, the NF welcomed burgeoning interest from teenagers and used its opponents' tactics by starting Rock Against Communism (RAC) to promote its ideology to the wider public through abrasive music.[1] After a slow start, RAC went from being in the background of the NF's recruitment efforts to being at the forefront of the party's activities following internal NF problems resulting from the 1979 general election. The ingenuity and energy of the NF youth had a transformative impact on fascist tactics, and the youthfulness and exploration of new ideas modified British fascism with an influx of foreign extremist thought.

This chapter explores the challenges posed by leftists who started the ANL and RAR in order to criticize the NF's ideology and electoral gains through a variety of outlets ranging from street demonstrations to music. While the ANL put intense public pressure on the NF by demonstrating its marginality and highlighting its fascist components through youth

The original version of this chapter was revised: Footnote reference placement has been corrected. An erratum to this chapter is available at DOI 10.1007/978-3-319-59668-6_9

R. Shaffer, *Music, Youth and International Links in Post-War British Fascism*, Palgrave Studies in the History of Subcultures and Popular Music, DOI 10.1007/978-3-319-59668-6_3

culture, the NF also drew lessons from the ANL that laid the ground for the transformation of British fascism. At the time of the ANL's campaign, a group of rebellious youth joined the NF and formed the Young National Front, which developed RAC to promote music that expressed its own sympathies, including neo-Nazism, racism and anti-Semitism. The NF's national leadership lacked an overall strategy for the youth, favoring doctrinal training over a clear outreach campaign that embraced youth culture. Consequently, the NF youth took it upon themselves to innovate British fascism by merging youth culture with extremism. This chapter shows how the NF was influenced by the anti-fascist movement, turning the anti-racist music around and giving itself new life in the 1980s. In 1979, the first large racist concert was poorly reviewed in the press, but the NF continued its music outreach and drew large numbers of youth who sang along with political slogans, bought music from the NF and generated publicity for the next decade. The high point for interest in post-war fascist youth subculture, however, marked a low point for the NF's electoral impact, as fewer elections were contested and party splits diluted its already limited electoral returns.

Anti-Nazi League and Rock Against Racism

Throughout 1977, the NF continued to organize marches that generated publicity and violence. The NF won 119,000 votes during the May Council and Greater London Council elections by running more than four hundred candidates, beating the Liberal Party in thirty-three seats in London.[2] Scholar Paul Whiteley explained that the number of NF candidates in "local and national elections has increased at each successive election since it was founded."[3] The media reported, to the worry of many, that the NF might overtake the Liberals as the largest third party. Webster said, bluntly, that the NF's election return that year "gave the establishment the shits."[4] In August 1977, the NF staged a demonstration to "clear the muggers off the streets," which immediately provoked opposition.[5] There were calls to ban the NF from its "deliberately provocative marches in areas with a large immigrant population," such as Lewisham in South East London.[6] Members of the SWP, which was known as the International Socialists prior to 1977, as well as other Marxist groups announced they would "stop" the NF, while the Front said it would not be intimidated.[7] The NF claimed to have drawn 2000 supporters to the event in which photographs showed different city branches of the NF marching and fighting with opponents in Lewisham.[8]

In November 1977 the ANL was formed to unite Labour, Liberal and SWP activists in reaction to the NF's electoral returns in the 1977 Greater London Council elections, which reached 10%.[9] The elections, along with the violence that was a constant feature of NF activity, inspired SWP member Paul Holborow, anti-apartheid activist Peter Hain, and Labour Party member Ernie Roberts to lead the ANL.[10] Hain, who became the ANL's national spokesman, had been threatened with violence and had his meetings disrupted by the NF due to his anti-racist activism.[11] He was drawn into the movement by Holborow, who argued for a massive movement against the NF and used the "Nazi" label in highlighting the NF's affinity to Nazism.[12] The anti-racists warned the public that the NF influence could serve as a spoiler and determine the results of several elections.[13] The Revolutionary Marxist Group, which argued for more radical policies, wrote that the ANL sees "the struggle against the NF as so urgent that it is necessary for all who oppose the NF to unite."[14]

The ANL used a variety of outreach methods to stop the NF and hobble its recruitment efforts.[15] The SWP issued a pamphlet arguing that the way to prevent the NF from "developing into a mass fascist movement" was not to "ignore them," but to challenge them in the workplace and also "stop them marching and organising."[16] These efforts ranged from street confrontations to preventing the NF from getting publicity and printing its own literature. Not all critics of the NF joined the ANL, as the Board of Deputies of British Jews initially condemned the ANL's street confrontations with the NF.[17] The ANL also argued for silencing the NF and called for ending the British Broadcasting Corporation (BBC)'s airing of the NF election party broadcasts.[18] This earned the group accusations of censorship, including from NF member Tom Mundy, who denounced the ANL's efforts and its linking of the NF with Nazism.[19] The ANL also campaigned to prevent the NF from hosting meetings at schools, which the NF was legally and frequently allowed to do.[20]

One of the ANL's significant activities was distributing literature throughout the country that highlighted the NF's policies and its leaders' extremist pasts. The most notable and widely circulated was *A Well-Oiled Nazi Machine*, of which the ANL printed 500,000 copies, which illustrated Tyndall's and Webster's National Socialist activities and whose title was taken from a statement by Webster in 1962 about building "a well-oiled Nazi machine."[21] With more than a dozen pages of photographs and details about the history of fascism, the pamphlet was a devastating exposé that linked the NF to anti-Semitism, Nazism, Holocaust denial, racism and violence.[22] In response, Webster compiled a pamphlet titled *Lifting the Lid Off the Anti-Nazi League* that called the ANL "a front for rampant Marxism, and a launching platform for hysterical violence."[23] In June 1978, four fires were ignited at the ANL main office in Soho, London, destroying 50,000 copies of *A Well-Oiled Nazi Machine* and causing more than £20,000 in damages.[24] Peter Hain blamed the NF, but the Front in turn accused the ANL of setting the fire on its own property.[25] The NF denied responsibility despite graffiti left behind that read, in part: "NF rules."[26] The NF responded by referring to the ANL with the acronym ANAL, describing the event as "a suspicious bit of 'arson' at ANAL's office, in which a few posters were scorched," and criticized most of "the national press" for not reporting the attempt by "ANAL terrorists" who "tried to burn down the home" of an NF organizer.[27] However, two years later Kenneth Matthews, the NF Southwark branch chair, was sentenced to six years in prison for "trying to set fire to a printing works used by the Socialist Workers' Party" when he and two others attacked the business with "a bang and a flash" so people "would notice that NF slogans had been painted on the walls."[28] Yet the ANL was not the only group whose criticism the NF had to contend with. Other local groups of Labour, Liberal and Conservative Party members teamed up to distribute "hundreds of thousands of leaflets" against racism and the NF.[29]

The ANL turned to culture, specifically music, to mobilize masses of people and attract youth to its movement.[30] A few years earlier, in the summer of 1976, RAR was started by the SWP "as a direct result of" the street battles involving the NF and comments made by Eric Clapton and David Bowie.[31] Clapton "made a few remarks that seemed to support Enoch Powell's view on repatriation," and in a 1978 interview in which Clapton denied he and Powell were racists, said Powell's "diplomacy is wrong, and he's got no idea how to present things. His ideas are right. You go to Heathrow any day, mate, and you'll see thousands of Indian people sitting there waiting to know whether or not they can come into the country."[32] Similarly, in May 1976 David Bowie said, "I believe Britain could benefit from a fascist leader. After all, fascism is really nationalism."[33] The following week he arrived at Victoria Station appearing to give a Nazi salute from a car, and the *New Musical Express* ran a photo of the event along with the quote about fascism.[34] In response to the words of two popular musicians and the gains made by the NF, the

SWP hoped to attract youth to its politics and challenge racism through music.

The activities of RAR consisted of organizing concerts, publishing a magazine called *Temporary Hoarding* and spreading literature. The first RAR concert was held in December 1976 at the Royal College of Art, with hundreds of youth gathering to hear the music.[35] The music press was reluctant at first to promote the events, as they were averse to mixing music and politics, which required the RAR to be innovative and develop its own outreach methods and "propaganda."[36] Posters from RAR, for instance, superimposed portraits of Hitler and Powell on images of Bowie.[37] *Temporary Hoarding* published interviews with bands such as the Sex Pistols and The Clash that seemingly supported its messages and gave instructions for people to organize concerts with the RAR message.[38] In addition, it issued articles about racism and fascism.[39] Ultimately it formed RARecords, which released a compilation album titled "Rock Against Racism's Greatest Hits."[40] Yet RAR's true power was in hosting regular concerts, which led people to begin associating RAR and its themes with their favorite bands.

The SWP developed RAR as a political campaign. As *Sounds* journalist Garry Bushell explained, RAR was created in 1976 by SWP members Roger Huddle and Red Saunders to serve as "an umbrella organization" and attract youth to leftist politics—which it succeeded in doing.[41] As David Renton has shown, the influence of the SWP within the ANL was a problem for Labour Party members because of the SWP's radical politics, leading some Labour Party members to later abandon the group.[42] Indeed, the political message in *Temporary Hoarding* went beyond racism, stating "the left is right" and "the right is wrong," and the reader "better decide what side you're on."[43] Bushell described how the RAR managed to build a network of music support because RAR concerts were the only platform given to countless bands, since many local councils banned punk events.[44] At the same time, SWP membership grew rapidly and its newspaper, the *Socialist Worker*, was selling 50,000 copies a week.[45] The power of RAR to mobilize youth for a political cause was harnessed by the ANL when the two organized large festivals together to protest the NF.

The link between music and race was a subject in which the wider public was interested. In March 1978, *Sounds* ran a story about the NF with the title "Racism and Your Music," with the cover featuring photographs of famous black musicians with a red stamp reading "deported" printed over their images.[46] It included an interview with Webster and discussed the NF's policies of repatriation, concluding that "the National Front will stop the music."[47] It went on to discuss popular "fascinations" with Nazism, including "swastika chic" and The Clash anti-racist song "White Riot," which was open to "misinterpretation."[48] Highlighting Webster's previous quotes supporting Hitler, the interview examined Webster's views on race and his opinion that rock music is a "massive con trick."[49] The article concluded, "over 150,000 people voted for the National Front," which was "a lot of votes against *your* freedom and life style" and it "got all that attention by default—because you (or those who disagree with what they stand for) were too apathetic to make yourselves heard."[50]

The ANL and RAR combined their efforts to host two large music festivals in 1978 that featured some of the most popular musical acts at the time. According to Hain, the organizations remained separate, but worked as siblings because the ANL could organize large events and RAR could get musicians involved.[51] The first concert in April 1978, featuring Steel Pulse, the Tom Robinson Band and X-Ray Spex, was advertised as "a stand of multi-racial solidarity" and intended to "disprove the brick throwing image that things like the Lewisham confrontation have foisted on anti-fascist demonstrations."[52] Other groups, including The Clash, were added to the bill and the public was told to meet at Trafalgar Square for speeches then march through the East End to the concert in Victoria Park.[53] The carnival was a success, drawing large crowds and publicity, including the RAR effigies of Tyndall and Webster making the cover of the *New Musical Express*.[54] Attendance ranged between 50,000 and 80,000, and anti-fascist leaders commented that it was only the beginning of a youth transformation.[55] The reaction spread, with photographs of the concert and rallies appearing in music magazines, and about 30,000 RAR badges were sold throughout the country.[56] Garry Bushell, who attended the concert, described it as a "fantastic event" and the greatest achievement of the ANL.[57] The attention and large crowds prompted RAR and the ANL to partner again for another concert. In September 1978, the second RAR festival attracted 30,000 people, with a march from Hyde Park to Brockwell Park in South London.[58] At the end of the march, the audience watched musical acts including Aswad, Elvis Costello and Misty perform their hits.[59] The crowd included "intense and whispy-bearded" leftists, and the marchers shouted and displayed slogans such as "stop," "smash," "crush" and "stamp out." Though the march was ostensibly against racism, the "mainly under 25 and mainly white" crowd targeted the NF with "large grotesque glass fibre heads" of Tyndall, Webster and Hitler.[60]

The NF's response was to mobilize its own supporters and taunt RAR supporters. Keith Axon, who joined the NF in 1976 and served as the North Birmingham branch organizer, said the ANL did serious damage to the NF by linking the party to Nazism.[61] Indeed, he reflected that the NF was slow to understand the impact the anti-racist movement was having on the party and to respond.[62] On the day of the the September RAR carnival, the NF held a march with 2000 supporters in the East End.[63] According to senior NF activist Richard Verrall, the timing and location were "deliberately" chosen, with *The Times* noting that it was "one of the most racially sensitive areas in the country."[64] According to reporter Robert Parker, "many" of those in the march "were youths with 'crew-cut' hair" who "wore heavy boots and jeans with braces."[65] Likewise Joe Pearce, a young NF activist, described how he and other NF youth would shout at white youth, telling them to support their own and not attend RAR events.[66]

Confrontations between the NF and its critics continued throughout the next year. Trade unionists and anti-racist groups staged demonstrations and counter-demonstrations, with police mobilized to prevent violence.[67] In the "most vigorous" demonstration against the Front in the Greater Manchester area, where 3500 local trade unionists and Labour members protested against the NF's meeting and became violent, 6000 police fought to separate the groups and arrested nineteen people.[68] Months later thirty-four people, including Webster, were arrested in Brixton, in south London, where hundreds of ANL activists protested against two hundred NF supporters.[69] Webster was charged and found guilty of obstruction for encouraging his supporters to disobey police.[70] A few days later, several more arrests were made at a similar NF meeting in High Wycombe.[71] Indeed, the violence was not limited to street confrontations; the press reported arrests of NF members for fighting and even members possessing "bomb materials."[72]

Young National Front

While the SWP was attracting youth to its movement through music, the NF also experienced an influx of teenagers who attended their events.[73] According to the mother of a supporter, the NF appealed to her teenage son because of political disillusionment based on the "coloured problem," and he "believed the NF … that the economic problems of the world were caused by high financiers who wished to make countries indebted to them."[74] After the unsuccessful attempt to harness anti-immigrant sentiment among white workers by starting NF trade unions, the new interest among youth came at an opportune moment. Indeed, the trade union outreach proved largely unsuccessful and the NF was unable to change the leftist face of organized labor. At first, the NF did not know how to respond to youth joining their ranks, so it turned its focus to education and responding to "liberal" education in schools. Yet its major policy goals went unrealized as the youth took it upon themselves to chart their own course and reach out to their peers with new publications and music.

The NF leadership responded to interest from teenagers by launching a section of the party devoted solely to youth and their interests. Though youth branches of fascist movements were not a new development, with the Hitler Youth being the most famous example, the NF's plan was the first serious British fascist youth mobilization effort since the Second World War. Moreover, the concepts and plans for teenage involvement came from the youth themselves. In summer 1977, Derek Holland, himself a student, called for the creation of a youth "wing" to serve as a liaison with young people and "fight" for the minds of students.[75] He noted that youth sections had been set up by British groups previously, but those attempts failed because the leaders "did not understand the nature and aims of this wing."[76] The proposals coming from interested youth mirrored the pre-existing issues raised by established NF activists. In 1975, Richard Edmonds, a Tulse Hill Comprehensive School teacher, was pressured to quit his job after being photographed at an anti-immigration rally.[77] Edmonds resigned, claiming he "was a victim of a campaign by other teachers," and later "resumed" his career in industry.[78] In *Spearhead*, he described the important "teaching profession" unions as heavily influenced by the "extreme left" and communists, and called for education to be "free from communist subversion."[79] This issue later resurfaced when young people joined the NF and denounced their teachers.

Young people joined the NF for a variety of social, political and psychological reasons. Pearce described his father as an autodidact with anti-Semitic and anti-Irish sentiments who believed that "Hitler's anti-communism trumped the less savory aspects of his politics."[80] Disliking formal education and feeling contempt for his teachers, Pearce began writing the NF logo on walls and books and joined the NF in 1976 as an activist selling the party newspaper.[81] A rebellious youth opposed to the communist politics of his teachers, at age 17 he published an article in *Spearhead* titled "Red Indoctrination in the Classroom."[82] Nick Griffin, who joined at the same age two years earlier, became interested in politics when his father, Edgar, took the family to local Conservative Party meetings.[83] Initially active with the Young Conservatives, Griffin heard about the NF and after several attempts was finally able to attend an NF meeting and listen to its speakers. He came away from the gathering impressed with the NF's honesty about its opinions, which he compared with the Conservative Party's tip-toeing around issues, and joined in 1974.[84] Ideologically, Griffin was attracted to the party's anti-European Economic Community (EEC), anti-immigration and anti-IRA rhetoric as well as its opposition to Zionism and international banking.[85]

At the October 1977 Annual General Meeting, the NF Directorate approved the creation of the Young National Front (YNF) to "counterbalance 'Marxist bias'" in schools.[86] Joe Pearce claimed this was not a case in which youth were manipulated by older people; rather, it was a result of the NF's realization that so many young people, including himself, wanted to join the NF.[87] According to Martin Webster, when the young people joined the party they sought a youth group devoted to their interests that would allow them to have some influence.[88] Following speeches about expanding the NF to include youth, the audience celebrated the motion.[89] In private, however, activists such as Edmonds and Tyndall were not sold on the idea of a separate youth division, believing that youth who were politically mature enough should be normal members.[90] Regarding political youth organizations, Edmonds said "when I came into nationalism, I opposed them at every turn" as "it provides a platform for hotheads who are irresponsible partly because they know nothing."[91] Instead, "young people should mix with the adults" and become part of the broader organization.[92] That is to say, the NF leadership welcomed the young people as members, but did not have an overall objective to incorporate them in a separate outreach strategy. In fact, demonstrating a desire not to give the youth autonomy, Andrew Fountaine, a former League of Empire Loyalist member who fought for Francisco Franco during the Spanish Civil War, was selected to lead the YNF and lasted about a year, followed by Philip Gegan and then Joe Pearce.[93] Shortly after its launch, the YNF announced its campaign to counter "pro-race mixing brainwashing" and to have multiracial films "banned" from schools.[94]

The youth section was developed during an all-day conference of about one hundred "young members," ranging in age from thirteen to twenty-five, who met with Tyndall, Webster and Richard Verrall to discuss goals and organizational structure.[95] The new organization, it was decided, would replace the older and less active National Front Students Association to have a wider influence and include lower-level and higher education students as well as young workers.[96] Indeed, the NF had a long-standing interest in delivering its message to the next generation. In 1973 Richard Lawson led the National Front Students Association and edited its newspaper, *Spark*. According to the NF, the paper was distributed in schools with content "to ridicule and debunk," which would also "enrage the student left" and underline "the radical aspects of NF ideology."[97] There were also other smaller subsections of the NF, such as the Cambridge Students' National Front Group, which published *Rite-Up*.[98] However, such efforts failed to make any wider impact and gain attention, especially with the younger audience.

In contrast, the launch of the YNF was successful in expanding youth membership and publicity. Indeed, one of its rallying points was the self-produced local bulletins that advertised youth activities.[99] Joe Pearce, who joined the NF as a fifteen-year-old in 1976, began his own publication, titled *Bulldog*, with help from his local branch in Barking.[100] Borrowing the attention-grabbing style of *The Sun*, *Bulldog* quickly became popular for its provocative articles on race and made Pearce a key youth in the NF.[101] The seventh issue, for example, included the headline "White Youth Unite and Fight" with a photo of a fight, and discussed "white youths" at football grounds supporting the NF.[102] The magazine also featured a regular column chronicling NF youth activity. For example, one issue discussed Nick Griffin at Cambridge University being criticized in the university's student newspaper and his "amused" response.[103]

To spread the NF ideology to the average person, activists sold NF publications on the streets and in areas with large crowds. Pearce explained that the NF would target the Chelsea football grounds for its large white working-class supporters and would regularly sell seven hundred copies, with about 10% of the crowd buying *Bulldog*.[104] NF member Colin Todd recalled selling two hundred copies at Newcastle games and some fans giving £10 per copy, with the money going back to the local party branch.[105] Schools were also targeted. For example, Pearce sold copies of *Bulldog* outside the school of musician and outspoken fascist critic Billy Bragg in the 1970s.[106] In 1981, the *Times Educational Supplement* described how schools had "a tiny group of pupils who are genuine believers," but "a much larger group are loosely sympathetic because of their support for particular football teams or rock groups."[107] Yet this activity was not without risk. Selling NF publications, such as *Bulldog* and the *National Front News*, could be dangerous as it led to violent confrontations with opponents and even arrest by police.[108]

The YNF grew exponentially during 1978. In fact, Pearce described the youth wing as "the most important development" of the NF in "many years."[109] The NF received a "flood of enquiries" from youth, which produced "excitement" throughout the country.[110] The youth wing planned to continue generating interest through sports and organize "socials which will cater primarily to the musical tastes of young members."[111] Its first "counter-offensive" was the publication of anti-communist material on topics including history, sociology, economics and race.[112] A leaflet titled *How To Spot a Red Teacher* claimed that "commie teachers will tell you that all races are 'equal'," but "tell the red teacher ... this is rubbish."[113] It also stated that readers should "tell the red teacher that poor whites during the Great Slump of the 1930s didn't commit muggings on defenceless old women."[114] Moreover, Joe Pearce wanted the teaching of social history to be replaced with a focus on British military feats and denounced the introduction of "pagan religions."[115]

The youth campaign generated attention from the press and elevated the status of key NF youth members. At a news conference, "16 year old editor of *Bulldog* Joe Pearce" told journalists the "campaign was a method of resisting the invasion of the classroom by politics which has already taken place as a result of the activities of Marxist teachers."[116] A February rally drew hundreds of young supporters who listened to speeches by YNF leaders such as Pearce and Nick Griffin, as well as senior leaders including Brons, Tyndall and Webster.[117] In May 1978, the *National Front News* proudly reported that the YNF's campaign to expose "Marxist teachers" had generated "dozens" of local press reports.[118] In June, the NF stated that it had received local Conservative council support in West Sussex because of concern about Marxist "infiltration" of education.[119] In the summer, the NF reported that "hundreds" of youth were still "flocking to join the Young National Front."[120]

The youth began gaining a larger influence in the movement with more initiatives from the YNF. Nick Griffin, who joined the NF as a fifteen-year-old in 1974, became the YNF's student liaison officer and editor of its newsletter, *Front Page*, from his home in Halesworth, Suffolk.[121] He explained that previous NF campaigns at universities had "left much to be desired" and that the new campaign would lay the groundwork for "real influence in our universities and colleges."[122] The goal was to coordinate the activity of the NF at British universities, and it ended up attracting about one hundred registered members.[123] Yet the influence of older members remained an important part of the NF structure. In July 1978, forty NF youth took part in "leadership training" that discussed the "drive for World Government" and "the case for racialism" led by Martin Webster, Andrew Brons and Richard Verrall.[124] Subsequent seminars, claiming to attract two hundred youth, offered lessons in "producing a local NF newsletter" or "nationalist economics."[125]

Aside from direct political activity, the YNF organized a football league for several London locations.[126] The championship consisted of the "first ever" John Tyndall Shield football finals, with Tyndall and his wife as guests of honor.[127] With teams from Norwich, Enfield, Bristol and Loughton, the final match saw Hackney beat the Barking YNF.[128] The YNF then announced it was looking to expand the league.[129] By the end of the year, the effort included more teams, showing a growing radical youth movement in the NF. *Spearhead* noted that at the start of the year "there were not even enough teams to form a league," but with a "massive" drive by groups in London, there was enough involvement to play fortnightly for eight months.[130] After the new league was launched, the team standings appeared as a regular feature in *Bulldog*.[131]

Locations for youth activity, including football games and concerts, proved to be a popular space for NF promotion and recruitment. As Pearce noted of football games, "we knew this was where the white working class gathered together" and "very few non-whites attend football games so it was a good place to have maximum impact."[132] Starting in 1978, *National Front News* and *Bulldog* were sold at Stamford Bridge, Chelsea Football Club's stadium, and hundreds of papers were purchased "every time."[133] Meanwhile, the fans made "racist and nationalist chants" that echoed on the fields, and the NF began selling Chelsea NF t-shirts.[134] This sentiment spread to other teams, such as Leeds United and Norwich.[135] Indeed, the news reported racist shouts of "nigger" as well as fans chanting "National Front! National Front" at games.[136]

Concerts also were a prime location for NF newspaper sales. *Bulldog* reported that NF activists sold two hundred issues at a Bad Manners concert despite police attempting to stop them.[137]

The first year of the YNF was described by Pearce as a success with "great expansion," and there was "much to celebrate" on its first anniversary.[138] He noted the involvement of other youth, including Griffin and Nick Wakeling, who showed "talent" and "courage" in their efforts for the movement.[139] Indeed, throughout 1978 news outlets were reporting on the NF's success in recruiting young football supporters.[140] A *New Society* survey of three hundred white youth in East London concluded: "A typical young NF supporter is male, left school at 16 with no qualifications and is prepared to use violence."[141] The report explained that in a random sampling in traditionally Labour areas, Labour was the most popular party, but the NF was tied with the Conservatives as the second choice.[142] The article went on to explain that while the NF was not an electoral threat, it had failed to fully "capitalise" on the youth's "racialist feelings."[143] The changing age of the party was also illustrated in the NF's reporting on its Remembrance Parade. No longer mentioning a specific number, the magazine discussed "thousands" that joined the NF march, but described YNF activist Griffin speaking alongside Tyndall and Fountaine.[144]

Rock Against Communism

When the young extremists saw the SWP's success in attracting new members through music, the NF youth started its own movement, RAC, to recruit teenagers to the NF.[145] However, fascists evoking passion and nationalism through music was not a new idea, as the "Horst Wessel Song," the Nazi's anthem about a Nazi martyred by communists, recounted a story that was a significant symbol for a new generation of Germans and was sung by millions.[146] Eddy Morrison, a long-time NF activist in Leeds, split from the party in 1975 and created a small group, the British National Party, which was short-lived but issued a monthly, *British News*, which by 1977 was telling its members to join the NF.[147] In 1978, Morrison and several others decided that in response to the SWP they needed to either "condemn" punk rock or "use it."[148] As he later wrote, there was a need to organize "our own white nationalist 'alternative society'," including social clubs to build a support base for their politics.[149] Morrison and others created a fanzine, a publication produced by fans, titled *The Punk Front*, which featured the NF logo and quickly became popular among young radicals.[150] Word spread rapidly among supporters at the largest music clubs, notably the F Club, which drew more people into the fold. *British News* told readers "to help end the domination of music" by supporting "RAC."[151] With Morrison, the fascists in Leeds started RAC and two local bands that expressed their ideology in music, The Ventz and The Dentists, joined the RAC effort. In September 1978 Alan Peace, singer of The Ventz, said that RAC was becoming more serious and discussion began about creating "a right-wing music monthly and a concert with about three or four anti-communist bands."[152]

The major music magazines were writing about the young punk phenomenon and its association with fascism. According to Morrison, *Sounds* journalist Garry Bushell went to Leeds to report on the movement.[153] In March 1979, Bushell discussed a local RAC Leeds concert, writing that "Rock For Fascism" would be a more appropriate title and that Morrison, "the self-styled leader of the young Nazi scene in Leeds," was actively recruiting youth at concerts.[154] Decades later Bushell recalled that the local groups were "talentless" and only played small pubs.[155] With extremism injected into aggressive music, fights started over political affiliation, including anti-NF bands being attacked with beer glasses.[156] The Mekons, for example, were assaulted by a crowd that was calling the band "commie bastards."[157]

Rock Against Communism became the centerpiece of the YNF and a national movement with the backing of Pearce and the NF. In addition to the YNF's outreach via schools and sports, music served as a vehicle for fascists to develop their own subculture that could entice youth to join and express NF ideas. In spring 1979, *Bulldog* told its readers that RAC would "hold concerts, roadshows and tours" in the following months.[158] No longer would "white" British youth have "to put up with left-wing filth in rock music" because "RAC is going to fight back against left-wingers and anti-British traitors in the music press."[159] The YNF was coordinating the venue, sound systems and musical acts for a large concert in London that would appeal to youth with fascist politics.

In August 1979, the first large RAC concert promoted and organized by the NF drew about two hundred youth. The mostly male audience gathered in front of a stage with a banner that read RAC at Conway Hall, a popular venue that the NF was able to book due to the party's relationship with the South Place Ethical Society, which supported free speech.[160] There were only two bands, The Dentists and White Boss, who were relatively unknown local acts. Mainstream journalists went to the concert to review the music and discuss the event. Mark Ellen and a photographer from the *New Musical Express* attempted to enter, but were kept outside reporting on details about crowd size and bands from concertgoers who successfully made entry.[161] Vivien Goldman, however, reported that a mere five women were in the crowd, and was able to speak with local NF organizer Tony Williams.[162] Nick Griffin attended the concert as well and recalled that the music was "absolute shit," but the attention it received helped to recruit people.[163] However, *Bulldog* reported that "the first RAC concert … really rocked the music establishment" and the major papers "squealed" in response.[164] Even though the RAC lacked bands with notoriety, the NF declared "that RAC is a movement of ordinary white rock fans, and they know that it is growing in support all the time."[165]

Aside from the concert, the YNF started RAC as a club with a quarterly magazine, *Rocking the Reds*, sold only to members.[166] Edited first by Joe Pearce, *Rocking the Reds* was a crude and poorly formatted four-page magazine.[167] An editorial explained that the publication "is going to fight back against the scum of the music papers, which are owned by big business and which support communist organisations like RAR."[168] According to Patrick Harrington, who also worked on the publication and later received a YNF merit badge, the purpose was to promote specific bands and music news in contrast to the more football- and race-orientated *Bulldog*.[169] The goal was to connect established bands with NF themes, such as citing a song by the Angelic Upstarts about unemployment and implying that it would support the NF's perspective.[170] Interested fans could join the club to receive a membership card as well as a badge. Eddy Butler learned about the organization as a young teenager, sending his money away and receiving a membership card in late 1979. According to Butler, his member card was number five, and upon seeing that he was surprised to learn it was such a small movement.[171] However, he grew increasingly interested in politics and joined the NF in September 1980.[172] Indeed, the youth movement remained small but continued to grow, and the fanzine was soon absorbed into a regular column in *Bulldog*.

The 1979 Election and the British National Party

As the Young National Front (YNF) expanded into music during 1979, the country faced a general election that the NF hoped would cement the electoral inroads it had made over the previous decade. Long before the election date was announced, in 1976 the NF declared its intention to run 318 candidates in the next national election, even though Tyndall expected "virtually all the deposits would be lost."[173] At a cost of £150 per candidate and 318 candidates, the total was a substantial sum to raise. It was seen as an investment, however, as Webster said the number of candidates would prevent the BBC from refusing "to give us more television time than they have in the past."[174] Many of the rank-and-file NF members and the public expected significant electoral gains, which was reflected in the NF polling large numbers for its growing party status. Indeed, the NF's election-specific material stated that the reason it "fights" elections is "to win them."[175]

In early 1979, John Tyndall spoke at the NF's Annual General Meeting about the "election year" being a "supreme test" after years of preparation.[176] The NF felt it had momentum following gains in the London elections, and the organized opposition from the ANL gave the NF the impression that it was on the verge of a breakthrough. Local branches had been soliciting campaign contributions to run a "first class" election and contest as many seats as possible.[177] Tyndall announced that the membership had multiplied by more than eight times since 1972 despite opposition and being "banned" from meeting halls.[178] Other speeches continued in a similar vein about the upcoming election constituencies and audiences received activity reports from Pearce, Griffin and Philip Gegan.[179]

The NF ran a campaign on issues that echoed those of its previous campaigns, including the themes that originally helped the party gain attention in the aftermath of Enoch Powell's 1968 speech. In a brochure about NF policy, the party described itself as dedicated to "the preservation of Britain's national identity," which included ending "all coloured immigration" as well as repatriating "coloured immigrants already here."[180] In addition to race and immigration, the party also issued vague ideas about economics and international policy. The NF campaigned on leaving the Common Market; opposition to capitalism, Marxism and international free trade; encouraging "self-reliance" in the national economy; and re-establishing close ties with Commonwealth countries.[181]

While the NF's election platform stayed the same, so did the tactics that had resulted in street violence between the fascists and anti-fascists. In April 1979, a clash in culturally diverse Southall between the NF and its opponents, including the ANL, also saw police fighting to keep the sides apart and resulted in the death of Blair Peach, a teacher and anti-fascist demonstrator.[182] The NF's critics, including union workers and Asian organizations, came out to protest the Front's scheduled meeting as several thousand police officers tried to control the flow and the people who were assembling.[183] Following Peach's death from a fractured skull, several eyewitnesses reported having seen the police hitting him.[184] However, no one was prosecuted.[185]

The NF's activists were busy campaigning with a mix of leafleting, newspaper sales and street marches. However, these efforts were wildly unsuccessful compared to the automated and professional systems used by the major parties. In the May 1979 general election that propelled Margaret Thatcher into power for more than a decade, the NF gained its highest number of votes ever. Despite the NF celebrating the number, the results were underwhelming in the context of its expectations and the votes received by the major parties. As *Spearhead* asserted, more than 190,000 "hardcore" voters supported the NF in more than 300 contests and "analysis of voting trends throughout the country indicates that a large number of pro-NF voters decided to vote Conservative in the election."[186] The NF argued that if the election had not been a "success," it had demonstrated "a real basis of mass support."[187] Yet the reality, as scholars Christopher Husbands and Jude England wrote at the time, was that the results were "humiliating," as the 191,706 votes "were little better than those regularly given to perennial joke candidates."[188] While the total was greater than in the October 1974 general election, the party had not increased its relative support since that election.

One area where the NF did succeed was on race and immigration, which brought the issues up among the broader public and forced them onto the streets of England. In polling, 24% favored involuntary repatriation and only 14% approved entry of relatives of immigrants already living in the country.[189] Indeed, the Conservative Party was publicly sympathetic to the issue. In 1978, Margaret Thatcher, during an infamous *World in Action* television interview, said that the public was "afraid that this country might be rather swamped by people with a different culture" and the government must "allay peoples' fears on numbers."[190] She specifically mentioned the public's attraction to the NF, saying some people "do not agree with the objectives of the National Front, but they say that at least they are talking about some of the problems."[191] The NF saw this as a dog whistle to their supporters. Nick Griffin said "all the noise of the anti-racist movement didn't do a fraction of damage Maggie Thatcher did when she said, 'I understand you feel swamped.' That one word did more damage than everything the far left did."[192] Richard Edmonds explained that Thatcher had played the "race card" to win the election; the NF peaked at that moment with a membership of 14,000, as following the speech Conservatives made inroads with NF members.[193] Likewise, scholar Christopher Husbands discussed the NF's loss of votes in urban constituencies as due in part to "the successful and unobtrusive appropriation by the Conservatives of the NF's theme on race and immigration," because the Conservatives would have a greater political impact than the NF.[194] Indeed, after about 500 attempts to win a parliamentary seat, the NF had not even come close to one victory.[195]

Despite the face of the NF publicly spinning the loss as a success, disappointment was rampant in the party and blame was being put on various party members. Weeks after the election, the party held a meeting where Directorate members, some who had thought they would win elections, were "demoralized."[196] By October 1979, the disputes and struggles within the party became public. Webster wrote about "factional problems" and "personal attacks" directed against him, but declined to "discuss my private life" with anyone beyond "personal friends."[197] He asserted that Fountaine had sought to become chair of the NF and had even at one time offered the chair to Anthony Herbert-Reed because Tyndall's past image as a Nazi hurt the party.[198] Indeed, *Spearhead* reported that since the summer, "the NF has passed through a series of internal convulsions" and a "takeover bid" was "thwarted" when Fountaine was expelled.[199] According to Webster, for several years Tyndall was trying to impress his father-in-law, Charles Parker, and give him influence in the party. When Webster and Verrall repeatedly rebuffed Tyndall's attempts to give Parker a ranking position or to change party policy to benefit landlords such as Parker, Tyndall "blew his top."[200] At the Annual General Meeting in Great Yarmouth in October, Tyndall blamed the election results on the "media" and Thatcher's comments "about the British people getting swamped."[201] Tyndall proposed two resolutions that would give the NF chair more control and reduce the Directorate from twenty members to six, with only the chair and deputy being elected positions.[202] Andrew Brons, the deputy chair, seconded the motion even though he personally opposed it because he did not want to be disloyal to Tyndall.[203] The membership overwhelmingly opposed this and it was voted down eighteen to two.[204] Tyndall, responding to charges that the resolutions were undemocratic, explained that the alterations would "restore" the "health" of the party.[205] Despite affirmations of party unity, the NF was experiencing serious dissension, which caused the party to split in four ways.[206]

The disharmony was magnified by accusations of conspiracy and wrongdoing. Following his expulsion in the autumn of 1979 Fountaine started the Constitutional Movement, whereas Anthony Herbert-Reed, an NF Directorate member since 1974, left the NF to create the British Democratic Party from the NF's Leicester branch.[207] The NF, meanwhile, continued to operate even as its headquarters, Excalibur House, were closed down in the face of financial and ownership issues.[208] Matters grew worse when Tyndall resigned from the party and started the New National Front. In December, Tyndall reported that Fountaine had discussed member misconduct, including Webster's homosexuality, and accused the NF leadership of "mishandling" finances.[209] Many people already knew Webster was gay, and the Directorate voted against removing him from his position.[210] That month Tyndall left the party, calling for "strong" leadership and complaining about the NF's twenty Directorate members voting on "each decision."[211] The NF's governance, he wrote, "deprives me of any effective power to act," and he explained he was "prepared to resume my duties as head of the party if I am given the power to act."[212] The new chair was Andrew Brons, then a thirty-one-year-old lecturer in Harrogate, Yorkshire who was deputy chair and had been involved in the NF early on.[213] Just a month earlier Brons had written about his vision of the state, including its "ethnic foundation," which reflected previous ideas of ethno-nationalism.[214] With Brons being only thirty-one years old, the NF was recognized as now being led by young men, but by comparison Griffin and Pearce were even younger, and they were gaining party support.[215]

Tyndall had not returned to the NF by the summer.[216] In June 1980 he launched the New National Front, which was "founded as a movement" to reform the NF.[217] At street level, there was a mass exodus of members who were frustrated with the poor election returns and party divisions. Keith Axon, for example, said that only one branch in Birmingham remained intact, with only about fifteen members attending monthly meetings, until it followed Tyndall out of the NF.[218] Replacing the *National Front News*, Tyndall's organization issued *New Frontier* to "support the policies, reflect the views and report the activities of the New National Front."[219] In articles about the new organization, Tyndall explained that he had severed political relations after years of "insufferable behaviour" and "public embarrassment,"[220] with the immediate issue involving "a homosexual network" on the Directorate, referring to but not naming Webster and his partner Michael Salt, and Tyndall being "overruled" by the Directorate in his decision to remove Webster.[221] For the next few months, Tyndall reached out to the NF leadership and hoped to resume his role as leader.[222] Yet accusations and blame continued to be cast in every direction.[223] Meanwhile, the New National Front stopped participating in marches and demonstrations, including Remembrance Day, which reflected its marginal status.[224] In December 1980 it started the Young Nationalists wing of the party for youth between the ages of fourteen and twenty-five, which would be involved in sports and social gatherings.[225] Unlike the youth movement in the NF, it was more tightly controlled by Tyndall to ensure that youth did not gain too much influence. After several failed attempts to reunite with the NF, Tyndall and his supporters reorganized the New National Front and it became the British National Party following a vote in April 1982.[226]

Foreign Connections

As the NF remained politically marginal in Britain and its leadership was in disarray, the party developed foreign connections with like-minded expatriates. However, during the 1970s these links were extremely limited in comparison with those of other fascists. Notably, Graham Macklin's research documented Oswald Mosley's post-war "European" shift wherein after 1966 Mosley "concentrate[d] on portraying himself as an elder statesman of European politics."[227] In contrast, the NF pursued a policy that was narrower than Mosley's goals and outreach to Europe, because the NF merely sought closer bonds with white Britons in the Commonwealth, which drew upon an older, imperial way of thinking. Reflecting its origins and membership in the League of Empire Loyalists, the NF wanted to build ties among English-speaking countries with common ancestry and develop political associations with sympathetic people who shared its views. The NF, as John Tyndall described in 1978, was not just for the British people in the United Kingdom, but for the British in the Commonwealth and former empire.[228] He noted that the goal was to develop an "exclusive, closely-knit association of white states" and have "world-wide impact."[229] However, in his view Britain would remain the centerpiece of any network, and the like-minded associations in other countries would exist to promote British policy.

When A.K. Chesterton was leader of the NF he made yearly visits to Africa, the continent of his birth, and his writing on the subject reflected imperial nostalgia. Chesterton had traveled to several African nations during wartime and peace, including visits to South Africa, Rhodesia and Kenya. While Tyndall's view of the world also mirrored Chesterton's imperialist line of thought, his own foreign experience was far narrower. Prior to the 1970s, Tyndall's international travel was limited to three visits to continental Europe, including being stationed in West Germany and a visit to Soviet Russia.[230] Though he had shown an interest in traveling to the "white" Commonwealth and "white"-ruled governments in southern Africa, he never made any visits.

When the NF was started in 1967, it limited overseas membership in an agreement between all the organizations that merged to make the Front. The goal was for the NF to be a political party, which meant focusing on citizenship and national issues, rather than being an international political club. Yet this changed many years later. After Chesterton's death and the rise of new leadership, international groups became involved in the NF. In summer 1974, the first NF overseas branch was started in South Africa.[231] There was little information available about it and it ceased operations thereafter for unknown reasons. Then in 1978, *Spearhead* announced the formation of a new NF branch in South Africa based in Johannesburg and led by Jack Noble that aimed to "preserve the white man's role in South Africa" and help in the "formation of a new commonwealth of white nations."[232] The branch issued its own magazine, *Hitback*, in English and Afrikaans, which focused on Rhodesian and South African issues related to race and politics.[233] Ray Hill, a British expatriate, then served as chair with Noble becoming secretary. Hill followed NF events in London closely, even publishing a letter in *Bulldog* about how "delighted" he was with the youth in the YNF.[234]

The NF in South Africa began attracting domestic support, which undoubtedly inflamed the South African government, already under siege both nationally and internationally. In 1979, the NF claimed it was suffering from "persecution" by "Zionist" groups in South Africa.[235] Tyndall planned a speaking trip to the country in order to meet with the

South African branch, but was refused a visa to enter South Africa.[236] In the wake of the announcement, a "mob" of "Zionists" tried to enter Noble's house.[237] Meanwhile, the NF in South Africa feared that it might be prosecuted for inciting hatred and noted that the "heat is now on the NF" as British-born members left the country following police raids and threats of prosecution.[238] In 1979, Hill returned to England and later became instrumental in bringing a group to join Tyndall's new British National Party, but made news in the 1980s when he claimed to have been a mole for the anti-fascist magazine *Searchlight*.[239]

The NF continued to attract overseas support. In May 1977, the New Zealand NF was launched under David Crawford from Christchurch with the goal of informing New Zealanders about "the NF in Britain and its policies of solidarity towards the White Commonwealth."[240] The NF also announced goals to open more branches throughout Australia, Canada and southern Africa.[241] Crawford wrote that the New Zealand branch had developed from overseas contact in the League of Empire Loyalists and that it was moving forward with implementing the same immigration and industrial policies that the British National Front was seeking.[242] Then in spring 1978, it was announced that there were plans for an Australian National Front with policies aimed at becoming economically self-sufficient and improving the military.[243] *Spearhead* told readers that "patriotic Australians wishing to assist in the formation of a National Front of Australia" should write to the listed address.[244] One of the Melbourne-based group's key figures was Rosemary Sisson, who studied at a university in England and printed leaflets about building closer ties to Britain and repatriating all non-whites.[245] David Greason, who made the motion to officially start the Australian branch, described the inaugural meeting in June 1978 as consisting of Sisson giving a speech, after which she read a letter from David Crawford of the New Zealand NF and then "played a rather creaky taped message from John Tyndall."[246] *Front Line* magazine was launched in 1978 as a joint publication by the Australian and New Zealand NF branches covering NF history as well as domestic and international political news.[247] The publication continued to support the organizations for seven years until it separated from the NF in 1985.[248] In 1979, Sisson attended the NF's annual conference, appearing as a speaker on the topic of Australian NF growth and the media response.[249] Yet the reality behind the articles, as Richard Edmonds described, was that the foreign groups were "a shadow of a shadow" and had approximately "no more than a dozen people."[250]

At the end of the 1970s, Tyndall made his first visit to the United States, traveling mostly in the southern states and meeting with pro-segregation Americans. The May 1979 general election was a busy time for him. Not only was he the leader of a political party running hundreds of candidates, but his wife gave birth to a daughter a few weeks after Thatcher's victory.[251] Then the following month Tyndall traveled to the United States "to make contact with a very broad spectrum of racial nationalists and fighters against communism."[252] His trip included visits to Atlanta, where he met Sam Dickson, Edward Fields and Wilmot Robertson and spoke to an audience about the NF and the "future of the white race."[253] He then met with the local Citizens Council and Elmore Greaves in Memphis before traveling to Washington DC to meet William Pierce of the National Alliance at a party, but he found the capital, with its 80% black population, "depressing."[254] While Pierce, a former American Nazi Party member, later garnered fame for inspiring terrorism, he had already been known to Tyndall for several years. In January 1974, Tyndall's *Spearhead* reprinted an article by Pierce, which became a fairly regular occurrence in the coming decades.[255]

There were also more informal connections between transatlantic racists. David Duke, then Knights of the Ku Klux Klan leader, said he supported "pro-white groups such as the National Front and National Party" and sought to build support for the Klan by visiting Britain in March 1978.[256] Richard Verrall publicly denied any official NF links to Duke, and said he met with "friends" in ten different groups, including the British Movement and League of Saint George.[257] The League of Saint George was started as a political club around 1974 by several Union Movement members to unite people who were to the right of the Conservatives.[258] According to one of its founders, Keith Thompson, the members wanted to be more active than the mostly dormant Union Movement.[259] It organized visits to art galleries and showed films such as *Birth of the Nation* and *Triumph of the Will*, which many NF members attended. While Tyndall was friendly with the group and contributed articles to the club's *League Review*, Webster disliked the organization and wanted to denounce any NF member who attended a League event.[260] As the League hosted many events of interest to NF supporters, this proved difficult for Webster to do. Thompson hosted Duke's visit, which drew a large number of NF members and led to Duke speaking at a local NF branch.[261] Moreover, the League also invited other Americans to speak, including J.B. Stoner and Edward Fields of the National States' Rights Party, which also attracted a large number of Front supporters.[262]

The Rebirth of Rock Against Communism

Following the 1979 general election, British fascism was suffering from the consequences of splintering which had divided electoral contests, finances and membership. In many ways the teenage members remained unaffected by the election. They continued to pursue their activism and interests sympathetic to the NF, such as hosting football games.[263] Moreover, extremism was increasingly becoming an element of skinhead music and youth subculture during this time of party factionalism. The older generation was not happy with the new image of youth that attended its demonstrations, which included "braces" and "bovver boots."[264] In fact, while the older NF members blamed "the mass media" for a "bad image," they noted that while previous marches had included "a wide cross section" of people, during the previous year "the proportion of skinheads among NF marchers has risen to a point at which there is danger of its becoming predominant."[265] More critically, concern was voiced in *Spearhead* that the "youth" section "has been allowed to get out of proportion," with the "prominent figures" in NF audiences being the "young generation."[266] Tyndall's post-NF groups instructed organizers not to bring "scruffs" or "punks" so that it would be like the "best days of 1976–78."[267]

The NF's youth filled the vacuum left by Tyndall and those who followed him to the New National Front. At the time, several key YNF activists had been in the party for several years and had been giving speeches, editing publications and organizing events. Nick Wakeling, for example, was the editor of several publications, including *Anglian News* about race, immigration and economics.[268] The youth used these skills in conjunction with new roles that became available once Tyndall and his supporters left the party. In March 1980, Griffin and Pearce launched a new magazine, *Nationalism Today*, which included "a cross-section of contemporary British nationalist opinion."[269] Griffin explained that he was not at the magazine's first meeting, which included Pearce, Steve Brady and Nick Wakeling, but was brought in because of his educational background and writing skills.[270] Produced out of Griffin's home in Halesworth, Suffolk, the first issue announced it would "represent a radical set of values and ideas."[271] Griffin and Pearce had spent the previous year developing the publication, which was called an "ideological magazine produced by young members of the party."[272] Edited under Griffin and then Pearce, *Nationalism Today* showcased material by other YNF members including Derek Holland, Patrick Harrington and Ian Stuart Donaldson.[273] The magazine borrowed directly from earlier NF publications, such as a feature titled "Rite-Up" that was originally an independent NF youth publication, and the "Industrial Front" feature that had appeared previously in *Spearhead*.[274] The content of *Nationalism Today* demonstrated the Strasserite thinking of the youth, with features about "nationalist" economics and white workers. In contrast, Webster and Verrall, two older NF members who remained in the party, published *New Nation* in support of the NF, which reflected more traditional extremist ideas surrounding the media, race and anti-Semitism.[275]

The new YNF publishing endeavors notwithstanding, the most visible change within the NF was its mobilization of youngsters. In 1981, journalist Philip Venning wrote that fascist organizations "increasingly" found support among young people and "switched their recruiting away from schools to football matches and rock concerts."[276] Specifically referencing the NF as well as the British Movement, founded by fascist Colin Jordan in 1968, the groups recruited white working-class youth.[277] Among football clubs, West Ham and Chelsea were particularly fruitful ground, where 1000 copies of *Bulldog* were sold, and another 700 were sold at a Madness concert.[278] The article then detailed specific instances of racial violence by skinheads who were attracted to the groups. Other organizations also reported on the NF recruiting youth through music and football, causing the National Union of Teachers and Football Association to criticize the activity.[279] The main focus for youth attracted to the NF centered around skinheads. Aside from football activity, Asian business owners and leftist book shops complained about NF skinheads in Brick Lane disrupting and damaging their operations.[280] Journalist Richard North claimed that NF and British Movement skinheads could be differentiated because the NF had red laces in their boots and the British Movement used white laces.[281] Garry Bushell recalled instances of violence where the British Movement assaulted opponents at concerts, which shaped public associations of skinhead music with Nazism.[282]

Indeed, the public perceived young skinheads as connected to violence and fascist politics. Yet the origins of skinhead culture and music were actually in multiculturalism and Jamaican music. George Marshall has described how the first skinheads emerged as early as 1967, where white Mods and West Indian communities in pubs combined the latest music with the rude boy gangs culture from Kingston, and by 1969 represented a distinct working-class movement.[283] The skinhead look of cropped hair, jeans, t-shirts and heavy boots was spread from town to town by football fans.[284] In 1978, there was a skinhead revival in reaction to the decline of punk music from the mid-1970s.[285] Meanwhile, rising unemployment and industrial conflict around the country generated a bleak outlook among the working class in the late 1970s and 1980s. In the context of the re-emergence of skinheads and their image meshing with racist politics, unemployment reached "unprecedented post-war proportions" for the urban working class, while Thatcher took a "conservative approach to immigration" and introduced policies to promote "self-interest."[286] Following her election, Thatcher challenged union power because she believed organized labor hurt economic growth and "optimism about the beneficent effects of government intervention had largely disappeared."[287]

Race and politics became a flashpoint at football games for NF supporters. At first there was no strict racist connotation associated with skinheads, but as the NF gained in local elections it gradually had "the edge" in gaining skinhead support due to its associations with football, such as the League of Louts feature in *Bulldog*.[288] The publication, for instance, dubbed Chelsea and West Ham as "top of the 'League of Louts'," praising NF activity at the games as well as claiming that the NF's support at football games in Northern Ireland was growing.[289] Later the feature was renamed the "Racist League," which ranked the top ten racist football fans by club.[290] Indeed, racism was a feature at games as black football players joined teams and were targeted with monkey chants and spitting.[291] For instance, Paul Canoville, Chelsea's first black footballer who joined in 1981, recalled Chelsea's own fans throwing bananas and chanting: "We don't want the nigger."[292]

The most important YNF musician to emerge on the scene was Ian Stuart Donaldson, best known as Ian Stuart, whose skinhead band Skrewdriver garnered local fame in late 1978.[293] Skrewdriver, originally a Rolling Stones cover band named Tumbling Dice, morphed into a skinhead band that released its first album, *All Skrewed Up*, in 1977 through Chiswick Records.[294] Garry Bushell, a writer for *Sounds*, described the non-political album as "good" and specifically praised the song "Anti-Social."[295] According to Joe Pearce, Graham McPherson, better known as Suggs who later became the singer for Madness, was a Skrewdriver roadie in 1977, but Suggs denied this and said he stopped speaking with Stuart when he started writing neo-Nazi songs.[296] Concert reviewers, such as Emma Ruth, reported how the band's tour was "wrecked by the skinhead reputation that preceded them" and wrote that Skrewdriver "could use some lessons in integrity and commitment."[297] In March 1978, Stuart wrote a letter published in the *New Musical Express* that stated, "Skrewdriver are no longer a skinhead band due to the increasing violence at our gigs" and "I do not mind who attends our gigs whoever they are so long as they are there to enjoy the music."[298] However, after continuing to have trouble booking concerts, the band broke up in 1978, but reunited briefly in late 1979. In 1980 *Sounds* reported that Stuart was "unable to shake off the nauseous NF connotations" and Skrewdriver again disbanded.[299] Bushell described how Stuart visited the *Sounds* office to convince the newspaper that he was not political, but after his "eighth pint" he would have "an upright arm."[300]

Stuart and Pearce, then head of the YNF, became close friends in London. Pearce had been a fan of Skrewdriver's first album and Stuart, long sympathetic to the NF, joined the party as a YNF recruiter in 1979 and went on to become a member of the Directorate.[301] *Nazi Rock Star*, one of four hagiographies about Stuart, described how he joined because he "had no love of blacks" and was around other skinheads who shared that view so he "joined up" with the NF.[302] By autumn 1981, Stuart had moved to King's Cross in London, and Pearce as well as other friends urged him to reform Skrewdriver.[303] Stuart agreed and with a new line-up, Skrewdriver released the song "Back with a Bang" with lyrics that celebrated the 1978 skinhead revival.[304] This period also proved important in cementing the band's racist connections with NF and British Movement youth. Skrewdriver performed at live concerts, proudly associated with young fascists and increasingly wrote songs that promoted racism and Nazism during the 1980s.

The NF and skinhead reputations for inciting racial tension only gained more attention from violence and prosecutions. In July 1981, a skinhead concert with The 4-Skins, The Last Resort and The Business in Southall, West London turned into "a fully-fledged race riot" that left the venue burned to the ground as whites and Asians fought outside.[305] Skinheads from outside the area attacked Asian shops, which prompted a group of four hundred "Asian youths" to visit the pub, where police escorted the skinheads out as Molotov cocktails ignited the venue.[306] Micky Fitz, singer in The Business, recalled that the bands had no idea of the extent of the rioting even as petrol bombs were being thrown through the windows, and by the time the band escaped the venue, "we were helping the police to the ambulances, as they were dropping like flies."[307] The concert made national news on television and in print, with the *New Musical Express* running a photograph of the destroyed venue on its cover above the headline "The Gig That Sparked a Race Riot."[308]

Like the culture and music associated with the NF, the material published by the YNF was controversial. In fact, some of the statements were illegal under the Race Relations Act. In June 1980, Pearce was told by authorities that they were considering filing charges under the Race Relations Act for comments published in *Bulldog*.[309] Pearce's editorial "challenged the Commission for Racial Equality to prosecute" him over *Bulldog* reports about black crime and mailed copies to "leading MPs and a special copy was delivered personally to arch-race-traitor David Lane," concluding the column with "white power forever."[310] One year later, *Bulldog* claimed the Race Relations Act "makes it illegal for whites to fight the black invasion of Britain" and that "Pearce is prepared to go to prison rather than back down."[311] That same issue also stated, "coloured immigrants can seriously damage your health."[312] In April 1981, Pearce received a summons to appear before the magistrates for "incitement to racial hatred."[313] NF activists staged several events in support of Pearce, including one where Webster "burst into a Young Conservative meeting" as "orange smoke filled the room" to chants of "scab" while William Whitelaw was speaking, which the NF concluded "showed the race traitors they have no place hiding."[314] The following year, he was found guilty by an all-white jury and sentenced to six months by a judge who called the publication "evil and dangerous rubbish," and Pearce shouted that the judge was "an enemy of the English people."[315] According to Pearce, he then began editing *Bulldog* under the pseudonym "Captain Truth," but the Special Branch later gathered evidence that he was the editor and he was again prosecuted.[316] Pearce wrote in *Nationalism Today* that he had "no regrets" and was "encouraged" by the support he received from inside and outside prison.[317]

Following Pearce's release from prison, he joined forces with Ian Stuart to relaunch RAC and seize the full potential of music in radical politics. In 1982, Pearce urged Stuart to allow the newly reformed Skrewdriver to become the flagship band for RAC, which was mostly moribund following the NF's internal disputes.[318] Stuart agreed and soon *Bulldog* highlighted that Skrewdriver had been "in the forefront of the skinhead revival in 1978" and, along with Sham 69, had "led a legion of racist youth," but Skrewdriver "never betrayed their supporters."[319] Sham 69's concerts initially were apolitical, attracting anti-racists and NF skinheads, but the band began playing RAR concerts and Sham 69 vocalist Jimmy Pursey publicly condemned racism.[320] When Sham 69 criticized racism, some fans considered it a betrayal, with Stuart saying Pursey "was a traitor to his country and a traitor to his fans."[321] Scholar Matthew Worley explained that around the time Skrewdriver reformed, "Oi!" music emerged in opposition "to Thatcher's assault on the industrial and cultural cornerstones of British working-class life whilst simultaneously baulking at the stultifying bureaucracy of Labour social democracy and rarefied identity politics of the left."[322] This reflected wider political issues that the NF hoped to challenge through music. The NF's new version of RAC built from YNF and Skrewdriver supporters, and planned large music festivals, better publications and its own record label.

In 1983, the NF created White Noise Records to release music that reflected its own views. The interest in forming its own record label originally started with NF fans sharing bootlegged tapes of their favorite songs that they interpreted to have racial connotations. Songs by David Bowie and Elton John that involved fighting or were thought to have fascist sympathies were copied onto tapes that were passed to other youth who might find inspiration from the songs.[323] According to the NF, it started a record label because the music industry was "dominated by alien influences who thought they achieved a stranglehold which would prevent the development of truly White British music."[324] The record label's first release was Skrewdriver's *White Power* EP that featured the self-titled track mirroring the racist themes long promoted by the NF.[325] Drawing from a book of the same name by American Nazi Party leader George Lincoln Rockwell (1918–1967), the racist lyrics criticized immigration and bemoaned the loss of world influence with lyrics that included: "We're letting them takeover, we just let'em come" and "once we had an Empire, and now we've got a slum."[326] Advertised in publications such as the *National Front News*, the release was immediately successful.[327] The NF reported that it was "selling by the thousand" with copies sold in Germany, Holland, Sweden and the United States.[328] Meanwhile, the first RAC concert in over three years was held in Stratford, East London and was the biggest concert yet hosted by the NF.[329] The live events were also being promoted by the NF, with *Bulldog* telling its readers "to support Britain's best known white racist band" by going to the November 1983 RAC concert.[330] The NF's influence in music was just beginning, and soon the youth subculture developed by the party would have international consequences and an ideological impact on British fascists.

Conclusion

This chapter discussed the impact anti-fascist organizations, including the ANL and RAR, had not only in challenging the NF, but also in inspiring the NF's youth to attract supporters with music. A surge of youth support among those with radical views who wanted to rebel by joining a fascist party had provoked the party to start its own youth wing. Yet the youth were largely left alone to publish their own periodicals and merge their interest in politics with youth culture. The YNF co-opted the left's music outreach by starting RAC, but the fascist mobilization of youth in the late 1970s was no match for the coalition of anti-fascists. The 1979 general election helped fracture the NF, causing it to split into four groups and many supporters to question the future of the movement. However, the seeds of fascist transformation were planted. The NF youth's activity, interest in foreign links and connections to racist music would grow into an international multidimensional youth movement free from party control. At the time, the meekness of RAC was clear from the public reception of its first large concert, but the NF harnessed music with a more established act, Skrewdriver. In the following years, fascist music reached audiences in new areas. As the next chapter explains, the youth were drawn into NF activities, and this outreach eclipsed the traditional fascism of John Tyndall's British National Party and prompted the NF to turn to foreign figures for new ideas and tactics.

Notes

1. "Rock Against Communism," *Bulldog* no. 14 (1979): 3.
2. "NF Wins 119,000 Votes in London," *Spearhead* no. 105 (May 1977): 18.
3. Paul Whiteley, "The National Front Vote in the 1977 GLC Election: An Aggregate Data Analysis," *British Journal of Political Science* 9, no. 3 (July 1979): 370.
4. Martin Webster, interviewed by Ryan Shaffer, audio recording, 3 June 2010.
5. "National Front: Major March and Rally in Lewisham, S.E. London," *Spearhead* no. 107 (July 1977): 15.
6. John Mendelson, "The National Front Must Not Be Allowed to Carry on This Dangerous Provocation," *The Times*, 19 August 1977.

7. Martin Webster, "Establishment Conspirators and Red Mobs Fail to Stop National Front Advance," *Spearhead* no. 109 (September 1977): 8; Robert Parker, "Front Chief Accuses Socialist Workers' Leaders Over Violence in London," *The Times*, 17 August 1977.
8. "The Reds Said 'They Shall Not Pass,' but We Marched Through Lewisham," *Spearhead* no. 109 (September 1977): 6.
9. Peter Hain, *Outside In* (London: Biteback Publishing, 2012), 118.
10. "The League to Stop the Front," *The Economist*, 25 February 1978, 20.
11. Peter Hain, interviewed by Ryan Shaffer, audio recording, 16 October 2014.
12. Ibid.
13. "Poll Warning on Front Contenders in Marginals," *The Times*, 31 August 1978.
14. *The Anti-Nazi League and the Struggle Against Racism* (London: Revolutionary Communist Group, n.d., circa 1978), 5.
15. For more details see: David Renton, *When We Touched the Sky: The Anti-Nazi League 1977–1981* (London: New Clarion Press, 2006).
16. *National Front: The New Nazis* (London: Socialist Workers Party, n.d., circa 1978), 8, 11, 12.
17. Martin Savitt and Jacob Gewirtz, "The Anti-Nazi League," *The Times*, 11 October 1978.
18. Bernard Levin, "Let Them Speak, If Only for Five Minutes," *The Times*, 20 September 1978.
19. Ibid.; Tom Mundy, "Reports on National Front," *The Times*, 11 October 1978.
20. "Anti-Nazis to Stop Front Meeting," *The Times*, 21 April 1978.
21. *A Well-Oiled Nazi Machine* (London: A. F. and R. Publication, n.d., circa 1978).
22. Ibid.
23. Martin Webster, *Lifting the Lid off the Anti-Nazi League* (London: National Front News Press, 1978), 3. Peter Hain sued Webster for libel in the publication. See: "Help Martin Webster Fight the Race Act Case and Hain Libel Action," *National Front News* no. 19 (October 1979): unpaginated 2.
24. "National Front Slogan Found on Wall After Office Fire," *The Times*, 26 June 1978.
25. "What We Think," *Spearhead* no. 119 (July 1978): 3.
26. "National Front Slogan Found on Wall After Office Fire," *The Times*, 26 June 1978.
27. "'Anti-Nazis' Step up Terrorism," *National Front News* no. 15 (15 September 1978): 4. Webster claimed credit for dubbing the ANL as ANAL in NF reports.

28. "Six Years' Jail for National Front Man," *The Times*, 23 May 1980.
29. "Anti-Racialism Campaign Backed by Dozen Groups," *The Times*, 10 July 1978.
30. Interview with Hain.
31. Chris Welch, "Portrait of the Artist as a Working Class Man," *Melody Maker*, 9 December 1978, 35.
32. Ibid., 35–36. He further claimed, "I believe he is a religious man. And you can't be religious and racist at the same time. The two things are incompatible."
33. Tony Stewart, "Heil and Farewell," *New Musical Express*, 8 May 1976, 9.
34. Ibid.
35. David Widgery, *Beating Time: Riot 'n' Race 'n' Rock 'n' Roll* (London: Chatto & Windus, 1986), 56, 58.
36. Ibid., 61.
37. See "Love Music, Hate Racism Poster," Modern Records Centre, MSS.284.
38. "Guidelines for RAR Gig Organisers," *Temporary Hoarding* no. 1 (1977).
39. For example: Dave Widgery, "What is Racism," *Temporary Hoarding* no. 1 (1977); *Temporary Hoarding* no. 6 (Summer 1978); Lucy Toothpaste, "Sex vs. Fascism," *Temporary Hoarding* no. 7 (Winter 1979).
40. Lynden Barber, "Albums: Various Artists—'Rock Against Racism's Greatest Hits'," *Melody Maker*, 13 September 1980, 35.
41. Garry Bushell, interviewed by Ryan Shaffer, audio recording, 6 June 2010. See also: Roger Huddle and Red Saunders (eds.), *Reminiscences of RAR: Rocking Against Racism 1976–1979* (London: Redwords, 2016). Huddle discussed the genesis of RAR in detail, noting Clapton's comments and the context of racist violence on the streets.
42. Renton, *When We Touched the Sky*, 95.
43. Untitled, *Temporary Hoarding* no. 3 (1977): 7.
44. Interview with Bushell.
45. Ibid.
46. "Racism and Your Music: Face-to-Face with the Front," *Sounds*, 26 March 1978, 25–33.
47. "It Can't Happen Here, Or Can It," *Sounds*, 26 March 1978, 25.
48. Ibid., 28.
49. Ibid., 31.
50. Ibid., 32.
51. Interview with Hain.
52. Paul Rambali, "Anti-Nazi Rally—Free Gig," *New Musical Express*, 8 April 1978, 11.
53. "Carnival Details," *New Musical Express*, 29 April 1978, 12.

54. Cover of *New Musical Express*, 6 May 1978.
55. Chris Salewicz, "Carnival," *New Musical Express*, 6 May 1978, 31.
56. Ibid.
57. Interview with Bushell.
58. Trevor Fishlock, "Anti-Racialism Trudge Proves Good Natured," *The Times*, 25 September 1978.
59. Modern Records Centre, MSS.284, *Carnival 2: Souvenir Programme* (London: Anti-Nazi League, 1978).
60. Fishlock, "Anti-Racialism Trudge Proves Good Natured."
61. Keith Axon, interviewed by Ryan Shaffer, audio recording, 11 October 2014.
62. Ibid.
63. Robert Parker, "Police Presence at Marches Cost £400,000," *The Times*, 26 September 1978.
64. Robert Parker, "Front Plans 'Deliberate' March into East End," *The Times*, 21 September 1978.
65. Robert Parker, "Police Tactics Ensure that National Front March is Peaceful," *The Times*, 25 September 1978.
66. Joe Pearce, interviewed by Ryan Shaffer, audio recording, 9 November 2009.
67. "Fresh Clash with National Front Feared Tameside," *The Times*, 12 January 1978.
68. John Chartres, "19 Arrests in National Front Rally Clashes," *The Times*, 11 February 1978.
69. David Nicholson-Lord, "34 Held After Incidents at Front Rally," *The Times*, 17 April 1978.
70. "Front Organizer Denies Charges of Obstruction," *The Times*, 28 June 1978; "National Front Organizer Fined," *The Times*, 29 June 1978.
71. "12 Arrested at Front Meeting," *The Times*, 19 April 1978.
72. "National Front Members on Affray Charge," *The Times*, 24 October 1978; "Crown Says Front Man Had Bomb Materials," *The Times*, 15 November 1978; "National Front Man Gets 3 Years," *The Times*, 17 November 1978.
73. Interview with Pearce.
74. Mrs. J. Fearne, "National Front Manifesto: Effect on the Young," *The Times*, 1 September 1977.
75. Derek Holland, "The National Front—A Youth Wing?," *Spearhead* no. 106 (June 1977): 9.
76. Ibid.
77. "National Front Man Resigns Teaching Job," *The Times*, 8 July 1975, 4c.
78. Ibid.

79. Richard Edmonds, "Anarchy at Tulse Hill," *Spearhead* no. 85 (July 1975): 9.
80. Joe Pearce, *Race With the Devil: My Journey from Racial Hatred to Rational Love* (Charlotte: Saint Benedict Press, 2013), 29, 30.
81. Ibid., 52.
82. Ibid., 42.
83. Nick Griffin, interviewed by Ryan Shaffer, audio recording, 8 October 2014.
84. Ibid.
85. Ibid.
86. Robert Parker, "Front Plans a Section for Young People," *The Times*, 13 October 1977.
87. Interview with Pearce.
88. Interview with Webster.
89. Video of the Annual General Meeting appears online. "National Front History—part 2—NF Annual General Meeting 1977," YouTube, 10 December 2009; available online at https://www.youtube.com/watch?v=XcJAhJjCimw; accessed 1 July 2016.
90. Richard Edmonds, interviewed by Ryan Shaffer, audio recording, 15 September 2011.
91. Ibid.
92. Ibid.
93. Interview with Pearce. For more on Fountaine's life, see: John Tyndall, "Obituaries: Andrew Fountaine," *Spearhead* no. 345 (November 1997): 20.
94. "YNF Campaign is Launched," *Spearhead* no. 111 (November 1977): 4.
95. "NF Youth Organisation Created," *Spearhead* no. 108 (August 1977): 19.
96. Ibid., 19.
97. "NF Students' Paper," *Spearhead* no. 64 (May 1973): 9.
98. "Editorial," *Rite-Up* no. 3 (Autumn 1976): 1. The author was listed as "Pizdorf Vizdeleft."
99. *Spearhead* wrote that the first Young National Front rally should be promoted "in local bulletins." "Young National Front Rally," *Spearhead* no. 112 (December 1977): 18.
100. Interview with Pearce.
101. Ibid.
102. "White Youth Unite and Fight," *Bulldog* no. 7 (May 1978): 1.
103. "Youth in Action," *Bulldog* no. 8 (June 1978): 4.
104. Interview with Pearce.
105. Colin Todd, interviewed by Ryan Shaffer, audio recording, 3 October 2014.

106. Andrew Collins, *Still Suitable for Miners: Billy Bragg* (London: Virgin Books, 2007), 148.
107. Philip Venning, "The Front Line Targeted," *The Times Educational Supplement*, 13 March 1981, 18.
108. Interview with Pearce; "Newsround Up," *National Front Member's Bulletin* no. 2 (Belfast group bulletin) (September 1981): 3.
109. Joe Pearce, "The Importance of the Young National Front," *Spearhead* no. 114 (February 1978): 5.
110. Ibid.
111. Ibid.
112. "YNF Launches Anti-Communist Counter-Offensive," *Spearhead* no. 113 (January 1978): 19.
113. Modern Records Centre, MSS.21/1571/9, *How to Spot a Red Teacher* (1978).
114. Ibid.
115. Joe Pearce, "Red Indoctrination in the Classroom," *Spearhead* no. 117 (May 1978): 9.
116. "YNF Launched Anti-Communist Counter-Offensive."
117. "Onward March of the Young National Front," *Spearhead* no. 115 (March 1978): 19.
118. "Local Press Reports Show Nationwide YNF Campaign," *National Front News* no. 13 (May 1978): 2.
119. "Councilor Supports YNF anti-Communist Schools Campaign," *Spearhead* no. 118 (June 1978): 18.
120. "Support for YNF Still Growing," *Spearhead* no. 120 (August 1978): 19.
121. "Students," *Spearhead* no. 121 (September 1978): 8.
122. Nick Griffin, "University Challenge," *Spearhead* no. 121 (September 1978): 15. According to Griffin, Webster wanted Ian Anderson, then a recent University of Oxford dropout, to head the organization, but Griffin moved ahead and steered the organization. Interview with Griffin.
123. Interview with Griffin. See also "Youth in Action," *Bulldog* no. 10 (November 1978): 4.
124. "Young National Front Keeps On Growing," *National Front News* no. 15 (September 1978): 4.
125. "Hundreds of Youths at YNF Rally," *Bulldog* no. 14 (1979): 6.
126. "Goals Galore," *Bulldog* no. 8 (June 1978): 4.
127. "Young National Front 5-A-Side Football Finals," *Spearhead* no. 118 (June 1978): 19.
128. Ibid.
129. "YNF Soccer League Set to Go," *Bulldog* no. 5 (February 1978): 4.

130. "Young NF Football League Cup," *Spearhead* no. 124 (December 1978): 19.
131. "YNF League Kicks Off," *Bulldog* no. 10 (November 1978): 4.
132. Interview with Pearce.
133. "Football Front," *Bulldog* no. 16 (n.d., circa 1980): 6.
134. Ibid.
135. Ibid.
136. Ibid.; "We All Agree … The National Front is Magic," *Bulldog* no. 11 (January/February 1979): 1.
137. "RAC News," *Bulldog* no. 21 (n.d., circa 1980): 3.
138. Joe Pearce, "The Young National Front: One Year On," *Spearhead* no. 122 (October 1978): 20.
139. Ibid.
140. "Stop the Talking: Its High Time for Action," *Sunday Times*, 5 March 1978, 31.
141. "Front Followers Accept Violence, Magazine Says," *The Times*, 27 April 1978.
142. Stuart Weir, "The National Front and the Young: A Special Survey; Youngster's in the Front Line," *New Society* 44, no. 812 (27 April 1978): 189.
143. Ibid., 193.
144. "Thousands March on NF Remembrance Parade," *Spearhead* no. 124 (December 1978): 18.
145. Ryan Shaffer, "The Soundtrack of Neo-Fascism: Youth and Music in the National Front," *Patterns of Prejudice* 47, nos. 5/6 (2013): 458–482.
146. Jay W. Baird, "Goebbels, Horst Wessel, and the Myth of Resurrection and Return," *Journal of Contemporary History* 17, no. 4 (October 1982): 633–650.
147. Eddy Morrison, *Memoirs of a Street Soldier: A Life in White Nationalism* (London: Imperium Press/White Nationalist Party, n.d., circa 2002), unpaginated 10.
148. Ibid., 14.
149. Eddy Morrison, "Why the Left is Winning," *Spearhead* no. 139 (May 1980): 15.
150. Morrison, *Memoirs of a Street Soldier*, 14.
151. "Rock Against Communism," *British News* no. 43 (October 1978): 10.
152. "The Ventz & RaC," *British News* no. 42 (September 1978): 7.
153. Morrison, *Memoirs of a Street Soldier*, 15.
154. Garry Bushell, "Rock Against Cretinism," *Sounds*, 10 March 1979, 10.
155. Interview with Bushell.
156. Morrison, *Memoirs of a Street Soldier*, 15.
157. Bushell, "Rock Against Cretinism."

158. "Rock Against Communism," *Bulldog* no. 14 (1979): 3.
159. Ibid.
160. "RAC News," *Bulldog* no. 15 (1979): 3. Peter Rushton wrote that "Conway Hall belonged to Bloomsbury's long-established South Place Ethical Society. To his enormous credit the Secretary of the Society, Peter Cadogan, consistently defended the NF's right to freedom of speech and assembly, despite his own far left affiliations." Peter Rushton, "40 Years of the National Front: Part II," *Heritage and Destiny* no. 31 (January–March 2008): 3.
161. Mark Ellen, "No Fun with the Front," *New Musical Express*, 25 August 1979, 17.
162. Vivien Goldman, "Seeing Red at RAC," *Melody Maker*, 25 August 1979, 9.
163. Interview with Griffin.
164. "RAC News," *Bulldog* no. 15 (1979): 3.
165. Ibid.
166. "Rocking the Reds," *Bulldog* no. 15 (1979): 3.
167. Interview with Pearce.
168. *Rocking the Reds* unknown (n.d., circa 1980): unpaginated 5. *Rocking the Reds* included no date or numbers. This issue's cover has images of news clippings about the Southall punk riot.
169. Patrick Harrington, interviewed by Ryan Shaffer, audio recording, 29 May 2010. Harrington was awarded a YNF merit badge. "YNF Merit Badge," *Bulldog* no. 21 (n.d., circa March 1980): 2.
170. Interview with Harrington.
171. Eddy Butler, interviewed by Ryan Shaffer, audio recording, 16 September 2011.
172. Ibid.
173. Robert Parker, "National Front to Field 318 Candidates in General Election," *The Times*, 2 July 1976.
174. Ibid.
175. *National Front Elections Handbook* (n.p.: National Front Education and Training Department, n.d., circa 1979), 1.
176. John Tyndall, "We Are the Coming Storm," *Spearhead* no. 126 (February 1979): 6.
177. "Announcements," *Front-Line: Voice of the Cornwall National Front* no. 6 (July 1978): unpaginated 4.
178. Tyndall, "We Are the Coming Storm," 7.
179. "NF AGM in Election Year is Biggest Ever," *Spearhead* no. 126 (February 1979): 19.
180. *Statement of Policy* (Croydon: National Front, 1979).
181. Ibid.

182. A jury ruled the cause of Peach's death was "misadventure." Nicholas Timmins, "The verdict has not settled the role of the special patrol group and the rights of citizens," *The Times*, 28 May 1980.
183. "Call for new law after London riot," *The Times*, 30 April 1979; see also: *Young Rebels: The Story of the Southall Youth Movement* (n.p., 2014) (DVD Recording).
184. For example, Nicholas Timmins, "Blair Peach was hit twice, witness says," *The Times*, 20 May 1980.
185. In 2014, David Renton called for a new inquest and reported discrepancies in police accounts. David Renton, *Who Killed Blair Peach* (n.p.: unknown, n.d., 2014).
186. "General Election," *Spearhead* no. 128 (May/June 1979): 18.
187. Ibid.
188. Christopher Husbands and Jude England, "The Hidden Support for Racism," *New Statesman*, 11 May 1979, 674. The cover of this issue featured Tyndall and Webster goose-stepping with a Nazi salute.
189. Ibid.
190. "Margaret Thatcher, TV Interview for Granada World in Action ('rather swamped')," Margaret Thatcher Foundation, 1978; available from http://www.margaretthatcher.org/document/103485; accessed 1 July 2016.
191. Ibid.
192. Interview with Griffin.
193. Interview with Edmonds.
194. Christopher Husbands, "The Decline of the National Front: The Elections of 3rd May 1979," *The Wiener Library Bulletin* 32, nos. 49/50 (1979): 62.
195. Ibid., 66.
196. Interview with Edmonds.
197. Martin Webster, "A Personal Commentary on Factional Problems," *Spearhead* no. 132 (October 1979): 5.
198. Ibid., 4.
199. "What We Think," *Spearhead* no. 133 (November 1979): 2.
200. Interview with Webster.
201. John Tyndall, "Our Movement Lives to Fight Again," *Spearhead* no. 133 (November 1979): 7.
202. "The Resolutions," *Spearhead* no. 133 (November 1979): 12.
203. Andrew Brons, interviewed by Ryan Shaffer, audio recording, 11 October 2014.
204. Interview with Webster; Interview with Edmonds.
205. John Tyndall, "A New Leadership System for the NF," *Spearhead* no. 133 (November 1979): 14.

206. See "Unity Affirmed at Gt Yarmouth AGM," *Spearhead* no. 133 (November 1979): 18.
207. "Co-Options to National Directorate," *Spearhead* no. 77 (July 1974): 19; Nigel Fielding, "Change on the Ultra-Right," *Marxism Today*, April 1982, 5.
208. Excalibur House was at 73 Great Eastern Street, London EC2. In a brochure asking for renovation donations, Tyndall described buying the property as "a major landmark in the progress of our party." John Tyndall, *A Personal Appeal from the Chairman of the National Front* (n.p.: unknown, n.d., circa 1978).
209. John Tyndall, "The Battle for the NF," *Spearhead* no. 134 (December 1979): 6.
210. Interview with Webster.
211. John Tyndall, "Resignation: A Personal Statement," *Spearhead* no. 135 (January 1980): 18.
212. Ibid.
213. "NF Chairman," *Spearhead* no. 136 (February 1980): 19.
214. Andrew Brons, "The Nationalist State," *Spearhead* no. 134 (December 1979): 12.
215. The caption of a 1981 photograph reads, "[y]oung men leading a young party. Left: NF Chairman Andrew Brons. Right: NF Deputy-Chairman Richard Verrall." "NF Organisers Get Down to Business at London Conference," *National Front News* no. 30 (March 1981): 2.
216. According to Brons, he did not meet Tyndall in person again until 1986 because they were in different organizations. Interview with Brons.
217. "New National Front: Campaign Objectives," *Spearhead* no. 140 (June 1980): 12; "New National Front," *Spearhead* no. 141 (July 1980): 9.
218. Interview with Axon.
219. "New year—New Paper—New Frontier," *New Frontier* no. 1 (January/February 1981): 1. This paper was edited by Ronald Rickford.
220. John Tyndall, "Why We Had to Act," *Spearhead* no. 140 (June 1980): 13.
221. "How it Came About," *Spearhead* no. 140 (June 1980): 10.
222. See letters printed in *Spearhead* no. 142 (August 1980): 10, 11.
223. John Tyndall, "John Tyndall Replies to Rubbish from Mr. Verrall," *Spearhead* no. 144 (October 1980): 12.
224. "Remembrance Day 1980," *Spearhead* no. 144 (October 1980): 19.
225. "Introducing the Young Nationalists," *New Frontier* no. 1 (January/February 1981): 4.
226. Interview with Edmonds.
227. Graham Macklin, *Very Deeply Dyed in Black: Sir Oswald Mosley and theResurrection of British Fascism After 1945* (New York: I.B. Tauris, 2007), 138.

228. John Tyndall, “Establishing the NF Overseas,” *Spearhead* no. 113 (January 1978): 6.
229. Ibid., 6, 7.
230. John Tyndall, *The Eleventh Hour: Call for British Rebirth* (Revised) (Welling: Albion Press, n.d., circa 1998), 329.
231. “National Front in South Africa,” *Britain First* no. 22 (July/August 1974): 4.
232. “National Front Affiliate Formed in South Africa,” *Spearhead* no. 118 (June 1978): 19.
233. “Editorial,” *Hitback* no. 3 (October 1978): 1; Allen Fotheringham, “Waar Staan U, Witman,” *Hitback* no. 3 (October 1978): 2.
234. Ray Hill, “Letter from South Africa,” *Bulldog* no. 10 (November 1978): 2.
235. “Zionists Declare War on NF in South Africa,” *Spearhead* no. 127 (March 1979): 18.
236. Ibid.
237. Ibid.
238. Ibid.
239. Ray Hill and Andrew Bell, *The Other Face of Terror: Inside Europe’s neo-Nazi Network* (London: Grafton Books, 1988), 49. Hill’s claims have been controversial as former NF and BNP members have doubted his published story. Mark Cotterill, who was a member of the BNP faction led by Hill, described him as a “hardline” racist who switched to help *Searchlight* for legal and financial reasons. Mark Cotterill, interviewed by Ryan Shaffer, audio recording, 6 June 2010. (Abbreviated as “Interview with Cotterill 1.”)
240. “New Zealand NF Forms,” *Spearhead* no. 105 (May 1977): 13.
241. Ibid., 13.
242. David Crawford, “The National Front of New Zealand: One Year On,” *Spearhead* no. 115 (March 1978): 14.
243. Jeremy May, “Towards a National Front of Australia,” *Spearhead* no. 117 (May 1978): 17.
244. “All Patriotic Australians,” *Spearhead* no. 117 (May 1978): 9.
245. Keith Thompson, interviewed by Ryan Shaffer, audio recording, 18 September 2011. (Abbreviated as “Interview with Thompson 2.”); David Greason, *I Was a Teenage Fascist* (Victoria: McPhee Gribble, 1994), 171.
246. Greason, 171.
247. The cover of the magazine described itself as “the magazine of the National Fronts of Australia and New Zealand.” *Front Line* no. 5 (October 1978): 1.

248. The cover of the magazine described itself as "in support of the nationalist cause in Australia and New Zealand." *Front Line* no. 67 (Autumn/Winter 1985): 1.
249. "NF AGM in Election Year is Biggest Ever," *Spearhead* no. 126 (February 1979): 19.
250. Interview with Edmonds.
251. "A Daughter for JT," *Spearhead* no. 129 (July 1979): 19.
252. John Tyndall, "American Journey," *Spearhead* no. 130 (August 1979): 12.
253. Ibid.
254. Ibid., 13.
255. William Pierce, "Rottenness in High Places," *Spearhead* no. 72 (January 1974): 8.
256. Derek Humphry and Walter Isaccon, "K-K Klansmen to Visit Britain," *Sunday Times*, 12 February 1978.
257. Ibid.; Derek Humphry, "Klansman Would Fight Deportation," *The Times*, 5 March 1978.
258. Keith Thompson, interviewed by Ryan Shaffer, audio recording, 2 June 2010. (Abbreviated as "Interview with Thompson 1.").
259. Ibid.
260. Ibid.; Martin Webster, "The League of St. George: A Front for 'European Nationalism'," *Spearhead* no. 86 (August 1975): 6–7. In fact, Thompson and Tyndall were so friendly that Thompson later operated Tyndall's Spearhead Books, which was a two-page book listing in the back of *Spearhead*. Tyndall did not actually have a book inventory, but the orders would by filled with Thompson's inventory from the League's Steven Books and get a commission.
261. Interview with Thompson 1.
262. Ibid.
263. "Brent Wins YNF 5-a-Side Soccer Final," *Spearhead* no. 129 (July 1979): 18.
264. "NF Given False Image," *Spearhead* no. 138 (April 1980): 18.
265. Ibid.
266. "National Front: Youth Policy or Youth Cult?," *Spearhead* no. 143 (September 1980): 7.
267. John Tyndall, "Chorley March Sets New Standard," *Spearhead* no. 146 (December 1980): 19.
268. See *Anglian News* no. 13 (September/October 1979).
269. "Nationalism Today," *Nationalism Today* no. 11 (n.d. circa 1981): 2.
270. Interview with Griffin. Griffin said that it was designed by Wakeling and based on *The Guardian*.

271. "Introducing Nationalism Today," *Nationalism Today* no. 1 (March 1980): 2.
272. "YNF Merit Badge," *Bulldog* no. 16 (n.d., circa 1980): 2. This article noted that Griffin was awarded the second YNF merit badge.
273. *Nationalism Today* no. 11 included articles by Steve Brady, Derek Holland, Nick Griffin and Joe Pearce as well as letters from Ian Stuart Donaldson and Patrick Harrington.
274. "Rite-Up," *Nationalism Today* no. 11 (n.d. circa 1981): 17; "Industrial Front," *Nationalism Today* no. 11 (n.d. circa 1980): 18.
275. For example, see Richard Verrall's editorial. "Editorial," *New Nation* no. 2 (Autumn 1980): 2. It should be noted that the magazine also ran an advertisement for the *Journal of Historical Review.*
276. Philip Venning, "The Front Line Targeted," 18.
277. Michael McLaughlin later led the British Movement from 1974 until 1983 and wrote that media focused on the skinheads in the group. Mike Walsh McLaughlin, *Rise of the Sun Wheel: Mike Kampf* (n.p.: CreateSpace Independent Publishing Platform, 2016), 39, 40.
278. Venning, "The Front Line Targeted."
279. Lucy Hodges, "Racists Recruit Youth through Rock Music," *The Times*, 3 August 1981; Richard Garner, "Union Protest over Young National Front 'Vendetta' Against School Teacher," *Times Higher Education Supplement*, 31 October 1980; Richard Ford, "FA to Investigate Alleged Racialist Recruitment," *The Times*, 14 February 1981.
280. Richard North, "The Brain Beneath the Bristle," *The Times*, 22 July 1981.
281. Ibid.
282. Interview with Bushell.
283. George Marshall, *Spirit of'69: A Skinhead Bible* (Argyll: S.T. Publishing, 1994), 12, 14.
284. Ibid., 15.
285. Ibid., 73.
286. Mark S. Hamm, "Hammer of the Gods Revisited: Neo-Nazi Skinheads, Domestic Terrorism, and the Rise of the New Protest Music," in *Cultural Criminology* eds. Jeff Ferrell, Clinton R. Sanders (Boston: Northeastern University Press, 1995), 198.
287. Margaret Thatcher, *Downing Street Years* (New York: Harper Collins, 1993), 92.
288. Marshall, 134; Interview with Pearce.
289. "Chelsea and West Ham Are Top of the 'League of Louts'," *Bulldog* no. 21 (n.d., circa March 1980): unpaginated 5.
290. "Football Front," *Bulldog* no. 40 (n.d. circa 1985): unpaginated 5.

291. Jon Garland and Michael Rowe, *Racism and Anti-Racism in Football* (New York: Palgrave Macmillan, 2001), 40.
292. Paul Canoville, *Black and Blue: How Racism, Drugs and Cancer Almost Destroyed Me* (London: Headline Publishing Group, 2008), 129, 130.
293. For an account of the band's early days, see: Mark Radcliffe, *Show Business: Diary of a Rock 'N' Roll Nobody* (London: Sceptre, 1998), 105–153.
294. *Chargesheet Zine* [*sic*] Skrewdriver interview reprinted in "Chargesheet Zine issue 4: Skrewdriver in the 1970s Interview," *The White Dragon* no. 16 (April 1999): 13; Alex Gottschalk, "The Roots of Skrewdriver: Interview with first drummer Griny," *NADSAT* (Spring 2005): 20–21.
295. Garry Bushell, interviewed by Ryan Shaffer, audio recording, 6 June 2010. He said this in the context of the music at the time and added that knowing their Nazi sympathies now impacts people's attitudes towards the music. For more about Bushell's music journalism career, see: Garry Bushell, *Bushell on the Rampage: The Autobiography of Garry Bushell* (Essex: Apex Publishing, 2010).
296. Joe Pearce, *The Early Years* (n.p.: Agitator Records, 2001), 12. This is an unauthorized reprint of Pearce's *The First Ten Years* (1987). "Suggs Blasts Skrewdriver Roadie Rumour," ContactMusic.com, 30 October 2012; available online at http://www.contactmusic.com/madness/news/suggs-blasts-skrewdriver-roadie-rumour_3350001; accessed 1 July 2016. Ian Stuart actually appeared in two scenes in Madness's 1981 film *Take It or Leave It*. He was one of several people to chase Madness, recreating an event for the movie, and received £60 for his role. Paul London, *Ian Stuart: Nazi Rock Star* (Gothenburg: Midgård, 2002), 38; *Diamond in the Dust: The Ian Stuart Biography* (n.p.: Racial Volunteer Force, 2001), 18.
297. Emma Ruth, "Skrewdriver: Leeds," *New Musical Express*, 9 September 1978, 54.
298. "100% Pure Pork Porky Prime Cuts, Beefy Chops, Skinless Bag," *New Musical Express*, 18 March 1978, 62.
299. "Skrew You," *Sounds*, 19 April 1980, 16.
300. Interview with Bushell.
301. Pearce, *The Early Years*, 5.
302. Paul London, *Ian Stuart: Nazi Rock Star* (Gothenburg: Midgård, 2002), 35. The other books about Ian Stuart include *Diamond in the Dust: The Ian Stuart Biography* (n.p.: Racial Volunteer Force, 2001); Mark Green, *Ian Stuart Donaldson: Memories* (Chemnitz: PC Records, 2007); Joe Pearce, *Skrewdriver: The First Ten Years—The Way It's Got to Be!* (London: Skrewdriver Services, 1987).

303. Interview with Pearce.
304. See the "Back With A Bang/I Don't like You" single released by Skrewdriver.
305. Paul Du Noyer, "The Burning of Southall," *New Musical Express*, 11 July 1981, 3.
306. Ibid.
307. Garry Fielding, *The Business: Brought to Book: Loud, Proud 'N' Punk* (Argyll: ST Publishing, 1996), 17. Despite The Business being linked by the press with racist skinheads, the group performed at events that were against racism. Ibid., 22.
308. See cover of *New Musical Express*, 11 July 1981.
309. "Joe Pearce Faces Race Act Charge," *National Front News* no. 24 (July 1980): 4.
310. "Is The Race Board Going to Prosecute," *Bulldog* no. 16 (n.d., circa 1980): 2.
311. "Smash the Race Laws," *Bulldog* no. 22 (n.d., circa 1980): 1.
312. "Warning!: Coloured Immigrants Can Seriously Damage Your Health," *Bulldog* no. 22 (n.d., circa 1980): 5.
313. "Editor Summoned," *The Times*, 8 April 1981.
314. "Free Speech, Free Joe Pearce," *South London Patriot* no. 1 (n.d., circa 1982): unpaginated 4.
315. "NF Paper Racially Insulting, Court Told," *The Times*, 8 January 1982; "NF Paper Editor is Jailed," *The Times*, 13 January 1982; "Let Joe Go," *National Front News* no. 36 (October 1981): 1.
316. Interview with Pearce. During his second prison sentence another member began editing as "Captain Truth." According to Griffin, he did some *Bulldog* editing, but that person was supposed to be Nick Wakeling who did it infrequently. Interview with Griffin.
317. Joe Pearce, "Prison Has Strengthened My Resolve," *Nationalism Today* no. 11 (n.d. circa 1981): 8.
318. Interview with Pearce.
319. "RAC News," *Bulldog* no. 22 (n.d.): 3.
320. Sham 69's criticisms about racism have been described as ambiguous. Roger Sabin, "I Won't Let That Dago Go: Rethinking Punk and Racism," in *Punk Rock: So What?: The Cultural Legacy of Punk* (New York: Routledge, 1999), 210.
321. "Why Do the Reds Hate Skrewdriver," *Rocking the Reds* unnumbered (n.d. circa 1980): 4. This unnumbered issue features a cyborg with the letters "NF."
322. Matthew Worley, "Oi! Oi! Oi!: class locality and British Punk," *Twentieth Century British History* 24, no. 4 (2013): 628.
323. Interview with Pearce.

324. "Rock Against Communism," *National Front News* no. 60 (October 1984): unpaginated 6.
325. "Our Own Record Label," *Bulldog* no. 33 (May 1983): 4. *Bulldog* explained that the NF was starting an "independent record label" that will issue "records by patriotic White bands. It will be called White Noise Records and the first single will be *White Power* by Skrewdriver."
326. George Lincoln Rockwell, *White Power* (Dallas: Ragnarok Press, 1967); *Skrewdriver Song Book* (n.p.: unknown, n.d., circa 1988), 19. In possession.
327. "White Noise Records Brings You," *National Front News* no. 57 (June 1984): 4.
328. "Selling by the Thousand!," *Bulldog* no. 36 (1983): 3.
329. Pearce, *The Early Years*, 23.
330. "See Skrewdriver Live!," *Bulldog* no. 36 (1983): 3.

CHAPTER 4

An International Youth Movement, 1983–1990

During the 1980s, the National Front (NF) expanded its reach throughout Europe and North America, becoming an international source for fascist music and literature. The relaunch of Rock Against Communism (RAC) proved highly successful due to the new songs and fame brought by Skrewdriver. With White Noise Records, youth from around the world sent the NF money in exchange for records. The NF responded by creating the White Noise Club to seize the youth's interest and promote foreign groups that shared its views.[1] Though it was at the forefront of the international fascist movement, domestically the NF's appeal became increasingly restricted to young neo-Nazis. By the late 1980s, the NF's electoral prospects were so limited that it moved away from election campaigns and built relations with the Libyan government as well as foreign Arab and black nationalists.

This chapter explores how the NF expanded its youth outreach through music and began adopting ideas from foreign radicals who shared its fascist and ethno-nationalist views. The NF and the British National Party (BNP) faced many struggles during the early 1980s with abortive attempts to unify and mounting NF infighting, which allowed Tyndall's BNP to surpass the NF in membership in late 1989.[2] By the time of the NF's disintegration during the 1980s, it had already lost marginal support while the leadership searched for new ideologies, which alienated supporters.[3] Building on these issues, this chapter explains how in the 1980s the NF was led by impressionable youth who had political ambitions but also wanted to transform cultural and social institutions.

R. Shaffer, *Music, Youth and International Links in Post-War British Fascism*, Palgrave Studies in the History of Subcultures and Popular Music, DOI 10.1007/978-3-319-59668-6_4

It further shows how the young NF leaders, unlike their older counterparts, looked to non-fascist foreigners from the past and present as well as borrowed ideas from the left. Some of these ideas created tension within the group and limited its broader domestic electoral appeal, but they also expanded the group's international reach and built associations with organizations that could help with new financing.

Political Soldiers

The NF youth's collection of eccentric philosophies began in the early 1980s with the introduction of Third Positionist ideas from Italian fascists. Young National Front (YNF) member Derek Holland explained that following the 1979 "electoral disaster," the youth "decided there needed to be a total reappraisal not merely about how we went about things, but also how we express what we believe and in fact what we believe."[4] These ideas included Third Position concepts adapted from the Terza Posizione (Third Position) movement in Italy, distributism from Hilaire Belloc and G.K. Chesterton, as well as the introduction of a spiritual element into NF politics. Broadly, these philosophies were about opposing both communism and capitalism and creating self-sustaining local communities. While some of these ideas alienated NF activists, the continuing search for new ideas led to meetings with the Libyan and later Iraqi governments as well as the Nation of Islam in the United States.

The earliest influence of this group was marked by the arrival of several Italians who had fled Italy following the August 1980 bombing of Bologna's main train station, which killed dozens of people and injured hundreds. Scholar Anna Cento Bull has discussed Italian fascists engaging in the Strategy of Tension, which involved assassinations and violence, to blame their opponents and undermine the democratic government.[5] Members of the Nuclei Armati Rivoluzionari (Armed Revolutionary Nuclei) were convicted of the bombing while several more Italian fascists were wanted by authorities.[6] After the bombing in 1980, Terza Posizione figures were under pressure from authorities, and Roberto Fiore and Massimo Morsello fled Italy to escape arrest and arrived in England, staying in the country for nearly twenty years as they fought Italian government demands for extradition.[7] During this time, Fiore and Morsello remained close and active in politics, even later launching an Italian political party, Forza Nuova (New Force), in

England.[8] In autumn 1980, a group of about a dozen Italians showed up unannounced at NF member Steve Brady's home because they knew Brady through his involvement in the League of Saint George, which had a network of international contacts.[9] According to Fiore, after making contact with NF activists, he was "introduced by friends to Nick Griffin" and then met others to see if "there was similarity in the politics of the NF and of Terze Posizione [*sic*]."[10] In 1981, Holland and Fiore met, bonding over their interest in the traditionalist Catholicism of Marcel Lefebvre, who opposed changes from the Second Vatican Council that allowed Catholic masses to be conducted in English. Holland, a traditional Catholic influenced by his Irish parents, had joined the NF at age eighteen in 1975 and was open about his faith, including writing in *Spearhead* that the "main planks of fossil evidence" for evolution were "fraudulent."[11] Such claims were criticized by other NF members and even prompted the editor, Richard Verrall, to respond that the examples were not fraudulent and "no scientist of repute today is an anti-evolutionist," arguing that the discussion for Christians was "unnecessary" because "evolution and a creative power, or God, are not incompatible."[12]

In the following years, the Italian figures had a profound impact on young NF members. Griffin remarked that the Italians were ahead of the young NF leaders in terms of political vision and ideology, and the Italian influence helped the NF develop intellectually.[13] Fiore, for example, attended the editorial meetings of *Nationalism Today* at Rosine de Bounevialle's Forest House in Liss Forest, where he played the piano in front of an NF audience. A group of NF youth also attended Latin Mass with Fiore, including Phil Andrews, who did not know Latin.[14] Moreover, Fiore's ideological influence, including his brief time as a "pagan" and interest in Julius Evola's writing, helped transform the direction of British fascism.[15] More Catholic concepts appeared in NF platforms, such as opposition to usury based on the writings of Hilaire Belloc, and the expansion of ownership of property based on G.K. Chesterton's distributism principles.

The NF did not immediately launch a project focused exclusively on these ideas as it remained devoted to race and immigration. Yet the NF's organs, such as *New Nation*, published articles and cover stories about Belloc's distributism, opposing capitalism and communism.[16] In 1981, Holland worked with Fiore to launch *Rising*, a small publication that was "for the Political Soldier."[17] Reflecting on its impact in 1998, an anonymous author argued *Rising* was "a decisive turning point" due to its "tactical, strategical, ideological and practical points of view."[18] Nigel Copsey described it as a "semi-clandestine publication" with "esoteric ideas of fascist philosophers."[19] Moving away from an electoral focus, *Rising* was devoted to "forging and harmonizing all elements" to bring about a "lasting" revolution.[20] The goal was to introduce young radicals to a "Political Soldier" mentality as dedicated and learned militants engaged in organizing businesses, schools and community projects for a new political, spiritual and economic approach.[21] With articles titled "The Meaning of Life on Earth," "The Rural Revolution" and "The Spiritual Revolution," *Rising* took a much different approach from that of previous NF publications. Though influenced by A.K. Chesterton's *The New Unhappy Lords*, Holland's writings had a far more religious tone that saw Christianity and land as vital concepts to the movement, as opposed to the more biological and imperial outlook promoted by figures such as Tyndall.

The circulation of *Rising* was small and only five issues were ever produced. Yet it served as the incubator for the most important British fascist tract of its era, Holland's *The Political Soldier: A Statement* (1984). Written in about two hours, his goal was to offer "simple ideas to totally areligious [*sic*], aspiritual [*sic*] people with good hearts" in order for them "to change themselves."[22] Other racist and fascist religions were circulating among the NF, such as Ben Klassen's Church of the Creator, which was a non-theistic belief system wherein the "white man" was the "creator" with the religion's ultimate goal being anti-white genocide.[23] Holland, however, wanted to introduce Christian principles to give the fascist revolution a spiritual dimension. Drawing on the inter-war fascist Iron Guard from Romania, a Political Soldier had virtues that included patience, calmness, self-discipline and a sense of humor.[24] Specifically, Holland gave examples of getting "priorities right" by "attending an NF function" over a football match or party.[25] The tract was advertised in the *National Front News*, explaining "why the nationalist movement needs Political Soldiers and how to attain the level of a true Political Soldier's commitment to the cause."[26] The fifth issue of *Rising* told readers the "task" of the publication was "to get our militants out of the sterile, materialist rut that they have been led into and to think in a new way."[27] The *Political Soldier* tract targeted impressionable youth with advertisements in Young NF publications to change the minds of readers and get them more committed to the NF.[28] The tract's success spawned a 1989 sequel that told readers, "we stand before the apocalypse! Gird yourself and prepare for battle!"[29] Proving to be a popular work, the first tract was translated into several languages, was republished in 1994 and excerpts appeared in an Oxford University Press anthology about fascism.[30]

In addition to new writings, the NF also released historical literature to "win the war of ideas." This included works by Hilaire Belloc, G.K. Chesterton, Corneliu Codreanu, William Morris and Otto Strasser on topics ranging from Jews to economics.[31] In a booklet titled *Yesterday & Tomorrow*, excerpts from works by fascists and Catholics were reprinted because, as "the final conflict approaches the duty of every militant is to read, to study and to find his roots in tradition" while also taking "control of the streets of England and of Europe."[32] Aside from excerpts and reprints, NF periodicals simply published a full page of quotes from Belloc detailing his stance on capitalism, communism, Judaism and private property.[33]

While Holland was spreading Political Soldier ideas, Pearce was also theorizing about doctrine and freedom. Influenced by his first prison term for violating the Race Relations Act, he wrote *Fight for Freedom*, which argued that "the British people have been dispossessed of their freedom" and "[a]s British people living in a multi-racial capitalist Britain during the 1980s we may have been born into slavery."[34] During his second prison term for similar charges, he started writing *Nationalist Doctrine*, which defined "nationalism" as a triangle of national freedom, racial preservation and social justice.[35] Though these tracts were not as influential as Holland's work in the long term, Pearce's regular writings for NF publications, involvement in RAC and prison convictions made him a significant figure, with contacts in the NF's football and music communities. Moreover, his working-class background was compelling for many activists, especially with his promotion of Strasserite fascism that involved organizing union workers.[36] Quotes from Otto Strasser were published in *Nationalism Today*, arguing for "liberation from the social and economic monopolies."[37] In addition, the anniversary of the murder of Otto's brother, Gregor Strasser, by Hitler was marked with articles celebrating their ideas about National Socialism.[38]

White Noise Club

The relaunch of RAC in 1983 was immediately successful, with hundreds of teenagers gathering for Skrewdriver concerts under the auspices of the NF. In April 1983, more than four hundred youth attended the RAC concert in London with Skrewdriver, The Ovaltinees, and Peter and Wolves.[39] The music generated a popular underground phenomenon, with the vocalist of The Ovaltinees, for example, claiming that demand for the music meant the band performed twice a week.[40] Meanwhile, the NF also restarted union initiatives from the 1970s, but compared to the estimated seventy people that attended the NF's Trade Union Association, the NF's music outreach was mobilizing and attracting hundreds more individuals at each concert.[41] A bulletin by Pearce announced the first meeting of the National Workers' Movement, an NF union, to take the "fight against the enemies of Britain onto the shopfloor,"[42] whereas the NF Trade Unionists existed to "promote the NF among members of the trade union movement."[43] Pearce's duties, such as editing *Bulldog*, union work and organizing RAC, proved too much and Pearce resigned as head of the YNF to focus exclusively on writing for *Bulldog* and organizing music events.[44]

The new RAC was far more successful than its predecessor. According to Patrick Harrington, once Skrewdriver became involved the movement "started to be seen more seriously."[45] Coupled with a band that had preexisting notoriety and the taboo nature of songs such as "White Power," Skrewdriver's music and concerts were readily welcomed by hordes of youth. As Phil Andrews, an NF activist from Hounslow, explained, RAC with Skrewdriver helped bring "more and more working-class white youths into the reach of the NF."[46] In fact, the NF reported that "Skrewdriver are back with a bang and their patriotic music is really skrewing [*sic*] the establishment."[47] The band hosted concerts despite law enforcement and opponents' attempts to prevent the events from happening, which only further enticed rebellious youth.

Security and organization were important elements in hosting the concerts, which initially took place in small clubs and later expanded to large outdoor festivals. Not only did the NF have to contend with opponents that wanted to find out the location of the venue and force the event's cancelation, but violent anti-fascists organized secretly to disrupt events with force. Notably, Anti-Fascist Action was formed in July 1985 and later fascist concerts became one its targets.[48] Indeed, mainstream concerts required much effort to organize, but the need for secrecy to ensure a concert was not canceled or disrupted caused the NF to refine its practices. Rival groups were a major concern, and at one concert six people were stabbed.[49] At another event, a summer festival, the Hells Angels Motorcycle Club were tasked with providing security.[50] Moreover, a common image from Skrewdriver concerts was males with shaven heads wearing "Skrewdriver Security" t-shirts; among them was Nicky Crane, a prominent skinhead and British Movement organizer.[51] In addition to the physical security of the crowd, the NF hired concert security to safeguard money, music equipment and merchandise.[52] As Harrington recalled, the NF did not always pick the largest or physically strongest, but selected people who were loyal, worked as a team and had a strong mentality.[53]

The NF used false names to book concerts at church halls and pubs under the pretense that they were hosting engagement or birthday parties.[54] Harrington described how an "advancement group" that included about twenty people would meet with the owners ahead of time to secure the hall. Later the music equipment would be loaded in and would often include two sets of sound gear, with one being a backup in case of failure or damage. This template was followed for the next decade, telling Skrewdriver fans, for example, to meet at an underground station where they would then be re-routed to the location of the concert.[55]

Aside from the live performances, music news and lyrics were printed in *Bulldog* so fans could spread the music's message, and scene reports generated excitement with details about future activities. The publication also included photographs, concert reviews and events devoted almost exclusively to Skrewdriver. Lyrics from Skrewdriver's "Smash the IRA" capturing NF themes in music form were printed so readers could absorb the lyrics in a different way than if they just heard the song.[56] Another addition to *Bulldog* was the publication of "RAC Charts" with top ten songs, compiled by readers who shared their favorite songs. Not surprisingly, Skrewdriver's song "White Power" was a frequent entry on the list.[57] Moreover, the publication also served as an outlet for Ian Stuart, whose letters to readers told supporters to "boycott" Asian and Jewish stores that sold skinhead items.[58]

During 1984, Skrewdriver's fame and role in the NF grew.[59] In fact, the NF reported that "Rock Against Communism has exploded onto the British music scene over the last twelve months" and drew hundreds of people to its events due to Skrewdriver.[60] When *Bulldog* incorporated *Rocking the Reds* as a regular feature, the music news became the heart of the publication and it even added an extra page focusing on music.[61] The new feature argued that Skrewdriver was popular because the band spoke "the language of the white working class."[62] Following the success of *White Power*, White Noise Records released another Skrewdriver single, "The Voice of Britain," with lyrics that included: "now Britain belongs to aliens" and "it's about time the British went and took it back."[63] That same year the NF organized the first annual outdoor RAC festival, held on property owned by Nick Griffin's parents in the Suffolk countryside. Griffin's parents gave him permission to host the event, and cheap Royal Dutch lager supplied by Tony Williams was sold to the crowd.[64] The NF reported nearly four hundred "mainly skinhead" attendees "from all over Britain" saw bands, including Last Orders, Buzzard Bait, Offensive Weapon, Public Enemy, Brutal Attack and Skrewdriver, perform.[65] Recorded on video, the concert drew a crowd of youth giving the Nazi salute to "White Power" and chanting "nigger, nigger" during the chorus of "When the Boat Comes In" as Skrewdriver performed on a makeshift stage donned with Union Jacks and NF flags.[66] The festival proved very popular and became an annual event for the next few years, providing solid revenue for the NF.[67] In addition, the NF reported that Skrewdriver's "White Christmas" concert on December 16, 1984 in East London drew about five hundred fans and "was the highest turn-out for any RAC concert so far."[68]

In contrast to the socio-political essays in other NF publications, *Bulldog*'s articles continued to focus on music and tabloid-style content. Pearce, under the Captain Truth pseudonym, taunted authorities after his release, writing that the authorities were "watching the houses of NF organisers, for weeks before, to try and get some clues as to Captain Truth's identity" and then "raided" the homes of Pearce and Ian Anderson, the NF deputy chair, to "stop" the publication.[69] In November 1984, the two received summonses for violating the Race Relations Act by publishing material "likely to stir up racial hatred."[70] Meanwhile, Pearce was also promoting other RAC bands, such as Brutal Attack, which released music for White Noise Records as well. Ken McLellan, the band's singer, told readers "we should fight for white rights."[71] Similar to Skrewdriver's lyrical content, Brutal Attack's ideas mirrored those promoted by the NF that had gotten Pearce and Anderson in legal trouble, and were at the heart of the NF's public demonstrations. In August 1983, for instance, the NF held a "Defend Rights for Whites" rally, drawing eight hundred people with speeches from Griffin, Brons and Webster in response to the anti-racist Notting Hill Carnival.[72]

Skrewdriver was becoming an international phenomenon with words that transcended political parties and borders. Thousands of copies of Skrewdriver's *White Power* EP were sold domestically and "dozens" more were bought by people in Belgium, Denmark, Holland, France and Sweden.[73] By 1985, the NF reported Skrewdriver had a "world-wide following" with skinhead support in the United States, specifically in New Jersey and Philadelphia.[74] American fans were a key element of the NF's foreign support with a large population of white, English-speaking youth. In fact, *The Spotlight*, an American anti-Semitic publication, included an article by Michael Hoffman II about skinhead music that discussed "white patriots" making music and told Americans "to correspond with Ian Stuart" by writing to the NF's Croydon address.[75] Beyond the United States and Britain, about one thousand copies of Skrewdriver recordings were also sold to fans in Germany.[76]

The international support did not go unnoticed by people who wanted to make money. Skrewdriver and White Noise Records did not have a signed contract or even a formal agreement on residuals from sales.[77] Pearce explained how he would "meet Ian Stuart on Friday nights and we would go out and have far too many beers. He would just hand me a huge wad of cash. There were no accounts."[78] In contrast to the NF's informality, Rock-O-Rama, a West German record label owned by Herbert Egoldt, purchased Skrewdriver singles from White Noise Records and sold them to German fans.[79] In 1985, Egoldt contacted Pearce about producing a full Skrewdriver album, which led to Skrewdriver signing a record contract with the West German company.[80] This news was welcomed by the NF, which explained "White Noise Records are hoping to import this record when it becomes available."[81] White Noise Records also continued producing its own records, such as *This is White Noise* with songs by Skrewdriver, Brutal Attack, ABH and The Die-Hards.[82] In the NF bulletin to members, chair Andrew Brons explained that threats from authorities had not "deterred White Noise Records from producing more discs. The next disc—featuring four bands—is due to be released in mid June."[83] The album, *This is White Noise*, became a popular release and its cover featured a memorable image of two children with the NF's logo. Continuing with NF and Skrewdriver themes, the lyrical content was centered on whiteness, such as The Die-Hards' song "White Working Class Man."[84]

With Skrewdriver's international audience, the NF grew into an international organization. This reflected a desire by Stuart, writing from prison in early 1986, that "[w]e must continue to create and cement ties with our kindred organisations in Europe, to make sure that none of the great achievements of European culture and history are forgotten."[85] While serving his prison sentence for assault, he continued to write new music and even an unpublished novel.[86] Skrewdriver's album *Hail the New Dawn*, released by Rock-O-Rama and including transnational themes, was sold by the NF.[87] The lyrics of the song "Europe Awake" included "Europe awake for the white's man sake" and "Europe awake before it gets too late."[88] *Nationalism Today*'s review of the album described it as an "excellent" record that inspires "optimism" through the "dream of a 'new dawn' and the hope which springs from it."[89] That same year Stuart's contributions drew so many people to the NF that he received "the branch recruitment cup from Andrew Brons."[90]

Seizing on the new-found power of international white youth, the NF rebranded its youth and music outreach. In late 1985, *Bulldog* ceased publication and *New Dawn* was created in its place, which the NF described would take "a much more positive stance" and emphasize "racial pride and unity."[91] While *Bulldog*'s last issue contained a column that ranked football fans "as the most racist," *New Dawn* was much more subdued, with news about YNF "anti-drug" marches.[92] Indeed, the NF described *Bulldog* as having been "very negative," saying that the party needed to build "a new, younger, more idealistic and positive leadership."[93] The new paper replaced the "Rocking the Reds" section with "White Noise," described as three pages of "RAC News."[94] It also promoted electronic music acts, such as Above the Ruins and Final Sound, but was still heavily devoted to Skrewdriver, which was preparing for the release of its album *Blood and Honour*.[95] Borrowing its title from the Hitler Youth slogan, the song "Blood and Honour" discussed "Europe" pushing back against Wall Street and "never" becoming a "puppet state."[96] Skrewdriver was the undisputed vanguard of fascist skinhead music, as demonstrated not just by its music sales but also by its prominent and featured role in the NF summer concerts. The 1985 festival included ten bands, doubling the number in the first concert, and drew hundreds of fans "from all over the British Isles."[97] In 1986, six hundred people, mostly skinheads, attended the White Noise festival in Suffolk.[98] Skrewdriver and nine other bands received a "great reception" from the crowd, which drank beer and ate food.[99] The event also served as a launching platform for new acts, such as Sudden Impact, which was associated with the Croydon NF branch and performed its first RAC concert at the festival.[100]

The NF exploited the growing international interest in skinhead music by starting the White Noise Club (WNC) in 1986. Though still using the RAC name, White Noise was used to describe music promoting racist and fascist views. Under the leadership of Derek Holland and Patrick Harrington, the WNC was a part of the NF that organized concerts, published the *White Noise* magazine, produced merchandise and crafted a plan "to produce records and tapes on a regular basis."[101] Harrington explained that given the controversial nature of the music, it was difficult to get distributors for the music, so the NF created "parallel" avenues to promote and distribute the music through its magazines and mail order enterprises.[102] Any white American or European could join the club and receive a membership card, a subscription to *White Noise* magazine and discounts on WNC concerts.[103] *White Noise* magazine's first issue featured a photograph of Ian Stuart on the cover with the words "stronger than before" and published an exclusive interview with him in which he predicted White Noise would have "a great future ahead."[104] The magazine also published articles about foreign bands, such as an interview with a member of Ultima Thule from Sweden that discussed the band's political views.[105]

The magazine demonstrated a shift away from a narrow "nationalist" view towards an "internationalist" outlook on race and politics. The NF leaders, such as Harrington, who studied philosophy at university, read Antonio Gramsci's work about intentionally using cultural forms to influence political development.[106] The NF hoped not only to have a domestic impact but also to shape change in other countries. Thus, the WNC built a network of more than thirty fanzines that both promoted White Noise music and acted as "talent scouts" that contacted the club about upcoming bands, while *White Noise* reached a peak worldwide circulation of 5000, not including issues photocopied by supporters.[107] The third issue was dedicated to "Music for Europe" and discussed WNC's concert in London featuring Skrewdriver, Sudden Impact, No Remorse and the German band Boots & Braces.[108] The magazine contained interviews with bands from Britain, France and Sweden and explained it was "a nationalist music organization promoting European nationalist groups."[109] In 1986, White Noise Records released a new compilation album titled *No Surrender* with songs from eleven bands, including Skrewdriver.[110] The WNC also sold videos and music, which allowed foreign supporters to not just listen to, but also see, British skinhead bands and mimic their sound and style throughout the world.[111]

By 1986 Harrington had become more heavily involved in nationwide political matters for the NF. Phil Andrews, who originally joined the YNF in 1977 and joined the party Directorate in 1984, served as the "front man" for the White Noise Club by mailing out record orders, but did not make key decisions involving the label.[112] Andrews recalled that he was mailing out "hundreds" of records to individuals in countries around the world, including Australia, Canada, the United States and Western Europe.[113] Those records, in turn, made their way into the hands of people such as Clark Martell in Chicago, who dubbed Skrewdriver music on cassettes and sold them from a post office box music operation. Martell also started the Chicago Area Skinheads (CASH), reportedly the first American neo-Nazi skinhead group, which went on to have a major influence on the American skinhead subculture.[114] Indeed, Andrews noted that while the music was "fringe," it was a "big fringe" and was the main component that kept the NF going.[115] Membership fees, for example, were barely enough to pay for mailing membership cards, and newspaper sales were eclipsed by record sales.[116] The money from the WNC would go into the party's fund, and while the bands would receive a share, Andrews said "I think the bands really were being ripped off."[117] Music sales and concert tickets were not the only ways the NF raised money. For example, the outdoor concerts had food stalls and sold beer, which also generated significant revenue for the party.

The WNC's concerts and promotional activities united European youth with similar ideas, but also brought them together at events. According to Griffin, "there was no other place to do it other than my parent's place" in rural Suffolk, and the NF began hosting concerts in 1984.[118] The NF activists helped prepare for a large festival by repairing the barns and cleaning up the property to make it suitable for a concert.[119] Weeks later, hundreds of skinheads traveled to the countryside and gave the *Sieg Heil* salute in front of a barn as Skrewdriver preformed "White Power."[120] A similar concert was held in 1986 with Skrewdriver headlining.[121] The White Noise festival in 1987, however, was a truly international event, with hundreds of fans attending from all over Europe, including Austria, Belgium, France and Germany.[122] One of the key organizers was Phil Andrews, who recalled it generating a large amount of revenue, with tickets costing around £6 or £7 sold to hundreds of fans, and Royal Dutch lager that was past the sell-by date, donated by Tony Williams, sold for £1 each.[123] The money, however, was not shared evenly. Despite high revenue from tickets, some of the bands complained about receiving a nominal payment of about £30.[124]

While most of the audience attended the festival to see Skrewdriver and Brutal Attack, the first foreign band to be involved with the annual event, Legion 88 from France, performed on a stage draped with White Noise and NF flags.[125] During Skrewdriver's set, Stuart spoke frequently between songs about the international crowd, including mentioning that the concert was being recorded on video for broadcast on American cable access television by Tom Metzger, leader of the White Aryan Resistance (WAR).[126] The concert was recorded by Michael Hoffman II, who was in contact with Metzger and was known to NF activists for his book about the trial of Holocaust denier Ernst Zündel.[127] Hoffman appeared at NF events to document the subculture, and the NF even published an interview with Hoffman while Harrington reviewed his book.[128] According to Metzger, Hoffman provided him with the tape and then made copies, which raised Metzger's profile with American skinheads and encouraged Metzger to host his own events in the United States called Aryan Festivals.[129] In 1989, Metzger and Bob Heick, who founded the American Front after visiting Britain in 1984, hosted a controversial "Aryan Woodstock" concert in Napa County, California.[130] Heick modeled his American Front, which remained small and mostly included skinheads, after the NF and worked with Metzger to organize the festival.[131] A court prohibited amplified music at the event, leading to skinheads calling it "Aryan Woodflop," but it still successfully united skinheads from around the country who listened to Metzger's message.[132] Metzger's son John was head of WAR's Aryan Youth Movement and claimed Aryan Woodstock led to the hosting of more concerts around the United States, notably Metzger's annual Aryan Festival in Oklahoma later that year.[133]

Indeed, the WNC developed an extensive range of local and foreign contacts. The NF's club was promoted in local newsletters for NF supporters, such as in Leeds, that told readers to "build the nationalist music and cultural industry now."[134] In June 1987, White Noise held its "first ever gig in Sweden" with bands from Denmark, England, Finland,

Norway and Sweden.[135] Aside from the concert review, a photograph of 150 skinheads dancing was featured in *White Noise*. Meanwhile, a new White Noise Records release titled *White Noise: We Want the Airwaves* was promoted and the club announced it was "developing" branches in Germany, Portugal and the United States.[136] An American branch of the WNC was briefly opened in Arlington, Virginia that focused on American bands and sold "white nationalist music."[137] Despite making international contacts and exporting British fascism to dozens of countries, however, internal disputes were impacting the NF organization in negative ways.

Internal Disputes

The 1979 split had a dramatic impact on British fascism by dividing resources and membership between those who stayed with the NF and those who left the party with Tyndall, joining what became the BNP. Increasingly, the younger NF leaders saw the group as less of a political party and more of a movement for national revolution. Consequently, the NF was developing its ideology and outreach through foreign contacts and music instead of political campaigns. However, some of the older members who had been with the party during the early days were resistant to abandoning the political tactics that had earned it support and media attention during the previous decade. In the early 1980s, the party underwent several internal conflicts that dramatically impacted its methods and ideology for the next decade. This included focusing on cultural and social programs to influence politics and, later, abandoning electoral politics.

The most well-known party figure who had remained with the NF since the late 1960s was Martin Webster. As the activities organizer, Webster earned praise and scorn for his street battles and election campaigning during the clashes of the 1970s. Following Tyndall's exit and as the youth adapted to the new environment, Webster remained fixated on the street marches and demonstrations to garner publicity.[138] Yet the marches were drawing only a few dozen people, such as one with fifty participants in Wolverhampton in 1981, which was far fewer than the hundreds or thousands who had participated in the 1970s.[139] Moreover, this created problems among the youth, who were focused on changing minds in other ways. Derek Holland, responding to an article by Webster, wrote that during the 1970s "the NF acted as though the road to power were a one away street—marches, elections, Parliament and power," but national revolutions must be "prepared through the development of a cultural revival, a revival that ties the people to soil, identity and tradition."[140] Additionally, Webster's views on politics, such as the absence of spiritualism, was the antithesis of the direction in which the young NF members were moving.[141] The differences were not only ideological. Nigel Copsey wrote that beyond the issue of opposing unity with the BNP, "Webster's bid to inhibit ideological radicalism and factionalism within the Front" was also a source of conflict.[142] Webster's homosexuality and his relationship with Michael Salt, who was also on the NF Directorate, made some members uneasy, due to both his lifestyle and the negative publicity surrounding it. Webster's brash personality was an additional problem because many of the younger people, including Griffin, Pearce and Holland, were friends and participated in many activities together without the older figures. According to Webster, he confronted Griffin and Pearce about the "secret" youth gatherings with Fiore at Forrest House, arguing that meetings should be public.[143] This provoked an angry response from the increasingly influential youth who did not want to be subjected to Webster's control.

In December 1983, the younger members of the NF engineered Webster's expulsion from the party. Webster and Salt were removed from their paid positions with support from Ian Anderson, who had previously worked with the two in expelling other members. Yet Webster's removal was not executed in accordance with the NF constitution and he sued in the High Court, with the judge finding in his favor and ordering that he be reinstated.[144] The nine-month lapse between the expulsion and the judge's ruling meant that it "did nobody any good" as the party had changed and his role diminished.[145] According to Andrews, the judge actually explained the proper way to remove Webster and the party then followed those instructions, removing him from his post legally.[146] Webster said the expulsion and the changes left "lunatic kids" in the Front who would go on to do "nutty stuff."[147] He then started Our Nation, a splinter group, taking dozens of NF members with him, and though it was rumored that he received money from Françoise Dior to fund the organization, he denied this.[148] Our Nation described itself as "a private society or club" rather than "a political party seeking to win votes" and therefore "it is under no obligation to encumber itself with democratic institutions."[149] Instead, the group's focus was on "internal education meetings" with goals to build links with youth.[150] Ultimately, it failed to attract large numbers and Webster abandoned the group after two meetings, turning his efforts to editing Lady Jane Birdwood's anti-immigration newspaper, *Choice*.

The party leadership in the early 1980s was headed by Andrew Brons, but because he lived a great distance from London, many of the Directorate members were given increased powers to act at the main headquarters in London. More than that, Brons was busy, with a full-time teaching position and a family, and also served as the editor of *New Nation*.[151] As chair, Brons had different deputy chairs who helped him, including Ian Anderson as well as Richard Verrall and later Nick Griffin.[152] His leadership of the party took a toll on his life, including pressure to get him fired from his job.[153] Then in February 1984, Brons was charged with threats or words likely to breach the peace.[154] After five years of leading the party, which was undergoing ideological and tactical change, Brons resigned from the chair in early 1985 and Anderson took over the position.[155] Brons explained that after two decades in politics, activists can get "jaded," but he remained a member of the NF throughout the 1980s with a less prominent role.[156] Though Brons and Anderson were not enthusiastic about the direction the party was taking, turning its back on traditional political campaigning in favor of efforts such as the Political Soldier outreach, these transformations were tolerated as products of youth activism.

The younger NF members banded together, not just around political views but as friends. Thrust into key positions in a political party during their formative years, Griffin and Pearce were close friends, neighbors and influenced each other ideologically, with Pearce even serving as Griffin's best man at his wedding.[157] At social events, including drinking at pubs and even boxing matches, the young members developed close bonds. By this time Griffin had emerged as one of the leaders. Journalist Bill Buford wrote about attending a pub party at Bury St. Edmunds in Suffolk with Andrews and Griffin, and described Griffin as "a well-mannered young man with an intelligent face" who was with a "pretty" girlfriend.[158] As the attendees drank, Griffin stood against the wall and occasionally "whispered an instruction," such as waiting "to play the White Power music" at the end of the party.[159] When the music was played following Griffin's approval, the crowd listened to Skrewdriver and Brutal Attack songs until someone went "berserk," knocked over glasses and "crashed into a table."[160] Then Buford explained, "Griffin went over and stopped the record and turned off the stereo. The party ended."[161]

Those associated with the Political Soldier ideas, including Andrews, Harrington, Holland, Griffin and Colin Todd, saw the new ideology as the way to change society and lay the groundwork for electoral victories in the future. In 1985, the NF started a Heritage Group devoted to "studying our cultural heritage" in order to give a "positive side to the party" and spark "idealism" among supporters.[162] The focus was on a spiritual battle against materialism that borrowed from Strasserism's working-class orientation.[163] The first events, held in March and April, involved members viewing paintings of English landscapes at the Hayward Gallery and the British Museum.[164] Griffin, then deputy chair, remarked that "ideological development" was one of the NF's great achievements and began training the party members in countryside seminars on ideology, but also about how to campaign and sell papers.[165]

The party's new ideological direction caused fascists who were interested in traditional political parties to join the BNP and perceived the NF weakened. In June 1985, the NF held an Extraordinary General Meeting (EGM) in response to members being charged with violating the Race Relations Act and media criticism. According to Griffin, the party unanimously adopted a new constitution that changed members' voting rights and set term limits for the chair.[166] It created a two-tier membership system in which old members had voting privileges, but new members' voting rights had to be approved in order to ensure "the NF always remains in the hands of an elite of ideologically aware activists."[167] Ian Anderson argued this had been needed years earlier to prevent "infiltration" and "subversion" of the party.[168] Meanwhile, citing security concerns, the NF changed its administration to separate memberships and publication subscriptions from RAC merchandise.[169] Griffin later wrote that this was done to get "Anderson away from the central funds and internal organisation."[170] In January 1986, Martin Wingfield, who edited the *National Front News* and *Sussex Front*, was elected party chair.[171] A long-time activist, Wingfield had made news the previous year for violating the Race Relations Act and was sent to prison for refusing to pay the fine.[172]

By summer 1986, the most serious party dispute since 1979 occurred between the National Front's Political Soldiers and the National Front Support Group (NFSG). Though some of the disagreements between the factions were ideological, there were also personality conflicts that shaped the opposing sides. According to Griffin, some of the ideological differences were "superficial," with the Political Soldiers seeing themselves as revolutionaries while at the same time the government was concerned with the NF hardline campaigns in Northern Ireland.[173] In fact, Nigel Copsey explained that part of the intra-party tension was over "reneging on its long-standing commitment to Ulster," banning scientific racism from the NF magazine and opposition to paramilitary-type exercises.[174] The Support Group became more commonly known as the "Flag" faction, drawing that name from the publication edited by Wingfield, and consisted of Anderson, Brons, Wingfield, Tom Acton and Steve Brady. Griffin accused some members, including Anderson, of financial misconduct and of working for the security services in his book *Attempted Murder* (1986), which detailed his perspective on events.[175] Griffin also alleged that Anderson had a "dirt file" with information that targeted people such as Mark Cotterill and Ian Stuart.[176] Additionally, Griffin criticized Tom Acton for failing to print party material in a timely manner and Steve Brady for mailing "sensitive" material in such a way that the Special Branch could copy it.[177] Clashes between Wingfield as chair and Griffin over Ulster and American policy further eroded unity.

In May 1986, the Political Soldiers called for Anderson's suspension, which cemented the divide between the Political Soldiers and the Flag group.[178] Pearce, a good friend of Griffin, had not been as intensely active in the party during 1985, and by 1986 he was serving another sentence for violating the Race Relations Act with material published in *Bulldog*.[179] However, he remained in contact with the party and even thanked supporters in *Nationalism Today* for their cards and letters.[180] While in prison he maintained his Directorate vote, and thanks to him and the Flag faction, the party discipline charges against Anderson were dismissed by a majority vote.[181] In another meeting later that month, the Political Soldiers won a vote that dismissed Wingfield's executive leadership and made Griffin the chair and Graham Williamson his deputy, and kept Andrews, Holland, Harrington and Pearce on the Directorate.[182] Brons explained that the crux of the dispute was about disciplining Anderson for alleged theft, and when that vote failed the Political Soldiers, in a "sinister" move, sought to expel those who did not support the charge against Anderson.[183] Both sides visited Pearce in jail to win his support, including Andrews as a representative of the Political Soldier faction.[184] Elected to the Directorate with hopes that he would rejoin his ideological mates and friends, Pearce eventually supported Wingfield's and Anderson's faction, which officially called itself the National Front Support Group.[185]

The Political Soldiers led the NF with its publications and resources, while the National Front Support Group operated *The Flag*, allegedly with a print run of 4000, and launched *Vanguard* magazine.[186] Started in June 1986, the Support Group was created "as a loyal opposition to the unrepresentative clique" on the NF Directorate with the goal of "saving" the party.[187] Indeed, *Vanguard*'s content was similar to *Nationalism Today* with articles on race, G.K. Chesterton and fascist activity.[188] Yet it also contained calls for "scrapping" the NF constitution to "efficiently" run the party by giving local branches powers.[189] Griffin then published *Attempted Murder* in August 1986, accusing "the state" of undermining the NF due to its "adoption of revolutionary ideology."[190] The Flag group drafted a newsletter in response to Griffin titled "Attempted Murder/Actual Insanity," directly rebutting several points and describing *Attempted Murder* as "long on allegations, but short on facts" with "paranoia, malice, gossip and insufferable self-righteousness."[191] Though he ran in a by-election, Pearce increasingly distanced himself from the NF until he dropped out of politics completely. He later denounced racism, converted to Catholicism and became a Catholic writer in the United States.[192]

As the NF and Flag group traded charges, both personal and political, they alienated members. Yet another split in the NF further demoralized the rank and file, who had to choose sides and lost confidence in the administration of the party. The Croydon branch of the NF, for example, led by Chris Merchant, declared its support for Griffin and wrote "that Ian Anderson, Martin Wingfield, Tom Acton, Andrew Brons, Steve Brady and the Nash brothers do not have the best interests of the NF at heart."[193] Meanwhile, the Crowborough and North Weald branch of the NF described the Support Group as a "gang of crooks, reactionaries and state agents" who were "no more than racist Tories" and should be "shunned."[194]

Not everyone who disagreed with the NF's new leadership and the direction of the party joined the National Front Support Group. Eddy Butler, an NF organizer in Tower Hamlets, explained, "British nationalist ideology is Nazism to be honest about it and it always has been," and the Political Soldier group "were trying to find an alternative source, but instead of finding something homegrown they looked for an alternative that was not as popular as Nazism, but equally as weird foreign models."[195] He also described the Support Group as containing many people whose personalities clashed but who were together solely due to their opposition to the Political Soldiers.[196] Considering neither option good, he joined the BNP as it had a stable leadership and its "Nazified" ideology was far more appealing than the NF in its then current form.[197] Butler's 1986 defection to Tyndall's party was mentioned in *Spearhead* where Butler described how "[a] party that once claimed to represent social justice has been transformed into a cross between the puritanical witch-hunts and the Spanish Inquisition."[198] Indeed, many other activists moved from the NF to the BNP, including entire organizations such as the Wirral branch of the Support Group, which was trumpeted by the BNP as proof of its growth.[199]

Blood & Honour

Personality clashes and political splits were not limited to the NF's leadership, and by 1987 the dispute between Ian Stuart and the WNC had become public and increasingly bitter. For several years, Stuart worked closely with the central branch of the NF, including Harrington, Holland and Pearce. Indeed, Stuart was not on the periphery of the movement, but his articles and letters were published in the NF's main magazines.[200] Skrewdriver's last appearance at the 1987 White Noise festival, where he praised American fascists, demonstrated his international outlook and that he sought a white global audience for his music. The WNC heavily promoted Skrewdriver, but it also benefited from the band's fame in a symbiotic relationship. The WNC was, nevertheless, a small operation compared to the corporate backing of the major music labels, and what money the NF received, even less was paid to Skrewdriver.

In summer 1987, Stuart publicly announced he was splitting from the WNC and the NF. According to Harrington, Stuart came to believe he no longer needed the NF as a "middleman" between Skrewdriver and Rock-O-Rama and "there was an economic motive that was justified politically."[201] Though they were previously friends and members of the same NF branch in London, their attacks on each other became personal, including accusations concerning money.[202] Stuart left the NF and formed Blood & Honour with assistance from his friends with NF connections and copied mailing lists to circulate the new organization's eponymous magazine, *Blood & Honour*.[203] The first issue accused the WNC of being "dishonest" with its customers, specifically saying it opened an account in the name of Skrewdriver Services at Harrington's local Chelsea Building Society.[204] Moreover, the magazine *Blood & Honour* declared it would reflect "the views of all nationalist music fans" and would not promote "one party's political message."[205] The NF responded that Stuart's claims were "false and malicious" and that the party had given him "free" advertisements for his personal profit, and that he had received money from the NF administration in addition to music royalties.[206] The party argued that Stuart's "real complaint" was Holland and Harrington telling him "exactly what they thought of his reactionary Nazi views, and instant cry of 'I want more'."[207] The NF then officially "proscribed" its members from involvement in Blood & Honour and shifted its support from Skrewdriver to Skullhead.[208]

While *Blood & Honour* magazine was similar to *White Noise* in terms of focus and format, it was more radical and overtly promoted neo-Nazism in ways that other British fascist publications avoided. Named after Skrewdriver's 1985 album *Blood and Honour*, it was a direct reference to the Hitler Youth slogan and drew inspiration from Nazism. In addition to photos of Rudolf Hess, the magazine unabashedly published photos of audiences giving the Nazi salute.[209] In fact, the front page of the eleventh issue was simply a black swastika on a red cover.[210] Yet it mirrored the layout of *White Noise* and *Bulldog* with "RAC Charts" of fans' top ten songs, concert reports and band interviews. *Blood & Honour* magazine's first issue simply eight pages, including the cover and a full page of advertisements, with the actual substance being two interviews with Ian Stuart about Skrewdriver and Paul Burnley of No Remorse.[211] In the interview Burnley said "the greatest man in history" was Adolf Hitler, as well as Bob Mathews, a violent militant who died in a shoot-out with American law enforcement.[212] Stuart's interview, meanwhile, featured comments about "a big" Skrewdriver concert in September with Brutal Attack, No Remorse and Sudden Impact to officially "launch" Blood & Honour.[213]

The Blood & Honour organization replaced the WNC, not just with news and merchandise, but in organizing concerts. The first of what became infrequent concerts under the Blood & Honour name was held in September 1987 at the Croydon Star in London, with hundreds of mostly male attendees chanting "Sieg Heil" and dancing to songs with Nazi, racist and anti-immigrant themes.[214] The organization blamed the NF for getting other events canceled, but Blood & Honour persevered and began hosting large concerts throughout the late 1980s in Britain.[215] For example, a large 1988 concert in London featured Skrewdriver playing in front of hundreds of people with displays of Union Jacks and Nazi flags.[216]

The organization's message was passed by word of mouth as well as a network of fanzines that promoted each other's publications. *Blood & Honour* magazine had a column titled "zine scene" that listed the addresses and prices of more than a dozen like-minded publications from Australia, Belgium, Britain, Italy, Norway, Portugal and the United States.[217] The international attention continued to build with Blood & Honour's affiliated bands signing contracts with Rock-O-Rama, which expanded the magazine's audience.[218] American *Blood & Honour* subscribers, for example, learned about American magazines through an advertisement in the British publication, creating an interwoven tapestry of content and promotion. The editors of the publications were in contact with one another, and provided content and news that gave the magazines an international dimension.

Skrewdriver's music was developing the same contours as Blood & Honour, with both international themes and overt Nazi messages. Indeed, the fury and anger in the music fit with the rage and anxiety of the street violence. It aptly reflected the desire to overcome the feeling of weakness in the face of social changes and political opposition by repeating international slogans of strength and support. In 1988, Skrewdriver released *After the Fire*, which included the song "European Dream" that reflected angst and international themes:

> Hey brother across the sea
>
> What future for you and me
>
> I want to know where we stand
>
> We fight the reds in all our lands[219]

Skrewdriver played several concerts in Britain in support of the album, but also embarked on an international "break the chains" tour in 1989 that included Belgium, West Germany and Sweden, with one concert in West Germany attracting 1000 fans.[220] Ian Stuart commented on the last decade of "racial nationalism" by noting the gains in France and Germany and social events that mixed NF, BNP, Ku Klux Klan and League of Saint George members that "bodes well for the future."[221] In the early 1990s, Skrewdriver performed many more concerts in continental Europe, including several in Germany, and led hundreds of youth in giving the Nazi salute during a 1991 show in Italy.[222]

Unlike the national confines of a political party, Stuart saw his music as both "patriotic" and international. According to Pearce, "the skinhead movement was becoming a global phenomenon" and given his prominence with Skrewdriver, Stuart became an "icon globally."[223] When launching the *Blood & Honour* magazine, he said that Skrewdriver received "support" from Germany, Holland, Sweden and the United States as well as "Denmark, Norway, Belgium, France, Italy, Finland, Canada, Hungary, Poland, South Africa, Austria, Bavaria and Australia."[224] The fifth issue declared *Blood & Honour* an "international success" because its "circulation has risen enormously" all across the "white world."[225] It reported that the previous issue's sales by region from largest to smallest were: England, Holland, America, Ulster, West Germany, Sweden, Wales, Belgium, Scotland and France.[226] The cover of the seventh issue displayed foreign unity with the image of a young skinhead shaking hands with a Ku Klux Klan member in front of a Confederate flag and a photograph of Hitler.[227] The magazine's pages included reprints of newspaper articles about skinheads being "welcomed" to the Aryan Nations' headquarters in Idaho as well as Stuart's connections to the Ku Klux Klan.[228] Indeed, the connections were truly remarkable because the American groups previously had little to no contact with skinheads because they were not considered a political force. Later, the Aryan Nations began recruiting skinheads, but this led to problems as the "skinheads caused nearly all the trouble" at the compound and most Aryan Nations members "were turned off by skinhead culture," which caused the group to stop hosting skinhead concerts.[229] Though Skrewdriver did not perform in the United States, Paul Burnley of No Remorse played at Tom Metzger's third annual Aryan Festival in 1990 near Tulsa, Oklahoma and later at the 1992 event in California.[230] He performed alongside American skinhead groups and received an enthusiastic reception to songs such as "This Time The World," with the lyrics:

> There's a new hope for the youth today
>
> It's not black power or communism

What it is I will now say

It will be carried out with pure precision.[231]

Blood & Honour became the young neo-Nazi community's uniting force, which continued expanding with subscribers until there were branches in nearly every Western European country during the 1990s. Spread by mail and bands when they toured, it motivated youth to create their own branches of Blood & Honour that paid tribute to Stuart's vision and highlighted their own local music scenes. Meanwhile, the WNC tried to continue to operate, but with internal NF problems and changing ideology, the music aspect of the NF was pushed into the background in the face of international visits. In February 1989, the NF voted to "disband" the WNC, citing the problem of being "smeared" as Nazis due to people "who were more interested in Germany 50 years ago than they are about the peoples of Britain in the 1980s."[232] By the time the NF ceased selling records, it had distributed tens of thousands of records around the world, including more than 10,000 copies of *White Power*.[233] In its place the NF started a new organization called Counter Culture with a journal about fashion, art, films and poetry.[234] The NF also started Counter Culture Records, which released music by Violent Storm and Skullhead.[235] This was not the only action activists took that distanced the NF from Skrewdriver. Other NF members, such as Troy Southgate and Gareth Hurley, edited *Welsh Leak*, which proclaimed it was not "a fanzine for the likes of Skrewdriver, No Remorse and other Nazi groups," but instead was completely "free from Nazi-type filth."[236]

With Stuart's decade of fame and the music being released by Rock-O-Rama from West Germany, Blood & Honour was the undisputed leader and promoter of fascist music by 1989. Readers from all over the world sent their money to London for Skrewdriver music and *Blood & Honour* magazines to learn more about the latest neo-Nazi music trends. In these magazines, young fascists also read criticism of the NF. Denouncing the official NF with Holland and Harrington as "the Nutty Fairy Party," *Blood & Honour* told readers interested in British politics to contact the BNP, the National Front Support Group and the Ulster Defence Association.[237] In a more pointed ideological criticism, *Blood & Honour* mocked "the *National Front News* which is now full of articles praising blacks and is more like a communist paper than a nationalist one."[238]

The White and Black International

British fascism's transition away from focusing on domestic campaigns towards appealing to an international audience was not confined to the realm of music, and international topics and links became increasingly important to the NF as domestic membership declined. Harrington explained that NF activists were looking for alternatives to capitalism and communism, leading them to search for ideas and political philosophies in other parts of the world.[239] He said the ultimate goal was to spread the NF leadership's new revolutionary concepts among the rank-and-file membership.[240] Unlike Tyndall's old imperial views that limited NF foreign links mostly to the Commonwealth, the NF looked to black separatists in the United States as well as the Iraqi, Iranian and Libyan governments. Indeed, the ideas they borrowed from foreign governments and groups were unlike the NF's earlier ideas but still broadly included separatism, revolution and anti-Semitism. Nigel Copsey described how this would appear as "rank heresy" to "those brought up on a daily diet of anti-black racism."[241] Importantly, this change did not occur in a vacuum, but was built by the youth involved in the NF based on their connections with the Italians and the WNC.

By the mid-1980s, international affairs had become a prominent feature in NF publications. Though NF publications had previously reported on international events, it was mostly done through the lens of its domestic policies and racism. The NF led by youth increasingly came to see itself as having a role to play in global politics. Early issues of *Nationalism Today* carried a "world affairs" section that discussed "white Australia" and "white workers" in South Africa.[242] Yet within a few years there was an increasing emphasis on geopolitics, with an interest in taking sides and demonstrating sympathy based on its own prejudices. Some articles, such as those on politics in Germany, discussed familiar international topics such as anti-Americanism and German unification.[243] Yet other subjects strayed from the previous decade's themes and compared the NF to foreign movements. For instance, Holland wrote about Palestine, describing "intentional" media distortions about Israel's aggressions and concluded the article, "Britain for the British" and "Palestine for the Palestinians."[244]

Israel was a rallying point and provided common ground for the NF and Arab groups. As Pearce described, dislike of Israel and Jews fostered friendship between the NF and pro-Palestinian groups.[245] This was reflected in the pages of *Nationalism Today* when it addressed "why the NF supports the Palestinians," telling readers: "anti-Zionists of the world unite and fight."[246] Other articles were sympathetic to authoritarian rulers. Muammar Gaddafi, for example, was defended from criticism over Libyan involvement in Chad by blaming problems in the country on "multi-racialism."[247] In more direct praise, Holland hailed the 1979 Iranian revolution and Ruhollah Khomeini by saying "we have mutual enemies" and "anti-imperialists and anti-Zionists must stand together."[248]

The NF maintained its ethno-nationalism but broadened its outlook on international fascist cooperation. In 1984, the NF announced that the "White International" column in *Nationalism Today* would "take a look at the struggle of white people in all four corners of the world."[249] According to Pearce, it drew on the "Black International" from the 1930s and "the whole idea was to build a network of connections with like-minded groups and organizations around the world to operate internationally."[250] Pearce wrote in the column about race relations laws in Australia, New Zealand and the United States with information about "our racial comrades" and legislative battles.[251] A subsequent article by Holland discussed the National Democratic Party of Germany (NPD), which had "remarkable parallels" to the NF "on the environment, immigration, the economic system and the cultural emasculation of Europe."[252] He explained that "[i]ncreased understanding and co-operation between our movements are useful not only from the point of view of morale," but "we can learn from one another" which "is crucial to the future of Europe."[253] Likewise, Holland wrote that "further, extensive contacts with our Australian compatriots will serve in time to iron out some of our differing ideological perspectives."[254] He also wrote about Jean-Marie Le Pen and the Front National (FN), critically calling it "a reactionary, right wing Tory organisation," and went on to praise the French National Revolutionary Movement.[255] By 1985, Holland had concluded that the White International showed the NF's "maturity" and that its "anti-Europe mentality of the 1970s has evaporated."[256] Though "still militantly pro-British," he found that "our brothers in the Western World" were "integral" in the struggle.[257] This was not limited to non-violent political parties, as Holland also praised the National Action Movement in Portugal, despite its links to violent crime, and wrote that "all NF members" should "follow" the direction of the party.[258]

NF activists acted on their associations and embarked on foreign visits. The main person in contact with foreign groups was Holland, who was the overseas liaison for the NF.[259] In addition to meeting with like-minded people in continental Europe to distribute music, NF leaders also traveled to the United States. Around 1985, Griffin made his first visit to the United States, staying with Robert "Bob" Hoy for several weeks in Virginia.[260] Griffin first met Hoy, a professional photographer, when Hoy visited the United Kingdom and took photographs that later appeared in NF publications such as *New Nation*.[261] Griffin delivered several talks during his visit and met with American extremist figures such as Gary Gallo in Maryland.[262] In fact, Griffin spent the last two weeks of the trip writing *Power*, an unpublished book about the movement's goals, in Gallo's spare bedroom.[263] During his visit, Griffin also interviewed White Aryan Resistance leader Tom Metzger about his ideology and activities, including developing a computer-based bulletin board to attract youth.[264] Upon returning to Britain, Griffin wrote about similarities between American and British radicals, as "a number of American patriots have turned to violence," which was similar to how the media switched from portraying the NF as "evil middle-aged Hitler-worshippers" to "terrorists."[265]

While NF members traveled to the United States, Americans visited Britain and studied the NF in order to develop similar parties. Following his meeting with Griffin, Gary Gallo, a lawyer and later medical doctor, visited England and stayed with several NF figures in order to learn about the organization and create a similar group in the United States.[266] When he first returned to the United States around 1985, Gallo started the National Democratic Front (NDF) in Gaithersburg, Maryland as a white separatist party with ties to the Ku Klux Klan.[267] Though the party was later disbanded, Gallo introduced American supporters to Third Positionist writings and Holland's *The Political Soldier: A Statement*.[268] At the 1985 Annual General Meeting, the NF read aloud messages of support from like-minded groups, including Gallo's NDF in the United States, the NPD in Germany and supporters from Northern Ireland, Italy, Romania and Sweden.[269] In fact, Matt Malone, a representative from Gallo's NDF, spoke at an NF meeting in July 1987 alongside Griffin and Harrington about working with like-minded black racial separatists.[270] At the gathering Griffin stepped down as chair and was replaced by Holland, while the meeting focused on the NF's new racial policies, including moving beyond Webster's and Tyndall's "imperial" views on race and comparing race issues in the United Kingdom with those in the United States.[271]

The discussion about militancy and revolution in the NF was not simply rhetoric. While the Political Soldier had a spiritual mission message, in 1986 the NF instituted a "cadre" formation and organized training camps that included exercise and seminars about how to campaign in elections. According to Griffin, the new structure was established because its previous form was "antiquated" and the NF needed "intensive training" to "integrate new recruits" under a centralized authority and ideology.[272] Cadre members had to apply and be approved after a trial period, which included educational training. The NF's *Cadre!* booklet, for example, included excepts from Holland's *Political Soldier: A Statement*, Griffin's *Attempted Murder* and Gaddafi's *The Green Book.*[273] The NF described the "Cadre Summer Camp" of 1987 as including "political activity as well as lectures, discussions and cultural outings" and required "all" cadres and candidates to attend.[274] The event was an outdoor social affair that expected attendees to bring sleeping bags, cookers and even pens.[275] Mark Cotterill, the NF's Southwest England regional organizer, recalled attending a camp with between fifty and sixty people, including Ian Stuart, and bunked with Fiore at the Griffin farm in Suffolk.[276] Cotterill described the event as useful, with attendees discussing party principles and learning how to run a campaign and design literature, but also with Political Soldier writings spread among the group.[277] The reason for the revolutionary ideas, according to the NF, was that "[o]nly an elite can build and control a mass movement" and the "new structure fulfills the main requirements of an organization which seriously aims to contend for political power."[278]

The activities were interpreted by some as having a nefarious purpose. Cotterill explained that the NF was getting bigger and "its worldwide contacts were probably scaring the state."[279] In 1987 the NF started the Friend of the Movement section in response "to the growing number of enquiries from overseas."[280] Critics and the media picked up on the Political Soldier name, the cadre structure and the NF's international connections, painting the group as would-be terrorists. *From Ballots to Bombs*, published by the anti-fascist magazine *Searchlight*, traced the development of the NF in the 1980s and connected the party to foreign extremists, including terrorists, and to political violence.[281] The anti-fascists were not the only ones to make the link. During the early 1980s,

NF members were accused and convicted of a range of racial attacks and arson.[282]

Within a few years, the White International developed into a far more encompassing movement. The British government broke off relations with Libya following the April 1984 diplomatic crisis that arose when police officer Yvonne Fletcher was killed during a protest against the Libyan government at its London embassy and the suspects, Libyan officials, fled the country without punishment.[283] By then, the NF had already made contact with the Libyan embassy and was defending Gaddafi while criticizing the Reagan administration for trying "to plant the seeds of doubt in the Colonel's mind" and undermine his "revolutionary command."[284] Gaddafi was not the only Arab icon praised by the NF. In addition to books by A.K. Chesterton and G.K. Chesterton, the NF started selling *Islam and Revolution* by Imam Khomeini.[285] The party also sold posters of Louis Farrakhan with the words "he speaks for his people, we speak for ours."[286] *Nationalism Today* published articles about Farrakhan and the Nation of Islam's history and ideas, including an article by Abdul Wali Muhammad, described as Farrakhan's "right hand man."[287] The *National Front News* itself underwent a change, with the Celtic cross replacing the Union Jack as well as a green background and a red banner that proclaimed "a Third Way beyond capitalism and communism."[288]

The NF also incorporated ideas about the environment into its policy. Linking landscape preservation to social composition, the NF told its members about a potential "environmental disaster" from acid rain hurting agriculture and industry.[289] Critical of the Conservative government for giving international aid to India for planting trees, the NF wanted domestic environmental investment.[290] The NF connected "international capitalism" to the countryside being "raped" and "pillaged," with woodlands, wetlands and ponds being destroyed as poisons killed plants and animals.[291] Other articles focused on radioactive waste and nuclear power as "threats" to British children.[292] Regional branches praised the "green wave" as "a brand new, independent concept supported by the National Front" focused on "the preservation and enhancement of our organic communities."[293]

In March 1988, the NF announced that it was forming the "New Alliance" to include "[r]evolutionary nationalist groups, racial separatists and the anti-Zionist nations of the Middle East."[294] With photos of Gaddafi, Farrakhan and Khomeini next to the NF logo, the NF explained "we must all work to spread the positive side of the Third Way in our own countries."[295] Highlighting Gaddafi's ties to the Provisional Irish Republican Army (IRA), "it needs to be made clear that the NF does not support Colonel Qadhafi as an individual, rather we support the broad principles of the International Third Position which he has ably explained in the *Green Book*."[296] These ideas resonated among some NF branches that described *The Green Book* as "controversial, but stimulating."[297] Kev Turner, vocalist for Skullhead, wrote to the NF about it being "a good sign that our repatriation stance is now being recognized by Black Separatists."[298] Troy Southgate, commenting on the "New Alliance," described the NF's links "with peoples of different races" and spreading the Third Way ideology as part of the "green revolution" concept.[299] Other activists were worried that the links with and images of Muslims and Arab leaders would make it harder to recruit "everyday" people.[300]

In late 1988, the NF leaders were invited to Tripoli by the Libyan government as official guests. The NF and Libyan government were in communication through Robert Pash, an Australian who published a newsletter supportive of Gaddafi.[301] In September 1988 Harrington, Holland and Griffin travelled to Tripoli via Malta on an aging Libyan commercial airplane with the goal of obtaining Libyan money after reports circulated that the IRA had received support from Gaddafi.[302] The three were all leaders of the NF due to a structural change where the leadership was equally rotated between Griffin, Holland and Harrington.[303] Harrington explained that while they did not meet Gaddafi, they met "high-ranking people," including officials in the foreign ministry and security ministry.[304] Harrington said, "what I wanted was a radio station broadcasting from Tripoli to Europe and what the other people who went there wanted was money."[305] According to Griffin, they were free to travel around the city and later presented the Libyan government with a £50,000 shopping list for what the NF needed.[306]

The NF celebrated the visit with a photograph of Griffin and Holland standing in front of a large Gaddafi billboard on the cover of *National Front News*.[307] The NF published photos of Griffin and Holland touring Tripoli to learn about the city's history and economic development under Gaddafi, such as meeting with "the manager of one of five big retail supermarkets" to discuss "co-operative theory and practice."[308] Indeed, the trip was described to NF members as "not a mere junket," but a detailed study of the Third Position being applied by Gaddafi.[309]

The three men learned about education and home ownership in Libya and visited a supermarket in Tripoli that included "family run stalls."[310] Despite the celebratory NF news, the visit did not win the party support and they were told Gaddafi was unavailable and not in Libya.[311] As Griffin explained, the NF received no financial support, but instead were given two crates of Gaddafi's *The Green Book*, most of which were lost or taken by British customs, leaving only the books in their suitcases as the remaining gift from the Libyan government.[312] The book, however, became a standard text for the party. NF members, such as Troy Southgate, argued that the theme of Gaddafi's book was "representative democracy" that serves broader social interests, whereas the system of electing politicians was "open to abuse."[313] The NF distributed *The Green Book* freely among its members and put copies in libraries, but had a hard time generating wider public interest in it.[314]

The NF's development was not merely cosmetic, but paved the way for more evolution. In summer 1988, the NF's summer cadre conference focused on developing the party's Campaign for Palestinian Rights and the duties of a cadre.[315] At the NF's cadre meeting in early 1989, it announced goals for overseas expansion, becoming debt-free, and starting a new magazine and record company with the overall objective to "improve the image of the movement among the public."[316] This included reaching out to black separatists in Britain so that both groups would jointly advocate "racial separatism" in a 1989 Vauxhall parliamentary by-election.[317] The NF's "altered image" was a move away from negative themes, and the party hoped to become associated with "popular participation" as well as cooperation with Asian and black separatists.[318] In October 1989, Harrington issued a press release to the *Jewish Chronicle* admitting to "serious ideological errors" in relation to the "Jewish community" and said the NF would "publicly apologise for and take active steps to correct any manifestation of anti-Semitism."[319] Moreover, he announced the party would expel people who voiced anti-Semitism. Harrington met with a group of Orthodox Jews, including Rabbi Mayer Schiller, in New York City to discuss common issues.[320] This was a radical departure for an organization and its newspaper, the *National Front News*, which earlier that year had criticized Jews and "[t]he main organ of Zionism in this country, the *Jewish Chronicle*."[321] According to Harrington, "whilst they had been prepared to open up dialog with the black community," the statement about Jews caused "hell to break loose."[322]

The statement about making peace with and apologizing to the Jews was the final straw in the party's downward spiral. The NF's membership, only dozens of people, was a mere shadow of what it had been a decade earlier.[323] Griffin, Holland and Todd were upset by the apology, and resigned to establish the International Third Position (ITP) with the goal of continuing the Third Position policies through an international network.[324] Griffin also believed that the NF was such a small organization at that point, they no longer had any interest in fighting to keep it.[325] Similarly, Todd said there were only about a hundred cadres left, but those people were the hardcore members.[326] Aside from the ideological disagreements, Holland complained about the NF's structure and strategy, and Griffin criticized the "bureaucratic clique."[327] The NF briefly continued to operate until December 1989, when Harrington and the remaining members of the NF Directorate voted to disperse the NF, and it was officially disbanded in January 1990.[328] The *National Front News* announced the decision by explaining that "yes," the "disbanding" of the NF was "admitting failure."[329] In particular, the NF decided its negative image, including associations with "violence," "Nazism" and "anti-Semitism," were damaging and that a new group needed to be formed without the political baggage.[330] The party's publications, the *National Front News* and *Nationalism Today*, were "shut down," with subscribers to receive publications that supported the Third Way to carry on an alternative to communism and capitalism.[331]

The late 1980s witnessed major ideological and tactical change among the fascists. Throughout 1987, not only did British fascism suffer from splits, but the NF, the Support Group and the BNP did not contest any seats, aside from a handful of self-run candidates, in the June general election. Tyndall explained that the BNP did this to "conserve" what little party funding they had to develop the organization, including acquiring a headquarters building.[332] Scholar Nigel Copsey detailed how the BNP lacked party activists and funding to adequately campaign during the election, which caused supporter morale to drop.[333] Meanwhile, the NF wanted to inspire change through social and cultural outreach rather than the ballot box. Harrington wrote that "[e]ven if the NF were rich enough, it would still be difficult to find a public relations firm willing" to positively promote the NF in the election.[334] Indeed, the NF Directorate agreed not to participate in the election because it would not be a cost effective way to attract members, television campaign coverage would not matter and money should be invested for long-term growth.[335] In a local Leeds bulletin, it explained that elections first required the group to "build and strengthen our OWN [*sic*] mass media and communications network. Therefore it makes a lot more sense that we put our hard earned funds into worthwhile assets that will set us on the road to securing our own voice, and we should use that time to sink local roots and establish ourselves in local politics."[336] The June 1987 *National Front News* cover told readers: "Elections are a Con" and "Don't Vote" in large print with the article claiming the "real power" was not with "politicians" but with the media, so there was "no real choice" on the ballot.[337] This alienated NF members who had joined a political party and expected to contest elections. As its membership dwindled, the further ideological developments and unusual associations were mocked by former colleagues.

The BNP and Blood & Honour openly condemned the NF's changes. Indeed, the ideas of Gaddafi and the Nation of Islam spread by the NF leadership did not resonate with the broader skinhead scene or with other fascist political parties. In a battle between *Spearhead* and the *National Front News*, the former described how the NF "progressed from the inane to the puerile" by claiming "that Front policy now is that Britain should possess no independent nuclear defences."[338] In the following month, the new design of the *National Front News*, which omitted the Union Jack, was denounced as "the reddening of the NF" while the NF's call for abolishing British nuclear capability was labeled a leftist policy.[339] The harshest criticism concerned the NF wanting to move away from "negative" racial policies, which led the anonymous author to conclude: "the task of defeating this treason against the nationalist movement and cause in Britain will be longer and harder."[340] The BNP also referred to Harrington's outreach to the Jewish population as "joining the opposition."[341] *Blood & Honour* was likewise critical, printing a "White Noise" anthem with the words: "black is beautiful, Nazis are shits, commies are cool, stuff the Brits."[342]

The NF led by Griffin, Harrington and Holland officially no longer existed in the 1990s. The "Flag" NF led by Ian Anderson continued with the name once its rivals, the Political Soldiers, disbanded the NF. However, Anderson and Wingfield also came to believe the name was toxic, and in a 1995 EGM the majority decided to change the name to the National Democrats, which in turn caused another group to spin off and use the NF name.[343] The National Front Support Group maintained international stances similar to those of the Political Soldiers. In October 1989 Ian Anderson and Richard Barrett, leader of the Mississippi-based Nationalist Movement, signed the New Atlantic Charter in Birmingham, England as official representatives of their respective groups.[344] The goal was for "the spiritual and cultural unity and advancement of Anglo-American heritage, language and destiny."[345] Yet Barrett's American influence was far more marginal by fascist standards, and Anderson's group was being eclipsed in membership by Tyndall's BNP. Cotterill helped organize an NF meeting in Exeter for Barrett, but recalled the Nationalist Movement being small and the event not amounting to much.[346] Thus despite its goals, the New Atlantic Charter had no transatlantic impact and did not foster any further development or organizational growth for either group.

Conclusion

The NF embarked on a new radical direction during the 1980s. Developing contacts with foreign figures first from Italy and later relationships with the Nation of Islam and the Libyan government, these contacts had direct ideological impact. The connections through music were financially rewarding and helped to develop a complex network of extremist youth that included racist conservatives and neo-Nazi figures. These music and international connections sometimes worked in parallel and other times in tandem, which increased youth interest in the NF. Yet the ideological changes and personality conflicts were not readily welcomed by all Directorate and party members. First in 1983, then in 1986 and finally in 1989, internal splits hurt party morale and led to an exodus of members from the NF, which the BNP seized on by welcoming new members into its fold. Indeed, the NF's music initiatives enhanced its appeal among the youth and generated revenue, but the more unusual ideological shifts alienated the traditionally minded fascists. As the next chapter shows, those who wanted conventional fascist politics and did not appreciate skinhead music having such a large role in British fascism increasingly turned to Tyndall and the BNP.

Notes

1. "Introducing the White Noise Club," *White Noise* no. 3 (1987): 8.

2. Nigel Copsey, *Contemporary British Fascism: The British National Party and the Quest for Legitimacy* (Basingstoke: Palgrave Macmillan, 2008), 33, 37, 45.
3. Alan Sykes, *The Radical Right in Britain: Social Imperialism to the BNP* (Basingstoke: Palgrave Macmillan, 2005), 122, 123, 125.
4. Derek Holland interviewed by Judith Sharpe, "The Middle East Tragedy from a Catholic, Political, and Historical Perspective: Understanding the Reasoning Behind Mass Murder (Part I—Introducing Derek Holland)," *In the Spirit of Chartres Committee*, 1 April 2008 (CD Recording).
5. Anna Cento Bull, *Italian Neofascism: The Strategy of Tension and the Politics of Nonreconciliation* (Oxford: Berghahn, 2007), 4, 7.
6. According to the National Front, the bombing was "blamed" on Terza Posizione and resulted in more than 100 arrests. "The Truth About Those Italian 'Terrorists'," *National Front News* no. 68 (July 1985): 5.
7. Roberto Fiore interviewed by Judith Sharpe, "Roberto Fiore: Catholic Statesman or Terrorist: You Decide!," *In the Spirit of Chartres Committee*, 1 September 2008 (CD Recording). In a tribute to Morsello, Fiore wrote: "In August 1980, he begins his life in hiding, provoked by a warrant for arrest which will end in the dustbin of history. Morsello flees abroad, arriving in London, where he begins a life of economic hardship." Roberto Fiore, "The Death of Massimo Morsello: A Tribute," *Final Conflict* no. 26 (2001): 6.
8. "Forza Nuova's Statement," *Final Conflict* no. 26 (2001): 6. The statement included describing Morsello as "leaving behind his indelible mark as a fascist, a Catholic and a militant of Forza Nuova."
9. Nick Griffin, interviewed by Ryan Shaffer, audio recording, 8 October 2014.
10. "Robert Fiore: Thoughts & Actions," *Nationalism Today* no. 46 (July 1989): 15.
11. Derek Holland, "Letters," *Spearhead* no. 132 (October 1979): 16.
12. Richard Verrall, "Editor's Comment," *Spearhead* no. 132 (October 1979): 16.
13. Interview with Griffin.
14. Phil Andrews, interviewed by Ryan Shaffer, audio recording, 1 June 2010.
15. Fiore interviewed by Sharpe.
16. Andrew Brons, "The Restoration of Property: A Review of Hilaire Belloc," *New Nation* no. 3 (Autumn 1983): 3.
17. *Rising: A Booklet for the Political Solider* (Hampshire: Legionary Press, 1998), 2.
18. Ibid.
19. Copsey, *Contemporary British Fascism*, 34.

20. *Rising: A Booklet for the Political Solider* (Hampshire: Legionary Press, 1998), 2.
21. Ibid.
22. Holland interviewed by Sharpe.
23. Eddy Butler, interviewed by Ryan Shaffer, audio recording, 16 September 2011; Ben Klassen, *Nature's Eternal Religion* (Lighthouse Point, FL: Church of the Creator, 1973), 7. The copy of this book includes a sticker that reads it was from "British Suppliers, B.P. Publications" with an address in North Wales. Personal possession. Tyndall's *Spearhead* even published an article by Klassen. Ben Klassen, "The Glory Catastrophe that was Rome," *Spearhead* no. 208 (February 1986): 8–10.
24. Derek Holland, *The Political Soldier: A Statement* (Croydon: Nationalist Education Group, 1984), 15.
25. Ibid., 14.
26. "Nationalist Books," *National Front News* no. 71 (October 1985): 6.
27. "Introduction," *Rising* no. 5 (1985): 2.
28. "Books," *New Dawn* no. 2 (1986): 8.
29. Derek Holland, *Political Soldier: Thoughts on Sacrifice and Struggle* (London: Burning Books, 1989), 25; later reprinted as Derek Holland, *Political Soldier: Thoughts on Sacrifice and Struggle* (London: A.K. Chesterton Trust, 2013), 42.
30. Derek Holland, *The Political Soldier: A Statement* 2nd ed. (London: International Third Position, 1994); Roger Griffin, *Fascism* (Oxford: Oxford University Press, 1995), 359–360.
31. Tom Acton, "Yesterday and Tomorrow," *Nationalism Today* no. 18 (n.d., circa 1982): 8.
32. *Yesterday & Tomorrow: The Tradition of National Revolution* (Liss Forest: Legionary Press, n.d.), 4.
33. "Hilaire Belloc," *Nationalism Today* no. 20 (n.d., circa 1983): 9.
34. Joe Pearce, *Fight for Freedom* (Croydon: Nationalist Books, 1984), 37, 39.
35. Joe Pearce, *Nationalist Doctrine: National Freedom, Racial Preservation and Social Justice* (London: Freedom Books, 1987), 3.
36. Joe Pearce, "Nationalism: Moving Forward into the 1980s," *Nationalism Today* no. 1 (March 1983): 8; Nick Wakeling, "Trade Unions: Our Task," *Nationalism Today* no. 1 (March 1983): 10.
37. "Otto Strasser on Communism," *Nationalism Today* no. 15 (n.d., circa 1984): 8.
38. Derek Holland, "A Revolution Betrayed," *Nationalism Today* no. 23 (July/August 1984): 12.

39. "400 Rock Against Communism," *National Front News* no. 47 (May 1983): 4.
40. "The Ovaltinees: The Godfathers of English Racial Rock Interviewed," *Final Conflict* no. 22 (Summer 1999): 7.
41. "NFTU Rally Boosts Blackburn Group," *National Front News* no. 47 (May 1983): 4.
42. Joe Pearce, "Select Organisers. …," *National Front Special Activities Bulletin*, 24 September 1981. Personal possession.
43. *Constitution for the National Front Trade Unionists* (n.p.: National Front Trade Unionists, n.d.). Personal possession.
44. Joe Pearce, "A Personal Statement," *Nationalism Today* no. 2 (1980): 19.
45. Patrick Harrington, interviewed by Ryan Shaffer, audio recording, 29 May 2010.
46. Phil Andrews, "YNF—The Future Calls," *Nationalism Today* no. 20 (n.d., circa 1983): 8.
47. "Skrewing the Establishment," *Bulldog* no. 34 (August 1983): 3.
48. Sean Birchall, *Beating the Fascists: The Untold Story of Anti-Fascist Action* (London: Freedom Press, 2010), 107, 151.
49. Interview with Harrington.
50. Ibid.
51. Crane became a common sight at Skrewdriver concerts, but was leading a secret life as a gay man. Before his 1993 AIDS-related death, he publicly announced he was a homosexual. In response, Ian Stuart said "it's a big shame that he turned out to be a homosexual because he could have been a good nationalist . . . I got no respect for that bloke." "Ian Stuart Interview," *Last Chance* no. 14 (1992): 15–16; Martin Wroe, "Reformed Fascist Ready to Admit Homosexuality," *The Independent*, 27 July 1992.
52. Interview with Harrington.
53. Ibid.
54. Ibid.
55. "See Skrewdriver Live," *Bulldog* no. 36 (n.d., circa 1983): 3.
56. "Smash the IRA," *Bulldog* no. 34 (August 1983): 3.
57. For example, see: "RAC Chart," *Bulldog* no. 34 (August 1983): 3.
58. Ian Stuart, "Don't Help Your Enemies," *Bulldog* no. 36 (1983): 3.
59. Ryan Shaffer, "British, European and White: Cultural Constructions of Identity in Post-War British Fascist Music," in *Cultures of Post-War British Fascism* eds. Nigel Copsey and John Richardson (Abingdon: Routledge, 2015), 142–160.
60. "Rock Against Communism," *National Front News* no. 60 (October 1984): 6.

61. "Rock On!," *Bulldog* no. 37 (1984): 4.
62. "White Music Fights Back!," *Bulldog* no. 37 (1984): 5.
63. "Skrewdriver Records," *Bulldog* no. 37 (1984): 5; "Stop the Press," *National Front News* no. 56 (May 1984): unpaginated 4.
64. Interview with Griffin.
65. "RAC Summer Festival," *National Front News* no. 61 (November 1984): unpaginated 5.
66. *Classic British RAC Volume 4: Skrewdriver, Suffolk 1984* (Denison: NS88, n.d.) (DVD Recording).
67. Interview with Griffin.
68. "Skrewdriver's White Xmas!," *Bulldog* no. 37 (1984): 4.
69. "They Can't Stop the Truth," *Bulldog* no. 38 (n.d. circa 1985): 1.
70. "Race Act Charges," *National Front News* no. 61 (November 1984): unpaginated 1.
71. "Brutal Attack," *Bulldog* no. 38 (n.d., circa 1985): 5.
72. "Defend Rights for Whites' Rally," *National Front News* no. 51 (November 1983): 4.
73. "A World-Wide Following," *Bulldog* no. 38 (n.d., circa 1985): 4.
74. Ibid.
75. Michael A. Hoffman II, "UK White Youths Proud of Heritage," *The Spotlight* (19 March 1984): 8.
76. "A World-Wide Following," *Bulldog* no. 38 (n.d., circa 1985): 4.
77. Interview with Pearce.
78. Ibid.
79. Joe Pearce, *The Early Years* (n.p.: Agitator Records, 2001), 50. This is an unauthorized reprint of Pearce's *The First Ten Years* (1987).
80. Interview with Pearce.
81. "Skrewdriver News," *Bulldog* no. 39 (n.d., circa 1985): 5.
82. "Coming Soon on White Noise Records," *Bulldog* no. 39 (n.d., circa 1985): 4; "Rock Against Communism," *National Front News* no. 60 (October 1984): unpaginated 6.
83. Andrew Brons, *The Chairman's Bulletin* no. 2 (27 April 1984): 1.
84. "White Working Class Man," *Bulldog* no. 40 (n.d., circa 1985): 5.
85. Ian Stuart, "Faith in the Struggle," *Nationalism Today* no. 37 (March 1986): 8.
86. "Rough Justice," *National Front News* no. 74 (n.d., circa 1986): 7. It was later published against his wishes in 2013. Ian Stuart Donaldson, *Invasion* (London: White Hart Publishing, 2013), 190, 191.
87. "Hail the New Dawn," *Bulldog* no. 40 (n.d., circa 1985): 4.
88. "Europe Awake," *Bulldog* no. 40 (n.d., circa 1985): 5.
89. "'Hail the New Dawn' by Skrewdriver," *Nationalism Today* no. 31 (July 1985): 23.

90. "Europe Awake," *Bulldog* no. 40 (n.d., circa 1985): 5.
91. "Hail the New Dawn," *New Dawn* no. 1 (n.d., circa 1985): 2.
92. "The Racist League," *Bulldog* no. 40 (n.d. circa 1985): 7.
93. "Front Launch New YNF Paper," *National Front News* no. 71 (October 1985): 7.
94. "White Noise," *New Dawn* no. 1 (n.d., circa 1985): 3.
95. "Skrewdriver News," *New Dawn* no. 1 (n.d., circa 1985): 5.
96. "Blood and Honour," *New Dawn* no. 2 (1986): 5.
97. "Skrewdriver Top RAC Bill," *National Front News* no. 71 (October 1985): 7.
98. "White Noise: 10 Bands ... 600 Made It," *New Dawn* no. 2 (1986): 3.
99. Ibid.
100. *Croydon National Front Bulletin* (n.d., circa December 1986), 2. Personal possession.
101. "Get Involved with White Noise," *White Noise* no. 1 (1986): unpaginated 8.
102. Interview with Harrington.
103. "Get Involved with White Noise," *White Noise* no. 1 (1986): unpaginated 8.
104. "The Ian Stuart Interview," *White Noise* no. 1 (1986): unpaginated 2.
105. "Ultimathule Interview," *White Noise* no. 1 (1986): unpaginated 7.
106. Interview with Harrington.
107. Ibid.
108. "Into 1987 with White Noise," *White Noise* no. 3 (1987): unpaginated 3.
109. "Introducing the White Noise Club," *White Noise* no. 3 (1987): unpaginated 8.
110. "No Surrender," *New Dawn* no. 2 (1986): 3.
111. "White Noise Shop," *White Noise* no. 4 (1987): unpaginated 6.
112. Interview with Andrews
113. Ibid.
114. "White Supremacists Indicted in Attack," *Chicago Tribune*, 20 February 1988; Matt O'Connor, "Skinhead Gets 11 Years in Beating," *Chicago Tribune*, 22 June 1989; Christian Picciolini, interviewed by Ryan Shaffer, audio recording, 19 January 2012. Picciolini later became leader of CASH after Martell went to prison and was vocalist for White American Youth when it was signed by Rock-O-Rama. Moreover, Picciolini was the singer for Final Solution when it became one of the earliest American skinhead bands to perform in Europe. The group, along with Bound for Glory, played one concert in Weimar, Germany with German bands Störkraft and Radikahl in 1992.
115. Interview with Andrews.

116. Ibid.
117. Ibid.
118. Interview with Griffin.
119. Ibid.
120. *Classic British RAC Volume 4: Skrewdriver, Suffolk 1984* (Denison: NS88, n.d.) (DVD Recording).
121. "From Acorn to Oak," *The Rune* no. 12 (1996): 15.
122. "St. George's Day," *White Noise* no. 4 (1987): unpaginated 4.
123. Interview with Andrews. Both Griffin and Pearce recalled having to grind rust off the beer cans to make them presentable. Interview with Pearce; Interview with Griffin.
124. Interview with Andrews.
125. "St. George's Day," *White Noise* no. 4 (1987): unpaginated 4.
126. *White Noise Live in Suffolk 1987* (n.p.: White Aryan Resistance, 1987) (DVD Recording). It is not clear if the concert was broadcast on Metzger's show.
127. Ibid. See the copyright notice on the video.
128. "The NT Interview," *Nationalism Today* no. 39 (n.d., circa 1987): 14–15; Patrick Harrington, "The Great Holocaust Trial," *Nationalism Today* no. 39 (n.d., circa 1987): 26.
129. Ryan Shaffer correspondence from Tom Metzger, 29 October 2009; "Through Thick and Thin: Interview with Tom Metzger," *Resistance* no. 23 (Fall 2004): 22.
130. Mark S. Hamm, *American Skinheads: The Criminology and Control of Hate Crime* (Westport: Praeger, 1993), 40, 70. Heick founded the American Front and published *Aryan Warrior* as its journal until 1989, but later launched a new journal titled *Revolutionary Nationalist.* Robert Heick, "Introduction," *Revolutionary Nationalist* no. 1 (n.d.): 2.
131. Robert Chow, "Judge Bans Rock Music at 'Aryan Woodstock'," *Los Angeles Times*, 4 March 1989. As it turned out, a Jewish man who had fled Nazi Germany signed the agreement with Heick, who hid the purpose of the gathering. Stephen Bloom, "He Fled the Nazis, Now This," *Sacramento Bee*, 4 March 1989.
132. Arno Michaels, interviewed by Ryan Shaffer, audio recording, 13 January 2012. Michaels, also known as Michaelis, was the vocalist for a Wisconsin band and attended the event. See also: Arno Michaels, *My Life After Hate* (Milwaukee: Life After Hate, 2010). The gathering was filmed and broadcast on Metzger's southern California cable access show, *Race and Reason.* "Aryan Woodstock," *Race and Reason* no. 724 V (n.p.: WAR, 1989) (DVD Recording). *Race and Reason* was first

broadcast in 1984. "Ex-KKK Leader Metzger Hosts TV Show," *White American Resistance* 2, no. 5 (1984): 1.

133. "The History of W.A.R. part 1," *White Aryan Resistance* no. 777 V (WAR, 1989) (DVD Recording). See also: "Aryan Festival' 88," *White Aryan Resistance* 7, no. 4 (1988).
134. "White Noise," *Frontline: The Voice of Leeds NF* no. 1 (Summer 1987): 4.
135. "Sweden, June 6th," *White Noise* no. 6 (1987): unpaginated 4.
136. "Club News," *White Noise* no. 6 (1987): unpaginated 6.
137. "The Beat Hits the USA," *White Noise* no. 7 (1987): unpaginated 12.
138. Interview with Andrews.
139. "Two Local Marches in West Midlands," *National Front News* no. 30 (March 1981): unpaginated 4.
140. Derek Holland, "Reader's Letters," *Nationalism Today* no. 18 (n.d., circa 1982): 16.
141. Paul Matthews, "Reader's Letters," *Nationalism Today* no. 19 (n.d., circa 1982): 16.
142. Copsey, *Contemporary British Fascism*, 33.
143. Martin Webster, interviewed by Ryan Shaffer, audio recording, 3 June 2010.
144. Ibid.
145. Ibid.
146. Interview with Andrews.
147. Interview with Webster.
148. Ibid.
149. "How We Are Organised," *Our Nation* unnumbered (n.d. circa 1984): unpaginated 4.
150. "What We Do," *Our Nation* unnumbered (n.d. circa 1984): unpaginated 4.
151. "Up Front' 84," *National Front News* no. 53 (February 1984): 6.
152. For example, see: "Up Front' 84," *National Front News* no. 53 (February 1984): 6.
153. Andrew Brons, interviewed by Ryan Shaffer, audio recording, 11 October 2014.
154. "NF Chairman Arrested on 'Catch-All' Charge," *National Front News* no. 55 (April 1984): 1.
155. "End of the Brons Age," *Nationalism Today* no. 27 (March 1985): 13; "Report from the Front," *British Nationalist* no. 44 (February 1985): 4.
156. Interview with Brons.

157. Pearce's memoir devoted a chapter to Griffin. Joe Pearce, *Race With the Devil: My Journey from Racial Hatred to Rational Love* (Charlotte: Saint Benedict Press, 2013), 69–78.
158. Bill Buford, *Among the Thugs* (New York: Vintage Books, 1991), 150.
159. Ibid., 150.
160. Ibid., 156.
161. Ibid., 156.
162. "The Heritage Group," *Nationalism Today* no. 31 (July 1985): 24.
163. Joe Pearce, "The Spiritual Struggle," *Nationalism Today* no. 32 (August 1985): 13.
164. "Heritage Group," *Nationalism Today* no. 29 (May 1985): 23.
165. Nick Griffin, "The Way Forward," *Nationalism Today* no. 31 (July 1985): 8.
166. Nick Griffin, "The EGM—An Important Step Forward," *Nationalism Today* no. 32 (August 1985): 21.
167. "Important New Membership Requirements," *Nationalism Today* no. 36 (February 1986): 23.
168. Ian Anderson, "The Way Forward," *Nationalism Today* no. 28 (April 1985): 9.
169. "NF Admin Changes," *Nationalism Today* no. 36 (February 1986): 23.
170. Nick Griffin, *Attempted Murder: The State/Reactionary Plot Against the National Front* (Norwich: Nationalism Today Press, 1986), 3.
171. "New NF Chairman," *Nationalism Today* no. 36 (February 1986): 19.
172. Ibid.
173. Interview with Griffin.
174. Copsey, *Contemporary British Fascism*, 37.
175. Griffin, *Attempted Murder*, 14.
176. Ibid., 17.
177. Ibid., 22.
178. Larry O'Hara, "The 1986 National Front Split, Part I," *Lobster* no. 29 (June 1995): 3–9.
179. "News From Joe," *Nationalism Today* no. 37 (March 1986): 23.
180. "News From Joe," *Nationalism Today* no. 38 (April 1986): 23.
181. Griffin, *Attempted Murder*, 41.
182. Ibid., 52.
183. Interview with Brons.
184. Interview with Andrews.
185. Griffin, *Attempted Murder*, 54, 57.
186. This number was according to Griffin. Ibid., 62.
187. "NFSG: What We Stand For," *Vanguard* no. 1 (August 1986): 16.
188. See *Vanguard* no. 1 (August 1986).

189. Joe Pearce, "Branching Out: A New Dawn for the National Front," *Vanguard* no. 2 (September 1986): 8.
190. Griffin, *Attempted Murder*, unpaginated 1.
191. "Attempted Murder/Actual Insanity," *National Front Support Group Newsletter* (East Sussex: National Front Support Group, n.d., circa 1986), unpaginated 1. Personal possession.
192. Interview with Pearce.
193. *Croydon National Front Bulletin* (August/September 1986), 1. This was signed by Chris Merchant, Stuart Strachan, Gavin Hall and Adrian Woods. Personal possession.
194. "Warning," *Crowborough and North Weald NF: Official Bulletin* no. 1 (n.d., circa 1988): unpaginated 2. This was edited by Troy Southgate.
195. Interview with Butler.
196. Ibid.
197. Ibid.
198. Eddy Butler, "The 'Radical' Myth," *Spearhead* no. 214 (December 1986): 13. He went on to contribute several more articles, including "Imperial Visionary," *Spearhead* no. 217 (March 1987): 10.
199. "Front Branch in Wirral Comes Over to BNP," *Spearhead* no. 224 (October 1987): 19.
200. For example: Ian Stuart, "Reader's Letters," *Nationalism Today* no. 25 (November 1984): 20.
201. Interview with Harrington.
202. Ibid.
203. Harrington explained that Ian Stuart had the NF hire his friend "Des," who copied the White Noise Club mailing list.
204. "Editorial," *Blood & Honour* no. 1 (1987): 2.
205. Ibid.
206. "Ripping Yarns," *National Front News* no. 100 (1988): 3.
207. Ibid.
208. Ibid.
209. "Editorial," *Blood & Honour* no. 1 (1987): 2, 4.
210. Cover of *Blood & Honour* no. 11 (n.d., circa 1989).
211. "Blood & Honour Interview: Paul of No Remorse," *Blood & Honour* no. 1 (1988): 8. Paul Burnley's real name is Paul Bellany. Paul and his brother, John, are the sons of famed Scottish painter John Bellany. Steve Silver, "Blood & Honour, 1987–1992," in *White Noise: Inside the International Skinhead Scene* eds. Nick Lowles and Steve Silver (London: Searchlight, 1998), 19.
212. "Blood & Honour Interview: Paul of No Remorse," *Blood & Honour* no. 1 (1987): 8.

213. "Blood & Honour Interview: Ian Stuart of Skrewdriver," *Blood & Honour* no. 1 (1987): 6.
214. *Blood & Honor Croyden Star, London September 1987* (Denison: NS88, n.d.) (DVD Recording).
215. "Editorial: International Success," *Blood & Honour* no. 5 (n.d., circa 1989): 2.
216. *Skrewdriver Live in London* (Denison: NS88, n.d.) (DVD Recording).
217. "'Zine Scene," *Blood & Honour* no. 6 (n.d., circa 1988): unpaginated 9.
218. "Editorial: International Success," *Blood & Honour* no. 5 (n.d., circa 1989): 2.
219. Skrewdriver, *After The Fire* (Rock-O-Rama Records, 1988) (CD Recording).
220. "Skrewdriver: Break the Chains Tour," *Blood & Honour* no. 9 (n.d., circa 1989): 3.
221. "Ian Stuart Skrewdriver," *Blood & Honour* no. 10 (n.d., circa 1989): 6.
222. *Skrewdriver Ritorno a Camelot 1991* (Denison: NS88, n.d.) (DVD Recording).
223. Interview with Pearce.
224. "Blood & Honour Interview: Ian Stuart of Skrewdriver," *Blood & Honour* no. 1 (1987): 6.
225. "Editorial: International Success," *Blood & Honour* no. 5 (n.d., circa 1989): 2.
226. "Sales League," *Blood & Honour* no. 5 (n.d., circa 1989): 10.
227. Cover of *Blood & Honour* no. 7 (n.d., circa 1989).
228. "News," *Blood & Honour* no. 7 (n.d., circa 1989): 3; "B&H Hits the Headlines," *Blood & Honour* no. 7 (n.d., circa 1989): 12.
229. Robert W. Balch, "The Rise and Fall of Aryan Nations: A Resource Mobilization Perspective," *Journal of Political and Military Sociology* 34 (Summer 2006): 104.
230. "Kicking ZOG Across America," *Blood & Honour* no. 11 (n.d., circa 1990): 8–9; "No Remorse Plays Aryan Fest '90," *White Aryan Resistance* 9, no. 3 (1990): 1; "Aryan Fest '92," *Blood & Honour* no. 14 (n.d., circa 1992): 4.
231. *Aryan Fest 1990* (n.p.: White Aryan Resistance, n.d.) (DVD Recording); *No Remorse Song Book* (London: No Remorse, n.d., circa 1989), unpaginated 2.
232. "Editorial," *White Noise* no. 8 (1989): 2.
233. Interview with Harrington.
234. "Editorial," *White Noise* no. 8 (1989): 2. A later publication of the same name with contributions from Harrington published reviews of books, art and music. Tim Bragg, *An Anthology of Counter Culture* (n.p.: Black Cat Distribution, 2006).

235. "Just Released," *National Front News* no. 122 (September 1989): 8.
236. "New Fanzine," *Wealden Warrior* no. 5 (n.d., circa 1987): unpaginated 2. This was edited by Troy Southgate.
237. "National Front: The Situation," *Blood & Honour* no. 7 (n.d., circa 1988): 7.
238. Ibid.
239. Interview with Harrington.
240. Larry O'Hara wrote the NF "failed because their ideology was too sophisticated for the audience that would listen." Lawrence Michael O'Hara, *Creating Political Soldiers?: The National Front 1986–1990* (Ph.D. Dissertation. Birkbeck College, University of London, 2000), 2. He quoted Harrington saying, "in the last couple of years there was drift on the part of the leadership . . . partly incorrect ideas, partly becoming out of touch with what the membership actually wanted."
241. Copsey, *Contemporary British Fascism*, 46.
242. "Worlds Affairs," *Nationalism Today* no. 2 (n.d., circa 1980): 6.
243. Joe Pearce, "Towards a Re-united Germany," *Nationalism Today* no. 23 (n.d., circa 1984): 10.
244. Derek Holland, "Justice for Palestine," *Nationalism Today* no. 11 (n.d., circa 1982): 13.
245. Interview with Pearce.
246. "Why the NF Supports the Palestinians," *Nationalism Today* no. 15 (n.d., circa 1982): 12.
247. "Chad: Another Race War," *Nationalism Today* no. 18 (n.d., circa 1983): 7.
248. Derek Holland, "Iran's National Revolution," *Nationalism Today* no. 21 (n.d., circa 1983): 12.
249. "The White International," *Nationalism Today* no. 25 (November 1984): 10.
250. Interview with Pearce.
251. Joe Pearce, "Australia, New Zealand and America," *Nationalism Today* no. 27 (March 1985): 10.
252. Derek Holland, "NPD: The New Nationalism," *Nationalism Today* no. 28 (April 1985): 10.
253. Ibid.
254. Derek Holland, "Advance Australia Fair," *Nationalism Today* no. 29 (May 1985): 18.
255. Derek Holland, "MNR: The Real Nationalism," *Nationalism Today* no. 31 (July 1985): 10.
256. Derek Holland, "The Global Struggle," *Nationalism Today* no. 32 (August 1985): 18.
257. Ibid.

258. Derek Holland, "Portugal's Future," *Nationalism Today* no. 37 (March 1986): 14.
259. Interview with Harrington.
260. Interview with Griffin.
261. R.J. Hoy, "The Women's War: A Photo Essay," *New Nation* no. 7 (Summer 1985): 11. Hoy and National Democratic Front activists were also involved in the Friends of the Movement that fostered ties between Americans and the NF. "NF Representatives Attend Separatist Conference," *National Front News* no. 115 (February 1989): 5. The Friend of the Movement initiative allowed overseas supporters to subscribe to the *National Front News.* See: "Become a Friend of the Movement," *National Front News* no. 114 (January 1989): 2.
262. Interview with Griffin.
263. Ibid.
264. Nick Griffin, "An Interview with Tom Metzger," *Nationalism Today* no. 31 (July 1985): 12.
265. Nick Griffin, "The Deadly Trap," *Nationalism Today* no. 29 (May 1985): 16.
266. Interview with Griffin; Interview with Andrews.
267. Gary Gallo, "A Personal Note on the Media," *The Nationalist* 3, no. 2 (February 1987): 2. According to an NDF business card, it was located at 444 N. Frederick Ave Suite L290 in Gaithersburg, Maryland. Personal possession.
268. "Essential Reading for the Nationalist," *The Nationalist* 3, no. 2 (February 1987): 11.
269. "Greetings to the NF," *Nationalism Today* no. 36 (February 1986): 17.
270. "Update on the NF's Race Campaign," *National Front News* no. 95 (September 1987): 4.
271. Ibid.,; Untitled National Front Meeting on July 24, 1987 (n.p.: Unknown, 1987) (Cassette Recording). In possession. This recording, along with many others, was received from a former NF member.
272. Nick Griffin, "Adapt or Die," *Nationalism Today* no. 39 (n.d., circa 1987): 9. See also: "Cadre/Candidates," *National Front News* no. 82 (n.d., circa 1986): 4.
273. *Cadre!* (n.p.: National Front Education and Training Department, 1987).
274. "What is to be Done," *National Front News* no. 92 (July 1987): 3.
275. "What is to be Done," *National Front News* no. 94 (August 1987): 3.
276. Mark Cotterill, interviewed by Ryan Shaffer, audio recording, 6 June 2010. (Abbreviated as "Interview with Cotterill 1.")
277. Ibid.
278. "Cadre Hope," *Nationalism Today* no. 40 (n.d., circa 1987): 11.

279. Interview with Cotterill 1.
280. "Calling Comrades Overseas," *National Front News* no. 94 (August 1987): 4.
281. *From Ballots to Bombs: The Inside Story of The National Front's Political Soldiers* (London: Searchlight, 1989).
282. Barindar Kalsi, Duncan Campbell and Zaya Yeebo, "Terror," *City Limits* (20–26 September 1985): 6. This publication was obtained from Tony Lecomber.
283. The British National Party condemned the Thatcher government for its actions. "Pathetic," *British Nationalist* no. 38 (May 1984): 1.
284. "Foreign Policy," *National Front News* no. 81 (n.d., circa 1986): 4.
285. "All Available From Burning Books," *National Front News* no. 96 (October 1987): unpaginated.
286. "Racial Realities," *National Front News* no. 94 (August 1987): 5.
287. Abdul Wali Muhammad, "Nation of Islam," *Nationalism Today* no. 39 (n.d., circa 1987): 16–20. Mattias Gardell wrote that the Nation of Islam "can be seen as a Third Positionist organization." Mattias Gardell, "Black and White Unite in Fight?," in *The Cultic Milieu: Oppositional Subcultures in an Age of Globalization* eds. Jeffrey Kaplan and Heléne Lööw (Walnut Creek, CA: Altamira, 2002), 163.
288. Cover of *National Front News* no. 95 (September 1987).
289. "On the Green Front," *Nationalism Today* no. 20 (n.d., circa 1984): 10.
290. Ibid.
291. "Rape & Pillage," *Nationalism Today* no. 38 (April 1986): 18.
292. "Two Threats to Our Children," *National Front News* no. 81 (n.d., circa 1986): 2.
293. "Editorial," *Isleworth Democrat* no. 5 (n.d., circa 1989): 2.
294. "The New Alliance," *National Front News* no. 103 (March 1988): 1.
295. Ibid.
296. "Comment," *National Front News* no. 105 (June 1988): 6. The NF later praised Libya's "condemnation of IRA terrorism and imperialism." "The Libyan Visit," *National Front News* no. 111 (1988): 6.
297. "Education and Ideology," *Isleworth Democrat* no. 5 (n.d., circa 1989): 11.
298. Kev Turner, "Dear Editor: Shocking the Bigot Brigade," *National Front News* no. 105 (June 1988).
299. "New NF News," *Wealden Warrior* no. 6 (n.d., circa 1988): unpaginated 1.
300. "Dear Editor," *National Front News* no. 107 (January 1988): 6.
301. Interview with Andrews; Interview with Harrington; *The Green March* 2, no. 1 (Brunswick: International Green March, 1989).

302. Interview with Griffin; Interview with Harrington. Holland's letter to Gaddafi and the response to *Searchlight* is in "NF 'Loonies' say UDA and Libyans," *Searchlight* no. 168 (June 1989): 3.
303. Interview with Griffin.
304. Interview with Harrington.
305. Ibid.
306. Interview with Griffin.
307. "NF Chiefs Visit Libya," *National Front News* no. 111 (1988): 1.
308. "Mad Dogs and Englishmen," *National Front News* no. 111 (1988): unpaginated 5.
309. "Libya: A Study of the Third Position in Practise," *Nationalism Today* no. 44 (January 1989): 8.
310. Ibid., 9.
311. Interview with Harrington.
312. Interview with Griffin. The Libyan leader did give money to fascists. Warren Kinsella wrote Gaddafi's government funded Donald Andrews's Nationalist Party in Canada "since at least April 1987, when a number of his members travelled to Tripoli for a 'peace conference' to commemorate a U.S. bombing raid." Warren Kinsella, *Web of Hate: Inside Canada's Far Right Network* (Toronto: Harper Collins, 1994), 223.
313. Muammar al-Qathafi, *The Green Book* (London: Black Front Press, 2015), 3, 4.
314. Interview with Andrews.
315. "Summer Cadre Conference," *National Front News* no. 110 (1988): 9.
316. "Cadre Meeting: Eight Aims for '89," *National Front News* no. 116 (March 1989): 4.
317. "Movement Aims to Contact Black Community in Vauxhall Election," *National Front News* no. 119 (June 1989): 4; "Black Separatists Back Front Candidate," *National Front News* no. 120 (July 1989): 1.
318. "Altered Images," *National Front News* no. 112 (November 1988): 6.
319. Interview with Harrington; "NF About-Turn is 'Not Serious'," *The Jewish Chronicle*, 13 October 1989, 21. Harrington said: "We now recognize that serious ideological errors have been made concerning the approach of the movement towards the Jewish community. For moral reasons the NF must be prepared to publicly apologise for and take active steps to correct any manifestation of anti-Semitism."
320. Interview with Harrington.
321. "Will the Jews Join the Culture Club," *National Front News* no. 114 (January 1989): 2.
322. Interview with Harrington.
323. Interview with Griffin.
324. Interview with Todd.

325. Interview with Griffin.
326. Interview with Todd.
327. Troy Southgate, *Nazis, Fascists, or Neither?: Ideological Credentials of the British Far Right 1987–1994* (Shamley Green: The Palingenesis Project, 2010), 77, 78.
328. Interview with Harrington.
329. "For A Third Way," *National Front News* no. 126 (January 1990): 2.
330. Ibid.
331. Ibid.
332. John Tyndall, "The General Election: Why I Acted as I Did," *Spearhead* no. 221 (July 1987): 16.
333. Copsey, *Contemporary British Fascism*, 42.
334. Patrick Harrington, "Elections: Uses and Abuses," *Nationalism Today* no. 40 (n.d., circa 1987): 26.
335. "Election Meeting," *National Front News* no. 88 (April 1987): 3.
336. "Realism: The National Front and the General Election," *Frontline: The Voice of Leeds NF* no. 1 (Summer 1987): 2.
337. "Elections are a Con," *National Front News* no. 90 (June 1987): 1.
338. "Latest Idiocies from the Front," *Spearhead* no. 227 (January 1988): 20.
339. James Thurgood, "The Reddening of the National Front," *Spearhead* no. 228 (February 1988): 11, 12.
340. Ibid., 13.
341. "The Front Joins the Opposition," *British Nationalist* no. 96 (December 1989): 7.
342. "The 'White Noise' Anthem," *Blood & Honour* no. 6 (n.d., circa 1988): unpaginated 9.
343. George Ashcroft recalled the meeting was a "mighty row" between the sides and Anderson had already printed literature with the new name. George Ashcroft, interviewed by Ryan Shaffer, audio recording, 30 May 2010. According to Martin Wingfield, he proposed "a resolution to change the name of the National Front to the National Democratic Party (to be known on all our literature as the National Democrats)." Modern Records Centre, MSS.412/ND/3, "Letter from Martin Wingfield to *The Flag* Subscriber," 8 June 1995. John McAuley, then Anderson's deputy, opposed the resolution and split off with a group using the NF and served as its chair. Modern Records Centre, MSS.412/ND/3, "Special Meeting to Debate Name Change," *National Front Member's Bulletin* (1995).
344. "The New Atlantic Charter," Nationalist Movement, 1989 (Video Recording). "Why Not Just an American," *All the Way* 1, no. 5 (November 1987): 1. John Tyndall wrote about Barrett's *The Commission*, calling it one of the "most interesting" books on

"contemporary affairs." John Tyndall, "From Vietnam to Politics," *Spearhead* no. 180 (October 1983): 17.

345. Ibid. "The American Friends' Fiasco," Nationalist Movement, 2008; available from https://web.archive.org/web/20081107211121.html http://www.nationalist.org/docs/reports/2001/123101.html; accessed 1 July 2016. Barrett gave a speech at the Flag NF's September 1989 Annual General Meeting in Birmingham, England. Richard Barrett, "Raise Your Excalibur," Nationalist Movement, 2008; available from https://web.archive.org/web/20080603121550/http://www.nationalist.org/speeches/foreign/excalibur.html; accessed 1 July 2016.
346. Mark Cotterill, interviewed by Ryan Shaffer, audio recording, 14 October 2014. (Abbreviated as "Interview with Cotterill 2.")

CHAPTER 5

Building a Street Force, 1990–1999

During the 1990s, British fascism underwent contradictory developments. At the same time a skinhead organization was wreaking havoc on London streets, the British National Party (BNP) won its first election with improved campaigning and a refined local message. With the increased attention and re-emergence of British fascist demonstrations in the early 1990s, the BNP started an organization to protect its members from attacks. Combat 18 was developed by the party leadership to provide security, and its rank and file included violent neo-Nazi skinheads with close ties to Skrewdriver. The group gained headlines for its violence, including links to the April 1993 murder of Stephen Lawrence, which caused problems for the BNP's new image. That same year in September, Derek Beackon, who was the chief steward of the BNP's security group, was elected in the Millwall ward of Tower Hamlets, becoming the BNP's first elected representative. Beackon's position in the party and successful election demonstrates the issues British fascism faced in the 1990s. According to Richard Edmonds, the election "changed" the party by legitimizing it, but the BNP members were slow to recognize its impact.[1] Indeed, the fascists struggled to transition from what Eddy Butler described as a "Nazi book club" to an organized political party that could win elections.[2]

This chapter examines the emergence of the BNP as a more electorally successful party than the National Front (NF). During the early 1990s, the BNP's evolution saw one local election victory in East London, but it proved to be a mere "false dawn" that they were not able to replicate.[3]

R. Shaffer, *Music, Youth and International Links in Post-War British Fascism*, Palgrave Studies in the History of Subcultures and Popular Music, DOI 10.1007/978-3-319-59668-6_5

The victory and losing the seat the next year caused local groups to lose faith in the BNP, but other party members saw the local "community-based strategy" as the future.[4] This chapter examines the BNP's local election strategy at the same time a small group of people continued with the NF. In fact, after the NF disbanded in 1989, the former NF leaders started several unsuccessful movements during the early 1990s. This included Nick Griffin and Derek Holland's International Third Position, which attempted to build colonies in continental Europe, and Patrick Harrington's Third Way efforts to spread the ideas of the NF without the skinhead negativity. Ultimately, when the BNP won its first local election—something the NF had failed at—its gains proved attractive to former NF figures, including Griffin, who then joined the BNP. By the end of the decade, the culmination of these efforts resulted in a new face for British fascism and the need for a political operation devoid of the skinhead image.

British National Party Evolution

While the BNP, led by John Tyndall, eclipsed the NF in the late 1980s in membership, the BNP began in the NF's shadow and initially struggled for several years. Months after Tyndall's January 1980 resignation from the NF, he wrote that the NF was not "ready" to be "reunited" due to "internal division" and "crippled morale."[5] Tyndall started an organization named the New NF with the hope that he could again lead the NF. The split hurt the parties tremendously, with Tyndall only getting about five out of every hundred former NF members to follow him in the early 1980s.[6] Launched in June 1980, the New NF was started with the goal of pressuring the NF to reform by giving the leader more power and thereafter unite the two groups.[7] As the former NF chair, Tyndall had support from a faction of the party and by the end of the year reported having "between 55 and 60 affiliated local organisations of various sizes" with expectations that it would accelerate in 1981.[8] One year after its creation, the New NF claimed an "increase in total membership of 100% at least."[9] Entire NF branches defected to the New NF, meaning that a "substantial part" of the new organization consisted of the "old" NF membership.[10] This trend continued and by late 1981, hundreds of former NF members had defected to Tyndall's group.[11]

The New NF's methods and reporting mirrored those of the NF. Tyndall's organization had its own youth wing, called Young

Nationalists, and kept "scuffs" and "punks" away from its marches.[12] Led by Richard Edmonds, the group had its own publication, *Young Nationalist*, which listed his name as editor, but in actuality he had little to do with the publication.[13] Less controversial than *Bulldog*, the content of *Young Nationalist* was more subdued and consisted of articles that called the Conservative Party "liars" and listed the aims of "British nationalism."[14] By early 1981, the youth division was "ready for action" with local groups in Grimsby, Durham and Leeds.[15] For the adults interested in political news, the New NF published *New Frontier* to serve as the group's newspaper and unite the different factions.[16] The publication had "three objectives," including to "persuade" Britons to join, "inform readers of our policies" and report on the group's activities.[17] As the New NF gained support and the NF continued with a different leadership, the New NF began shifting away from being a mere holding name to becoming a competitor party, with the rank and file calling for a different name.[18]

In March 1982, the New NF was renamed the BNP following a vote by supporters in a London hotel room and the party was launched in early April. Edmonds described how there was discussion about naming it simply the National Party, but BNP had more support.[19] The meeting followed months of informal contact with other groups, including the NF and the British Movement, to "reunite" "nationalists" under a larger party led by Tyndall.[20] About seventy people attended the meeting, including Ray Hill's faction of the British Movement, the British Democratic Party and figures from the League of Saint George.[21] The amalgamation of the different groups led Tyndall to describe the unification as "an important victory," but the group had "some way to go."[22] The party leadership consisted of Tyndall as chair, his father-in-law Charles Parker as national organizer, Violet Parker as administrator, David Bruce as activities organizer, Richard Edmonds as Young Nationalist chair, Ronald Rickford as *New Frontier* editor and Ray Hill as publicity officer.[23] By October 1982, the BNP reported that about three hundred people had attended a BNP rally with speakers discussing "nationalist unity," which marked a "big increase" from the year before.[24]

When the BNP was established, its ideology was identical to that of the NF, with policies directly drawn from the NF's activities of the 1970s. The BNP was founded as a "nationalist" organization opposed to the Common Market, communism and capitalism, and in support of forced non-white repatriation.[25] When asked about the differences between the BNP and the NF during the 1980s, Edmonds said, "we were successful and they weren't; we grounded them down."[26] The NF and BNP manifestos for the June 1983 general election demonstrated their common ideology. While the NF "rejected" multiculturalism and would "institute a policy of phased and orderly repatriation," the BNP would likewise initiate "a massive programme of repatriation or resettlement of coloured immigrants and their offspring."[27] The NF used its party resources to run sixty candidates in the election, but the BNP scrambled to raise money for more than fifty seats to receive broadcast time.[28] The election results for both parties were poor, with the NF receiving 27,065 and the BNP even fewer, with 14,621 votes.[29] In contrast, the Conservatives received 13,012,316 votes, which successfully re-elected Thatcher and gave the Tories 397 parliamentary seats.[30]

The similarities between the NF and the BNP extended not only to ideology and election returns, but also to cultural interests and problems. While the BNP tried to avoid the skinhead neo-Nazi image of the NF, the BNP was interested in music. Although the BNP engaged in a far tamer music genre, by the end of its first year it had three marching songs for members to learn as well as plans for a "nationalist song book."[31] Like the NF, the BNP sought to continue mobilization strategies by holding rallies centered around race and immigration that drew hundreds of people.[32] More than that, while Young National Front (YNF) leader Joe Pearce was found guilty of violating the Race Relations Act, BNP activists Tyndall and John Morse were convicted of similar charges and went to prison in 1986.[33] During his time in prison, Tyndall wrote a political treatise titled *The Eleventh Hour* that was both autobiographical and a statement of the movement.[34] That same year, the BNP started its general election drive with plans to contest a minimum of twenty "properly financed campaigns," which if achieved would cause the party to expand the number to fifty.[35] With the election set for June 1987, the party announced it needed £15,000 for twenty to twenty-five seats and donating was "a chance for all our supporters really to show how high their dedication is."[36] Ultimately, neither the NF nor the BNP officially entered candidates in the election. Tyndall later explained that the BNP received only £3000 for the election and rather than spend the money on an increased £500 deposit for each candidate as well as paying for campaign literature, the resources would be better spent developing the party.[37]

One subject the BNP focused on more than the NF during the 1980s was the Holocaust. Leading BNP members, such as Richard Edmonds, wrote about what they called "Holocaust revision" but scholars describe as "Holocaust denial." Edmonds wrote that the Holocaust was a "political weapon" that connected extremists to genocide and called for "exposing the lie" because "there is in fact nothing to substantiate the claim that 6 million Jews were put to death by the Nazis."[38] The BNP members believed that one reason for their lack of support was the popular history of the Holocaust, which was linked to fascism. According to Eddy Butler, who thought the denial alienated people, the BNP felt that once people no longer believed the Holocaust happened, they would then be able to distribute party literature.[39] The BNP spread thousands of leaflets titled *"Holocaust" News* with headlines that included calling the Holocaust "an Evil Hoax," with no bylines.[40] In response, newspapers began inquiring about these activities and an article in the *Sunday Times* identified Edmonds as one of the people involved, causing him to lose his job from Cable & Wireless Ltd.[41] At the same time, the party was raising money for a headquarters, and Edmonds ultimately received a settlement from the company that was used to purchase a building that would be both a bookstore and party headquarters in Welling, East London in spring 1989.[42] The store went on to sell books printed by Anthony Hancock that denied the Holocaust, but also publications from foreign groups, such as the National Alliance in the United States.[43]

In the late 1980s, the NF was focusing on international ties, but the BNP was concentrated on positioning itself as the premier fascist party in Britain. In 1988, Tyndall described how the party's success depended almost entirely on local efforts, with hard work and a "positive attitude" to spread party ideas.[44] As the NF suffered from internal turmoil, an exodus from the party to the BNP continued, with the "first few weeks of 1988" bringing "a noticeable increase in the rate of new recruits coming into the BNP."[45] The October 1988 rally was called one of the "best ever," with about two hundred people donating £1749 as they listened to speeches critical of Thatcher.[46] The following year Tyndall wrote that the goals for 1989 included "training" activists, publishing a book about the aims of the movement, increasing membership and establishing the BNP as the leader of the "British nationalist movement."[47] With the dissolution of the official NF in January 1990, the BNP achieved its goal of becoming the undisputed largest British extremist party. In early 1990, Tyndall reflected that 1989 "was probably the best year" the party had and as it entered 1990, "we must make double the effort to get our message out."[48]

Rights for Whites

In March 1990, John Stoner, a sixteen-year-old white student, was attacked by Bangladeshi pupils in Bethnal Green, East London. The family held a march to draw attention to the assault and BNP members, arguing it was a racist attack, joined in support of the white student.[49] Nigel Copsey explained how the boy's foster grandfather "denied that the family was racist and publicly disowned the BNP."[50] At the same time, BNP activists were inspired by the local Liberal Democrats' "racial" policies, such as the local government providing priority housing for the sons and daughters of residents, and the BNP also turned to local race issues.[51] Following the march to raise awareness about Stoner's assault, the BNP called for more events in support, which was welcomed by his foster parents who wanted more public pressure to be put on the school.[52] In response, Eddy Butler developed a "Defend Rights for Whites" campaign with leaflets and marches to draw attention to what the BNP argued was "reverse" racism. The leaflets declared that Britons "have become second class citizens" and in some areas were "the ethnic minority" as it promoted BNP policies and "demanded" rights for whites.[53] This differed from BNP leaflets in other areas, where anti-immigration policies were promoted alongside anti-Irish Republican Army (IRA) and anti-European Community policies.[54] Like the NF, the BNP's literature focused on racist propaganda with claims about "race war in the nineties," but the BNP's new strategy focused its marches and elections in specific areas where the racist message could be attached to a local event.[55] The party claimed to be "defending whites" in areas where racial attacks were reported as it sought inroads into local community politics.[56]

The BNP aggressively campaigned in East London with growing electoral results. In support of a May 1990 BNP campaign, the party organized a rally in the East End that drew about two hundred opponents and an equal number of BNP supporters who clashed.[57] The party started receiving a higher percentage of votes and in a Bermondsey and Epping Forest election the party reported its 9.7%

return was "encouraging."[58] Then in July 1990, Steve Smith ran in Park Ward of Tower Hamlets, winning 130 votes or 8.4%, beating the Tory candidate by seventeen votes and the Green candidate with eighteen.[59] The BNP came in third, behind the Liberal Democrat candidate who earned 779 votes and Labour with 598. *Spearhead* described the results as "an important moral victory," with the campaign's high point being a rally that included speeches from Tyndall, Butler and Edmonds.[60] Moreover, the article gave special praise to East London organizer Butler for his "highly efficient and energetic campaign in the ward."[61] Aside from the local issues and campaigning, the BNP's rallies were credited with giving the party publicity through newspaper and television reports.[62] Yet the growing support in the East End was due to local initiative rather than support from the party leadership. Butler, for example, found Tyndall out of step with the changes and in fact he gave a speech about Sir Francis Drake at a meeting devoted to local instances of racial violence.[63]

The BNP turned its attention to building public support for the next general election. Butler wrote that the "immediate task" was "local election battles" which had to be "fewer" to get "good results and increased credibility."[64] The public demonstrations, leafleting and newspaper sales were "progressing," but the local work would be jeopardized if the general election results proved to be "poor."[65] The BNP continued to improve its percentage of votes in East London by-elections. In August 1990, Ken Walsh received 12.1% with 275 votes in St. Peter's Ward and would have done better if the Liberal Democrats had not used "a bogus 'racist'" campaign borrowing from the "BNP-style."[66] The BNP concluded that the results showed "the abysmal electoral period which was experienced by the nationalist movement in the 1980s" appeared to be at an end, while the BNP "provides the best hope" for "success in the future."[67] In autumn 1990, the BNP hosted its "most successful assembly ever" and the cover of *Spearhead* showed a photo of the event with the words: "triumph of the will."[68] Despite the positive gains, Butler was opposed to running fifty seats in the next election, citing concerns about spreading resources too thinly as the BNP had done in 1983.[69] Though the larger number of seats would enable the party to have a political broadcast on television, he argued that the perception of success would attract more votes than would broadcast time. Therefore, Butler proposed focusing on particular candidates and elections where the party would be most effective.[70]

In 1990, the BNP announced that its next general election plans had been approved by the leadership and that it would contest between ten and twenty seats.[71] With the reasoning reflected in Butler's arguments, the party would focus its resources on particular seats due to the costs involved in election deposits and printing literature, based on the belief that good results would generate positive press coverage.[72] Claiming that "the 'racist' Tory vote looks very unstable," BNP member Tony Wells argued that the combination of alienation from the two major parties and a populist message would gain more votes.[73] Wells, identified as director of propaganda, held seminars discussing the ability to get the Tory votes "lost" in 1979, saying the party had a "responsibility" as the "standard-bearer."[74] Butler, meanwhile, argued for canvassing house-to-house over just leafleting in public locations.[75] The first party candidates selected were Richard Edmonds and Steve Smith for seats in East London, while members were told to send their campaign donations to Butler.[76]

The BNP ultimately ran thirteen candidates in the April 1992 general election with the expectation that the party would eclipse its poor organization and marginal popularity in the 1980s.[77] BNP activist Peter Rushton, who helped canvass for votes in the constituencies, explained that one important factor for small parties in national elections was the free mailing of leaflets when parties had paid the election deposit.[78] He noted it was not until years later that people were regularly sent advertising for products, which meant the election leaflets had greater impact.[79] Tyndall described the BNP's 1992 election as focusing on issues such as the "racial threat to Britain" as well as leaving the European Community.[80] He denied the party was fascist or Nazi, explaining: "Fascism was Italian; Nazism was German; we are British. We will do things our own way; we will not copy foreigners."[81] The BNP's 1992 manifesto contained the previous calls for involuntary repatriation, but also proclamations for political reform that denounced British democracy as a "racket" ran by a "mafia" that needed to be replaced with a "strong executive" made by direct vote.[82] Butler wrote, "the BNP now faces the most favourable set of conditions for political success that nationalism in this country has known since the 1979 general election."[83] He argued that for the previous two and a half years, the BNP was "almost like a non-stop success story."[84] Butler wrote that Ian Anderson's NF, which was competing with the BNP, was "visibly falling apart" and its members were joining the BNP.[85] In addition, he described how the BNP was attracting new members who were involved with the Conservative Party and Blood & Honour.[86]

Despite high expectations, the party received fewer than 8000 votes, which was less than the support it received in 1983. Tyndall wrote that the lesson learned, which "should have been learned in previous general elections," was that "in the eyes of the vast majority of British voters small parties have no relevance."[87] Butler offered a case-by-case analysis of each BNP contest, explaining it was "the first time since 1979 that any nationalist candidate has polled over a thousand votes in a parliamentary election" and showed a positive trend of gains.[88] Meanwhile, Butler told BNP members at a post-election planning conference that the results were "encouraging," and Tyndall said the party needed to recruit more members "to be taken seriously by the voters."[89] Butler wrote in an article that the BNP's growth, while good, was still not enough "to expect high votes in a general election."[90] Still, the party's most successful candidates ran in areas where "the BNP has been campaigning almost exclusively on locally relevant issues."[91] Specifically, the "Rights for Whites" theme was prevalent in certain areas, while opposition to the Treaty of Maastricht and the European Union was stressed in other districts.[92] Door-to-door newspaper sales, he argued, were key to meeting people and discussing BNP issues.[93] Indeed, while race was a key issue, the BNP considered the Treaty of Maastricht treason and hoped to harness opposition to Britain joining the European Union.[94] In an appeal for donations to pay off its campaign debt, the BNP called the election spending "most certainly" worthwhile, with about 750,000 pieces of BNP literature spread around the country.[95] Likewise, the party reported that regular literature sales in East London, led by Edmonds, ensured street-level attention to BNP issues.[96] In the face of the poor election results, Rushton explained that newspaper sales served as a social point and networking site that provided regular activity and kept up morale among activists.[97]

While race remained at the forefront of fascism, so did anti-Semitism. Tyndall defended the party from news reports about the increase in racist attacks in London and wrote that he did not "know" about "any cause-and-effect relationship" from reading *"Holocaust" News*, which denied Nazi Germany had a policy to murder Jews.[98] The party's *Handbook on Propaganda* stated that it "has no position or policy on the 'Holocaust' at all because, true or untrue, it is a subject that belongs to Germany and German-occupied Europe half a century ago rather than to Britain today."[99] A *Sunday Express* report titled "Inside the HQ of Hate" included interviews with Tyndall and Edmonds as well as details about skinheads selling the BNP newspaper, but earned an angry response from Tyndall about the interviewer's "self-righteousness."[100] Meanwhile Steve Cartwright, one of thirteen BNP candidates in the 1992 election and later leader of Blood & Honour in Scotland, appeared in a documentary with Austrian, French and German radicals who denied the Holocaust and who were taken on a tour of Auschwitz.[101] In *Spearhead*, Cartwright described his experience meeting Kitty Hart, a Holocaust survivor, by putting the word in scare quotes and doubted it would air on television given the content.[102]

Though the BNP's results in the national election were weak, it continued to campaign in areas marked by racial tension. Peter Rushton explained that the party focused "on white working class areas that were becoming disillusioned with Labour."[103] In October 1992, Barry Osborne received 20% of the vote when he ran for a local seat in the Millwall ward of Tower Hamlets Borough, which was "the best ever BNP vote" and "best vote" of any fascist candidate since the 1970s.[104] Described in the press as "racist" and "neo-Nazis," the BNP relished the attention and compared it to the success of the 1970s, announcing: "we are back."[105] The party told its readers it could have done better "had not the Liberal Democrats attempted to steal the party's platform by pitching its campaign largely at the white anti-immigration voters."[106] Meanwhile, the BNP was also experiencing nationwide growth after the 1992 general election.[107] People such as Warren Glass, who had been an NF skinhead in the 1980s, joined the BNP in Hounslow after seeing the party's local impact in London.[108] Glass himself ran for a local Hounslow council seat in 1993 and another in 1995, with the national office printing leaflets and giving strategy advice for local elections.[109] The party also expanded the "Defend Rights for Whites" campaign to other parts of the country, such as Scotland.[110] Since its local outreach effort began in 1990, the BNP reported that in three years "local BNP units" had grown by 74% and the party had doubled its membership size since 1989.[111]

With the influx of new recruits, the BNP began focusing on training and educating its members. The leadership argued this was a transition away from the street violence and mayhem used in the 1970s to get publicity in the belief that attention would result in votes. The party planned monthly training events so that more people could be involved in spreading ideas and campaign successfully.[112] The lack of professionalization in the party was a serious problem. Butler led a ten-member team that was self-financed and developed a systematic canvassing campaign for the BNP where the party would track supportive people and avoid opponents to maximize its share of the vote.[113] Influenced in part by methods he had learned in the NF earlier, the BNP targeted areas with specific leaflets and talked one-on-one with residents.[114] To help streamline these methods, video tapes about how to prepare for elections and field media inquiries were made available to party members who could not attend the London training seminars.[115]

The culmination of more than a decade of BNP campaigning and intensive efforts in East London resulted in the party's first electoral victory and the third post-war fascist victory. After years of reporting about black-on-white attacks, the party intensified its focus on areas experiencing racial tension.[116] On September 16, 1993 BNP member Derek Beackon was elected in a Millwall by-election, beating the Labour candidate by a slim margin.[117] The headline of the BNP's *British Nationalist* newspaper was simply: "We Won," and the accompanying article claimed it was "just the beginning."[118] Though it was a local election and a single victory, the BNP's success became nationwide news, with leading officials from the major political parties condemning the result. Prime Minister John Major commented, "I think it was an unfortunate result. I just want to make it quite clear there is no place in our society for those sort of policies and I hope that will be readily understood by everyone."[119] Meanwhile, the Anti-Nazi League, newly relaunched in 1992 due to BNP gains, started focusing on the victory and held a large carnival during the spring of 1994 in Brockwell Park.[120] Nonetheless, the BNP announced it was "swamped" with inquiries as a result of all the publicity and was now in "a completely new league of politics."[121] In fact, its growth was so large and unexpected it needed more staff to handle the new recruits and press inquiries.[122] The election victory gave a boost to BNP events and its annual rally, with about seven hundred people, was the "biggest" to date.[123]

In addition to the negative press, the BNP faced physical attacks and was accused of violence. There was a scuffle between BNP members and critics outside the voting site.[124] Additionally, Edmonds and three others were arrested for "violent disorder" while selling newspapers in Brick Lane three days after the victory.[125] Then the BNP headquarters building was "raided" by police, but no items, aside from Edmonds's phone, were confiscated.[126] Edmonds maintained his innocence, but was convicted of throwing a glass at a white girl who was with her Indian boyfriend.[127] After the election, however, the party had gained official recognition by winning a democratic election. Edmonds said the election "legitimized us" and the party "had a slogan: No longer a street gang, but a political party."[128] Consequently, the party no longer had to sell the party newspaper at the corner of Brick Lane and Bethnal Green Road to get publicity, and he said "we never went back to Brick Lane" because the election "changed the party completely."[129]

Combat 18

As the BNP was transforming its image and making local electoral inroads in the early 1990s, neo-Nazi skinheads re-emerged with ferociousness. While the NF was connected with skinheads, Combat 18 (C18) was a BNP-associated group that promoted racial violence and its activists committed murder. As the NF faltered in the early 1990s and the BNP emerged as the premier extremist party, Ian Stuart continued recording music and performing for large audiences. At the same time, many skinheads and former skinheads from the 1980s were the BNP's new recruits in the early 1990s. Blood & Honour remained the organizing network that united neo-Nazi skinheads even though the publication of its magazine and its concerts were infrequent. Moreover, it remained a formidable skinhead group with foreign ties that promoted and hosted international concerts. In September 1993, the same month the BNP won its first election, Stuart died from injuries sustained in a car crash near Derbyshire, leaving Blood & Honour to face an uncertain future.[130] Following brief internal conflict, the leaders of Combat 18 took over the group and cemented its reputation as a racist, violent neo-Nazi organization.

While the official NF collapsed and was dissolved at the end of the 1980s, Ian Stuart continued recording albums and releasing music for a growing international audience. In addition to his concert performances with Skrewdriver, he recorded solo albums as well as new Skrewdriver albums *Warlord* (1989) and *The Strong Survive* (1990).[131] Though Blood & Honour remained the main conduit for neo-Nazi skinhead music, its magazine was not produced at "regular" time intervals.[132] When it was published, it boasted about violence and assaults. The magazine, for example, reported on clashes with BNP opponents, telling readers that the group Anti-Fascist Action went to a pub with extremists who were attending a BNP march and were beaten until they fled.[133] In an editorial, *Blood & Honour* magazine told its readers that "[a]s our [m]ovement grows so does the opposition" and ended the paragraph with "the laws that we recognise are the laws we were born with—white pride and survival."[134]

During 1991, Skrewdriver toured throughout Europe, allowing Stuart to network with fascists, and received international headlines. In early September, the band performed with Peggior Amico at the Return to Camelot concert, which was organized by the Veneto Fronte Skinheads in Italy.[135] According to Colin Todd, who filmed the event as a friend for Stuart, they were invited to Italy by Roberto Fiore and Massimo Morsello, who had contacts with the Italian skinheads.[136] Yet it was during the following month that Skrewdriver made international news. In October 1991, several members of Skrewdriver were arrested for a stabbing in Cottbus, former East Germany.[137] The band traveled to the city to perform when "[a] fight occurred between local rival gangs who then fled as police arrived" and then police "arrested all [the] English people in the near vicinity plus the German organiser of the concert."[138] According to journalist Robert Kellaway, a group of fifteen skinheads near a bowling alley taunted a smaller group who fled the scene, but when one man tripped he was stabbed and left "fighting for his life."[139] While Stuart and his fiancée were held by police, they were later released without charge.[140] The other Skrewdriver band members were eventually released and left the country, but the prosecutor later said, "[i]f they walk on German soil we'll arrest them."[141] Stigger, one of the arrested Skrewdriver members, explained in 1995 that "we were accused of stabbing up a local red, and were all put in prison awaiting trial. Most of us served up to three months and got out on bail. We are still wanted in Germany because we never went back for the trial."[142] Stuart, with his bandmates in jail, performed the concert with local German musicians and apologized to the crowd for the situation.[143] Relishing the publicity, *Blood & Honour* published various articles boasting about the international media attention.[144]

The following year Skrewdriver released a new album, *Freedom What Freedom* (1992), and performed what it planned would be one of the largest events hosted by Blood & Honour. On September 12, 1992, "more than a thousand" skinheads from several European nations gathered in London to watch Skrewdriver along with No Remorse and Dirlewanger.[145] The concertgoers were told to meet at Waterloo Station at 4:30 pm, where they were rerouted to the venue, The Yorkshire. Garry Bushell wrote that "Blood & Honour had deliberately made that night's planned concert… public knowledge."[146] Indeed, *Blood & Honour* magazine publicly disclosed the date of the concert and named Waterloo as the "re-direction point" to all subscribers in advance.[147] A large number of anti-racists traveled to the rendezvous site, including Anti-Fascist Action and Skinheads Against Racism and Prejudice (SHARP). The fascists, including the neo-Nazi Chelsea Headhunters, and their opponents began fighting in what became known as the "Battle of Waterloo."[148] Journalist William Shaw stood in the crowd as groups clashed, watching as police desperately tried to stop the violence.[149] However, police did not expect the "sheer vehemence" of the anti-fascists and Shaw described it as "a vile scene."[150] Police arrested dozens while the mayhem caused the Underground and British Rail to suspend services.[151] While many could not get to the concert, Stuart estimated that about seven hundred people traveled to the pub and attended the Blood & Honour event.[152] During the concert he discussed the violence and praised an obscure group, later known as Combat 18, and the man who became its leader, Paul David "Charlie" Sargent. Stuart dedicated a song "to a new group" that "the reds just" learned about during the fight.[153] He explained, "I'd like to dedicate this number to a new group called Redwatch and especially to a little bloke called Charlie [who] looks like a school boy, but I've never known anybody less like a school boy. This is for Redwatch and they're doing a fucking good job."[154] Stuart, while disappointed that the media did not report anything positive, later described the concert as a "good gig" that the attendees "enjoyed."[155]

The public was again reminded of the link between fascist music and youth violence, but the announcement about a group fighting the "reds" would usher in a new era of skinhead violence.[156] Charlie Sargent along with his brother, Steve, were important figures in the group that became known as Combat 18, which united neo-Nazi skinheads and promoted racial violence. In the wake of making gains in the East End, the BNP began a stewarding group to defend its members. Skinheads from Blood & Honour joined the "Defend Rights for Whites" protests and even Ian Stuart attended BNP meetings as the party was winning support in the local elections.[157] As the BNP's numbers grew, so did their opponents' numbers. Butler explained that the party "needed a stewarding group" to run the events and protect the membership from disruption and violence.[158] Coincidentally, Derek Beackon, the BNP's first elected councilor, was named head of the BNP's security.[159]

The BNP went through a period of organizing election campaigns that focused on local issues, but had a "cross-over" period where its members were regularly connected to violence.[160] A significant C18 member, who wished to remain anonymous, explained, "[e]very Sunday various right wingers and football hooligans used to drink in pubs around Bethnal Green, close to where the BNP/NF did their paper sales."[161] These men banded together and became known as Combat 18, with numbers ranging between fifty and one hundred people, including brothers Steve and Charlie Sargent, to provide the BNP protection from "left-wing gangs."[162] According to Butler, some of the people who became involved in C18 were BNP members who would go out for the night with the intention of finding opponents to assault.[163] Combat 18, referring to the first and eighth letters of the alphabet for the initials of Adolf Hitler, became increasingly more violent. C18 drew from BNP supporters, members of the British Movement in the 1980s and increasingly younger skinheads who were interested in neo-Nazism.[164]

Though Combat 18 did not initially have a single leader, in April 1993 *World in Action* aired a television report about the group, focusing on Charlie Sargent's large role.[165] Thereafter, he was looked at as a leader and more people tried to get in contact with him and the group.[166] The television program also examined other people connected to C18, including Gary Hitchcock and Harold Covington, an American neo-Nazi who lived in the United Kingdom.[167] Butler described Hitchcock as the most dominant figure in C18, dating as from the British Movement era and being a physically large person, but he dropped out after a year.[168] By the time Combat 18 began receiving publicity, Covington was living in North Carolina and his address was reportedly used to redirect mail from the United Kingdom to keep plans, names and addresses from being intercepted by law enforcement.[169] Steve Sargent, using the name Albion Wolf, edited a crude monthly newsletter, *Putsch*, that published press clippings about racial attacks, commentary on skinhead music and praise for Hitler and Nazism.[170] Meanwhile, Charlie Sargent edited *The Order* for two years until Steve took over, using the name Andy Saxon due to Charlie being arrested, and Steve discontinued *Putsch* in favor of just producing *The Order*.[171]

During 1993 the fascist movement underwent several changes including the seizure of fascist records, the death of Ian Stuart, the BNP's first electoral victory and the growth of Combat 18. In February 1993, law enforcement in Germany closed Rock-O-Rama, seizing tens of thousands of music recordings.[172] After a decade of releasing music with fascist and racist themes, Rock-O-Rama's owner, Herbert Egoldt, was rumored to have earned a million dollars from Skrewdriver albums before authorities put an end to the record label.[173] Yet the number of youths attending the BNP's events was growing. In fact, even the BNP's newspaper discussed reports about "skinhead terror" disrupting an anti-apartheid meeting by "storming" the meeting and chanting BNP slogans.[174] Then in September 1993, the same month Derek Beackon was elected in Millwall, Ian Stuart died in a car accident.[175] The death of the neo-Nazi skinhead movement's icon was seen as a great loss at a time when British fascists were jubilant over their first electoral victory in nearly twenty years.

Before his death, Stuart had little interest in the day-to-day operations of Blood & Honour and let other people operate it. As Combat 18 member Martin Cross explained, until March 1994 the *Blood & Honour* magazine was published infrequently, with only "a couple of issues" produced in the previous three years, and the organization lacked a "coherent plan" under the leadership of Paul Burnley, vocalist for No Remorse.[176] Cross accused Burnley of "stealing" money while working with Derek Holland and "Spike," former NF activists.[177] In 1994, a "radical shake up" occurred when a new group took over Blood & Honour in order to bring about "action" in the movement.[178] In April 1994, subscribers received a letter along with issue sixteen that stated: "A new group will now publish B&H, with a new approach and better finance."[179] This included Charlie serving as the editor for *Blood & Honour* magazine along with support from Will "The Beast" Browning, while they forced Burnley entirely out of the organization.[180] Combat 18 also started ISD Records, named after Ian Stuart Donaldson and controlled by Browning, to produce new music for Blood & Honour. With Browning and the Sargent brothers, key C18 figures were involved in editing and distributing extremist material, both in music and print form. In 1994, ISD Records' first release was Skrewdriver's final and posthumous album *Hail Victory* (*Sieg Heil* in German) featuring both the ISD Records and C18 names on the layout.[181]

When Combat 18 took over Blood & Honour, it combined the financing received from music sales with ambitious racist goals. In particular, Combat 18 sought to use money raised from music endeavors to finance an "Aryan homeland" in central Essex where the Sargent brothers lived. *The Order* explained it would be "a white only area within" the United Kingdom and it needed white males willing to move there and work seven days a week.[182] While Charlie was happy to receive some support for the idea, he complained "there is still a lack of belief or hobbyist syndrome affecting half of our movement."[183] He hoped that his dream of a "whites only" nation in Essex would become a reality in the near future, including a farm to feed "national socialists" and use of the property for "celebrations."[184]

After the BNP's 1993 election victory, police received word about opposition plans to attack the group, and the BNP responded by creating a "security fund" to protect members and its bookshop.[185] Tyndall also described an incident in which a group of opponents "six times the size of the BNP team" attacked party members selling papers and the BNP members were arrested.[186] In response, the BNP "formulated an elaborate plan" to host the annual rally by rerouting people by bus to hear party speakers as well as American lawyer Kirk Lyons and National Democratic Party of Germany leader Günter Deckert.[187] The concern was real. In April 1994, a bomb was mailed to the BNP bookstore and Alf Waite, head of party administration, "escaped major injury" when the bomb exploded in front of him.[188] Peter Rushton, who was in the bookshop later in the day after the bombing, recalled that Waite avoided serious injury by turning away when he saw a spark, causing his face to get singed instead of being blinded.[189] Other BNP figures reported attacks, such as one at Tyndall's home, and there was an assault on the BNP's building.[190] Likewise in June 1994, Michael Newland, BNP press officer, was assaulted at his home.[191] Despite the attacks and negative press, the BNP boasted it was gaining support and the press reported a "huge increase" in BNP votes in council elections throughout London.[192]

Street Terror

Combat 18 solidified as a group following media reports about racist violence and its open support for Nazism. The BNP's official policy stated that party members were expected to be "peaceful" with everyone, including ethnic minorities.[193] Similarly, the BNP South Wales branch stated that it "condemned" racial hatred and told readers to focus on "lawful action" against politicians.[194] Yet the reality was much different. In 1994, David Myatt, formerly a British Movement figure in the 1970s, re-emerged in fascist politics, explaining that "through" the BNP he aimed to "make my noble vision real."[195] Decades earlier he had been involved in violence and disrupting opponents' meetings. After joining the BNP in 1994, Myatt described how he "gave a personal pledge of loyalty to Combat 18's leader, Charlie Sargent, and his brother, Steve."[196] Myatt further explained, "Combat 18 had built up a fearsome reputation and done what no other group had done—gained street power from those opposed to National-Socialism."[197] He later wrote articles supporting Combat 18, including calls for "bringing down the system," and hypothesized about how the "Zionist Occupation Government" would respond.[198] Indeed, the ties between the BNP and violent plans were obvious, with media attention linking skinhead music and BNP members to racial violence.[199]

For members of the BNP and C18 whites were the victims, and BNP literature only fed that belief. In fact, readers who uncritically accepted the BNP's claims feared for their lives. With headlines such as "Murdered for Being White," *British Nationalist* described the death of a white teenager as "the latest in a series of race attacks against whites in Kings Cross."[200] Another headline, "Is This the Britain You Want?," featured a large photograph of a knife stuck into a white male's head.[201] The newspaper discussed "Asian race violence," with "lone whites" being attacked by dozens of non-whites.[202] Other BNP reports warned about "ethnic cleansing" involving "anti-white race hate extremists" and the "race-hate killing" of whites.[203] The BNP painted a picture that whites were under deadly threat and engaged in a war on the streets of England.

On April 22, 1993 Stephen Lawrence, a black teenager, was killed in a stabbing while waiting for a bus in southeast London by a group of white men who had made racial taunts. Police immediately identified the suspects, but they were not arrested, leading to increasingly harsh public criticism. In the context of other racially motivated attacks, accusations about police indifference and corruption became prominent themes for anti-racists. Lawrence's death, as a racially motivated crime, became a landmark case and was the subject of thousands of news stories about the police's inability to punish those responsible for the unprovoked racial murder of a teenager.[204] After the failure to prosecute the five suspects, who were publicly identified in the media, the government began an inquiry and its final report concluded that "institutional racism" within the Metropolitan Police Service led the authorities to mishandle the case and let the suspects get away.[205] The report made seventy recommendations for police to build better relations with ethnic communities, which led to changes in how the police operate.[206] In 2012, two of the accused were convicted of the murder, one of whom, Gary Dobson, had admitted killing Lawrence during a Combat 18 gathering.[207]

Violent activity was promoted and celebrated in C18's self-reporting. Alongside news clippings about racial violence and quotes from Adolf Hitler, Steve wrote: "The British government has clearly showed that terrorism does work if waged long enough… Imagine if the first blacks off the boats here had been stoned, and the Asian shops burnt to the ground."[208] The issue included "Ten Principles of National Socialist Thought" from Harold Covington's National Socialist White People's Party in North Carolina as well as newspaper reports about C18, "the Nazi terror group," burning a car owned by an anti-fascist.[209] Every subsequent issue contained news about Combat 18 violence, which increased in volume by several pages in later publications.[210] Meanwhile, police began intensifying their efforts against C18. In 1995, Steve wrote that ZOG, the Zionist Occupation Government, had raided C18 members' homes in London and Essex and confiscated CDs.[211] This did not stop its activities. By spring 1995, *Putsch* marked the start of its third year by discussing celebrations for Hitler's birthday and St. George's Day.[212]

Aside from random racial assaults on British streets, *Redwatch* and *Combat 18* magazines spread fear and promoted violence. *Redwatch*, a crude typewritten publication using a North Carolina post office box address in the United States, did not list any authors, but contained the names and alleged addresses of anti-fascist writers and Anti-Fascist Action supporters as well as details about their size and subgroupings. For example, *Redwatch*'s final issue claimed that Red Action in London had only sixty active members and after listing the names and locations, it told readers: "it is time these wretched scum got a dose of their own medicine."[213] Subsequently a new black glossy magazine with the Combat 18 name as the title and featuring the Totenkopf (death's head), explained, "we cannot fight them on their terms," but "all is not lost."[214] It continued, "we must build at grass root[s] level a movement which is not interested in playing political games" and get into peak physical condition "for the final conflict."[215] The magazine provided a "how to" for organizing a "cell" to avoid law enforcement detection by staying in small groups with personal friends and gathering information on "enemies."[216] It also contained ideological instruction, with articles about Ian Stuart and former American Nazi Party leader George Lincoln Rockwell (1918–1967) as well as about the BNP's building being attacked. More than that, the magazine also contained lists of names and phone numbers, and asked for information on "reds in your area."[217] Similar to *Redwatch*, no authors were listed, and the address was a post office box in North Carolina operated by Covington.[218] The second issue of *Combat 18*, which was erroneously labeled the third, "welcomed" readers to their "favourite hate-zine" and asked if the reader had the "bollox to fight."[219] The issue included articles about a man who murdered a homosexual, a page about killing a white woman who loved a black man, bomb making instructions, addresses of "traitors" and even alleged Anti-Nazi League membership lists.

As Combat 18 was promoting violence against its perceived opponents, Blood & Honour received new life. Its magazine was published on a regular basis, had more content and cross-promoted the C18 publications *Putsch* and *The Order*.[220] *Blood & Honour* magazine stimulated interest in the music sold by ISD Records, such as Razors Edge's album *Whatever It Takes*, which was featured on the magazine's cover with an interview explaining that the music was available for sale from *The Order*.[221] In addition, Will Browning became the vocalist for a new version of No Remorse, which released *Barbecue in Rostock* (1996), referring to hundreds of German far-right supporters burning an apartment building that housed asylum seekers in 1992.[222] The music was more violent and offensive than earlier Rock Against Communism music and linked C18 to murder. One song from the album was "Zigger, Zigger, Shoot Those Fucking Niggers" with lyrics that included: "C18 you're just a killing machine, whatever it takes you know what I mean" and "don't try and mess with the master race, 'cause if you do we'll smash your face."[223]

The C18-led Blood & Honour forged international links and exported its violent calls for racial revolution. In 1995, Blood & Honour claimed it was "growing faster" than "ever" and had branches in fifteen countries.[224] Though British bands were the focal point, many groups, such as RaHoWa (Racially Holy War) from Canada, were featured in the magazine, which ended with the words "victory or death."[225] Blood & Honour also built close ties with Swedish and Danish extremists, including NS88 Videos in Denmark, which sold videos of skinhead concerts through a crude computer-printed catalog.[226] NS88 Videos complimented ISD Records by releasing videos of the concerts and racial violence, but also operated an international "club house" for concerts in southern Sweden named Valhalla.[227] According to an American named Bart who lived at the location, NS88 Videos was started by Marcel Schilf, who also worked with Marko Jäsä Järvinen from Finland in releasing *Kriegsberichter*, a video series featuring music and glorifying skinhead violence.[228] Bart met Schilf in 1994 through another American contact and visited London, making friends with Combat 18 members such as Browning as well as musicians from Razors Edge and Squadron.[229] Bart became friends with Scandinavian skinheads and was invited to help Schilf and Erik Blücher with NS88 Videos, NS Records and Ragnarok Records.[230] After just a few years, several European documentaries featured Bart, Schilf and Blücher, including Bart's visit to an "international" meeting in Belgrade, Serbia around the time of the NATO bombing campaign.[231]

Country-specific magazines in support of the new Blood & Honour were printed throughout North America and Europe, even in locations where its racist content was banned.[232] Meanwhile Blood & Honour in England hosted large concerts, notably the September 1994 Ian Stuart Memorial, which included performers from Italy and France along with an audience of hundreds from Belgium, Denmark, France, Germany, Italy and Spain.[233] The group continued to organize annual concerts that attracted hundreds, with a 1995 Ian Stuart concert, a St. George's Day celebration in 1996 and an Oswald Mosley memorial in 1997 in addition to concerts in smaller venues throughout Britain. Yet the travel was not in one direction. In 1995, for example, Charlie traveled to Roskilde for a Rudolf Hess memorial event and met with Jonni Hansen, leader of the National Socialist Movement of Denmark.[234]

The prominence of violence and the association with skinheads was harming British fascism's already limited electoral prospects. As a result, the BNP publicly denounced both Combat 18 and skinhead music. Tyndall considered classical music to be the proper representation of "white" music, whereas BNP member Ian Christie wrote that country and western music, described as "the indigenous music of the Southern States of America," was "enjoyed by white people the world over."[235] He claimed that it was the music of the "majority" and an "emotive expression of white consciousness."[236] Tyndall criticized using rock music for political objectives, describing how the "large numbers of rebellious youngsters whose opinions leaned in a nationalist direction" ended up "more interested in entertainment than politics."[237] Tyndall favored the classical music of Ludwig van Beethoven and condemned the rock genre, arguing: "We are deluged with alien music because alien forces have captured the nerve centres of our culture."[238]

Though disapproving of rock music, Tyndall and the BNP's harshest criticism of C18 concerned its promotion of racial violence. As Combat 18 attracted newspaper coverage, the BNP worked to build on Beackon's successful election; although he failed to be re-elected in May 1994, he ran another campaign in a different ward.[239] The BNP leadership dispatched Edmonds to meet with C18 leaders with the aim of getting them to tone down their activities and work with the BNP in campaigns as they had done before.[240] However, this failed to alter C18's path.[241] Tyndall accused C18 of "doing the enemy's work" by "poisoning our party from within" when it should be "in better shape."[242] He denounced Combat 18's "policy of violence," which might be "seductive" to some but could cause the government "to imprison our leaders and close us down."[243] Tyndall also responded to C18's "lies" denying that BNP membership lists had been given to police and claiming that the BNP "welcomed transvestites" to join.[244] While he did not name the Sargent brothers, he wondered why the government did not prosecute C18 leaders and hinted that Harold Covington had fed information to law enforcement.[245] Tyndall concluded that "it is no accident" that "disruptive action against our party started" following Beackon's victory.[246] Nonetheless, C18 supporters continued to attend BNP meetings, notably the 1995 annual rally where they were accused of disturbing speeches, and it was said that their "bad manners" did not win "friends."[247]

C18, on the other hand, accused BNP members of working against its political goals. For example, Peter Rushton was accused of passing information to political opponents, and it was alleged that Butler and Tony Lecomber had turned Tyndall against C18.[248] In response, C18 aligned itself with the more radical National Socialist Alliance and included the group's logo on the covers of *Putsch*, and it grew increasingly negative about Tyndall and the BNP.[249] According to Nigel Copsey, the National Socialist Alliance was C18's "political wing," a June 1994 byproduct of dissension in the BNP's ranks.[250] In a subsequent article, Tyndall mocked C18's claims that elections were "a waste of time," telling readers that the "group's 'revolutionary' activity has consisted of the beating up of two women and a brick through an old man's window."[251] He concluded, "we hope very much that this is the last time" to write about "this group of criminals, mobsters and losers."[252]

Combat 18 started to fracture under internal and external pressure. By late 1995, Charlie and Browning had been charged with violating the Race Relations Act and *Putsch* was raising money for legal support.[253] Upon their release, the two clashed over revenue from record sales, which was estimated to be a minimum of £200,000.[254] In early 1997, Charlie wrote that ISD Records "has proved to be no more then [*sic*] another money making scam by its owner."[255] He explained that revenue could have been used to buy a headquarters and equipment, but instead went into Browning's "pocket."[256] In February 1997, Charlie and friend Martin Cross "lured" Browning to Charlie's home to exchange address lists and money.[257] Browning, who was driven to the residence by C18 member and musician Chris Castle, waited in the car while Castle made the exchange. Castle was stabbed in the lungs and heart as he left the home and later died at the hospital. Charlie and Cross were arrested and charged with murder.[258] As the two were being held for the murder, Browning, Charlie and Cross pled guilty to inciting hatred in the 1995 case and received sentences ranging from twelve to seventeen months.[259] In early 1998, Charlie and Cross were convicted of murder.[260] Yet *Blood & Honour* continued, with the ninth issue telling readers that the magazine had a new address because Charlie had been "forced" out for "gross misconduct within the movement, which we shall not go into."[261] Explaining to readers that the new staff had the subscription list, "[t] here is too much negativeness [*sic*] within our movement."[262] A subsequent new version of the magazine was friendly towards the people and groups it had previously criticized. This included praising Tyndall and the BNP for their efforts in the 1997 general election.[263] Meanwhile, with the C18 leadership in jail, ISD Records moved to Denmark and was operated by Schilf and Blücher, who kept the name but folded the operation into NS88 Videos, NS Records and Ragnarok Records.[264]

International Third Position and Third Way

Following the NF's collapse in the late 1980s, key NF figures searched for new ways to express their politics and spark cultural, political and social revolutions. Alan Sykes explained that while the NF's Third Position concept evolved out of a desire to establish a spiritual basis for revolution, it eventually grew to incorporate aspects of the anarchist tradition of the radical right, including "the need for sacrifice, ruralism and distributism."[265] Indeed, the former NF leaders were honing their international contacts and refining their Third Positionist ideas. On one side, Harrington and several others established the Third Way, which continued with the economic policies of the NF from the 1980s but adopted more liberal social views on Palestine and gay rights.[266] On the other side, Griffin, Holland and several former NF members formed the International Third Position (ITP), which turned its attention to international alliances and focused on a "back to the land" approach. At the same time, the NFSG, led by Ian Anderson, became the official NF and attempted to return the party to its glory of the 1970s.

In March 1990, Harrington, Graham Williamson and David Kerr started the Third Way, which retained some of the NF's Political Soldier principles. For this new group, the "third way" was "the Third Position, whose name reflects our opposition to both capitalism and communism."[267] Former NF member Troy Southgate described the group as "far more conservative" in some ways, such as "supporting anti-federalist and 'save the pound' campaigns."[268] Indeed, the Third Way focused on the nation, but remained opposed to the parliamentary system and expected a "battle" with capitalism.[269] Like the NF, the Third Way was interested in black nationalism because "[f]or black and white alike it means a return to one's innermost self."[270] Focused on green issues as well as music and literature, the group wanted to offer an alternative to mainstream politics and society.[271] Regional divisions of the Third Way were started in Liverpool, opposing the European Community with calls for Liverpool autonomy and "local democracy."[272] The group remained small, mostly led by Harrington, and its publications continued for the next decade albeit with increasing infrequency.[273] Following Prime Minister Tony Blair's adoption of the term "third way," Harrington differentiated his group from Blair by calling his ideas a "rehash" of the American New Deal and neo-Thatcherite economic policies while Harrington's Third Way politics sought "social solidarity" under state regulation with a highly skilled work force.[274]

In response to Harrington issuing a press release apologizing for the NF's anti-Semitism, in autumn 1989 Griffin and Holland left the party and began discussions with their NF supporters to form a new group for "revolutionary nationalism." Griffin and Holland organized the International Third Position with Robert Fiore and NF members Colin Todd, Phil Andrews, Gareth Hurley and Troy Southgate.[275] With some leaders, notably Fiore and Holland, supporting Marcel Lefebvre (1905–1991) and the Catholic Society of Saint Pius X that rejected the Second Vatican Council, the ITP "took the disastrous road towards reactionary fascism."[276] Griffin, Holland and Todd released a video, *Revolution in Action*, to attract NF supporters to the ITP.[277] In the video, Holland criticized Harrington's apology to the Jewish community as well as the NF's structure and strategy.[278] A sequel, *Revolution in Action II*, included ITP leaders as well as local and regional organizers, such as Hurley, who criticized Harrington for trying to "privatise" the NF.[279]

The ITP moved some of its operations to northern France, establishing a community by fixing "dilapidated farm buildings."[280] Holland relocated there to oversee the project as Todd and Fiore traveled around Britain to recruit members.[281] Started in early 1990, the property comprised ten acres purchased for a £30,000 mortgage, which included a barn and a chapel with plans for farming and a publishing operation.[282] An ITP newsletter, *News from Somewhere*, announced that the project's goal was to build a "co-operative" because "our society is now so revolting," naming drugs, AIDS, racial conflict and pollution as serious problems.[283] In detailing their progress, the unnamed author, likely Holland, described the difficulty of preparing the property for human habitation and solicited money to finish the printing area, rooms and chapel and to plant trees.[284] The newsletter included photographs of the property, including the landscape and the transformation of the buildings.[285] Todd, who later moved to France to help with the remodeling, described it as a beautiful property that needed workers to make it livable.[286]

In terms of purpose and ideology, the ITP was not a political party with electoral goals, but rather a socio-religious project with an international outlook. Andrews described the ITP as pitched to supporters as an "umbrella" organization to unify a variety of different extremists.[287] The ITP declared itself to be "a federation of nationalist individuals, groups, associations and movements from across Europe" that was united around the ITP's ten principles.[288] These principles included the "moulding" of a new spiritual man, the establishment of a moral order, anti-materialism, anti-Zionism, "popular rule," racial separatism, preservation of the environment, opposition to international finance, Third Positionism on ownership and a "national revolution worldwide."[289] Smaller groups, such as the ITP students, denounced student loans for causing debt, with criticism of usury, teachers' unions promoting "liberal" education and American "imperialism."[290] According to Southgate's review of its policies, structure and personalities: "the ITP was Fascist at its very core."[291]

The International Third Position proved unable to attain its goals and tension in the organization caused by distance between countries increased. The tactics and struggles were reminiscent of what had happened to the NF. In December 1990, just weeks before the Gulf War, Holland and Todd traveled to Baghdad, Iraq.[292] According to Southgate, they went with Malik Afzal from the Union of European Muslims, who reportedly disappeared after the trip.[293] The ITP members received an invitation from the Palestine Liberation Organization (PLO) and were official guests of Iraq's Ministry of Religious Affairs.[294] The visit lasted two weeks, during which they stayed in the Al Rasheed Hotel, which was hosting Jean-Marie Le Pen at the same time.[295] The men traveled to tourist sites, including a synagogue, and spoke with their hosts about "Jews" and Adolf Hitler.[296] In addition to the stay in Iraq, the men made a three-day side visit to Jordan, where they stayed with "Palestinian leaders" and visited "hospitalized Palestinian youth who had been wounded in the Intifada."[297] According to Todd, the goal was to acquire funding to support their activities, but as with the NF and Libya, no money was received.[298]

As for Griffin, he was injured in northern France and returned to England for several months to recover. He then received a phone call from Holland telling him to convert to Catholicism or burn in hell.[299] An email sent later by the ITP claimed Griffin had left the organization after a year and that he was very critical of the group, including its religious direction.[300] The ITP was financed by Fiore, who had several successful businesses in London, and most of the ITP's publications were focused on the local grassroots level, with little political activity.[301] The organization, throughout its existence, lacked a clear structure or "party line," which frustrated its "mishmash of neo-Nazi skinheads and bourgeois Catholics."[302] After four years, Southgate found that "none" of the group's plans for small businesses and workshops had been "put into operation."[303] The thousands of pounds invested by supporters were "lost," including money from people who had taken out second mortgages.[304]

In September 1992 the internal pressures, including disagreements about religion and complaints about money, caused the ITP to split.[305] Southgate, who had been a member of the NF since 1984, along with others criticized Fiore for his capitalist businesses in London, which included a travel agency.[306] Furthermore, Colin Todd said that Griffin had taken money for a printing press.[307] Holland and Fiore were accused of "stealing" financing for property in northern France.[308] Yet Southgate explained that the "most decisive factor" was the leadership's "obsession with Catholicism and its gradual descent into the reactionary waters of neo-fascism."[309] The ITP became the centerpiece of the *Final Conflict* magazine edited by Hurley, in close association with Fiore.[310] In February 1993, ITP members traveled to Croatia to deliver aid and learn about the conflict.[311] A video of the trip was made available to ITP supporters for £25, and plans were announced to continue providing aid and to build an orphanage.[312]

International Third Position activists branched out in many different directions. Some members, such as Southgate, went on to form the English Nationalist Movement, and the ITP publishing arm, the Rising Press, continued to print books about Catholicism, Strasserism and Holocaust denial.[313] In 1996 the ITP launched another "village project" by purchasing an "abandoned village in Spain," calling on supporters to make the new property habitable.[314] British and Spanish supporters sharing a similar ideology and goals joined forces to fix up the buildings.[315] A few years later *The Guardian* reported that Fiore had bought seven properties in Los Pedriches, a rural Spanish village that lacked running water and power.[316] In 1998, the English Nationalist Movement became the National Revolutionary Faction, rejecting Third Positionism, and Southgate later associated with the National-Anarchist movement.[317] After Rosine de Bounevialle's death on Christmas Day 1999, Todd became the editor of *Candour* and got involved with the A.K. Chesterton Trust.[318] Meanwhile, Holland left the ITP in 2001 and moved to Ireland at an unknown date, and the organization "disappeared a year or two later."[319] Filling the transnational void left by the ITP, in 2004 the European National Front was launched under Fiore's leadership as the general secretary and Adam Gmurczyk, head of Narodowe Odrodzenie Polski (National Revival of Poland) and an ITP activist, as chair of its Political Council.[320] The European National Front called for "reconstruction and development of sovereign national states, based on strong family and national property."[321] Gareth Hurley wrote that an ITP "reunion" in July 2004 marked the official foundation of the European National Front, which had an online presence until early 2009.[322]

As the NF leadership from the late 1980s developed new organizations, Ian Anderson's National Front Support Group became known simply as the NF and sought to challenge Tyndall's BNP for the position of leading fascist party. By this time, the NF was producing several publications, including *The Flag* newspaper and *Vanguard* magazine, and it started a new publication, *Lionheart*. *Vanguard*, which was launched shortly after the 1986 split, was edited by Tom Acton as an "independent" magazine, but "editorially" it supported Anderson's NF.[323] For instance, it published an article by Anderson, who wrote: "the NF has built itself as a viable political machine" that will continue to contest elections.[324] Shortly after the Political Soldier NF disbanded, Acton called for Anderson's NF to receive the "intelligent commitment of all our members" to build the party again.[325] Anderson, meanwhile, saw a need to have his own magazine and started *Lionheart* to publish political and social commentary from authors. In its third issue, *Lionheart* published the results of a poll about immigration conducted by *The Sun* that showed 98% of readers were against immigration.[326] Other articles argued that Oi! "was white, working class British rock music," which was "killed" by the Southall riot and its association with neo-Nazism from the release of *Strength Through Oi!* (1981).[327] Shortly thereafter, the NF purchased *Vanguard* and merged it with *Lionheart*, while The Flag was purchased from Martin Wingfield, becoming NF property in 1992.[328]

Despite having a widely recognized name, the NF did not succeed under Anderson during the 1990s. The BNP's growth, including its local council victory in 1993, attracted enthusiasm and financial support, and Anderson was unable to compete. In addition, Anderson's leadership style and negative rumors about his personal life did little to gain the confidence of the broader fascist community. Matthew Collins, an NF member who later worked for *Searchlight*, put the NF membership at no more than eight hundred members and described Anderson as "the most manipulative and greedy man I had ever known."[329] Without competition from a similarly named group, the NF announced in summer 1990 that it would run sixty seats in the next election and build its support from Martin Wingfield's campaign in the year's previous European Parliamentary election.[330] Yet the NF failed to raise enough money or generate sufficient enthusiasm to meet this goal. Mark Cotterill, a member of the NF who worked on a campaign in Birmingham, recalled that the election was a "complete flop" and party membership dropped below one hundred by mid-1992.[331] During the April 1992 general election, the NF contested only fourteen seats for a total of 3984 votes, which was an even poorer showing than the BNP's thirteen seats that won 7005 votes.[332] Its policies were similar to those of the BNP, which included "separating" races in education "pending" repatriation and opposing the European Community.[333] Yet the election result was proof of what the newspapers had been reporting: the BNP was now the most popular fascist party.

In the aftermath of the election, the NF struggled financially and membership continued to decline the following year, when the BNP won its September 1993 campaign in Millwall. The NF members thought their ideas resonated with the public, but the negativity attached to the party name was holding it back. In July 1995, the NF leadership, specifically Martin Wingfield, proposed "a resolution to change the name of the NF to the National Democratic Party (to be known on all our literature as the National Democrats)."[334] All the party literature, at the national and local levels, was changed to the National Democrats and a new manifesto and constitution were published in early 1996.[335] The constitution mirrored elements of the NF, including calling itself "a party of British racial nationalism" and stating that the nation "must be of exclusively European and predominately British racial descent."[336] Anderson remained the leader of the newly named organization and the party hoped to stir up interest by campaigning in local elections.[337] In May 1997, the National Democrats ran twenty-one candidates, including Anderson, and received 10,829 votes compared to the BNP's fifty-seven candidates and 35,832 vote total.[338] In a post-election analysis, Anderson admitted they expected "no breakthrough" and discussed targeting specific wards in local elections to build support.[339] However, 1997 was Anderson's last National Democrats campaign and he dropped out of national politics to focus on local community efforts, leading the Epping Community Action Group until his 2011 death.[340]

Despite Anderson's extended NF leadership, the NF's name still resonated with extremists. A group of members split from the National Democrats to keep the NF name, but this NF proved to be a mere shadow of the party's previous membership. John McAuley, who opposed the new name, became the leader and chair of a faction called the NF, with a publication titled *The Flame*. NF finances from May 1997, for example, revealed that its own leadership believed it was operating "as a second class outfit" without a computer or typewriter, and monthly donations totaled £166.50, with one person donating £100.[341] Nevertheless, this group survived through several leadership changes, despite its indirect links to the NF of the 1970s. In June 1997, the

NF was featured on ITV's *The Cook Report*, where NF member Wayne Ashcroft was documented working with Nick Griffin to pool extremist resources at a time when the NF was struggling in the BNP's shadow. Despite Ashcroft being filmed making offensive racist statements, the NF celebrated the attention and even sold video tapes of the broadcast at meetings to raise money.[342] The attempted merger failed and the NF remained a small group even for the fascist fringe. It ran six candidates in the 1997 national election, receiving 2716 votes, and in 2001 contested five seats to get 2484 votes.[343]

The Search for a New Image

After the BNP's September 1993 council seat victory, members believed they were on the verge of more successes throughout the country. Membership grew, donations increased and there was excitement about political opportunities that had not existed for the fascists since the 1970s. Yet as the decade continued, it did not win a single election, which discouraged some entirely, while others saw this failure as an issue of image, not an ideological problem. For those who wanted the organization to reform, transforming the party's image proved difficult as the conservative-minded members wanted to keep the BNP the same.

In the early 1990s, many members approved of Tyndall's leadership and the party's old-fashioned post-war fascist image, while Combat 18 opposed participation in electoral contests and sought out violence. When Nick Griffin joined the BNP, Eddy Butler and Tony Lecomber wanted to rebrand the BNP as a viable third party similar to the Front National in France.[344] Butler and Lecomber faced threats and attacks from C18 members for their attempts to enter the political mainstream. C18, for instance, published threats such as: "Butler your condition is terminal and we are going to put you out of your misery."[345] Butler was subsequently stabbed by Will Browning on Good Friday in 1994 at Anthony Hancock's printing factory.[346] As C18 received more negative publicity for its actions, many BNP members came to believe that a softer image would improve its electoral returns.

Throughout 1994, the party hoped to expand its campaign efforts in East London by concentrating on the Isle of Dogs. Tyndall explained, "for the first time ever a genuine nationalist and patriotic political party is making a serious bid to take control of a local authority."[347] The plan was that if all the BNP candidates were elected, the party would have a 3–2 majority and control £23 million.[348] Tyndall argued that such a victory would produce "vast" results that would bring it positive media attention and credibility.[349] The heavily promoted council elections were linked by the party to Derek Beackon, who told people to "vote BNP."[350] None of the party's candidates won. The loss was spun as a "success" based on improved election percentages, including an increase in Millwall where Beackon had won the previous year.[351] The BNP held a rally on the Isle of Dogs with over a hundred supporters to announce its "strategic and tactical aims for the remainder of 1994 and for 1995."[352] At the rally, Tyndall concurred with the other speakers about opposing "street-gang" tactics, but "emphasised that this did not mean that the BNP was becoming 'soft' or abandoning the firm cutting edge of its principles."[353] Tyndall, meanwhile, ran in the Dagenham by-election, earning 7% of the vote, and the party declared it a success with the "first ever deposit retained."[354] Tony Lecomber's analysis of the September Shadwell Ward by-election in Tower Hamlets concluded that the party could win by "benefitting from the Liberal/Tory decline" and "fewer non-whites will definitely mean fewer votes for Labour."[355]

Though 1994 started with great expectations for continued local victories, the year ended in disappointment, with every single BNP candidate failing to get elected, and even Beackon lost his bid for re-election that year.[356] Butler was frustrated that the BNP leadership was not adopting the changes and techniques used to win the Millwall election and was shocked that no one ever contacted him to ask how he ran the successful 1993 campaign.[357] In early 1995 Griffin re-entered politics, building ties with BNP members and writing a letter to *Spearhead*.[358] Even *Blood & Honour* magazine discussed news about Griffin, describing how he was "trying to worm his way back" and claiming that "Ian Stuart didn't trust him nor should you."[359] He began regularly contributing articles to *Spearhead*, such as one about the "Jewish" influence in Hollywood's "propaganda war waged against the white race."[360]

In 1995, the BNP announced it would run fifty candidates in the 1997 general election, believing that the continued success of Labour would help the BNP win Conservative votes and that this number of candidates would get it five minutes of radio and television broadcast time.[361] The first candidates selected for the election were Beackon and Tyndall, with the party targeting the East End.[362] This was a major announcement because it marked the first time in fourteen years that the party would run such a large number of candidates in an election, and it hoped that distributing two million pieces of BNP literature would aid in the recruitment of "many more members."[363] The BNP also launched its first website to publish an online version of British Nationalist, calling it a "momentous" occasion as more people were gaining access to the Internet.[364] Meanwhile, William Pierce, leader of the National Alliance in the United States, spoke at the BNP's annual meeting and signed copies of his book, *The Turner Diaries*, which made mainstream news earlier that year for inspiring Timothy McVeigh to bomb the Oklahoma City federal building.[365] The visit was celebrated with a photograph of Pierce sitting to Tyndall's right appearing on the cover of *Spearhead*.[366] The accompanying article described Pierce's speech as "stressing the differences in operating conditions between American and British patriotic movements" and discussing the National Alliance's operations.[367] Ultimately, however, Tyndall admitted that 1995 "proved not to be one of our best years."[368] He blamed the BNP failures on an "all-out war" from "combined forces" from the "establishment."[369] Though there were internal "enemies" within the BNP, people's expectations that the party would win local elections led "a higher-than-average number of people" to not renew their party membership.[370]

Other party activists were developing strategies to improve the BNP's image. Tony Lecomber explained that the reason for the party running fifty candidates in the next election was to recruit new members in "big numbers."[371] Given that the party gained eight hundred members shortly after the Millwall victory, the "publicity" from the election was "worth millions."[372] Yet other figures saw it as an issue of misinformation and ideology. Griffin explained that while there was little an organization "can do to influence the outcome of the battle of ideas," the party could play a role by gaining a "foothold in Britain's universities" and fighting against "the so-called 'Holocaust'."[373]

Griffin became increasingly involved with the party and started writing articles for several magazines. After leaving the International Third Position and seeing the BNP gain new members, he explained that he wanted to help the BNP avoid the mistakes that had been made in the 1980s.[374] After visiting the BNP Croydon branch, he was introduced to several people including Paul Ballard, editor of *The Rune* magazine.[375] Later Griffin became editor of *The Rune* and it was advertised in Tyndall's *Spearhead* as "produced in partnership" with the BNP's Surrey branch.[376] *The Rune* initially published articles about Jews being "a powerful compact racial minority with an influence out of proportion" and the rapid growth of Blood & Honour.[377] Later issues edited by Griffin discussed Nazi history and "six million" television viewers being "bored to death by a series of endless programmes about Auschwitz."[378] Another article by Griffin addressed critics opposed to contesting seats in the next general election, arguing that fifty lost deposits, costing £500 each for a total of £25,000, was cheaper than buying time on ITV for £1,500,000 and would "provide a great opportunity for recruitment on which to base solid progress."[379] He also continued writing articles for *Spearhead*, including one that "disputes the trendy thesis that the white heterosexual male is obsolete."[380]

After seeing the BNP grow stronger and attract a new generation of members, Griffin joined the party in 1995.[381] At the time, Butler and Lecomber were pushing for the BNP to moderate its policies and engage with more local communities to win office. In contrast, Griffin described himself as a hardliner who was brought in by Tyndall to support the leadership's uncompromising policy.[382] Soon Tyndall was paying Griffin £30 for an article each month, which once again put Griffin's name and ideas in front of extremist readers. In April 1996, this relationship expanded when Tyndall invited Griffin to become assistant editor of *Spearhead*, initially for £200, which allowed Tyndall to focus more on party matters and revising his book, *The Eleventh Hour*.[383] The relationship with Griffin provided Tyndall with support so that he could remain a hardliner and oppose the moderate tendencies of the others.

In summer 1996 the BNP started raising money for the 1997 general election, with a target of £10,000 to be used for the party broadcast, election literature, extra phones and party travel.[384] The party gains stagnated, which was explained as "an accelerating swing towards Labour which has greatly reduced opportunities for the BNP."[385] The party also "permanently" closed the BNP bookshop, owned by Edmonds, in the face of mounting legal fees over zoning issues that the party believed would be better spent on the next election.[386] Tyndall remarked that as 1997 began, the BNP saw the year as "more encouraging" after suffering from "tremendous internal harm" in 1994 and 1995.[387] Writing about a change in "propaganda," the BNP focused on a "broader section of the social spectrum" instead of limiting its literature to the politically "radical."[388] Policy would be "presented intelligently and addressed to a public now extending beyond the inner city 'racist' constituency."[389] Yet Tyndall stressed there would be "no softening up."[390] The party encouraged BNP members to watch the broadcast and tell others about it.[391]

In the May 1997 general election, the BNP ran in fifty-six constituencies and campaigned on Euroskepticism, anti-immigration, ending homelessness and supporting family values.[392] The party's sixty-page manifesto contained previous BNP and NF views on race and immigration, such as ending immigration and non-white repatriation as well as the usual refrain about social and economic decline.[393] Yet Tyndall's foreword to the manifesto was pessimistic, with the opening sentence stating the election "will itself solve nothing."[394] As the BNP and its critics predicted, the BNP failed to win any seats in the election with a total of 35,388 votes.[395] Nevertheless, the BNP declared "mission accomplished" by meeting its targets and received about 2000 requests for party information.[396] The peak performances were 7% in two East End seats as well as saving a deposit in Dewsbury.[397]

With continued election failures and not a single election victory in four years, party members were searching for new approaches to regain the momentum from the 1993 Millwall victory. Griffin wrote that the party could not depend on the strategy of large demonstrations to battle "the Reds," but needed "activities," such as "political guerilla warfare" that would be "short, legal, but noisy."[398] Griffin commented on the gains of Jean-Marie Le Pen's Front National in France, writing that there had been a tide of change in Europe and the BNP must overcome external and internal issues so Britain could follow the lead of France.[399] Griffin, in another article about the Front National, wrote that the BNP "will have to be better dressed and presented," become "more professional" and "sink" roots in the inner cities.[400]

The two key members involved in promoting a new image of the BNP were Butler and Lecomber. In spring 1997, the two launched *Patriot* magazine in support of the BNP, but argued that while similar European parties, such as the Front National in France, used "suits, smiles and good presentation," in Britain the party had not adopted "modern nationalism."[401] The publication featured an interview with Beackon about his 1993 victory as well as articles about election strategy by Lecomber and Butler.[402] The second issue featured Lecomber's analysis of the 1997 general election, which "exceeded" expectations by generating public interest and new members.[403] Moreover, Butler contributed a critical appraisal of NF and BNP history, discussing the negativity of Combat 18 as well as the Political Soldier NF, but he removed pointed criticism of Griffin at his request.[404] However, the magazine's objective, as reflected by the image of Le Pen on its cover, was to argue for a "populist" political approach with a "positive lead."[405] A few BNP members had a growing interest in Le Pen's party. Butler first visited the Front National's Paris office in the early 1990s, and also made visits between 1996 and 1999 to learn how the party had built a base of supporters.[406] In contrast, Tyndall addressed the April 1993 annual congress for the Nationalist Party of France and Europe (PFNE), a fringe "militant" group of people expelled from Le Pen's party, offering a short speech on behalf of the BNP.[407] Yet an article in *Patriot* by Michael Newland, former BNP press officer, and Edmonds discussed Le Pen and the Front National's relationship with the British press, arguing that the French party's increasing support showed the media misreporting.[408] The fourth issue of *Patriot* featured a discussion of Le Pen and the Front National's internal disputes.[409] In the same issue, an article by Jackie Cook argued the BNP needed to examine itself and put on a "caring face."[410] The interest in Le Pen's party was not limited to publications. In September 1997, the BNP accepted an invitation to attend the Front National's Red, White and Blue festival, with more than a dozen Britons traveling to Paris where BNP delegate Richard Edmonds was greeted at the event by Bruno Gollnisch.[411]

The need for a facelift was clear, due not only to previous neo-Nazi associations and Combat 18, but also the promotion of extremist literature. The BNP associated itself with books, such as American Nazi Party founder George Lincoln Rockwell's (1918–1967) *The Fable of the Ducks & the Hens*, which was promoted in *Spearhead* and sold by *The Rune*.[412] Rockwell's fairy-tale tract was a children's story about the failure of "ducks" and "hens" to assimilate and the "ducks" founding their own separate society.[413] Moreover, *Who Are the Mind-Benders*, an anonymous tract produced by Griffin, was launched at a 1997 BNP rally and designed "to spread the truth."[414] The publication claimed "that members of the Jewish community (whether practising or not) exercise a power of influence in Britain's mass media that are out of all proportion to their numbers in the population."[415] Meanwhile, on top of the usual anti-fascist campaigns, ITV's *The Cook Report* featured Griffin and the remnants of the NF trying to pool their resources.[416] The BNP still had a public connection to skinheads, not only through the lingering news about Combat 18 but also because local branches were helping to host Blood & Honour events.[417] The BNP promoted the performances in its publication as well as a BNP benefit CD titled *Our Europe... Not Theirs*, about which the *British Nationalist* stated: "If you've not had a chance to hear white resistance music before or have just been wary, now's the time to get hold of your first CD."[418] The collection included songs, with titles such as "To the Gallows" and "This Land is Ours," by several different skinhead bands including Celtic Warrior, Avalon and Warlord (featuring former Skrewdriver guitarist Stigger).[419]

After the election Griffin and Paul Ballard were informed they would be prosecuted for violating the Public Order Act over statements "likely to stir up racial hatred" about the Holocaust published in *The Rune*.[420] Specifically, *The Rune* had published a letter by Michael A. Hoffman II, an American Holocaust denier, and included a reply that stated: "Such is the status of the Holohoax tale today… we will remain convinced that Mr. Irving's newly revised guesstimate is as fictitious as the sacred six million."[421] In April 1998 the case went to trial, with Griffin conducting his own defense, which included having Robert Faurisson, a Holocaust denier, appear as a witness for Griffin.[422] Ballard pleaded guilty and Griffin was found guilty by a jury.[423] According to Ballard, the trial was delayed for months and he "had problems over the years with the Security Service, including close surveillance (entry of my property in my absence) and harassment of various sorts."[424] Following the controversy, Griffin was featured on the cover of the BNP's newspaper with the headline "No to Race Tyranny."[425]

The BNP leadership was not receptive to changes being pushed by members because it was concerned that the party would become "soft." Some activists in the party believed Tyndall was out of step with the members and had failed to capitalize on the improvements in BNP campaigning tactics.[426] Indeed, Tyndall discussed the 1998 leadership plan, which focused on the quality of leaflets, publicity and "options" for shaping government policies.[427] Yet the party was successful at attracting more than a hundred people who were part of Ian Anderson's National Democrats, including Simon Darby and Sharron Edwards.[428] Griffin became more active in the BNP, including heading a countryside recruitment program by editing the *British Countryman* newspaper.[429] The party described itself as fighting against immigration, which was expanding into the countryside, and to save family farms. During a large London protest by the Countryside Alliance, the BNP reported that 30,000 copies of *British Countryman* were distributed.[430] By 1998, Griffin was increasing his involvement in reforming the BNP in the direction sought by Lecomber and Butler.[431] According to Griffin, Lecomber and Butler's publications did not influence him to moderate, but the way Griffin was portrayed on *The Cook Report* as well as his arrest convinced him that softening the BNP's approach would help the party.[432] He specifically credited Jonathan Marcus's book about Le Pen and the Front National as offering a blueprint for reforming the BNP.[433] To BNP members, Griffin argued that BNP "propaganda" should focus on the concepts of freedom, democracy, security and identity that would build the party into a mass movement.[434]

Leadership Challenge

During 1999, the BNP underwent several strategic and personnel changes. For the first time, the BNP decided to run candidates in the June 1999 European Parliamentary election, an institution it opposed, and by early 1999 it had raised £38,598 of its £50,000 campaign target.[435] The reason it contested European elections, according to Butler, was that the publicity it generated would help in local and national elections.[436] More than that, the campaign generated enthusiasm and the BNP celebrated the "rapid progress" of donations to support the election effort.[437] The funds were used for a television broadcast, an "Internet conference," professional development and a weekend festival for families.[438] At the same time, the Security Service announced its plan to "infiltrate far right groups," which was no doubt related to violence from groups such as Combat 18 and the public inquiry into Stephen Lawrence's murder.[449] Tyndall reacted angrily in a letter to law enforcement, concluding that their actions were "appalling" as they were taking a "political role" instead of "fighting real genuine crime."[440]

In February 1999, Griffin told the BNP leadership that he planned to challenge Tyndall to become party chair.[441] Griffin initially wanted to wait until he had built more support, but decided to act when Tyndall discussed amending the constitution to make it more difficult to seek party leadership.[442] Griffin had joined Lecomber and Butler's calls to reform the party and change its image to appear as a "modernized" political party. In late 1998, Griffin denounced "irresponsible political Peter Pans" who lacked the "ability" and "intention" of actually mounting a challenge for political power.[443] However, the article was prefaced with an "editor's note" from Tyndall that stated: "I have some doubts about NG's suggestions," such as getting more support "if only we modify our repatriation policy."[444] Despite Tyndall's resistance, Griffin continued to push for "professionalism" and to invite people with particular skills and talent to inform party leadership.[445] In an analysis of the BNP's "modernization," Nigel Copsey described how some activists saw Tyndall as an impediment to making political gains, and a 1999 leadership challenge made Griffin a moderate leader despite many people earlier regarding him as an unlikely reformer.[446] Copsey argued "that at the root of the party's ideological modernization is short-term political expediency: not so much a change of course as an opportune change of clothing."[447]

In April 1999, a serial bombing spree that targeted homosexual and ethnic communities provoked fear throughout the country. For nearly two weeks an unidentified bomber planted nail bombs at public places, hurting dozens and killing three people. The security services initially suspected the White Wolves, led by former C18 figure Del O'Connor, of being behind the attacks.[448] Yet the terrorist turned out to be David Copeland, who was identified by a co-worker based on security camera footage of him placing the bombs that was shown on television.[449] As the story unfolded, Copeland's links to neo-Nazi groups and the BNP were widely reported. Copeland was briefly a member of the BNP in 1997 and had been photographed with Tyndall at a BNP march.[450] Subsequently, Copeland joined the National Socialist Movement, which was founded in August 1997, first led by David Myatt and later Tony Williams.[451] The group was promoted in Steve Sargent's *The White Dragon* magazine and was disbanded following Copeland's bombing spree.[452] In Copeland's subsequent confession to police, he said his goal was "to cause a racial war in this country" where "there'd be a backlash from the ethnic minorities, then all the white people will go out and vote BNP."[453] Griffin responded by calling the reports "smears" and "innuendo" from the "alleged 'neo-Nazi' bombing campaign," and explained Copeland was only "briefly" involved with the BNP in 1997 and then "disappeared."[454] Griffin further wrote that Combat 18 was a Security Service "honeytrap" and that British intelligence had been involved with groups that provoked violence.[455]

The bombing did not prevent the BNP from achieving its highest number of votes in an election. The party's European campaign plan was simple and "can be summed up in three words: 'Get Britain Out'."[456] In the June European election, the party received more than 100,000 votes, which Griffin noted was "[d]espite all the smear-mongering about the London nail-bombs."[457] The party distributed 15,000,000 leaflets, pushing its ideas and views on race in local communities throughout

Britain.[458] Comparing the number of votes in the 1999 European election with the same areas in the 1997 general election, the party's percentage "doubled or even nearly trebled."[459] The election also showed that the BNP "can finance and run a nationwide campaign" and escape the "local pressure group category."[460] Moreover, it helped the party gain new members "from the thousands of follow-ups," which meant the campaign would have a "substantial" impact on growing the party.[461] However, the BNP criticized the media for not reporting about the party in the election, but instead referring to the United Kingdom Independence Party (UKIP) as representing the anti-European Union position.[462]

In July 1999, Griffin received the formal nomination for BNP leader, causing the two opposing sides to engage in a bitter party election for control.[463] Griffin was featured on the summer issue of *Patriot*'s cover with the words "new millennium… new leader" and a sympathetic interview inside.[464] Griffin described his switch from an "old-style nationalist hardliner" to a "moderniser" as a response to seeing that Butler, Newland and others were trying to change the party, C18 was causing disruption and the French Front National was winning public support after its transition.[465] That month Griffin was no longer in charge of *Spearhead* and Tyndall reacted to Griffin's party campaign by criticizing his leadership of the NF during the 1980s, including his visit to Libya and his "weird alliances."[466] Tyndall wrote that by "July 1996, Nick was still not a member of the BNP" due to his "ideological" commitment but soon changed his mind, and that Tyndall had welcomed his help in editing *Spearhead*.[467] Tyndall was also critical of *Patriot*, claiming it created "imaginary conflict" between modernizers and those accused of resisting change.[468] Tyndall was joined by several other BNP leaders in condemning Griffin for challenging Tyndall while they campaigned for the European election.[469] Additionally, Martin Webster re-emerged, distributing a printed newsletter titled *Loose Cannon* that, among other things, accused Griffin of being bisexual and having an affair with Webster in the 1980s.[470]

Griffin mounted an aggressive campaign, traveling the country and meeting with regional and local organizers.[471] He promised that if he won the election, he would build the party by holding regular meetings about party strategy, hosting national planning conferences, conducting a "skills audit" and fixing the "amateurish" BNP administration by appointing a treasurer and auditor.[472] Moreover, part of this "modernization" also included divorcing party literature from neo-Nazism and skinheads, which hurt the BNP's image.[473] Nigel Copsey wrote that "Griffin turned his back on the party's traditional demands for compulsory repatriation, he refused to countenance a return to the macho confrontational street marches of the 1970s and recommended, as an alternative, the creation of numerous special interest circles, the holding of family festivals and the adoption of more subtle and professional campaigning techniques."[474] Griffin used his connections with various BNP branches, distributing a booklet and audio tape with endorsements from reformers and highlighting his biography. The booklet featured contrasting images of Tyndall dressed as a neo-Nazi and Griffin in a suit, with comparisons between Griffin's University of Cambridge education and Tyndall's three "O" levels.[475] In terms of reforms, Griffin pledged to polish the party's image and organization, which he argued was holding the party back from making inroads with the public.[476] The audio cassette in the packet included a discussion by Griffin about improving the BNP's image to make it more voter-friendly and using "modern music to spread the white nationalist message" because "it's a very powerful medium and the multi-racial devil mustn't be left with all the tunes, good or otherwise."[477] He also called Webster's claims about a homosexual relationship "lies," then described Webster as a "bitter old poof" who was still upset about his removal from the NF by the youngsters.[478]

In September 1999, Griffin won the leadership challenge with over 60% of the vote, forcing Tyndall from his two-decade role as BNP chair.[479] Following the election, Tyndall wrote that he would "accept" the will of the BNP members and "remain in the party as an ordinary member."[480] However, the strained and bitter contest meant that Tyndall wanted "some operational distance" from Griffin while he devoted time to writing.[481] *Spearhead*, which was personally owned by Tyndall, would remain loyal to the BNP and respond to criticism of the BNP's publications.[482] To ensure the magazine's continued publication, Tyndall asked supporters for financial help because the new BNP leadership no longer promoted *Spearhead* in the party literature.[483] Indeed, Griffin's leadership victory marked a watershed moment in British fascist history and left Tyndall without a significant party role for the first time in twenty years. Griffin would go on to take the BNP as well as British fascism to new highs and new lows.

Conclusion

British fascism again underwent several changes during 1990s. The extremists gained one election victory after failing to win any seats during the 1980s, but as in the previous decade the image of the neo-Nazi skinhead hurt British fascist electoral politics. Between the racial violence and news about Combat 18, the BNP had trouble portraying itself as anything more than a gang of thugs. Consequently, in the late 1990s several key figures, including Butler, Lecomber and Griffin, set about changing the party's face to appear as a respectable "rights" organization for white people. Overcoming the hardline fascists proved difficult, however, and produced a significant backlash. Yet in late 1999 Griffin replaced Tyndall as leader of the BNP and began efforts to improve its image by banning certain members, disassociating itself from some racist policies and trying new forms of outreach. Indeed, as Nigel Copsey has shown, the BNP's modernization was a superficial change, as many fascists remained in the party and the extremist rhetoric was toned down but not abandoned.[484] As the next chapter explains, Griffin led the BNP to new heights of electoral success and forged stronger international connections than any other radical in British fascism. Later, the BNP started disintegrating under increasing personal attacks, financial pressure and Griffin's international activities in Europe.

Notes

1. Richard Edmonds, interviewed by Ryan Shaffer, audio recording, 15 September 2011.
2. Eddy Butler, interviewed by Ryan Shaffer, audio recording, 16 September 2011.
3. Nigel Copsey, *Contemporary British Fascism: The British National Party and the Quest for Legitimacy* (Basingstoke: Palgrave Macmillan, 2008), 66.
4. Matthew J. Goodwin, *New British Fascism: Rise of the British National Party* (New York: Routledge, 2011), 47.
5. John Tyndall, "Can the National Front be Reunited," *Spearhead* no. 141 (July 1980): 5.
6. Interview with Edmonds.
7. "New National Front," *Spearhead* no. 140 (June 1980): 12.
8. "New National Front: Progress Report," *Spearhead* no. 146 (December 1980): 18.

9. "NNF Progress Continues," *Spearhead* no. 152 (June 1981): 18.
10. "More Joining NNF," *Spearhead* no. 154 (August 1981): 18.
11. "Old NF Gains a Convert," *Spearhead* no. 158 (December 1981): 18.
12. John Tyndall, "Chorley March Sets New Standard," *Spearhead* no. 146 (December 1980): 19; see also: "Young Nationalists Protest Against 'Romans'," *Spearhead* no. 146 (December 1980): 19.
13. Interview with Edmonds; "New Youth Paper Launched," *Spearhead* no. 161 (March 1982): 19.
14. "They Lied," *Young Nationalist* no. 2 (n.d., circa 1982): 1; "Things We Stand For," *Young Nationalist* no. 2 (n.d., circa 1982): 2.
15. "NNF Youth Division Takes Shape," *Spearhead* no. 149 (March 1981): 19.
16. "At Last—Our Own Party," *Spearhead* no. 147 (January 1981): 19.
17. "New Year—New Paper—New Frontier," *New Frontier* no. 1 (January/February 1981): 2.
18. Eddy Morrison, "Time for a Name Change," *Spearhead* no. 160 (February 1982): 7.
19. Interview with Edmonds.
20. "Parties Agree to Unite," *Spearhead* no. 162 (April 1982): 18.
21. Ibid.
22. John Tyndall, "A New Era Begins," *Spearhead* no. 163 (May 1982): 8.
23. "Know Your Party Officers," *Spearhead* no. 173 (March 1983): 17.
24. "Great London Rally," *New Frontier* no. 22 (November 1982): 4.
25. "Principles and Policies of the British National Party," *Spearhead* no. 163 (May 1982): unpaginated insert; *A New Way Forward: Political Objectives of the British National Party* (Hove: British National Party, n.d.).
26. Interview with Edmonds.
27. *Let Britain Live: The Manifesto of the National Front* (Surrey: The Directorate of the National Front, 1983), 5; *Vote for Britain: Manifesto of the British National Party* (Hove: British National Party, 1983), 14.
28. "BNP Gets Geared Up for Election," *New Frontier* no. 25 (February 1983): 4.
29. Jessica Yonwin, "Electoral performance of far-right parties in the UK," *Parliamentary Standard Notes*, 29 June 2004; available online at http://researchbriefings.files.parliament.uk/documents/SN01982/SN01982.pdf; accessed 1 July 2016.
30. "Politics '97," BBC, 1997; available online at http://www.bbc.co.uk/news/special/politics97/background/pastelec/ge83.shtml; accessed 1 July 2016.
31. "Start of a Nationalist Song-Book," *Spearhead* no. 169 (November 1982): 20; "Marching Songs," *New Frontier* no. 22 (November 1982): 4.
32. "London Rally Big Success," *Spearhead* no. 181 (November 1983): 18.

33. John Tyndall, "Captives of 'Democracy'," *Spearhead* no. 214 (December 1986): 4.
34. John Tyndall, *The Eleventh Hour: Call for British Rebirth* (London: Albion Press, 1988).
35. "Big General Election Drive," *Spearhead* no. 207 (January 1986): 19.
36. "Election Fund: £15,000 Needed," *Spearhead* no. 219 (May 1987): 18.
37. John Tyndall, "The General Election: Why I Acted as I Did," *Spearhead* no. 221 (July 1987): 13, 14, 16.
38. Richard Edmonds, "Exposing the 'Holocaust'," *Spearhead* no. 224 (October 1987): 10.
39. Interview with Butler.
40. Ibid.; See *"Holocaust" News* no. 1 (n.d., circa 1988).
41. Edmonds said he was given a "golden handshake." Interview with Edmonds; "Gutter Press Gets BNP Man the Sack," *Spearhead* no. 230 (April 1988): 18. According to Butler, Tyndall thought the Holocaust happened and it was good, but Edmonds believed it did not happen. The two would argue about it in election meetings. Interview with Butler.
42. "Building Fund: £3316," *Spearhead* no. 234 (August 1988): 18; "Our Building at Last," *British Nationalist* no. 89 (April 1989): 5.
43. Peter Rushton, interviewed by Ryan Shaffer, audio recording, 16 October 2014.
44. John Tyndall, "What We Must Do In 1988," *Spearhead* no. 227 (January 1988): 4, 5.
45. "Recruitment Up in 1988," *Spearhead* no. 229 (March 1988): 19.
46. "London Rally One of the Best Ever," *Spearhead* no. 237 (November 1988): 19.
47. John Tyndall, "1989: Tasks and Targets," *Spearhead* no. 239 (January 1989): 5.
48. John Tyndall, "1990s: Time of Destiny," *British Nationalist* no. 97 (January 1990): 7.
49. Interview with Butler.
50. Copsey, *Contemporary British Fascism*, 57.
51. Interview with Butler.
52. Ibid.
53. *Defend Rights for Whites* (Welling, n.d., circa 1990).
54. *Where We Stand* (Welling, n.d., circa 1990).
55. For example see "Race Riots," *British Nationalist* no. 111 (July 1991): 1.
56. "BNP Defends Whites in Walsall," *British Nationalist* no. 122 (July 1992): 8; "Defend Rights for Whites in Halifax," *British Nationalist* no. 123 (August/September 1992): 7.

57. "Great Rally in East End," *Spearhead* no. 255 (May 1990): 19.
58. Eddy Butler, "Election Time Again?," *Spearhead* no. 259 (September 1990): 11.
59. "Steve Smith Wins 8.4%," *Spearhead* no. 258 (August 1990): 18.
60. Ibid.
61. Ibid., 20.
62. "East End Rally Makes Big Headlines," *Spearhead* no. 259 (September 1990): 18.
63. Interview with Butler.
64. Eddy Butler, "Election Time Again?," *Spearhead* no. 259 (September 1990):12.
65. Ibid., 12, 14.
66. "Dramatic BNP Poll Success," *Spearhead* no. 260 (October 1990): 18.
67. Ibid.
68. "And We Held Our Rally," *Spearhead* no. 261 (November 1990): 18.
69. Eddy Butler, "Election Time Again," *Spearhead* no. 261 (November 1990): 12.
70. Ibid., 13.
71. "BNP Plan for General Election," *Spearhead* no. 262 (December 1990): 18.
72. Ibid.
73. Tony Wells, "The Next Election; What We Must Aim At," *Spearhead* no. 264 (February 1991): 13.
74. "London Regional Seminar and Social," *British Nationalist* no. 109 (May 1991): 5.
75. Ibid.
76. "First Election Candidates Selected," *Spearhead* no. 264 (February 1991): 16.
77. "Where You Can Vote BNP," *British Nationalist* no. 119 (April 1992): 8.
78. Interview with Rushton.
79. Ibid.
80. "Election Special: Our Platform," *British Nationalist* no. 114 (October 1991): 5.
81. Ibid.
82. *Fight Back!: The Election Manifesto of the British National Party* (Welling: British National Party, 1992), 4.
83. Eddy Butler, "A Call to Arms," *Spearhead* no. 277 (March 1992): 12.
84. Ibid.
85. Ibid., 13.
86. Ibid.

87. John Tyndall, "Where We Go From Here," *British Nationalist* no. 120 (May 1992): 4.
88. Eddy Butler, "BNP Vote Continues to Show Upward Trend," *British Nationalist* no. 120 (May 1992): 8.
89. "Post-Election Planning Conference," *Spearhead* no. 280 (June 1992): 18.
90. Eddy Butler, "Past, Present and Future," *Spearhead* no. 281 (July 1992): 7.
91. Ibid., 9.
92. Ibid.
93. Ibid.
94. *No to Maastricht and No to Europe* (Welling: British National Party, 1992); Simon Smith, "Maastricht Treaty: Death of a Nation, Birth of a Tyranny," *Spearhead* no. 290 (April 1993): 12.
95. "Post-Election Fund," *Spearhead* no. 280 (June 1992): 19.
96. Interview with Edmonds; "Selling the Party Means Selling the Paper," *Spearhead* no. 244 (June 1989): 13.
97. Interview with Rushton.
98. John Tyndall, "And They All Cried Wolf," *Spearhead* no. 261 (November 1990): 4.
99. *Spreading the Word: British National Party Handbook on Propaganda* (Kent: British National Party, n.d., circa 1992), 18.
100. John Tyndall, "The Moral High Ground and the Gutter," *Spearhead* no. 270 (August 1991): 5.
101. *The Psychology of Neo-Nazism: Another Journey by Train to Auschwitz* (Princeton: Films for the Humanities and Sciences, 1994) (VHS Recording).
102. Steve Cartwright, "A Trip to Holocaust Land," *Spearhead* no. 293 (July 1993): 12.
103. Interview with Rushton.
104. "Election Triumph," *Spearhead* no. 285 (November 1992): 18.
105. Ibid.
106. "Twenty Percent," *British Nationalist* no. 125 (November 1992): 1.
107. "Party Growth Continues Nationwide," *Spearhead* no. 286 (December 1992): 18.
108. Warren Glass, interviewed by Ryan Shaffer, audio recording, 7 October 2014. Nick Lowles wrote that Glass's brother Stuart Glass was a "convicted" Chelsea Headhunter. Nick Lowles, "Far Out With the Far Right," in *Hooligan Wars: Causes and Effects of Football Violence* ed. Mark Perryman (London: Mainstream, 2001), 111.
109. Ibid.

110. "BNP Defends Glasgow Whites," *Spearhead* no. 286 (December 1992): 19; "Rights for Whites' Campaign Comes to Scotland," *British Nationalist* no. 126 (December 1992): 8.
111. "1990–1993: BNP Expansion," *Spearhead* no. 287 (January 1993): 19; "BNP Launches Big Training Programme," *Spearhead* no. 293 (July 1993): 19.
112. "BNP Launches Big Training Programme," *Spearhead* no. 293 (July 1993): 19.
113. Interview with Butler.
114. Ibid. The BNP did this with the electoral register and when local Conservatives saw the system, they were surprised at how detailed it was.
115. "Successful Leadership Conference," *Spearhead* no. 294 (August 1993): 19.
116. John Morse, "Racial Attacks: White Victims," *British Nationalist* no. 132 (June 1993): 3.
117. "A Night to Remember," *Spearhead* no. 296 (October 1993): 18.
118. "We Won," *British Nationalist* no. 136 (October 1993): 1.
119. "Mr. Major's Joint Doorstep Interview with Prime Minister Keating," JohnMajor.co.uk, 1993; available online at http://www.johnmajor.co.uk/page1090.html; accessed 1 July 2016.
120. For example, the souvenir program mentions the Millwall election in many locations. "Carnival Against the Nazis," *Anti-Nazi League*, 28 May 1994. For details about anti-fascist activity in the 1990s, see: Nigel Copsey, *Anti-Fascism in Britain* (New York: Routledge, 2016).
121. "BNP Office Swamped with Enquiries," *Spearhead* no. 297 (November 1993): 19.
122. Ibid.
123. "Victory' 93," *British Nationalist* no. 138 (December 1993): 8.
124. "A Night to Remember," *Spearhead* no. 296 (October 1993): 18.
125. "The BNP Victory: 'Democracy' Reacts," *Spearhead* no. 296 (October 1993): 19.
126. Ibid.
127. "Edmonds Arrested," *British Nationalist* no. 136 (October 1993): 8.
128. Interview with Edmonds.
129. Ibid.
130. "Car Crash Kills 'Driver," *New Musical Express*, 9 October 1993, 3.
131. "Ian Stuart Skrewdriver," *Blood & Honour* no. 10 (n.d., circa 1990): 7.
132. "Editorial," *Blood & Honour* no. 11 (n.d., circa 1990): 2.
133. "Reds on the Run," *Blood & Honour* no. 11 (n.d., circa 1990): 10.
134. "Editorial," *Blood & Honour* no. 13 (n.d., circa 1992): 2.

135. *Skrewdriver Ritorno a Camelot 1991* (Denison: NS88, n.d.) (DVD Recording). Some Veneto Fronte Skinheads attended the NF's 1986 White Noise festival in Suffolk. *Sulla Strada Dell'Onore: Oltre 30 Anni Di Testimonianze Fotografiche e Di Vita Degli Skinheads Veneti* (N.p.: Associazione Culturale Veneto Fronte Skinheads, 2016).
136. Colin Todd, interviewed by Ryan Shaffer, audio recording, 3 October 2014.
137. "UK Skinheads Held in Stabbing," *The Vancouver Sun*, 22 October 1991.
138. "Skrewdriver News," *British Oi!* no. 21 (1991): 14.
139. Robert Kellaway, "Brit Skinheads Held in Nazi Battle," *The Sun*, 2 October 1991.
140. "Skrewdriver News," *British Oi!* no. 21 (1991): 14.
141. Mark Fritz, "Sounds of Violence: Europe's Skinheads United by Music," Associated Press, 6 November 1992; "Rock's Songs of Violence Unite Europe's neo-Nazis," *The Toronto Star*, 6 November 1992.
142. "Stigger," *Viking* no. 4 (November 1995): 9.
143. *Skrewdriver Cottbus, Germany 1991* (Denison: NS88, n.d.) (DVD Recording).
144. "Banned News," *Blood & Honour* no. 12 (n.d., circa 1992): 3.
145. "Saturday 12th September," *Blood & Honour* no. 14 (n.d., circa 1992): 6.
146. Garry Bushell, *Hoolies: True Stories of Britain's Biggest Street Battles* (London: John Blake, 2010), 251.
147. "Blood & Honour Present," *Blood & Honour* no. 13 (n.d., circa 1990): 16.
148. Louise Hidalgo, "Concert Awakens neo-Nazi Fears," *The Times*, 5 September 1992; see cover "Battle of Waterloo," *Blood & Honour* no. 14 (n.d., circa 1992).
149. William Shaw, "The Battle of Waterloo," *Select* (November 1992): 14; Martin Cloonan, "State of the Nation: 'Englishness,' Pop and Politics in the Mid-1990's," *Popular Music and Society* 21, no. 2 (Summer 1997): 47–70.
150. Shaw, 15, 16.
151. Bushell, *Hoolies: True Stories of Britain's Biggest Street Battles*, 250; Alison Cameron and Moira Whittle, "'Battle of Waterloo'—30 Charged," Press Association, 13 September 1992; "30 Held after Clash," *The Herald*, 14 September 1992; "Seven in Court after Waterloo Clash," *Evening Standard*, 14 September 1992.
152. Shaw, 17.
153. Skrewdriver, *Battle of Waterloo* (ISD Records, 1994) (CD Recording).
154. Ibid.

155. "Ian Stuart Interview," *Last Chance* no. 14 (1992): 14.
156. For more on descriptions of Blood & Honour, see: "Lots of Blood, Little Honour," *Searchlight* no. 164 (February 1989): 4.
157. Interview with Butler. He described Ian Stuart attending the meetings, but noted that many members were concerned about the skinheads hurting the party image and were "snobbish" in their treatment of skinheads.
158. Interview with Butler.
159. Ibid.; John Burns reported, "[i]n the movement, they all call him Daddy. Not that there is anything particularly paternal about Derek Beackon, veteran neo-Nazi and now London councilor. He gets his nickname from the teenage skinheads, the yobbish lower ranks of the organization… Filmed evidence of Beackon's activities as chief steward to the British National Party has been submitted to the Commons Select Committee on race violence." John Burns, "He's try to Disown Violence, but Fascist," *Daily Express*, 24 September 1993.
160. Interview with Butler.
161. Ryan Shaffer correspondence from anonymous, 28 June 2011.
162. Ibid.
163. Interview with Butler.
164. Ibid.; In 1993, Leo Regan photographed members of C18 and provided some context about their lives. Many years later, he produced a documentary about three former C18 members with attention to how their ideas and lives changed. Leo Regan, *Public Enemies* (London: Andre Deutsche Limited, 1993); *100% White* (n.p.: Channel 4, 2000) (DVD Recording).
165. "The Terror Squad," *World in Action*, April 1993; *State Enemy No. C18* (Denison: NS88, n.d.) (DVD Recording).
166. Correspondence from anonymous.
167. Interview with Butler. John Tyndall, who met Covington once in about 1981, wrote: "In our investigations into people with contacts with Combat 18 one name kept cropping up again and again. This was an American called Harold Covington, who… was closely involved with a number of people from whose ranks C18 emerged." John Tyndall, "Doing the Enemy's Work," *Spearhead* no. 319 (September 1995): 9.
168. Interview with Butler.
169. A "Dixie Press" post office box in Raleigh, North Carolina appeared on the back cover of *Combat 18* no. 1 (n.d., circa 1994). See also: "The Terror Squad," *World in Action*, April 1993; *State Enemy No. C18* (Denison: NS88, n.d.) (DVD Recording).
170. Nick Lowles, *White Riot: The Violent Story of Combat 18* 2nd ed. (London: Milo Books, 2014), 35.

171. Andy Saxon [Steve Sargent], "Editorial," *The Order* no. 15 (n.d., circa 1995): 2.
172. "Word for Word/The Skinhead International; Some Music, it Turns Out, Inflames the Savage Breast," *New York Times*, 2 July 1995; David Lewis, "Hate Rock," CNN, 21 May 1995 (TV Broadcast).
173. Bushell, *Hoolies: True Stories of Britain's Biggest Street Battles*, 253.
174. "Day of Action to Remember as BNP Storms Blackburn Terrorist Meeting," *British Nationalist* no. 131 (May 1993): 8.
175. "Car Crash Kills 'Driver," *New Musical Express*, 9 October 1993, 3.
176. M. Cross, "The Necessity for Change in Blood & Honour," *The Order* no. 9 (n.d., circa 1994): unpaginated 8.
177. Ibid.
178. Ibid.
179. Blood & Honour letter, April 1994. In possession.
180. *Blood & Honour* reported: "Ex-Blood & Honour musician Martin Cross, formerly of bands—Brutal Attack, Skrewdriver, Razors Edge, The Order and Empire, was sentenced to life imprisonment for murder. The same sentence was passed upon ex-Blood & Honour editor, and supposed European Nazi leader/C18 leader Charlie Sargent." "Murder," *Blood & Honour* no. 12 (n.d., circa 1998): 13. An undated tract by "original members of Combat 18" described Browning's personal dislike of Paul Burnley. Harry O'Lara, *Drowning Browning: Examining the Nature of the Beast* (n.p., n.d.), unpaginated 2, 3. In possession.
181. Skrewdriver, *Hail Victory* (ISD Records, 1994) (CD Recording). Stigger is thanked on the album and featured in the artwork. On the back of the CD, C18 claims that "Ian was murdered by enemies of our people," despite it being widely reported, including by his friends who were injured, that he died in an automobile accident.
182. "The Homeland Part Two," *The Order* no. 9 (n.d., circa 1994): unpaginated 5.
183. "The Editorial," *The Order* no. 12 (n.d., circa 1994): unpaginated 2.
184. "Getting Stronger," *The Order* unnumbered (n.d., circa 1994): unpaginated 3. This issue has no number and features Ian Stuart on the cover with the words "Heil Our Fuhrer."
185. "Security Fund Launched," *Spearhead* no. 296 (October 1993): 10.
186. John Tyndall, "When the Stone is Moved," *Spearhead* no. 297 (November 1993): 7.
187. "Superb Rally Triumph," *Spearhead* no. 298 (December 1993): 19. Lyons previously visited with Sam Dickson in 1992. "American Leaders Visit Britain," *British Nationalist* no. 122 (July 1992): 7.

188. "BNP's Opponents Take Fright and Get Vicious," *Spearhead* no. 303 (May 1994): 19; "Bomb Hits BNP Office," *Daily Express*, 8 April 1994.
189. Interview with Rushton.
190. "Riot," *British Nationalist* no. 132 (June 1993): 1.
191. "What We Think," *Spearhead* no. 304 (June 1994): 3.
192. "Tremendous Successes in Council Elections," *Spearhead* no. 304 (June 1994): 19.
193. *Activists' Handbook* (Welling: British National Party, n.d., circa 1994), 57.
194. BNP South Wales Nationalist Response," *Nationalist Response* no. 12 (Autumn 1990): 4.
195. David Myatt, "A Political Re-Awakening," *Spearhead* no. 307 (September 1994): 13.
196. David Myatt, *Myngath: Some Recollections of a Wyrdful and Extremist Life* (n.p.: CreateSpace Independent Publishing Platform, 2013): unpaginated 51.
197. Ibid.
198. D. Myatt, "An Analysis of the Zionist Response to System Breakdown," *The Order* no. 18 (January/March 1997): 7.
199. "Neo-Nazi Gang Jailed For Attack on Asians: Racist Assault Condemned as 'Unprovoked, Vicious and Cowardly'," *The Independent*, 3 July 1993; available online at http://www.independent.co.uk/news/uk/neonazi-gang-jailed-for-attack-on-asians-racist-assault-condemned-as-unprovoked-vicious-and-cowardly-1482628.html; accessed 1 July 2016.
200. "Murdered for Being White," *British Nationalist* no. 147 (September 1994): 1.
201. "Is This the Britain You Want?," *British Nationalist* no. 164 (February 1996): 1.
202. "Asian Gang Violence," *British Nationalist* no. 174 (December 1996): 1.
203. "Ethnic Cleansing…in Britain," *British Nationalist* no. 190 (April 1998): 1; "More Race Hate Attacks Against Whites," *British Nationalist* no. 195 (September 1998): 1.
204. Richard Stone, *Hidden Stories of the Stephen Lawrence Inquiry: Personal Reflections* (Chicago: Policy Press, 2013), 9.
205. William Macpherson, *The Inquiry Into The Matters Arising From The Death of Stephen Lawrence* (London: Stationery Office, 1999): 46, 27; available online at https://www.gov.uk/government/publications/the-stephen-lawrence-inquiry; accessed 1 July 2016.
206. Stone, 121.
207. Tom Pettifor, "Stephen Lawrence Verdict: Killers Gary Dobson and David Norris United in Race Hate," *The Mirror*, 4 January 2012;

available online at http://www.mirror.co.uk/news/uk-news/stephen-lawrence-verdict-killers-gary-157049; accessed 1 July 2016.

208. "Albion Replies," *Putsch* no. 17 (n.d., circa 1994): 5.
209. "Ten Principles of National Socialist Thought," *Putsch* no. 17 (n.d., circa 1994): 7, 8; Untitled, *Putsch* no. 17 (n.d., circa 1994): 8.
210. Untitled, *Putsch* no. 19 (n.d., circa 1994): 8; Untitled, *Putsch* no. 20 (n.d., circa 1995): 8; Untitled, *Putsch* no. 22 (n.d., circa 1995): 7–10.
211. Untitled, *Putsch* no. 21 (n.d., circa 1995): 1.
212. Untitled, *Putsch* no. 24 (n.d., circa April/May 1995): 1.
213. Untitled, *Redwatch* (n.d.): unpaginated 8. According to this unnumbered and undated issue, it was the last issue and had a circulation of five hundred copies.
214. "Aims of C18," *Combat 18* no. 1 (n.d., circa 1994): unpaginated 8.
215. Ibid., 8, 9.
216. Ibid., 10.
217. Ibid., 25.
218. The post office box address was printed in the magazine. However, a well-connected member of Blood & Honour said the address was not actually used, but was a "smoke screen."
219. "Editorial," *Combat 18* no. 3 (n.d., circa 1994): unpaginated 2.
220. Untitled, *Blood & Honour* 2, no. 5 (n.d., circa 1995): 5, 12.
221. "Whatever It Takes," *Blood & Honour* unnumbered (n.d., circa 1995): unpaginated 11.
222. This was promoted on the cover of *Blood & Honour* unnumbered (n.d., circa 1996). Burnley disbanded his version of No Remorse in 1996 to "end it with the dignity and respect it so rightly deserves." Paul Burnley, "A White Farewell to No Remorse," *Resistance* no. 8 (1997): 10.
223. No Remorse, *Barbecue in Rostock* (n.p.: 28 USA Records, 2010) (CD Recording).
224. "Blood & Honour Across The Globe," *Blood & Honour* 2, no. 6 (n.d., circa 1995): unpaginated 3.
225. "Interview with RaHoWa," *Blood & Honour* 2, no. 6 (n.d., circa 1995): unpaginated 4, 5.
226. *NS88 Videos* (Denmark, n.d., circa 1994); "Blood & Honour Distributors," *Blood & Honour* unnumbered (n.d., circa 1996): unpaginated 3. The cover featured *Barbecue in Rostock.*
227. "Blood & Honour News," *The Order* no. 12 (n.d., circa 1994): unpaginated 10.
228. Anonymous 4 (identified as "Bart"), interviewed by Ryan Shaffer, audio recording, 7 April 2014. This person did not want his surname used.
229. Ibid.
230. Ibid.

231. Interview with Bart; Daniel Schweizer, *Skinhead Attitude* (n.p.: Sunny Bastards, 2004) (DVD Recording); Daniel Schweizer, *White Terror* (n.p.: Sunny Bastards, 2006) (DVD Recording).
232. For example: *Blood & Honour Division Deutschland* no. 2 (1996); *Blood & Honour Danmark* 1, no. 1 (October 1998); *Blood & Honour Scandinavia* 1, no. 1 (Summer 1997); *Blood & Honour Espana* no. 1 (September 2000); *Blood & Honour Division Serbia* no. 6 (January 2000); *Blood and Honour California* no. 1 (n.d., circa 1993). In possession.
233. *1st ISD Memorial 1995 Kent England* (Denison: NS88, n.d.) (DVD Recording).
234. "C18 Pair Head for Old Bailey," *Searchlight* no. 248 (February 1996): 3.
235. Ian Christie, "Ain't Gonna Take it No More," *Spearhead* no. 267 (May 1991): 14.
236. Ibid.
237. John Tyndall, "The Music of Revolution and Counter-Revolution," *Spearhead* no. 231 (May 1988): 4.
238. Ibid., 20.
239. "Derek Beackon Fighting Tower Hamlets Ward," *Spearhead* no. 310 (December 1994): 14.
240. Interview with Edmonds.
241. Ibid.
242. John Tyndall, "Doing the Enemy's Work," *Spearhead* no. 319 (September 1995): 6.
243. Ibid.
244. Ibid., 7.
245. Ibid.,10.
246. Ibid.
247. "Rally Goes Ahead Despite Massive Sabotage Operation," *Spearhead* no. 322 (December 1995): 22.
248. "The BNP/C18 Split," *Combat 18* no. 3 (n.d., circa 1994): 29, 33.
249. Cover of *Putsch* no. 25 (n.d., circa May/June 1995): 1; "Hollywood Nazis," *Putsch* no. 28 (n.d., circa August/September 1995): 1; "Rat Tails', Rat Tales," *Putsch* no. 30 (n.d., circa November 1995): 1.
250. Copsey, *Contemporary British Fascism*, 67.
251. John Tyndall, "Combat 18: An Update," *Spearhead* no. 320 (October 1995): 10.
252. Ibid.
253. "No Surrender to the ZOG," *Putsch* no. 31 (n.d., circa December 1995): 1.
254. Correspondence from anonymous.

255. "Burdi & Dishonour," *The Order* no. 18 (January/March 1997): 11.
256. Ibid.
257. Nick Ryan, "Combat 18: Memoirs of a Street-Fighting man," *The Independent*, 1 February 1998; available online at http://www.independent.co.uk/arts-entertainment/combat-18-memoirs-of-a-streetfighting-man-1142204.html; accessed 1 July 2016; Nick Lowles and Nick Ryan, "Neo-Nazi gang war fear after murder," *The Independent*, 25 January 1998; available online at http://www.independent.co.uk/news/neonazi-gang-war-fear-after-murder-murder-1140723.html; accessed 1 July 2016.
258. Andy Saxon [Steve Sargent], "Editorial," *The Order* no. 18 (January/March 1997): 2.
259. Ibid.
260. Kim White, "Life neo-Nazi Cowards," *The Law: The Newspaper of the Essex Police* no. 292 (February 1998): 7.
261. John Davies, "Editorial," *Blood & Honour* no. 9 (n.d., circa 1997): 2.
262. Ibid.
263. "Blood & Honour Takes a White Look at the General Election 97," *Blood & Honour* no. 10 (n.d., circa 1997): 7.
264. "ISD in Exile," *Blood & Honour* no. 10 (n.d., circa 1997): 4; Interview with Bart.
265. Alan Sykes, *The Radical Right in Britain: Social Imperialism to the BNP* (Basingstoke: Palgrave Macmillan, 2005), 128.
266. Patrick Harrington, interviewed by Ryan Shaffer, audio recording, 29 May 2010.
267. "Dear Reader," *Third Way* no. 1 (1990): 2.
268. Troy Southgate, *Tradition & Revolution: Collected Writings of Troy Southgate* (London: Arktos, 2010), 120.
269. "Alternatives to Capitalism," *Third Way* no. no. 1 (1990): 10.
270. "Black Nationalism," *Third Way* no. 3 (August 1990): 14.
271. "Green But Not Naive," *Third Way* no. 3 (August 1990): 16; "Counter Culture," *Third Way* no. 3 (August 1990): 7.
272. *A Mersey Manifesto* (Liverpool: Committee of Liverpool Third Way, 1991): unpaginated 3.
273. An article by Nick Griffin appeared several years after he became leader of the BNP. Nick Griffin, "Civil Liberty: The Indivisible Right," *Third Way* no. 35 (2005): 3.
274. Patrick Harrington, *The Third Way: An Answer to Blair* (London: Third Way Publications, 1998), 9, 10.
275. Southgate, *Tradition & Revolution*, 120.
276. Ibid.
277. Troy Southgate, *Nazis, Fascists, or Neither?: Ideological Credentials of the British Far Right 1987–1994* (Shamley Green: The Palingenesis Project, 2010), 77.

278. Ibid., 77.
279. Ibid., 78.
280. Ibid., 78.
281. Ibid., 78.
282. "What is the 'News from Somewhere' Project," *News from Somewhere* no. 2 (n.d., circa 1990): unpaginated 1.
283. Ibid., 1.
284. Ibid., 2, 3. According to Todd, this was written by Holland. Interview with Todd.
285. Ibid., 5, 6.
286. Interview with Todd.
287. Interview with Andrews.
288. *The International Third Position: An Introduction to the Movement of Tomorrow* (n.p.: International Third Position, n.d., circa 1990): unpaginated 2.
289. Ibid., 4, 5, 6.
290. "Student Loans," *The Anvil* no. 1 (n.d., circa 1992): unpaginated 1, 2, 3.
291. Southgate, *Nazis, Fascists, or Neither?*, 89.
292. Interview with Todd.
293. Southgate, *Nazis, Fascists, or Neither?*, 88.
294. Interview with Todd.
295. Ibid.
296. Ibid. A boxing fan, he noted that Muhammed Ali was there, and Todd also later visited the West Bank.
297. "Third Positionist Delegates Visit Iraq," *Third Way: Supporters Bulletin* (January 1991): 4. In addition, according to this article twelve hours of video were recorded of the entire visit.
298. Interview with Todd. According to Southgate, they received money from the Iraqi government, but Afzal took it and "disappeared." Southgate, *Nazis, Fascists, or Neither?*, 88.
299. Nick Griffin, interviewed by Ryan Shaffer, audio recording, 8 October 2014.
300. The ITP claimed he was told to "go away," but Griffin said he left. "Nick Griffin: An ITP Statement," *Spearhead* no. 367 (September 1999): 12.
301. Southgate, *Nazis, Fascists, or Neither?*, 79.
302. Ibid., 80, 81.
303. Ibid., 84.
304. Ibid., 84.
305. Southgate, *Tradition & Revolution*, 120.
306. Ibid., 121.
307. Interview with Todd.
308. Southgate, *Tradition & Revolution*, 121.

309. Ibid., 121.
310. Ibid., 120.
311. *Emergency Aid for Croatia* (London: International Third Position, 1993), 2.
312. Ibid., 10, 11.
313. Southgate, *Tradition & Revolution*, 121; *Rising Books: Winter'93–94 Catalog* (London: ITP, 1993).
314. "Spanish Special," *Final Conflict* no. 13 (Spring 1997): 5.
315. "An Introduction to the Movement," *Final Conflict* nos. 14/15 (Summer 1997): 19; "Heavy Lumps at Noon or Snippets from Spain," *Final Conflict* no. 17 (Winter 1998): 10, 11.
316. Vivek Chaudhary, "Neo-Nazis take over Spanish village," *The Guardian*, 19 November 1999; available online at https://www.theguardian.com/world/1999/nov/20/vivekchaudhary; accessed 1 July 2016.
317. Southgate, *Tradition & Revolution*, 122.
318. "I have to inform you that Miss Rosine Maria de Bounevialle passed away on Christmas Day of 1999. Rosine is to be buried in the grounds of her beloved Forest House." Colin Todd, "The AK Chesterton Trust," *Candour* 73, no. 1 (July 2000): 2; Interview with Todd.
319. Derek Holland interviewed by Judith Sharpe, "The Middle East Tragedy from a Catholic, Political, and Historical Perspective: Understanding the Reasoning Behind Mass Murder (Part I—Introducing Derek Holland)," *In the Spirit of Chartres Committee*, 1 April 2008 (CD Recording).
320. "Structure," European National Front, February 2005; available online at https://web.archive.org/web/20050310224403/http://www.europeannationalfront.com/?id=7; accessed 1 July 2016.
321. "Ideology & Programme," European National Front, 2005; available online at https://web.archive.org/web/20050312020800/http://www.europeannationalfront.com/?id=11; accessed 1 July 2016.
322. Gareth Hurley, "European Nationalists Meet in Slovakia," National Vanguard, 21 July 2004. https://web.archive.org/web/20041013165457/http://www.nationalvanguard.org/story.php?id=3382; accessed 1 July 2016; "Foundation Declaration of European National Front," Narodowe Odrodzenie Polski, 2006; https://web.archive.org/web/20060517212526/http://www.nop.org.pl/?artykul_id=83; accessed 1 July 2016; The website's last online archive was February 2009. 'European National Front Declaration of Foundation,' European National Front, 2009; available online at https://web.archive.org/web/20090225072411/http://europeannationalfront.com/; accessed 1 July 2016.
323. "Vanguard," *Vanguard* no. 28 (November/December 1989): 2.
324. Ian Anderson, "Nationalism: With a Friendly Face," *Vanguard* no. 28 (November/December 1989): 3.

325. Tom Acton, "Was the Last Split the Last Split," *Vanguard* no. 29 (January/February 1990): 15.
326. "The Sun Does a Bottle Job," *Lionheart* no. 3 (n.d., circa 1990): unpaginated 11. Matthew Collins wrote about a "Mr. X" who leaked the polling results, and Collins in turn reported the person's identity to *Searchlight*. Matthew Collins, *Hate: My Life in the British Far Right* (London: Biteback Publishing, 2011), 199, 203.
327. "Oi!: The Reality," *Lionheart* no. 3 (n.d., circa 1990): unpaginated 6, 8.
328. "Editorial: National Front Ownership," *Vanguard* no. 36 (n.d., circa 1992): 2.
329. Collins, *Hate: My Life in the British Far Right*, 129.
330. Steve Brady, "The 60 Seat Campaign," *Vanguard* no. 31 (July/September 1990): 9.
331. Interview with Cotterill 2. Cotterill and Steve Brady resigned from the party and Cotterill briefly joined the Conservative Party.
332. Jessica Yonwin, "Electoral performance of far-right parties in the UK," *Parliamentary Standard Notes*, 29 June 2004; available online at http://researchbriefings.files.parliament.uk/documents/SN01982/SN01982.pdf; accessed 1 July 2016.
333. *Caring for Britain: The Manifesto of the National Front* (Worthing: National Front, 1992), 9, 11.
334. Modern Records Centre, MSS.412/ND/3, "Letter from Martin Wingfield to *The Flag* Subscriber," 8 June 1995. Modern Records Centre, MSS.412/ND/3, "Special Meeting to Debate Name Change," *National Front Member's Bulletin* (1995).
335. "National Democrat Annual Conference," *The National Democrats: Members Bulletin* (January 1996): 1.
336. *The Constitution of the National Democrats* (n.p.: National Democrats, n.d., circa 1996): unpaginated 9.
337. "Local Elections," *The National Democrats: Members Bulletin* (March 1996): 1.
338. Jessica Yonwin, "Electoral performance of far-right parties in the UK," *Parliamentary Standard Notes*, 29 June 2004; available online at http://researchbriefings.files.parliament.uk/documents/SN01982/SN01982.pdf; accessed 1 July 2016.
339. Ian Anderson, "National Democrats: The Two Year Plan," *Vanguard* no. 51 (n.d., circa 1997): 14.
340. The results were mocked by the BNP. "Mission Accomplished," *Spearhead* no. 339 (May 1997): 5; Faye Duxberry, "Clean-up for Co-op," *Hillingdon Times*, 30 November 2005; available online at https://web.archive.org/web/20070927043231/http://www.hillingdontimes.co.uk/display.var.654744.0.0.php; accessed 1 July 2016;

"Obituary—Ian Anderson—1953—2011," Heritage & Destiny, 2011; available online at http://efp.org.uk/obituary-ian-anderson-1953-2011/; accessed 1 July 2016.

341. Modern Records Centre, MSS.412/HQ/2/1, "National Front Finance Report, May 1997."
342. George Ashcroft, interviewed by Ryan Shaffer, audio recording, 30 May 2010. Ashcroft was the regional organizer in West Midlands for the National Front, but quit the party following the report. He then changed his name from Wayne to George and went on to condemn racism. He was a member of the Conservative Party, becoming local councilor for Telford and Wrekin, but then left the party and served as an independent.
343. Jessica Yonwin, "Electoral performance of far-right parties in the UK," *Parliamentary Standard Notes*, 29 June 2004; available online at http://researchbriefings.files.parliament.uk/documents/SN01982/SN01982.pdf; accessed 1 July 2016.
344. Interview with Butler.
345. "The BNP/C18 Split," *Combat 18* no. 3 (n.d., circa 1994): 33.
346. Interview with Butler.
347. John Tyndall, "The Isle of Dogs: What is at Stake," *Spearhead* no. 303 (May 1994): 4.
348. Ibid.
349. Ibid.
350. "Vote BNP," *British Nationalist* no. 142 (April 1994): 1.
351. "Tremendous Successes in Council Elections," *British Nationalist* no. 144 (June 1994): 8.
352. "London Rally Puts Pep into New Campaign," *Spearhead* no. 307 (September 1994): 18.
353. Ibid.
354. "Election Boost for BNP," *British Nationalist* no. 145 (July 1994): 1.
355. Tony Lecomber, "The Shadwell By-Election," *Spearhead* no. 309 (November 1994): 11.
356. Butler did not run this campaign, but stepped back from politics following threats from Combat 18. Interview with Butler.
357. Interview with Butler.
358. Nick Griffin, "Letters," *Spearhead* no. 312 (February 1995): 19.
359. Martin Cross, "White Whispers," *Blood & Honour* 2, no. 6 (n.d., circa 1995): unpaginated 16.
360. Nick Griffin, "Battle for Hollywood," *Spearhead* no. 323 (January 1996): 13.
361. "General Election: BNP to Go For 50 Seats," *Spearhead* no. 318 (August 1995): 23.

362. "First Candidates Announced," *British Nationalist* no. 158 (August 1995): 1.
363. "BNP to Fight 50 Seats at Election," *British Nationalist* no. 158 (August 1995): 1.
364. The website's URL was http://ngwwmall.com/frontier/bnp/. "BNP Now on the Internet!," *Spearhead* no. 320 (October 1995): 22.
365. Interview with Ashcroft. Ashcroft attended the meeting and purchased the book from Pierce, who signed it. He said the signed book was later donated to the Modern Records Centre.
366. Cover of *Spearhead* no. 322 (December 1995): 1.
367. "Rally Goes Ahead Despite Massive Sabotage Operation," *Spearhead* no. 322 (December 1995): 22. The magazine also noted that Thomas Anderson of the Sweden Democrats spoke as well.
368. John Tyndall, "Verdict: 'Can Do Better'," *Spearhead* no. 323 (January 1996): 6.
369. Ibid., 6.
370. Ibid., 7.
371. Tony Lecomber, "The 50-Seat Campaign," *Spearhead* no. 323 (January 1996): 9.
372. Ibid., 10.
373. Nick Griffin, "'Populism' or Power," *Spearhead* no. 324 (February 1996): 12.
374. Interview with Griffin.
375. Ibid.
376. "The Rune," *Spearhead* no. 324 (February 1996): 23.
377. "Jews: A Spotter's Guide," *The Rune* no. 2 (n.d., circa 1994): unpaginated 3; G. String, "Nationalist Noise," *The Rune* no. 2 (n.d., circa 1994): unpaginated 4.
378. "Fighters for Fighting Sake," *The Rune* no. 10 (1995): 18; "The Sen File," *The Rune* no. 10 (1995): 4; Paul Ballard, "14 Days That Saved the World," *The Rune* no. 11 (1995): 14.
379. Nick Griffin, "At This Stage of the Game," *The Rune* no. 11 (1995): 10, 11.
380. Nick Griffin, "The Inevitable White Man," *Spearhead* no. 326 (April 1996): 12.
381. Interview with Griffin.
382. Ibid.
383. Interview with Griffin. *Spearhead* announced, "Tom North will be taking over as *Spearhead*'s Assistant Editor." "Assistant Editor Appointed," *Spearhead* no. 326 (April 1996): 23. The following *Spearhead* issue described *The Rune* as being edited by Griffin "and produced by the team responsible for the facelift of this issue of *Spearhead*." "The Rune," *Spearhead* no. 327 (May 1996): 12.

384. "General Election Fund Opened: Target £10,000," *Spearhead* no. 328 (June 1996): 23.
385. "BNP Vote Holds Up Well," *Spearhead* no. 328 (June 1996): 23.
386. "Public Enquiry Held Over BNP's Bookshop Appeal," *British Nationalist* no. 156 (June 1995): 7; "BNP Bookshop Closed," *Spearhead* no. 330 (August 1996): 22.
387. John Tyndall, "A Year of Huge Opportunity," *Spearhead* no. 335 (January 1997): 6.
388. Ibid., 7.
389. Ibid., 7.
390. Ibid., 7.
391. "BNP Election Broadcast," *Spearhead* no. 338 (April 1997): 27.
392. "Vote BNP," *British Nationalist* no. 178 (April 1997): 1.
393. *Britain Reborn: A Programme for the New Century, British National Party Election Manifesto, May 1997* (Kent: British National Party, 1997), 4, 44.
394. Ibid., 2.
395. Tony Lecomber, "The 1997 General Election," *Patriot* no. 2 (Winter 1997): 4.
396. "Mission Accomplished," *Spearhead* no. 339 (May 1997): 4.
397. "New Era for Nationalists," *British Nationalist* no. 179 (May 1997): 1; "British National Party Poll Results," *British Nationalist* no. 179 (May 1997): 7.
398. Nick Griffin, "Will No-One Rid Us of These Turbulent Reds," *Spearhead* no. 330 (August 1996): 12, 13.
399. Nick Griffin, "Still 'No Electoral Road'?," *Spearhead* no. 334 (December 1996): 13.
400. Nick Griffin, "When the Wall Comes Down," *Spearhead* no. 337 (March 1997): 16.
401. "Editorial," *Patriot* no. 1 (Spring 1997): 1.
402. Tony Lecomber, "Success and Failure: New Politics and the Old," *Patriot* no. 1 (Spring 1997): 16. Jack Truman [Eddy Butler], "60 Years of Nationalism: Strategies Analysed Part 1," *Patriot* no. 1 (Spring 1997): 20. While Lecomber and others used their real names, Butler published under Jack Truman. Interview with Butler.
403. Tony Lecomber, "The 1997 General Election," *Patriot* no. 2 (Winter 1997): 3.
404. Jack Truman [Eddy Butler], "60 Years of Nationalism: Strategies Analysed Part 2," *Patriot* no. 2 (Winter 1997): 14. Interview with Butler. Griffin described himself as initially being hostile to Butler and Lecomber's ideas and said he personally did not like Butler. Interview with Griffin.

405. Michael Newland, "The New Nationalism," *Patriot* no. 2 (Winter 1997): 23.
406. Interview with Butler.
407. John Peacock, "BNP Contingent Visits French Patriots," *Spearhead* no. 291 (May 1993): 19.
408. Michael Newland, "A Tale of Two Medias," *Patriot* no. 3 (Summer 1998): 18.
409. "France and the FN, Britain and the BNP," *Patriot* no. 4 (Spring 1999): 9.
410. Jackie Cook, "Friends?," *Patriot* no. 4 (Spring 1999): 10.
411. Nick Griffin, "BNP Delegation Sees the Future of France," *Spearhead* no. 345 (November 1997): 18; "100,000 Turn Out for Front National's Fete Bleu-Blanc-Rouge," *British Nationalist* no. 185 (November 1997): 5. Edmonds also attended the same event in 1999. Richard Edmonds, "BNP Activists Visit Front National Festival in Paris," *Spearhead* no. 369 (November 1999): 26.
412. A. Duck, "Hysterical 'Hens' Singe Own Feathers in Panic Attack," *Spearhead* no. 332 (October 1996): 9.
413. George Lincoln Rockwell, *The Fable of the Ducks & the Hens* (Uckfield: Media Concept, 1996).
414. "BNP Launches 'Operation Daylight'," *Spearhead* no. 336 (February 1997): 5; "New BNP Booklet," *British Nationalist* no. 177 (March 1997): 6.
415. Anonymous [Nick Griffin], *Who are the Mind Benders?: The People Who Rule Britain Through Control of the Mass Media* 2nd ed. (Stroud: The Right Impression, 1999), 6. Griffin later wrote that those "in charge actually wanted the *Mind-Benders* to appear. If this conclusion seems too far-fetched, reflect also on the fact that, although they clearly knew I was working on the project, the police left me with my computer, whereas both of Paul's were seized and taken away." Nick Griffin, "Agent Provocateurs and Destabilisation," *Patriot* no. 4 (Spring 1999): 17.
416. Nick Griffin, "The Cooked Report," *Spearhead* no. 341 (July 1997): 18.
417. For example, "BNP Benefit Concert," *Spearhead* no. 358 (December 1998): 19; "White Resistance Bands Play BNP Benefit Concert," *British Nationalist* no. 198 (December 1998): 6.
418. "BNP Euro-Election Benefit CD," *British Nationalist* no. 199 (January 1999): 6.
419. *Our Europe…Not Theirs* (Welling.: TYR Services, 1999) (CD Recording).
420. Ian Cobain, "Nick Griffin's vision for BNP-led Britain shown in 1990s police interviews," *The Guardian*, 6 May 2014; available online at https://www.theguardian.com/politics/2014/may/06/

nick-griffin-vision-bnp-britain-1990s-police-interviews; accessed 1 July 2016; "BNP Men in Race Act Prosecution," *Spearhead* no. 342 (August 1997): 18.

421. "Editor's Reply," *The Rune* no. 12 (1996): 21.
422. "Nick Griffin Free Speech Trial Starts 27th April," *Spearhead* no. 350 (April 1998): 17.
423. "The Rune Trial," *Spearhead* no. 352 (June 1998): 17.
424. Paul Ballard, correspondence with Ryan Shaffer, 4 September 2014.
425. Cover of *British Nationalist* no. 192 (June 1998): 1.
426. Interview with Butler.
427. "BNP Leaders Plan 1998 and Beyond," *Spearhead* no. 348 (February 1998): 4.
428. "Unity' 98," *Spearhead* no. 354 (August 1998): 9. In 1997, the Edwards family and Simon Darby were prominent National Democrats members. For example, see: "The National Democrats," *The Flag* no. 100 (1997): 1, 3. Darby, in fact, launched the National Democrats' first website at http://www.cityscape.cp.uk/users/fj00/index.html. "National Democrats Set Up New Communications Office," *The Flag* no. 90 (February 1996): 4.
429. Nick Griffin, "British Countryman," *British Countryman* (Spring 1998): 2.
430. "BNP Backs the Countrysiders," *British Nationalist* no. 189 (March 1998): 7.
431. Griffin contributed to *Patriot* at the time. Nick Griffin, "Agent Provocateurs and Destabilisation," *Patriot* no. 3 (Summer 1998): 10.
432. Interview with Griffin.
433. Ibid. Griffin objected strongly to the suggestion that he adopted moderate policies as an internal political maneuver. Rather, he said it was really about issues involving public image and the state. The book Griffin credited was Jonathan Marcus, *The National Front and French Politics: The Resistible Rise of Jean-Marie Le Pen* (New York: New York University Press, 1995).
434. Nick Griffin, "BNP—Freedom Party," *Patriot* no. 4 (Spring 1999): 7.
435. "BNP Euro-Election & General Funds," *Spearhead* no. 359 (January 1999): 17.
436. Interview with Butler.
437. "Euro-Election Fund," *Spearhead* no. 361 (March 1999): 9.
438. "Election Preparations Continue As The BNP Forges Ahead," *Spearhead* no. 362 (April 1999): 4, 5.
439. Hal Austin and Ian Gallagher, "MI5 to Smash Race Gangs," *Daily Express*, 8 February 1999.

440. John Tyndall, "Bambi's New Police State," *Spearhead* no. 361 (March 1999): 8.
441. Interview with Edmonds.
442. Interview with Griffin.
443. Nick Griffin, "No Time for Peter Pan," *Spearhead* no. 357 (November 1998): 19.
444. John Tyndall, "Editor's Introduction," *Spearhead* no. 357 (November 1998): 14. According to Griffin, Tyndall called to complain about it, but ultimately accepted its basic premise because he needed support in the party. Interview with Griffin.
445. Nick Griffin, "No Time Like the Present," *Spearhead* no. 360 (February 1999): 17.
446. Nigel Copsey, "Changing Course or Changing Clothes?: Reflections on the Ideological Evolution of the British National Party 1999–2006," *Patterns of Prejudice* 41, no. 1 (February 2007): 67.
447. Ibid., 80
448. "100% Violence: Del O'Connor," *Brogue Book II: Sinners and Saints* (March 2014): 15; available online at http://issuu.com/broguemagazine/docs/brogue_two_whole_publication_for_is; accessed 1 July 2016. According to an article in *Blood & Honour*, Del O'Connor was expelled from C18 by Will Browning. "The Harley Column," *Blood & Honour* no. 17 (n.d., circa 1999): 10.
449. For details, see: Graeme McLagan, and Nick Lowles, *Mr. Evil: The Secret Life of Racist Bomber and Killer David Copeland* (London: John Blake, 2000).
450. McLagan and Lowles, *Mr. Evil*, 20.
451. "First Meet," *The White Dragon* no. 4 (September 1997): unpaginated 2.
452. "Along with the disbandment of the NSM went the Column 88 magazine and the BCM BOX 335, which is now closed, so please do not write there." "Editorial," *The White Dragon* no. 17 (July 1999): unpaginated 2.
453. "The Nailbomber," *Panorama*, 2000; available online at http://news.bbc.co.uk/hi/english/static/audio_video/programmes/panorama/transcripts/transcript_30_06_00.txt; accessed 1 July 2016.
454. Nick Griffin, "Stranger Things Have Happened," *Spearhead* no. 364 (June 1999): 15.
455. Ibid., 15.
456. *Freedom for Britain and the British: A Voice for a Silent People, British National Party Election Manifesto, Euro '99* (Kent: British National Party, 1999), 2.
457. Nick Griffin, "Euro Mission Accomplished," *Spearhead* no. 365 (July 1999): 4.

458. The cover of this newsletter included the caption, "Preparation of just some of the 15,000,000 leaflets which were delivered throughout Great Britain." *BNP Newsletter* (July/August 1999): 1.
459. Nick Griffin, "Euro Mission Accomplished," *Spearhead* no. 365 (July 1999): 4.
460. Ibid., 5.
461. Ibid., 5.
462. "BNP Euro Election Results," *British Nationalist* no. 204 (June/July 1999): 7.
463. See nomination paper in "The BNP Leadership," *Patriot* no. 5 (Summer 1999): 13.
464. Cover of *Patriot* no. 5 (Summer 1999).
465. "Nick Griffin Interviewed," *Patriot* no. 5 (Summer 1999): 5, 6.
466. John Tyndall, "Why Now?," *Spearhead* no. 366 (August 1999): 4.
467. Ibid., 4, 5.
468. Ibid., 5.
469. Ibid., 5. Interview with Edmonds.
470. Webster wrote about Griffin's "hypocrisy" over "his bi-sexual nature." Martin Webster, "Come for an 'Outing' Down Memory Lane," *Loose Cannon* no. 1 (September 1999): 4.
471. Nick Griffin, "Looking to the Future," *Patriot* no. 6 (Autumn 1999): 13.
472. Ibid., 13, 14, 15.
473. Ibid., 15, 16.
474. Copsey, "Changing Course or Changing Clothes?," 69.
475. Nick Griffin, *Moving On, Moving Up: Campaign for British National Party Chair* (Ilford: NG Election Campaign, 1999), unpaginated 9.
476. Ibid., 6.
477. Nick Griffin, *Moving On, Moving Up: Campaign for British National Party Chair* (Ilford: NG Election Campaign, 1999) (Cassette Recording).
478. Ibid.
479. "BNP Elects New Leader," *British Nationalist* no. 207 (October 1999): 1.
480. John Tyndall, "Time to Get Back to Work," *Spearhead* no. 368 (October 1999): 4.
481. Ibid., 4.
482. "Spearhead and the BNP," *Spearhead* no. 369 (November 1999): 16.
483. "Friends of Spearhead," *Spearhead* no. 370 (December 1999): 14.
484. Copsey, "Changing Course or Changing Clothes," 80.

CHAPTER 6

Fascist Modernization, 1999–2005

Under Nick Griffin's leadership, the British National Party (BNP) developed a friendlier face and made inroads into government power through local elections. The party's close ties with Combat 18 were publicly severed and Griffin appeared on television singing traditional English folk songs with newly written racist lyrics to recruit members. Moreover, women were placed front and center not only to change the party's image as a male fascist club, but to encourage family participation.[1] Meanwhile, a new vocabulary was developed to appeal to a more mainstream audience, relabeling the organization a "democratic" and "rights" political movement. Older BNP publications were discontinued and the words "freedom" and "identity" replaced "British nationalist" and "spearhead." Nowhere were such changes more evident than in the BNP's music. With images and soft voices of women, the songs featured lyrics that spoke about democracy, tradition, rights and identity. Far from ushering in large sales, the music initiative failed to find an audience. However, the BNP found local and international audiences for its ideas through other avenues even as it remained a marginal political party in national elections.

This chapter examines the BNP's self-described "modernization" process in which it transitioned from a small group of hardcore extremists to a thinly veiled populist fascist party that secured minor electoral victories. Specifically, with Griffin as chair of the BNP, it softened its appeal in its publications, public interviews and meetings. Indeed, the BNP's "more radical and esoteric aspects" were "concealed behind a

R. Shaffer, *Music, Youth and International Links in Post-War British Fascism*, Palgrave Studies in the History of Subcultures and Popular Music, DOI 10.1007/978-3-319-59668-6_6

populist face as the party has latched on to panics over asylum, immigration and terrorism."[2] The convergence of several factors, including the asylum issue, mainstream debates about race and community politics, played a role in the BNP's electoral gains.[3] This chapter explores these local election victories in the context of wider BNP efforts to finance and build domestic support through cultural projects while making international links that raised the party's profile and injected racist ideas into society beyond leafleting. In some ways, this represented a more mature and advanced outreach campaign than the venture into music by the National Front (NF) in the 1980s, but other methods stayed the same. Griffin continued his associations with foreign radicals, including visits to the United States and closer contact with European fascists. By this time the leading party members were veterans of British fascism, and they focused on downplaying more radical and offensive ideas that harmed their image.

The "Modernized" British National Party

Following Griffin's successful 1999 leadership election against Tyndall, he made plans to push the party towards the political mainstream with ideas popularized by BNP members Butler and Lecomber. Yet these ideas were not entirely original; rather, they were borrowed from the French Front National's transition from a radical organization to a populist anti-immigrant party. Before the transition could be made, the BNP needed to distance itself from the past and show that the change was not a mere "fig leaf." At the Annual Rally and Members' Meeting in March 2000, amendments were made to the BNP constitution that required members to be in the party for five years before running for leader and added "an explicit acceptance of democracy" to prevent others calling it "fascist."[4] By adopting the term democracy, the party hoped to shed its anti-democratic image and change how the party was perceived by the public. Yet many scholars have shown that the change was purely cosmetic. James Rhodes, for example, explored how the BNP presented itself as a "subcultural movement" that used the language of more popular critiques of multiculturalism but was "totally opposed to the norms and values of the dominant culture and reliant on a racially exclusive, anti-democratic political ideology."[5]

The official Tyndall-era publications were discontinued and replaced with more professional and seemingly less controversial news periodicals.

The *British Nationalist* newspaper, published for two decades, was discontinued in late 1999 (the name became the title for the internally circulated members' bulletin) and in early 2000 *The Voice of Freedom* newspaper was started, with the tagline "for British tradition, identity and democracy." Edited by Tony Lecomber, the first issue "welcomed" readers to "the new broadsheet newspaper of the BNP," which was described as a "tremendous step forward for the BNP" that "looked" like a "mass" newspaper and could be distributed to a wider audience.[6] The party also promoted its new website, with a simpler web address and a "slick multi-media" web page, to spread a more professional political message.[7]

The BNP started the first party magazine, which was a professionally produced bi-monthly publication titled *Identity*.[8] While *Spearhead* previously served as the unofficial magazine and mouthpiece for the BNP, it was Tyndall's personal property and directly opposed Griffin's changes. Neither Griffin nor Tyndall wanted it associated with the new party. *Identity* was started, according to editor Paul Golding, in order for the party to own the magazine and so that it "benefited" from its profits, which would be "put back into building" the BNP "machine."[9] He explained that the name *Identity* showed the party was "now firmly committed" not to confrontation or "preaching to the already converted," but to campaigning on four themes: freedom, democracy, security and identity.[10] Griffin wrote in the magazine's first issue that the key to organization-building was developing groups that "will help us to bring on board and involve large numbers of people when external circumstances swing further in our favour."[11] John Richardson's analysis of the BNP's literature found that despite its language and proclamations of racial populism, it actually remained committed to the ideological core of British fascism from the 1960s.[12]

Among the methods used by the BNP to attract new and respectable people was the party's family organization. Within its first year under Griffin, the party had built on previous changes and started several new subgroups. In July 1999, Sharron Edwards organized the Renaissance Family Day, stemming in part from her involvement in the BNP's "family values" group, Renaissance.[13] With a total of two hundred attendees, children ate free food, played games and were entertained by a magician.[14] The party newspaper described it as a day for children because the BNP saw families as "the heart of a nation and children are the centre of any family."[15] After Griffin became leader, Edwards and her husband, Steve, gained more influence in the party. She became deputy chair under Griffin on January 1, 2000, with her duties being "shadowing" Griffin and serving as leader if he became "indisposed."[16] As key figures in the leadership, Edwards and her husband made speeches around England about elections and the role of local community politics.[17] In August 2000, the "Renaissance Family Day" was renamed the "Red, White and Blue Festival," mirroring the title of a similar event hosted by France's Front National, and was organized with help from Lecomber.[18] The event hosted political seminars, a "big" BNP meeting, fireworks, women's self-defense classes and children's activities, such as a "teddy bears' picnic."[19] Under the new name, the festival became an annual event and a yearly member highlight that promoted the BNP's softer image.[20] In 2000, Griffin described the Red, White and Blue festival in Shropshire as attracting "a few hundred people," while in 2001 it was hosted near his Welsh home with "about five hundred people" and continued to be organized by Griffin until 2005, when Nick and Suzy Cass took over as organizers.[21] To ensure a clean image and keep away unsavory people, the BNP initially banned alcohol and "bomber jackets or clothing which may cause embarrassment to the party."[22]

The party also launched the Young BNP and *Excalibur*, a youth paper edited by Paul Golding, that was named after "Arthur's legendary sword" as a "symbol" of resistance and honor.[23] Additionally, the BNP's Internet presence allowed young people to contact the party and become involved even if they did not have local branches in their area.[24] The Young BNP was started in January 2000 with plans to gather more ideas and build the group through the Internet.[25] Like the Young NF, the BNP's youth wing was focused on ideological "training" and activities. However, the BNP combined its outreach for youth with its family events, such as the Young BNP giving a presentation about "white slavery" at the 2001 Red, White and Blue festival.[26] Later in 2001, the Young BNP was featured on *BNP: Under the Skin*, a BBC *Panorama* episode that expressed skepticism about the BNP's transformation.[27] Specifically, the BNP was accused of being neo-Nazi and racist at a time when it was working to shed those labels.[28] Simon Darby, the BNP's director of technology, described the episode as a "smear" and called its claims that Griffin and other BNP members listened to "Nazi music" "lies."[29]

While the BNP under Tyndall limited youth involvement and the role of music, Griffin saw music was a way to finance and recruit for the party.

The first issue of *Identity* featured an article by Chris Telford, guitarist for the Blood & Honour band Nemesis, announcing the formation of "British Voices," a "nationalist musicians' and artists' circle" for creative party members to introduce political ideas, as Gramsci argued, through a political struggle in culture.[30] Specifically, Telford explained that many fellow BNP members wanted to see a British version of Carl Klang, an American extremist or "nationalist folk group."[31] He concluded the article by calling on members and supporters with artistic skills not only in music and art, but also literature and photography, to get involved.[32]

The BNP worked to shed the fascist and Nazi labels by distancing itself from people who openly embraced Nazism, but also by labeling its opponents "fascists" and "Nazis." For instance, Martin Wingfield described New Labour and union actions as being "in the best traditions of the Brownshirts" and dubbing them "'red' Nazis."[33] *The Voice of Freedom* ran headlines that read "New Labour = New Fascism," claiming the Blair government wanted "to frighten voters with the sack or homelessness."[34] Likewise, the BNP condemned its opponents by using other labels, such as calling the Anti-Nazi League demonstrators "thugs."[35] In terms of self-description, the party denied it was fascist and banned members from extremist groups and websites that promoted violence against critics, such as Redwatch.[36] By 2005, the BNP had "proscribed" its members from joining the National Alliance, British People's Party, NF, White Nationalist Party and Combat 18 because "[w]e don't need or want the skinhead and Nazi image."[37]

The BNP believed their ideas were widely held and hoped that changing the public's perception of the party would propel it to electoral victory. The BNP focused its electoral resources in England during the May 2000 local elections, with Michael Newland running in the mayoral race and six candidates contesting the Greater London Authority elections.[38] The 2000 London Assembly elections saw the party distributing 120,000 BNP "calling cards" and earning an election return of 47,670 votes, which Lecomber boasted was higher than the results of the "extreme left."[39] Likewise, Tyndall called the results "enormously encouraging," including Newland receiving 33,569 as first preference and another 45,337 as second preference for mayor, while Steve Edwards performed best with 23.6% in the West Midlands.[40] The BNP also gained its first local councilor since Millwall in 1993 when John Haycock, who joined the BNP in 1995, was one of sixteen candidates for eighteen seats on the Bromyard and Winslow parish council for the Herefordshire District Council.[41]

Despite seemingly positive steps forward, there was turmoil at the higher levels of the party. In autumn 2000, Newland as well as Sharron and Steve Edwards were expelled from the party. Sharron had been seen as an "excellent candidate" for the November 2000 West Bromwich West parliamentary by-election, but following her expulsion Griffin became the BNP's candidate.[42] A by-election leaflet supporting Griffin claimed: "Voting BNP tells [the] central government and Sandwell council that it's time they stopped spending our taxes on noisy minorities such as the homosexual 'rights' lobby and asylum-seekers."[43] Griffin received 794 votes (4.2%) in the election, but while this seems high for the BNP, *Spearhead* commented, "earlier this year it looked very much as if the party could do much better."[44] A minor party split occurred when Adrian Davies, Sharron and Steve Edwards formed the Freedom Party in late 2000.[45] According to the BNP members' bulletin, Griffin was the target of a "destabilisation" attempt in which he was accused of stealing money and would "be replaced by a self-appointed committee headed by Sharron Edwards."[46] The Freedom Party was described as a "Tory splinter group" and called the Edwards family "troublemakers" who were trying to "steal" money.[47] Tyndall, though critical of Griffin, urged his readers to "stand by the BNP" as "new" parties created as a result of factionalism "have immensely damaged the nationalist cause."[48]

Notwithstanding the party's internal problems, by 2001 the BNP was boasting about its growth being the "fastest," reaching more than one hundred groups and branches.[49] In fact, a year after summer 2000, the BNP found that party expansion had increased and "the BNP's more moderate low-threshold demands … are likely to be a large majority."[50] The BNP ran thirty-three candidates in the June 2001 general election, with Griffin contesting a seat in Oldham West and Royton. The party strategy was to "target" areas "where we stand a realistic chance of winning, or at least getting headline and credibility-grabbing votes of above 20%."[51] The BNP's 2001 manifesto contained many elements from the Tyndall era manifestos, such as withdrawing from the European Union and rejecting aid to Third World nations, but it did contain one important difference. Notably, the BNP called for ending immigration and deporting "criminal and illegal immigrants," but involuntary repatriation was changed to financial support for "voluntary resettlement" of "non-whites."[52] This change was merely cosmetic, as founding BNP member

Keith Axon explained: voluntary repatriation meant taking property and the right to vote away from "immigrants" to encourage them to leave the country.[53]

Meanwhile, in May 2001 a race riot broke out in Oldham, followed in June 2001 by clashes between Asians and whites in Burnley and, in July, between Asians and police in Bradford.[54] A government inquiry concluded that "far-right extremists" had "stoked" divisions within the communities.[55] The 2001 Ritchie Report found that long-standing racism in Oldham, a divided community, "separate development" and racist material from the BNP laid the groundwork for the disorder.[56] The rioters in Bradford, meanwhile, said they took to the streets expecting the NF and BNP to appear in the town center.[57] In contrast, Griffin wrote that the Oldham event showed "the multiracists" were "hoist[ed] by their own petard."[58] The BNP newspaper blamed the riots on "Muslim extremists" who preach "holy war" to Islamic youth to establish a Muslim dictatorship.[59] Additionally, the Burnley BNP issued a document that claimed the "probable cause" was "the attempted incursion by Muslim thug[s] into white areas" that "was met with resistance and a series of battles broke out."[60] At a meeting that month in Bradford, Tyndall told BNP supporters that there was a large "alien" population in the city and commented that one cannot argue with the "subhuman" BNP opponents, but can only "beat the daylights out of them."[61] Illustrating his point, Tyndall remarked that two "nationalists" had taken care of opponents earlier and then further argued that while the BNP should engage in civilized debate, the "alien" population only knows fighting.[62]

The BNP did well for a marginal party in the June general election, which it described as "the most electorally successful in the history of the BNP, or indeed in the history of British Nationalism," with 47,225 votes for thirty-three seats.[63] The highlights were saving five deposits, three results above 10% and saving more deposits than the United Kingdom Independence Party (UKIP).[64] The BNP told its organizers that new recruits were "flooding in" and the BNP's message was spreading to "millions."[65] The party believed it was building credibility, declaring that the "modernising" of the party was "continuing."[66]

On September 11, 2001 Islamic terrorists targeted American landmarks and killed thousands on the East Coast of the United States. Though the destruction was limited to sites in New York, Pennsylvania and Washington DC, the worldwide attention and support for the United States spread to Britain. In the October 2001 members' bulletin, the BNP announced a "campaign against Islam," writing "[a]ny real Muslim is, by Western standards of freedom and democracy, an extremist."[67] The party hosted "anti-Islam" demonstrations that included calls for the religion to get "out of Britain."[68] Islam had been targeted previously in NF literature, with the party claiming that the Salman Rushdie affair was proof that "the multi-racist dream is now nothing more than a rotting corpse whose burial is long overdue."[69] However, the BNP was more explicit in its criticism, with Paul Golding describing Muslims as a "fifth column" and Nick Griffin calling for the United States and Britain to stop "inflaming the Muslim world."[70] In fact, the BNP later added sections to its "introduction" packet that tied immigration and asylum to Islamic extremism.[71] While the United States received British military support for its operations to push the Taliban out of power in Afghanistan, Griffin wrote that President George W. Bush and Prime Minister Tony Blair "had no real evidence linking Bin Laden directly with the attacks," and while Griffin initially supported the West's bombing campaign, he then declared "no British blood for Afghanistan."[72] Though Tyndall's *Spearhead* published a conspiratorial article about 9/11, it also included an article claiming that multiracialism provided "a breeding ground for terror."[73] Griffin took this idea further and announced the BNP's "new national campaign against Islam" in response to the 2001 riots and the terrorist attacks to broaden the BNP's appeal.[74] In fact, the BNP stood two candidates for local Burnley by-elections in November, where the "average BNP vote rose to 21%, compared with 12% in May 2000 and 11.25% in this year's general election," motivating the BNP to work hard for a "historic breakthrough" in May 2002.[75]

The BNP aimed to win several local seats in the North West of England and saw the local government elections as the "best opportunity for a long time" to win an election.[76] Indeed, the BNP told its organizers "we can win in a number of seats up and down the country" and asked for help canvassing.[77] The party ran for sixty-seven seats in the East Midlands, West Midlands, London, North East, North West and Yorkshire during the May 2002 local elections.[78] The campaigns focused on public housing, corporal punishment and opposing asylum seekers and called for spending to be used "directly" for "local British people."[79] The social policies and anti-immigration platform began attracting people who held anti-EU and anti-asylum seekers views, including Labour Party members who were upset with Prime Minister Blair. Trevor

Maxfield, who joined Labour in the late 1980s, had grown increasingly disappointed with Tony Blair's New Labour, believing it had abandoned the working class, and joined the BNP in 2002.[80] Maxfield saw the BNP as an alternative to the two major parties, but then left the BNP and later rejoined Labour, getting elected as a Blackburn with Darwen Borough and Darwen Town councilor.[81] Likewise, Andy McBride, who later became a self-described "enforcer" for Griffin, joined the BNP in 2002 after being pushed out of the Labour Party for his views.[82] McBride joined the BNP out of interest in stopping immigration and leaving the EU, and by late 2007 became the South East regional organizer devoted to cleaning up the party image by banning people with Nazi sympathies.[83]

The 2002 results "shocked" commentators when three BNP candidates were elected to the Burnley government, marking the best election in party history.[84] Tony Lecomber claimed the BNP won because the Burnley council practiced "anti-white racial discrimination" and the party "listened" to the white middle and working classes.[85] Besides these election victories, Lecomber wrote that the BNP had done well in many other areas and that no other like-minded party in Britain was as successful.[86] Just weeks later, the BNP received bad publicity when Carol Hughes, one of the elected BNP Burnley councilors, "refused" to support a motion praising the Burnley football club "for banning fans involved in racial chanting and proclaiming that there was no room for racism in the town."[87] Hughes, however, was featured on the cover of *Identity*, which published an interview in which she described being a councilor as "fantastic" and "hoped" to be a "figurehead" who would encourage more women to get involved with the BNP.[88] The three elected BNP councilors were featured guests at the Red, White and Blue festival and received a standing ovation.[89] Griffin argued that "in the wake of our council victories in Burnley and rising support across the country, we have the leadership and potential to go much, much further."[90]

International Links

The BNP fostered international contacts and associations in ways that earlier British fascist groups did not. Like the NF in the 1980s, the BNP had an interest in building links with like-minded foreigners, but these connections were infrequent and did not result in any meaningful transnational organizations under Tyndall's leadership. Following Griffin's election as leader of the party, ideas and strategies associated with the NF under Griffin became part of the BNP. Discussions about distributism, for example, appeared in BNP publications, and for the first time British fascists raised money in the United States for British elections and hosted events with European extremists.[91] While Tyndall had made infrequent trips abroad, such as a 1979 visit to the United States, Griffin was far more interested in developing organizations with foreign radicals to promote transnational fascism and raise British fascism's profile in other countries. Tyndall, for instance, planned a visit to South Africa in the 1970s, but was denied entry and in 1990 he flew to Charlotte, North Carolina to speak with American extremists, only to be refused entry into the country.[92] Griffin, however, visited the United States several times and traveled to many European countries as BNP leader.

The development of a functioning transnational British fascist organization was centered on the American Friends of the British National Party. In January 1999, Mark Cotterill, a British expatriate living in Falls Church, Virginia, established the American Friends.[93] Cotterill, a veteran of the NF, New NF, British Movement and even a brief stint in the Conservative Party, had long been a political activist and was known for publishing *Patriot Forum* and serving as an organizer in several groups. Having lived in the United States since 1995, as leader of the American Friends he hosted BNP visits to the United States and arranged for British radicals to network with Americans. Inspired by the Friends of Sinn Féin in the United States, the group's objective was to unite the BNP with like-minded groups to raise money and support one another.[94] By remaining in contact with British groups while living in the United States and even welcoming Patrick Harrington to his home, Cotterill made the American Friends into the first actual transnational fascist British group to operate on American soil.

Cotterill launched *Heritage and Destiny* that same year to serve as the American Friends' newsletter, covering news about the BNP as well as other like-minded American and European organizations. The publication's first issue declared it was "devoted to the study and promotion of our Western culture," and that the United States "owes all of its short, but interesting history" to Britain "in particular."[95] The group also launched a website containing up-to-date information about the American Friends and the BNP and issued email bulletins.[96] The

American Friends' "mission statement" included preserving "British culture and heritage among Americans of British descent" and "educating" the Americans about "British nationalism."[97] Having started the organization months before Griffin became party leader, Cotterill supported Griffin's leadership challenge and Cotterill's endorsement appeared second, after that of Derek Beackon, in Griffin's campaign magazine.[98] Cotterill wrote in his endorsement, "I believe a younger man is now needed for this job and that man is Nick Griffin."[99]

The American Friends newsletter celebrated Griffin becoming BNP chair, with Cotterill writing that "[h]e has the full support of the American Friends of the BNP."[100] As Griffin built support in Britain, Cotterill organized several "well-attended" meetings, including attracting more than eighty people to the American Friends' second public event.[101] The speakers included Vincent Edwards, who was campaign manager for David Duke's congressional campaign, webmaster of Stormfront Don Black and journalist Lawrence Myers discussing the power of music in the movement.[102] Cotterill also attended a "Southern Heritage rally" that featured Duke as a speaker, and the American Friends newsletter published a photograph of the two together.[103] At another 1999 American Friends meeting William Pierce, author of *The Turner Diaries*, spoke about his previous BNP speech in London and discussed the differences between his National Alliance and the BNP.[104] Moreover, Black and Duke, along with Canadian Paul Fromm, gave speeches at a 2000 meeting, raising $1300 for the group.[105] Cotterill also promoted the American Friends at the American Renaissance Conference, organized by Jared Taylor, which included a talk about the Front National in France by one of its key figures, Bruno Gollnisch.[106] Following the conference, Gollnisch was a special guest at the American Friends' "Red, White and Blue Celebration."[107]

The American Friends helped British extremists mix with their American counterparts. In its first year of existence, several Britons met with American radicals through Cotterill. In spring 1999, Steve Cartwright, a BNP organizer in Glasgow and Scottish Blood & Honour leader, flew to Washington DC where he was met by his long-time friend Cotterill.[108] In an article about his visit, Cartwright explained that he was one of the speakers at the American Friends' March 1999 inaugural meeting, where he discussed the history of the BNP and the party's strategy in the 1999 European elections that raised $500 for the election.[109] Cartwright and Cotterill then attended a dinner with Duke, and the two were invited to visit NBC Studios where Duke was appearing on *Meet the Press*.[110] In addition, Cartwright traveled to Resistance Records' offices in West Virginia and had several meetings in New Jersey and New York City.[111] A few months later, in July, Simon Darby, a key BNP activist, was hosted by Cotterill and discussed the BNP at a private event.[112] Moreover, Darby filmed his visit, which the BNP published online, boasting of its international activity.[113]

The American Friends also facilitated several meetings between Griffin and American radicals. In April 2000, Griffin stayed with Cotterill on his second visit to the United States, following his first trip more than fifteen years earlier as an NF member.[114] Griffin's trip had three purposes, including speaking at the American Friends' St. George's Day event, meeting "key activists in the organization" and meeting "some of the main American nationalist leaders."[115] The trip "accomplished" these objectives and Griffin met with David Duke, Samuel Francis, Kirk Lyons and even "leading members of Pat Buchanan's campaign organization."[116] Though the American Friends contacted media in the Washington DC area, there were no press visits and no coverage of the events.[117] Despite the lack of media attention, about seventy people attended the American Friends event, listening to speeches from Griffin and Duke as well as Roy Armstrong, a member of the National Democratic Party of Germany.[118] Griffin called for Americans of British descent to support the American Friends and said that while whites were in "peril," the "battle can still be won."[119] Armstrong and Duke had driven by car from New Orleans, Louisiana to Washington DC to meet Griffin, with the American Friends newsletter proclaiming it "disgraceful" that other American leaders did not attend.[120] In May 2001, Griffin returned with his wife, Jackie, for a six-day speaking "tour" on the American East Coast, which was organized by Cotterill.[121] The first speaking engagement was a talk about the 2001 British general election in Richmond, Virginia, along with a tour of "the main Confederate landmarks in the city."[122] Griffin then spoke at another meeting alongside figures from the League of the South and Americans for Self-Determination, and at a final gathering with activists from the Council of Conservative Citizens.[123]

The American Friends protested on American streets while supporting the BNP's efforts in local British elections and presenting British fascist history to Americans. The campaigns were reported in its newsletters, remarking on the steady percentage increases and calling the

May 2000 returns "the best results received by nationalists in Britain since 1977."[124] Meanwhile, the BNP's 2001 general election results were hailed as "the most electorally successful" in the "history of British nationalism" with several pages of analysis.[125] Besides election coverage, articles about William Joyce of the inter-war British Union of Fascists and John Bean of the NF appeared in the newsletter.[126] In April 2001, the American Friends led a demonstration at the German embassy in Washington DC, protesting a proposed ban of the National Democratic Party of Germany, which was described by the American Friends as "the German equivalent of the BNP."[127]

Beyond the protests and dissemination of ideas, the American Friends raised money for local and national BNP elections. According to records, during its first year the American Friends reported donations totaling $3864 from supporters in more than a dozen states.[128] The group continued to build its support and reported $16,504 in 2000 and $13,817 in 2001 before ceasing its operations that year.[129] Donations, in turn, were sent to the United Kingdom for use in local elections, including $500 for Griffin's 2000 campaign in West Bromwich, a $500 donation for campaigning in Preston and £500 ($788.22) to the BNP's National Office for the West Bromwich election.[130] Later media reports claimed the American Friends raised between $85,000 and $200,000, but Cotterill stated in paperwork filed with the American government that such figures were "complete and utter lies … our tax returns for 1999, 2000 and 2001 clearly show that we raised only a fraction of this and of that fraction, only $1788.82 went directly from the AFBNP to the BNP," as well as about $4000 from individual Americans to the BNP.[131] The actual group membership totaled 120, with no more than eighty at one time.[132]

While Cotterill was leading the American Friends, he was also involved with the National Alliance in West Virginia. In 1999, the National Alliance purchased Resistance Records, a racist record label founded in 1993 by George Burdi and Mark Wilson to distribute the music of Burdi's band, RaHoWa (meaning Racial Holy War).[133] Burdi started *Resistance* magazine to promote like-minded bands and offer an outlet for fans to buy albums from Resistance Records' office in Detroit, Michigan.[134] After some initial success, several years later Resistance Records temporarily went out of business as a result of tax disputes and Burdi leaving the movement.[135] Mirroring Resistance's format, in late 1994 Nordland Records and *Nordland* magazine were established in Stockholm, Sweden, selling American, British, German and Scandinavian neo-Nazi music.[136] In 1999, the National Alliance purchased the Resistance Records name and inventory under the direction of William Pierce from Willis Carto and Todd Blodgett to promote extremism through music. In winter 2000, Pierce announced buying "the entire inventory of Nordland," which was "facing bankruptcy" and allowed Resistance to "double" its inventory and the "number of titles we are able to offer."[137] Cotterill was involved in relaunching *Resistance* magazine and used the pseudonym Andrew Miller in editing its ninth issue (the first issue published by the National Alliance).[138] Pierce, writing in the "resurrected" magazine, explained that he had worked with several others "to get Resistance Records back on its feet" because "our people need what Resistance Records can give them."[139] In addition to Cotterill's pseudonym, he, Steve Cartwright and several others were listed as contributors, with articles about the Political Soldier and the history of Skrewdriver based on Joe Pearce's book about the band.[140] The new issue also promoted the American Friends, published a photo of Cartwright with David Duke and included a review by Cotterill of Duke's *My Awakening*.[141] The next issue was published in winter 2000 and Cotterill was replaced as editor by Erich Gliebe, who was critical of Cotterill's involvement.[142]

The American Friends' final year was 2001. Cotterill ran into legal problems for failing to register the organization with the United States under the Foreign Agents Registration Act, which requires foreign political parties and governments to inform the authorities of their activities and income in the country.[143] Cotterill contacted the federal government after hearing rumors that American officials were investigating him and subsequently filed the proper paperwork.[144] Concurrently, it was found that he had overstayed his original tourist visa issued in July 1995 and he was fined by the government.[145] After living in the United States for more than seven years, Cotterill moved to Blackburn, Lancashire.[146] He suspended publication of *Heritage and Destiny* for a year and half, ultimately relaunching it with Peter Rushton in winter 2003 as a "cross-party" magazine.[147] A political hardliner, he left the BNP over disagreement with its direction and founded the England First Party in 2003, which sought the "repatriation of all immigrants to their lands of ancestral origin" as well as "the abolition of the Islamic faith and demolition of all mosques."[148] Besides a few councilors who joined the party, it had two candidates elected when Cotterill and Michael Johnson became councilors in 2006 for Blackburn with Darwen. However, in 2007 Cotterill resigned from office and Johnson joined the For Darwen party, and the England First Party became inactive in June 2012.[149] The American Friends, however, also made news in June 2009 when James von Brunn killed one security guard and wounded two others at the US Holocaust Museum in Washington DC, with newspapers reporting that he had links to the American Friends.[150] When asked about any association, Cotterill explained that von Brunn's name did not appear on the membership lists and he was not a member, but may have attended some meetings.[151]

Even with the dissolution of the American Friends, the BNP continued to engage with like-minded people in the United States. In 2002, Griffin was invited to speak at Jared Taylor's American Renaissance Conference in Washington DC, where he talked about "nationalist movements" gaining credibility in Europe by claiming the BNP and like-minded groups' successes were in response to liberals' "deliberate" attempt to "destroy" white culture with non-white immigration.[152] This marked Griffin's third visit in three years to the United States, which eclipsed his previous single visit as an NF member in the 1980s. Griffin, however, was not the first Briton to speak at an event organized by Taylor. Michael Walker, a former NF member in the 1970s, spoke at the 1998 conference about "nationalist movements in Europe."[153] In addition, John Tyndall was a featured speaker at David Duke's May 2004 "International European American Unity and Leadership Conference" in New Orleans, where he discussed the "need for power" and how even having "a little bit of power" changes how the party is perceived.[154] This was Tyndall's final visit to the United States, and included speeches at Duke's event in New Orleans, a talk in Arlington, Virginia (where he stayed with Jared Taylor) and a discussion with about twenty-five people in Atlanta, Georgia (hosted by Sam Dickson).[155] Unlike Griffin, Tyndall had little interest in American politics and *Spearhead* only published articles about the United States sporadically, including a piece by Edward Fields on Duke's successful 1989 election.[156]

In contrast, Griffin became a frequent visitor to the United States and met with a range of American radicals.[157] In 2005, Griffin, his wife and Simon Darby spoke to an enthusiastic audience at Duke's conference.[158] The following year Griffin returned, delivering a talk at the 2006 American Renaissance Conference about free speech in Britain.[159] Then in 2007 Griffin returned to the United States following invitations by campus groups to speak at Clemson University, Texas A&M and Michigan State University about free speech and Islam.[160] Indeed, while Griffin traveled to the United States once as an NF member, he made almost yearly visits in his early years as the chair of the BNP. This activity was not the only bond the BNP had with American radicals. In fact, the BNP paid its respects to American extremists, such as publishing an obituary for William Pierce (1933–2002) in *Identity*.[161] Likewise, Tyndall wrote that Pierce's death was "a major tragedy" and "he personified the true revolutionary."[162]

Beyond the American Friends' dissolution and the BNP's successes in local elections, the party turned its attention to Europe. The BNP developed more collaborative efforts with European political parties under Griffin. Though BNP reformers, such as Butler and Lecomber, had previously sought to emulate the Front National's methods, Griffin developed high-level relationships with European groups to raise the BNP's profile and fundraise for European Parliamentary campaigns. Griffin argued that the June 2004 European elections would greatly help the BNP, pointing out that if the party had five candidates elected to the European Parliament it would support full-time activists and professionalize the BNP with a £1 million "subsidy."[163] Similarly, the party was making plans for the 2004 London Assembly elections with hopes of having two candidates elected, which would then spawn a synergistic effect.[164] Yet Griffin declared that the European election should be the main focus rather than local elections due to the financial support the party would receive.[165]

The June 2004 European elections brought the BNP closer to continental extremists. In the preceding year the BNP had begun an intense effort to raise funds for campaigning and to pay deposits for the elections, and by February 2004 the party was £104,000 short of its £200,000 goal.[166] The party also needed funding for its campaigns that targeted specific areas with leafleting.[167] In response, the BNP turned to the French Front National for help. Simon Darby, BNP national treasurer, traveled with a BNP delegation "to take the advice of the experienced Front National team."[168] The BNP's magazine featured a photo of the event, with Simon Darby shaking hands with Bruno Gollnisch from the Front National.[169] In March donations increased, with £82,000 raised in just one month.[170] To help further fundraise, Jean-Marie Le Pen, the Front National leader, was a special guest at Griffin's side for an April 2004 "Anglo-French Patriotic Dinner."[171] The media attention and the donations received, with tickets for the dinner selling for £50, were used to support the BNP in the European elections.[172] The May 2004 cover of *Identity* featured Griffin and Le Pen with the title "Two Parties, One Passion."[173] The dinner was described as an event where the Front National was "proud to join with and support" fellow "nationalists in defence of our common interests."[174] In front of 250 people and several television reporters, Le Pen spoke to the audience about "nationalists who seek to preserve and build our national states."[175] The collaboration with Le Pen continued "modernizing" the party's image. The BNP distanced itself from fascism by circulating a *Freedom from the €U* newspaper, with an article titled "We are not thugs & we are not Nazis."[176] Subsequently, fundraising picked up and the press coverage drew more attention to the party.

While the BNP's hopes of winning seats in the European Parliament did not come to fruition, the party received more than 800,000 votes in the June 2004 election.[177] The party saved all of its deposits in the nine English and Welsh contests and received "record levels" of website traffic.[178] The BNP declared the election had given "Britain hope" but also made vague accusations of "electoral fraud," complaining that mail was not sent and election broadcasts were "banned."[179] Griffin boasted that the 808,000 votes were a triumph compared with the 104,000 votes received in 1999, and hoped that the "new recruits" would in turn help campaign for a record number of BNP contests in the 2005 general election.[180]

Aside from its vote share, the 2004 European elections were a breakthrough for the BNP, with public and high-profile European cooperation. Previously international interaction had been limited to low-level contact or individual travel, such as Edmonds's 2003 visit to Germany or a Front National member attending the BNP's 2003 Red, White and Blue festival.[181] Indeed, 2004 marked the first time Le Pen and Griffin appeared together in Britain, announcing a "common" fight for their own nations, while previously the French radicals had sought to distance themselves from their British counterparts. In addition, it was a conscious effort to focus BNP resources on Europe's transnational body over local interests. The following year Le Pen and Griffin met again, this time at the Front National's annual Joan of Arc parade, where Griffin toured the group's Paris office.[182] According to the BNP, the two men explored "ideas for future co-operation between nationalist parties united by opposition to the EU and globalisation, and the Islamification of Europe."[183] In October 2005, Griffin returned with several other BNP members to attend the Front National's festival near Paris and operated a stall with details about the BNP.[184] Griffin delivered a speech in French at the event and this was described as the first time the BNP were "officially invited guests."[185] Meanwhile, Jean-Michel Girard of the Front National was an official guest and speaker at the BNP's 2005 family festival, sharing encouragement from Le Pen "to carry on the work" and declaring that the Front National would "help" the BNP.[186]

The subjugation of local efforts to international politics did not sit well with the long-time BNP members. Tyndall's political and personal animosity towards Griffin spilled over to include criticism of the BNP's strategy. Tyndall wrote that "[t]he overwhelming priority was given to the Euro elections" and so "the party emerged with no Euro seats and just four council seats more than it had" in previous elections.[187] Using the money from the European elections, he argued, "could well have tipped the scales" in local elections and gotten more BNP candidates elected locally.[188] Tyndall also expressed his anger over proposals to alter the BNP's requirement that members be "white," which was being discussed by the legal department following claims about discrimination.[189] By summer 2004, he had had enough and Tyndall publicly announced he would challenge Griffin for the BNP leadership, citing several complaints including the recent "Euro failure."[190]

The connections with France were not the party's only links to continental Europe. In February 2001, the BNP published a call from the National Democratic Party (NPD) in Germany for "patriots from all over Europe" to travel to Germany and support the party against a proposed ban by the government.[191] In 2004, Chris Beverley served as a BNP representative at the annual congress for the NPD, explaining that "[t]he BNP acknowledges that nationalists across Europe can learn a lot from each other."[192] Beverley returned to Germany in February 2007, attending the NPD's European Youth Congress and "meeting various representatives" from Dutch, Italian, Portuguese, Spanish and Swedish groups.[193] The event also included 1500 people marching in commemoration of the bombing of Dresden during the Second World War, and he called it "the most productive foreign visit I have made to represent the party."[194] In 2005 Björn Söder, party secretary for the Sweden Democrats, spoke at the BNP's family festival, denouncing immigration and linking minorities to crime.[195] The following year in 2006, a BNP delegation traveled to Stockholm to help the Sweden Democrats, where

BNP activist Mike Bell remarked the party "face[s] the same struggles as the BNP."[196] Two years later Marc Abramsson, head of the National Democrats of Sweden, attended the 2008 Red, White and Blue festival where he was involved in judging the "best stall."[197] At the same event, guests from Sweden and the Czech Republic were also involved in the event's cooking tent with different food dishes, hosted by Griffin.[198] Meanwhile, in 2008 Griffin and Roberto Fiore, then an Italian Member of the European Parliament, traveled to Hungary to speak to Jobbik party members, and Griffin also spoke alongside members from the Czech National Party in the Czech Republic about opposing Islam.[199]

Internal Struggles and Burnley Victory

Despite the growing membership and high-profile meetings, there were internal disputes and heavy criticism of the BNP leadership from Tyndall. Griffin and his allies were accused of creating party "divisions" by preventing Tyndall from speaking and expelling members, which was "damaging" the organization.[200] In July 2002, Peter Rushton was "excommunicated" from the party without a hearing over accusations he had supplied information to *Searchlight*, and Keith Axon, former West Midlands organizer, was suspended for allegedly spreading false rumors about Griffin.[201] Rushton, a key activist who supported Tyndall, claimed Griffin expelled him when Rushton questioned how estates left to the party would be handled.[202] Axon was also a loyal Tyndall supporter who had followed him from the NF to the BNP, and said Griffin feared Tyndall's remaining party support, which provoked Griffin to officially suspend Axon for a year.[203] A reply about Axon's treatment issued to BNP organizers claimed that Axon had not been suspended but was prohibited from attending BNP events for implying Griffin was "a thief and a traitor."[204] Other people had been pushed out of the BNP earlier, including Simon Sheppard, who had drawn media attention when he and David Hannam were arrested for inciting hatred with a 1999 European election leaflet.[205] Sheppard continued to work with Tyndall, including web-hosting for *Spearhead* and writing *Spearhead* articles on topics such as "why many white women prefer non-white males."[206] Sheppard, who described his interests as including procedural analysis and sex "differences," wrote about Jewish "control" of the British government, and while his views were criticized by some BNP figures, he was the webmaster for a variety of political groups.[207]

While some people were expelled from the party, the changes made to the BNP under Griffin encouraged several former NF and National Democrats members to join. Notably, Martin Wingfield, a former NF chair in 1986, said he returned to politics because the votes Griffin received for Oldham in the 2001 general election showed him that the party could have a breakthrough and "the BNP were suddenly looking [like] a modern, challenging political party."[208] Wingfield became editor of *The Voice of Freedom* and his wife, Tina, who was also a former NF activist, became a BNP member.[209] In addition, John Bean, a founding member of the NF in 1967, joined the BNP and became editor of *Identity* in 2003.[210] Bean joined the party citing Griffin's leadership as widening the BNP's support base, and his time as *Identity* editor would last longer than his editorship of *Combat*, the magazine of the first BNP in the 1960s.[211] As Graham Macklin has shown, the BNP promoted John Bean's version of the history of British fascism, which whitewashed the anti-Semitism and extremism as well as marginalized Tyndall "to make it serviceable for future ideological exigency."[212]

The media also took an interest in the party. In November 2002, Young BNP leader Mark Collett was featured on Channel 4's *Young, Nazi and Proud* expressing Nazi sympathies in footage recorded by journalists.[213] One week before the broadcast Collett was on the cover of the *Sunday Times Magazine* standing in front of a mosque, and an accompanying article explained: "He says he isn't anti-Semitic, but he thinks Jews are a distinct, 'non-white' race, and he is in no doubt that the 'white race' (a clearly definable entity in his mind) is superior."[214] The coverage was a public relations disaster for the BNP as it was seeking to move away from the neo-Nazi and fascist label, and it resulted in Collett, who had been appointed by Griffin, losing his position.[215] In fact, the BNP called the program "a real stinker," but wrote Collett "was sacked from his position" and "[j]uvenile extremism has no place in our party and is no longer acceptable."[216] Despite the bad publicity, in November the BNP won a Blackburn council by-election with its candidate, Robin Evans, beating Labour by sixteen votes.[217] Evans's victory in the hard-fought local election brought the BNP's number of councilors to four.[218]

Throughout 2003, the BNP continued building local support and winning elections. After several years of consciously changing its brand, the organization declared it was "a family party" and "a party dedicated to restoring and preserving traditional values."[219] In January 2003,

Adrian Marsden won a council by-election for the BNP in Halifax, West Yorkshire.[220] Griffin commented that the victory "showed that our council wins in Lancashire were not the isolated protest votes that some media commentators had suggested, but the first examples of a seismic shift in British politics."[221] In discussing the direction of the party, Griffin wrote: "Our fundamental determination is to secure a future for white children but we don't hate anyone" because the nation "is first and foremost decided by ethnicity."[222] The BNP started a new campaign denouncing New Labour's support for the American invasion of Iraq, declaring the war was about Israel and oil, not terrorism.[223]

In the May 2003 council elections, the BNP contested more than two hundred seats and was gaining about one hundred new members each week.[224] This marked the "biggest" council campaign in the party's history as the branches engaged in intensive leafleting.[225] The party focused on issues including lower taxes, "saving" town centers, "shrinking" bureaucracy, fighting corruption and preventing the provision of housing to asylum seekers.[226] BNP activists spent weeks canvassing with candidates, hoping for more victories in areas where the party had done well the previous year. Opponents, including Asian organizations, unions and anti-racist groups, campaigned against the BNP.[227] Burnley BNP activists, such as Steve Smith, distributed thousands of BNP publications and mailers to residents as well as spreading the messages on the streets.[228] Griffin dismissed the idea that the leafleting made a decisive difference, instead crediting the increased interest to more public awareness on television about the BNP being a way to "kick" Labour out.[229] The result was not only an increase in votes, but eight BNP victories for the Burnley council, which made the party the official opposition against Labour.[230] In total, the BNP won thirteen council seats and received 104,037 votes nationwide as well as beating the Conservatives in eighty contests.[231] The BNP declared it was now a "mainstream" party.[232] Scholar Benjamin Bowyer analyzed the district voting data from the BNP's 2002 and 2003 elections and found that ethnic minority size was associated with BNP support, and that the party usually did best in white neighborhoods and poorer urban areas where real estate values shaped support.[233] Specifically, James Rhodes studied the BNP in Burnley, finding that "the spiralling political disaffection, particularly towards Labour, within socio-economically deprived boroughs, the politicisation of 'race', weak opposition parties, racialised geography and a BNP party or branch able to present itself as a 'respectable' political actor" were significant factors in the BNP gains.[234]

Yet everything was not perfect. As fundraising and preparations began for 2004, the BNP lost two by-elections in North England and was publicly embarrassed by BNP councilor Robin Evans, who told the press that BNP councilors in Burnley were "useless," resulting in his resignation.[235] However, a Conservative Party councilor in Halifax "defected" to the BNP over the "Tories' gutless stance on Europe."[236] Yet tension between Griffin and Tyndall increased throughout the year. In early 2003, the BNP banned *Spearhead* from its meetings and activities, claiming the magazine was causing dissension in the party.[237] For his part, Tyndall denied that the "softening" of BNP policies had helped the party win the elections, crediting instead public opinion against immigration, media reports critical of immigration and the decline of the Conservative Party.[238] Griffin denounced Tyndall's previous leadership and "selling himself as the 'hardline' guardian of nationalist principles," arguing that the victories never could have happened under his chairmanship.[239] The disputes were not simply ideological but were also personal, and the two argued over the use of BNP money.[240] Tyndall was then called to a BNP disciplinary tribunal over seven charges "relating to alleged actions prejudicial to the good of the party," but urged supporters to remain with the BNP.[241] Ultimately, four charges were dropped while Tyndall was acquitted of one and found guilty of two, including "slandering" Griffin, and the four-member tribunal moved to expel Tyndall.[242] Martin Wingfield remarked that Tyndall's expulsion "tells the public that the BNP is not stuck in the past and that his kind of racism has no place in the BNP."[243] However, Griffin later reinstated Tyndall's membership following arguments from Tyndall's solicitor that the charges would not withstand court scrutiny.[244]

Ladder Strategy and Tyndall's Death

The BNP hoped to benefit from its new membership and media attention in local election victories to make record gains in the 2005 general election. Tony Lecomber explained that the BNP's plan for "winning" involved a "ladder strategy" of focusing on lower sets of elections and then moving on to national elections, with activists "canvassing" areas where BNP voters live.[245] He described how the "best" chance at a parliamentary seat was in Burnley, where not a single ward had been canvassed.[246] Indeed, Nigel Copsey wrote that the party "used the general election" in order to campaign for "selected wards" and "reap the benefits at local elections the following year."[247] The party planned to make the most of its Internet presence by pushing its perspective to the masses. Internet efforts could reach more people, with the party's webmaster, Steve Blake, commenting that the BNP website was now "recognised" as a news source on Google.[248] Concerning the streets, Eddy Butler wrote that the ideal election campaign involves four sweeps through key areas, including visiting homes, revisiting homes that did not answer, another revisit and a "good morning" leaflet on election day.[249] The BNP sought to build from these tactics and refine its techniques.

In early 2005 Griffin announced that the BNP would contest more than one hundred constituencies in the general election.[250] The purpose was to "build up voter loyalty" in key areas, target wards for the 2006 council elections, air a television broadcast and achieve "headline winning votes."[251] He cautioned members that the BNP could not compete like a major party because "we are not in" the big league yet, but would position itself after 2005 with more members, skills and better leaflet production.[252] As Butler explained, the BNP had moved beyond what it once was and needed to focus on long-term success and contest an election with one hundred candidates "to confirm our position as a major player in the British political scene."[253] In April 2005, the BNP hosted an election rally in London to motivate organizers and fundraise for the campaigns.[254] The party's 2005 election manifesto, comprising more than fifty pages, included platforms that mirrored its previous positions, including "abolishing multiculturalism, preserving Britain."[255]

As the party moved towards the 2005 general election, Tyndall became increasingly focused on criticizing Griffin and once again becoming leader. After several years of condemning Griffin's leadership, Tyndall announced his intention to challenge Griffin in summer 2004 with backing from his long-time supporters, including Edmonds.[256] Tyndall's side published reports that Griffin was "gagging" Tyndall and Edmonds to prevent them speaking to BNP branches and accused Griffin of hypocrisy.[257] Other Tyndall backers included Peter Rushton and Eddy Morrison, and letters in *Spearhead* by people such as Keith Axon expressed anger at Griffin for "diluting" BNP policies.[258] Some supporters helped form the Spearhead Support Group, which was launched at a July 11, 2004 meeting in Leeds with Rushton, Morrison, Tyndall and

Tony Braithwaite giving speeches, to unite against Griffin's moderate policies.[259] Tyndall spent much of his time calling for unity, criticizing Griffin and hinting that the government was behind the party's problems.[260] The group issued an email publication titled *Nationalist Week*, which described Tyndall's speech at the meeting denouncing Griffin's willingness to allow "non-whites" to join the BNP and criticizing Griffin's "opportunism."[261] Likewise, Tyndall wrote about his vision of the party, including pledging that the BNP would be "a party of 100% racial nationalism" and opposing Griffin's focus on religion and "Islam as a special enemy of Britain" instead of "the overall threat of multi-racialism."[262] Tyndall also accused the BNP leadership, namely Griffin and Lecomber, of "crippling" the party by "antagonising almost everybody in sight, imposing bans, suspensions and prohibitions."[263]

In December 2004, Tyndall was again expelled from the party on a range of charges, including publishing "pro-Nazi" material in *Spearhead* and spreading "false and malicious rumours" about Griffin.[264] Tyndall denounced these actions but remained supportive of the party, planning a legal challenge against his expulsion and opposing the formation of a breakaway party.[265] Tyndall's supporters, including Axon, Rushton, Edmonds, Steve Smith and Eddy Morrison, held meetings to "save" the BNP.[266] A dinner, for example, was held to unite Griffin's critics, with Tyndall giving the keynote speech and other talks presented by Morrison, Rushton, and John Morse denouncing Griffin's "softening" of the BNP and allegations about his use of finances to win party support.[267]

The challenge from Tyndall and the 2005 national campaign were not the only issues facing the BNP. In December 2004, Griffin, Tyndall and Mark Collett were arrested for using "words" or "behaviour" that would "likely" incite "racial hatred."[268] The charges against Griffin and Collett came in response to *Secret Agent*, a BBC documentary that captured speeches by the two, and Tyndall's arrest was based on a separate event filmed by the television crew.[269] Griffin called the BBC program a "hatchet job" by the media, which was attacking the BNP because it was doing well.[270] The party organized "free speech" rallies in response to the charges, accusing the laws of being "draconian" and "politically-motivated."[271] Griffin even spoke alongside his family at the summer 2005 Red, White and Blue festival about the "painful" prospect of being jailed and taken away from his family.[272]

The May 2005 general election resulted in 192,745 BNP votes for its 118 candidates, compared with the winning Labour Party result of 9,552,436.[273] Even before the vote, Griffin said "we've already won the election," claiming that a twenty-five-year "taboo" that prevented the major parties talking about "immigration" had been broken and that the BNP had given voters a "real choice."[274] Tony Lecomber wrote that the BNP's vote share showed that the party had "improved" in "every respect," including saving thirty-four deposits and the party acquiring professional printing facilities for use in the future.[275] Likewise, *The Voice of Freedom*, the BNP's newspaper, claimed: "We are now Britain's 4th party" in terms of influence and organization.[276] Journalist Daniel Trilling described how the BNP sought inroads with working-class voters who were concerned about immigration, thereby appealing to traditionally Labour-aligned voters.[277] Tyndall was critical of the results, finding there was "no meaningful opposition in British politics" and concluding, "[i]f the BNP can somehow get its act together it can create that opposition and become a true contender for power."[278] A much harsher *Spearhead* article claimed that the BNP leadership "squandered" opportunities with "flawed" strategies and tactics.[279] The BNP's 2005 manifesto was condemned as containing "leftist-liberal buzz words" and "wrong" messages.[280] While Peter Rushmore wrote the results could have been better, he applauded the BNP vote tally of 192,745 in 2005, which "slightly" beat the NF record of 191,719 in 1979.[281] The BNP, wanting to further improve its election returns, held a meeting to discuss errors made in the campaign. They concluded that changes needed to be made, including improving candidate training and releasing the election manifesto internally before announcing it to the press.[282]

The original May 2005 court appearance for inciting hatred was pushed back citing the upcoming election, and a trial date was expected later in the year or the next year.[283] However, on July 19, 2005 Tyndall died unexpectedly, with *Spearhead*'s final issue, edited by Edmonds, published as a tribute to his life.[284] Condolences from British and international supporters were printed in the magazine as plans were made for a private funeral.[285] An obituary in *Identity* described Tyndall as a man with "legendary" courage who "spent a lifetime trying to warn his fellow Britons of the approaching danger."[286] A companion article by John Bean called him "headstrong and argumentative" but with "impeccable" "personal manners and courtesy."[287] With Tyndall's passing, Griffin's main remaining challenge to leading the party was a potential prison sentence.

Fascist Folk Music

As the BNP increased its election returns and developed foreign associations in Europe and North America, music remained an important element of British fascism. Neo-Nazi skinhead music continued to be a transnational conduit between foreign fascists as the main skinhead organizations, Blood & Honour in Britain and the Hammerskins in the United States, expanded their reach with publications and international concerts. Indeed, while Griffin was trying to "modernize" the BNP, the skinhead image continued to be pushed by the younger and more radical youth. Yet there was still overlap between Blood & Honour and the "modernized" BNP. Steve Cartwright, the first member of the BNP to travel across the Atlantic for the American Friends organization, was the head of Blood & Honour's Scottish division. As the group's *Highlander* publication noted, Cartwright attended the 2003 Rudolf Hess march in Bavaria and his brother, John, performed with Nemesis at the start of the event.[288]

Following the imprisonment of Charlie Sargent and the spring 1999 nail bombing spree, Combat 18 lost significant support. A new group behind Blood & Honour began organizing events and publishing its magazine, while ISD Records moved to Denmark.[289] In 2000, about eight hundred people attended the Ian Stuart memorial concert, and a thousand attended the 2001 concert with bands including Whitelaw and Celtic Warrior.[290] Annual memorials for the former Skrewdriver singer became a mainstay and centerpiece for Blood & Honour, which drew large international crowds.[291] Meanwhile, *Blood & Honour* magazine published a "BNP Update," praising the new leadership and discussing the Young BNP's activities.[292] The magazine's regular column covered BNP news, discussed the party's local election gains and published BNP contact information where readers could get more details.[293]

As the BNP expanded locally, Blood & Honour continued building support in Europe. In 1997, a Scandinavian branch of Blood & Honour was developed and its figures became some of the most active outside of Britain. The first issue of its magazine, published in English, featured a swastika with the words "Unity or Die."[294] In 1998, Blood & Honour's Denmark division began publishing a magazine, which featured images of Waffen-SS soldiers and Nazi leaders.[295] In 2000, a Spanish branch was started with news about British and Italian skinheads.[296] A Hungarian division opened in 2001, which also featured reports about international skinhead events.[297] In subsequent years, more branches in European countries were opened and began publishing national magazines.[298]

Though not as significant as Blood & Honour in Europe, the Hammerskins emerged as the most significant skinhead group in the United States. Founded in Dallas, Texas in 1987 as the Confederate Hammerskins, the group expanded across the United States despite several leaders being arrested for violent crimes.[299] By the early 1990s, Hammerskin branches existed in the north, south, east and west, where a group earned the name after becoming notorious for its violence.[300] In 1997, a semi-regular magazine titled *Hammerskin Press* was started as the "official source for collective activity amongst the Hammerskin Nation."[301] It also developed international chapters in Australia, Britain, Canada, the Czech Republic, Germany and Switzerland.[302] Events organized by the Hammerskins became sites for transnational expressions of fascism. In 2001, it organized Hammerfest in the American South with support from Resistance Records and a newer racist label, Panzerfaust Records.[303] A review of the event was published by *Blood & Honour* magazine, which praised Nemesis's performance and boasted about Europeans attending the festival.[304] The concerts continued to gain international notoriety. In 2004, four hundred skinheads from Britain, Canada, France, Germany and Poland attended a Hammerfest concert in Michigan where Brutal Attack from England played.[305] The 2005 Hammerfest gathering again drew an international crowd to Atlanta, Georgia, with Kremator from Canada and Whitelaw from England headlining the performance.[306] That same year Whitelaw embarked on a European tour and performed in Russia, spreading fascist music and creating a bridge between diverse skinhead organizations.[307]

The public association of international neo-Nazi skinheads with the BNP was not what the party wanted. If the BNP wanted to be seen as a legitimate party with a "modernized" image, it needed to distance itself from skinhead groups and extremist rhetoric. In reality, Blood & Honour promoted the BNP and key figures were involved in both groups, so the public did not have to delve deeply in order to find links.[308] In fact, Stigger, best known as the guitarist for Skrewdriver and a self-described National Socialist, performed at the BNP's Red, White and Blue festival in 2003.[309] Meanwhile, the BNP's *Identity* magazine highlighted and sold the CD *Extremist* by Carl Klang, whose songs promoted fringe perspectives, although Klang did not perform rock music or sing about Nazism.[310]

In 2005 the BNP, hoping to transform its image through music, started Great White Records (GWR) to release "folk" music that carried "softer" racial themes devoid of Nazi references. Griffin was a long-time fan of folk music and even in the early 1980s did not enjoy the heavier style of punk music.[311] This new initiative fit in with Griffin and Steve Cartwright's earlier abortive plans to start Radio White Europe, a radio station to be broadcast throughout Eastern Europe "aimed" at a "more cultural audience—folk and apocalyptic folk" as well as other forms of rock and skinhead music.[312] Great White Records' purpose, however, was limited to releasing softer music for the "patriotic cause."[313] The party funded its own recording studio and invited artists who wanted to be part of the effort to send music samples to Great White.[314]

In summer 2005, the BNP began to promote "English music of the past" to "celebrate our heritage and heroism through the imagination of composers."[315] That year Great White Records was incorporated by Dave Hannam as secretary and director, with Nick Cass serving as the other director and with two hundred shares of the company evenly divided between the two.[316] Great White's first release was *Time to Make a Stand* by Lee Haggan, whose title track the BNP newspaper explained was "the popular British nationalist anthem" about Gavin Hopley, who was killed in Oldham.[317] The collection also included "A Vision, Not a Dream," with lyrics by Griffin, which was a "powerful story of war and betrayal in this tribute to the fallen heroes of Europe."[318] In *Resistance*, the American skinhead magazine, a review of the CD styled it as "a soft-on-the-ear collection of acoustic folk music with an overtly pro-white flavor."[319] The album was promoted by the BNP as "a collection of patriotic British folk songs."[320] According to a review published in the BNP newspaper, the CD showed that "[t]he era of nationalist music being dominated by often badly performed and produced post-punk rock growling is definitely over."[321] Lastly, another review by Peter Ashford offered a positive song-by-song analysis, calling it "a must buy, a must hear."[322]

The Great White Records operation was profiled alongside neo-Nazi rock bands, such as Whitelaw, in the 2006 documentary *Nazi Hate Rock*.[323] Featuring interviews with Griffin and Hannam, the presentation contrasted the different styles of music and the BNP's efforts to move beyond skinhead associations. Among the performances shown in the documentary was a recording session with Griffin's youngest daughter singing "The Sun and the Moon," a Cornish folk song originally about a miner dying in an accident, but with new lyrics about a father dying in a racist assault. The media's response was not positive, as demonstrated in the *Sunday Mirror*'s description of the segment: "BNP chief Griffin gets his 15-year-old daughter to make a hate-filled pop song for kids."[324] Hoping to capitalize on newer forms of communication, Great White Records launched a website as well as social media outreach on MySpace that promoted its music, including free downloads and news about the controversy surrounding "The Sun and the Moon" song.[325]

The BNP's folk music was not just about promoting a new "positive" message, but also provided entertainment for party members. The 2005 Red, White and Blue festival was called the "best" yet, with hundreds of "campers" attracted by the entertainment and food.[326] The event also showcased BNP musicians, including Dave Hannam, who performed "a mixture of traditional folk and modern political protest songs" later released by Great White Records.[327] At the 2005 organizers' conference, announcements were made about a May 2005 folk festival in Halifax and there was discussion about linking "New Right" ideas with politics and culture.[328] Folk concerts were also used to raise money. In May 2005, four hours of entertainment were organized by the BNP to gather donations for BNP councilor Arthur Redfearn, who was appealing his job dismissal.[329] Several musicians performed "traditional British folk music from England, Scotland, Ireland and Wales," which included Dave Hannam and even a duet by Griffin and Yorkshire organizer Nick Cass.[330]

Folk music also served as the background to social functions at meetings, where activists sang along with the musicians.[331] At the 2006 Annual Conference, music performed by several BNP activists, including Colin Auty and Dave Hannam, provided party loyalists with entertainment.[332] In summer 2006, the BNP held its first "summer school" event, attracting more than two hundred people.[333] With "classes" about activism, BNP newcomers and veterans were entertained by music performed by Colin Auty and Frank Atack.[334] Both men were then featured performers at the Red, White and Blue festival that year, which was described as a "wonderful blend of folksy, humour, tinged with the serious edge of what we, the BNP, are all about."[335] In fact, the BNP newspaper proudly highlighted the mix of political campaigning, ideological classes and musical entertainment.[336] In 2006, Great White Records director Alan Smith spoke at the BNP's elite Trafalgar Club dinner about "the ability of music to touch peoples emotions like no other form of communication can do."[337] Smith specifically thanked the club's members for helping pay Great White Records' costs and "promised a new more professional approach in the promotion of their products."[338] Yet the reality was that Great White Records was failing as a business, with accounts showing £8 in total assets less liabilities in 2006.[339]

Great White Records released several albums during 2007 in hopes of turning the business around. As in 2006, when the company sold the audio recording of the Red, White and Blue festival, it also released a recording of the 2007 festival, including music and speeches.[340] More significant was the 2007 release of *West Wind*, which the BNP promoted as containing eleven tracks "written by Nick Griffin and professionally performed by different artists in several different styles."[341] *West Wind* was featured on the June 2007 cover of *Identity*, with a review by Peter Ashford calling it "a huge direction change for the label" and noting that "Great White Records are indeed now producing some of the finest nationalistic music in the UK."[342] No expense had been "spared" on the CD's packaging, and it marked "a new high in terms of quality for nationalistic music."[343] The album's lyrical content ranged from bemoaning American culture to criticizing the Blair government and supporting ethno-nationalism.[344]

Great White Records' music received widespread criticism for its racist themes, which linked local BNP officials to xenophobia. Colin Auty's 2007 album, titled *Truth Hurts*, included songs about changing racial demographics, and criticism of democracy as well as immigration.[345] Auty, a Dewsbury East councilor, was publicly criticized for his song about Savile Town that linked Muslims to changes he did not like.[346] More directly, critics accused Auty of stirring up hatred and community divisions with the song.[347] Great White Records released a statement on its website supporting the song and quoted Auty, saying: "The straightforward message behind the lyrics is that Savile Town is populated by foreigners who do not speak English, is a place where residents openly sell heroin, and that these people are paedophiles who have a preoccupation with girls aged 12."[348] One year later, Auty decided not to complete his term as councilor and in July 2008 resigned, which *The Press* reported left the BNP's "local credibility in tatters."[349]

Great White Records was seeking to grow its base not only with the music it produced, but with other items it sold as well. By 2008, Great White Records was selling shirts with its logo, a shark with the company's name, through the BNP's monthly magazine.[350] It also sold pens, stickers, posters and even computer mouse pads.[351] In summer 2008, Great White Records started a magazine, *Soundbites*, that highlighted the company's history and artists. Its first issue featured Joey Smith discussing the six-month process of recording his "electro-pop-rock" album *Not Just About the Music*.[352] Smith explained about his music: "If I can promote awareness of British heritage and pride in our people then that is what I am aiming for."[353] His lyrics consisted of reminiscing about a narrow view of British history and criticizing change, including in demographics.[354] *The Voice of Freedom* claimed "the opposition appears to be very worried at the growing influence of the BNP's music 'arm' Great White Records."[355] Smith went on to perform at the 2008 summer school, where more than two hundred activists listened to lessons on organizing and were then entertained by his music.[356]

Mainstream musicians resented the BNP's attempts to adopt folk music and inject racist themes into it. In August 2009, BNP critics responded to Great White Records with Folk Against Fascism "because many in the folk community wanted to say that you can be proud of England's music, traditions and customs without being a bigot or a racist."[357] Indeed, Karl Spracklen analyzed the folk music community's reaction online and concluded that folk music was "quick to resist fascism co-opting its traditions."[358] With well-known artists, such as longtime NF and BNP opponent Billy Bragg, Folk Against Fascism released music and held events to prevent the BNP from "co-opting" folk music for its political goals.[359] This campaign was launched at an interesting time, as months earlier Great White Records had been officially closed. As it turned out, there was a strong, albeit marginal, market for neo-Nazi skinhead music, which could sustain business despite attacks from antifascists. However, Great White Records attracted much more limited interest among radicals and in June 2009 the company was dissolved.[360] At the 2009 Red, White and Blue festival, Butler held a public auction to clear out "crates" of CDs that were cluttering up office space, and the whole endeavor represented a substantial financial loss.[361] As Patrick Harrington reflected later, "the NF had more influence on youth culture than the BNP had even though the BNP is much bigger."[362]

Music, however, was not the only cultural form the BNP used to promote its views. The Young BNP organized Camp Excalibur, which included figures such as Mark Collett and Griffin's daughter, Jennifer, hosting political discussions and entertainment activities.[363] Beginning in 2001, the camp was designed for members between the ages of sixteen and twenty-five and was "all but politics free," with special activities for girls.[364] Initially organized by Collett, it was designed for youth "to have some fun and enjoy the comradeship."[365] The BNP also sold busts of Admiral Nelson and an *England Expects* DVD about Nelson made with Griffin, Butler and Jonathan Bowden, the BNP's cultural officer.[366] The movie was described as an hour-long journey through Nelson's life and naval victories with "facts aplenty."[367] Similarly, *East Ended*, another BNP-produced "documentary" hosted by Butler, was about the changing ethnic make-up of London's East End and the BNP's role in "protecting" British nationalism.[368] Though none of these projects resulted in significant financial gain or cultural impact, they demonstrated the BNP's efforts to make a political impression outside the ballot box by introducing ideas to the public.

Conclusion

The BNP was significantly transformed under Nick Griffin's leadership. In his first few years as leader, the party won more elections than all previous efforts in NF and BNP history combined. To do so, it developed an ideological program that connected extremism with local communities and like-minded foreigners. While the NF disseminated its ideas through music internationally, the BNP maintained foreign organizations that raised money, and its supporters engaged with transnational politics in ways that were not possible in the 1980s. With success and some local political power, the party leadership faced increased pressure with its founder, Tyndall, being highly critical of Griffin's strategy, even as they both attracted attention from law enforcement for inciting hatred. The party failed to establish a new and friendlier form of fascist music, but the BNP was more successful at making international links than at any time previously. As the next chapter explains, the BNP continued to build international associations and made a breakthrough by winning two seats in the European Parliament. Yet with its electoral success, increased internal pressure caused the party to fracture, which had a profound impact on the subsequent direction of British fascism.

Notes

1. Nick Griffin, *Nationalist Movements and the Crisis of the Liberal Elite* (Marietta: American Renaissance, 2002) (DVD Recording). He also stated that "very often deeply political women are also deeply disturbed and you're probably better without some of them."
2. James Rhodes, "The Banal National Party: The Routine Nature of Legitimacy," *Patterns of Prejudice* 43, no. 2 (2009): 142.
3. Nigel Copsey, *Contemporary British Fascism: The British National Party and the Quest for Legitimacy* (Basingstoke: Palgrave Macmillan, 2008), 124.
4. "Constitutional Reform," *Patriot* no. 7 (Summer 2000): 35.
5. James Rhodes, "Multiculturalism and the Sub-Cultural Politics of the BNP," in *British National Party: Contemporary Perspectives* eds. Nigel Copsey and Graham Macklin (New York: Routledge, 2011), 75.
6. A. Lecomber, "The Voice of Freedom Says," *The Voice of Freedom* no. 1 (February 2000): 2.
7. The article stated, "visit the BNP Home Page at www.bnp.net and the BNP's slick multi-media site at: www.bnp.to." "On The Internet," *The Voice of Freedom* no. 1 (February 2000): 3.
8. "Identity," *The Voice of Freedom* no. 1 (February 2000): 7.
9. Paul Golding, "Editorial," *Identity* no. 1 (January/February 2000): 2.
10. Ibid.
11. Nick Griffin, "The Way Ahead," *Identity* no. 1 (January/February 2000): 7.
12. John E. Richardson, "Race and Racial Difference: The Surface and Depth of BNP Ideology," in *British National Party: Contemporary Perspectives* eds. Nigel Copsey and Graham Macklin (New York: Routledge, 2011), 58.
13. "BNP 'Day of the Family' An Outstanding Success," *Spearhead* no. 366 (August 1999): 26.
14. "Renaissance Family Day," *British Nationalist* no. 205 (August 1999): 8.
15. Ibid.
16. "BNP Appoint New Deputy Chairman," *Identity* no. 1 (January/February 2000): 26.
17. "Great Tipton Meeting Launches Drive for Midlands Growth," *The Voice of Freedom* no. 2 (March 2000): 12; "Deputy Leader Appointed," *Spearhead* no. 371 (January 2000): 27.
18. Red-White-and-Blue Summer 2000 Ticket. Personal possession. This ticket included Lecomber's phone number.
19. "Red White and Blue Summer Festival," *Patriot* no. 7 (Summer 2000): 17; "Red-White-and-Blue Summer 2000," *British Nationalist: Member's Bulletin* (June/July 2000): unpaginated 2.

20. *Red, White and Blue 2001* (n.p.: British National Party, 2001) (VHS Recording); *Red, White & Blue 2007 Live* (n.p.: Great White Records, 2007) (CD Recording).
21. Nick Griffin, "Showcase for Modern Nationalism," in *Red, White and Blue 2006: Official Program* (Herts: British National Party, 2006), unpaginated 7.
22. *Red, White and Blue 2006: Official Program* (Herts: British National Party, 2006), unpaginated 8. See also: "Code of Conduct," *British Nationalist: Member's Bulletin* (August 2001): unpaginated 3.
23. "BNP Launches Youth Newsletter," *The Voice of Freedom* no. 1 (February 2000): 12.
24. Ibid.
25. "Young BNP," *Identity* no. 1 (January/February 2000): 27.
26. Bob Gertner, "RWB 2001," *Spearhead* no. 391 (September 2001): 21.
27. "BNP: Under the Skin," BBC, 2001; available online at http://news.bbc.co.uk/hi/english/static/in_depth/programmes/2001/bnp_special/activities/young_bnp.stm; accessed 1 July 2016.
28. "The BBC Does its Worst," *Spearhead* no. 395 (January 2002): 4, 9.
29. Simon Darby, "Panorama," *Identity* no. 16 (December 2001): 9.
30. Chris Telford, "A Voice for the Silent," *Identity* no. 1 (January/February 2000): 25.
31. Ibid.
32. Ibid.
33. Martin Wingfield, "Comment," *The Voice of Freedom* no. 29 (August 2002): 8.
34. "New Labour = New Fascism," *The Voice of Freedom* no. 52 (August 2004): 10.
35. "The Real Face of New Labour," *The Voice of Freedom* no. 29 (August 2002): 11.
36. The members' bulletin wrote: "All members and party officials should be reminded that the Redwatch internet website has been proscribed for some time and this remains the case." "Redwatch Website Proscribed," *British Nationalist: Member's Bulletin* (April 2004): unpaginated 2. "What We Do Believe and What We Don't," *Identity* no. 101 (2009): 52.
37. "Proscribed Organisations," *British Nationalist: Member's Bulletin* (October 2005): unpaginated 6.
38. "Now's The Time," *Spearhead* no. 375 (May 2000): 21.
39. Tony Lecomber, "This May's Elections 2000," *Patriot* no. 7 (Summer 2000): 4.
40. John Tyndall, "May 2000 and After," *Spearhead* no. 376 (June 2000): 6.

41. "New BNP Councillor," *Patriot* no. 7 (Summer 2000): 4; "BNP Councillor," *Spearhead* no. 375 (May 2000): 26.
42. John Tyndall, "Open Letter to Nick Griffin," *Spearhead* no. 380 (October 2000): 4.
43. *At Last!: A Chance to Tell Tony Blair, "It's Time to Put Our Own People First"* (Tamworth: British National Party, n.d., circa 2000).
44. "Mixed By-Election Results," *Spearhead* no. 382 (December 2000): 27.
45. The Freedom Party consisted of Adrian Davies as chair, Sharron Edwards as deputy chair, Eddy Butler as campaign director and Jonathan Bowden as treasurer. *Introducing the Freedom Party* (London: Freedom Party, n.d., circa 2000), unpaginated 4. Butler later rejoined the BNP in early 2003. Eddy Butler, interviewed by Ryan Shaffer, audio recording, 16 September 2011.
46. "Coup Bid Fails—3 Expelled," *British Nationalist: Member's Bulletin* (September 2000): unpaginated 3.
47. "Freedom Party Tries to Steal £2800 From BNP and Fails," *BNP Organisers' Bulletin* (January 2001): unpaginated 3.
48. John Tyndall, "Stand By the BNP," *Spearhead* no. 382 (December 2000): 4. This message was similar to one published the following month. "Unite or Fail!," *Spearhead* no. 383 (January 2001): 4.
49. "Welcome to the BNP," *Identity* no. 9 (May 2001): 9.
50. "A Year of Progress," *Patriot* no. 8 (Summer 2001): 34.
51. "The British National Party and the General Election," *Identity* no. 9 (May 2001): 16.
52. "Time to Declare: Where We Stand," *Identity* no. 9 (May 2001): 6.
53. Keith Axon, interviewed by Ryan Shaffer, audio recording, 11 October 2014.
54. "Summer of Discontent," BBC, 12 July 2001; available online at http://news.bbc.co.uk/2/hi/uk_news/1435958.stm; accessed 1 July 2016.
55. Ibid.
56. "Panel Report," Oldham Independent Review, 11 December 2001; available online at http://www.tedcantle.co.uk/publications/002%20One%20Oldham,%20One%20Future%20Ritchie%202001.pdf; accessed 1 July 2016.
57. Janet Bujra and Jenny Pearce. *Saturday Night & Sunday Morning: The 2001 Bradford Riot and Beyond* (Skipton: Vertical Editions, 2011), 36, 38, 39.
58. Nick Griffin, "The Night Before the Storm," *Identity* no. 9 (May 2001): 5.
59. "Muslim Extremists Behind the Riots!," *The Voice of Freedom* no. 18 (August 2001): 1.

60. *Insight into the Disturbances in Burnley June 2001* (Burnley and Pendle: British National Party, 2001), unpaginated 4. See also: "The Riot Reports," *The Voice of Freedom* no. 22 (December 2001): 2.
61. *John Tyndall Speaks: Bradford BNP 2001* (Leeds: Far View Videos, 2015) (DVD Recording).
62. Ibid.
63. "General Election 2001," bnp.org.uk, 2001; available online at https://web.archive.org/web/20010815075530/http://bnp.org.uk/elections.html; accessed 1 July 2016.
64. Ibid.; detailed results also printed in "The Election Results," *Identity* no. 10 (June 2011): 10–11.
65. Untitled, *BNP Organisers' Bulletin* (July 2001): unpaginated 1.
66. "Standardisation of Letters," *BNP Organisers' Bulletin* (July 2001): unpaginated 2.
67. "BNP Launches Campaign Against Islam," *British Nationalist: Member's Bulletin* (October 2001): unpaginated 1.
68. "Anti-Islam Demonstration," *British Nationalist: Member's Bulletin* (December 2001): unpaginated 4.
69. "The Horns of the Dilemma," *National Front News* no. 116 (1988): 1
70. Paul Golding, "Time to Root-Out the Islamic Fifth Column," *Identity* no. 15 (November 2001): 3; Nick Griffin, "Chairman's Article," *Identity* no. 15 (November 2001): 5.
71. *Britain First!: Your Introduction to the British National Party* (Wigton: British National Party, n.d., circa 2006).
72. Nick Griffin, "No British Blood for Afghanistan," *Identity* no. 16 (December 2001): 4, 5.
73. Michael Walsh, "September 11th Outrages: Questions Unanswered," *Spearhead* no. 395 (January 2000): 18; James Thurgood, "Multi-Racial Britain a Breeding Ground for Terror," *Spearhead* no. 395 (January 2000): 20.
74. "Annual College 2001," *Identity* no. 15 (November 2001): 7.
75. "Excellent Burnley By-Election Results," *Identity* no. 16 (December 2001): 14. The result was also celebrated in *Spearhead*. "Very Good Burnley Results," *Spearhead* no. 395 (January 2002): 26.
76. "Local Government Elections, May 2nd: Big Effort Needed," *Spearhead* no. 397 (March 2002): 27.
77. "Win or Lose?: It's For You to Choose," *BNP Organisers' Bulletin* (March 2002): unpaginated 1.
78. "BNP to Contest 67 Seats," *Spearhead* no. 399 (May 2002): 27.
79. "BNP Bids for Council Seats on May 2nd," *Spearhead* no. 398 (April 2002): 27.
80. Trevor Maxfield, interviewed by Ryan Shaffer, audio recording, 10 October 2014.

81. Ibid.
82. Andrew McBride, interviewed by Ryan Shaffer, audio recording, 19 September 2011.
83. "Andy McBride is Our New Regional Organiser for the South East," *The Voice of Freedom* no. 94 (2008): 9.
84. "BNP gain three seats in local election shock," *The Telegraph*, 3 May 2002; available online at http://www.telegraph.co.uk/news/1393068/BNP-gain-three-seats-in-local-election-shock.html; accessed 1 July 2016.
85. Tony Lecomber, "An Overview of the Council Elections," *Identity* no. 20 (May 2002): 20.
86. Ibid., 22.
87. David Ward, "BNP councillor refuses to back anti-racism motion," *The Guardian*, 12 July 2002; available online at http://www.theguardian.com/uk/2002/jul/12/race.thefarright; accessed 1 July 2016.
88. "Interview with Burnley BNP Councillor Carol Hughes," *Identity* no. 23 (August 2002): 14, 15.
89. "Sun Shines for RWB 2002," *Spearhead* no. 403 (September 2002): 27.
90. Nick Griffin, "Editorial," *Identity* no. 22 (July 2002): 3.
91. For example: Anthony Holroyd, "Using Distributism to Re-Build Our Communities," *Identity* no. 29 (February 2003): 12.
92. "Tyndall to Visit US This Month," *Spearhead* no. 255 (May 1990): 18; "Tyndall Barred from US," *Spearhead* no. 257 (July 1990): 18.
93. "American Friends of the BNP," *Spearhead* no. 360 (February 1999): 9; "American Friends of the BNP," *British Nationalist* no. 200 (February 1999): 8.
94. Mark Cotterill, interviewed by Ryan Shaffer, audio recording, 6 June 2010. (Abbreviated as "Interview with Cotterill 1.")
95. "Introducing Heritage and Destiny, and the American Friends of the BNP," *Heritage and Destiny* no. 1 (Summer 1999): 1.
96. The American Friends website was at http://www.americabnp.net and available from 1999 to 2001.
97. "Mission Statement of the American Friends of the BNP," *Heritage and Destiny* no. 2 (Fall 1999): 2.
98. Nick Griffin, *Moving On, Moving Up: Campaign for British National Party Chair* (Ilford: NG Election Campaign, 1999), unpaginated 2.
99. Ibid.
100. "Griffin Wins BNP Chairmanship," *Heritage and Destiny* no. 2 (Fall 1999): 1.
101. "Recent Events and Activities," *Heritage and Destiny* no. 2 (Fall 1999): 3.
102. Ibid.

103. Ibid., 4.
104. Ibid., 5.
105. "Recent Events and Activities," *Heritage and Destiny* no. 4 (Summer 2000): 3, 4.
106. Ibid.; Bruno Gollnisch, *The Nationalist Movement in France* (Marietta: American Renaissance, 2000) (DVD Recording).
107. "Recent Events and Activities," *Heritage and Destiny* no. 4 (Summer 2000): 5.
108. Steve Cartwright, "Another Journey by Plane," *Spearhead* no. 363 (May 1999): 10.
109. Ibid.
110. Ibid., 11.
111. Ibid.
112. "Recent Events and Activities," *Heritage and Destiny* no. 2 (Fall 1999): 5.
113. Ibid.
114. "BNP Chairman Visits America," *Heritage and Destiny* no. 4 (Summer 2000): 1.
115. Ibid.
116. Ibid.
117. Ibid.
118. Ibid., 5.
119. Ibid.
120. Ibid., 6.
121. "Chairman Nick Griffin Completes Successful American Tour," *Identity* no. 10 (June 2011): 12. Jackie was also a National Front member when the two married in June 1985. "Congratulations Nick and Jackie," *National Front News* no. 68 (July 1985): 2.
122. "Recent Events and Activities," *Heritage and Destiny* no. 8 (May/June 2001): 5.
123. Ibid., 6, 7.
124. "Best Election Results Since 1977," *Heritage and Destiny* no. 4 (Summer 2000): 7.
125. "British Election 2001—Mission Accomplished," *Heritage and Destiny* no. 9 (July/August 2001): 1, 3–5.
126. "The Life and Death of William Joyce I," *Heritage and Destiny* no. 6 (January/February 2001): 18–20; "The Life and Death of William Joyce Part II," *Heritage and Destiny* no. 7 (March/April 2001): 18–19; "Responses to our Review of the Many Shades of Black," *Heritage and Destiny* no. 6 (January/February 2001): 8.
127. "Recent Events and Activities," *Heritage and Destiny* no. 8 (May/June 2001): 4.

128. "Registration Statement of the American Friends of the BNP," U.S. Department of Justice Form CRM-153, 2002.
129. Ibid.
130. Ibid.
131. Ibid.
132. Ibid.
133. George Burdi, interviewed by Ryan Shaffer, audio recording, 12 June 2012.
134. Ibid.; According to its first issue, "Resistance is sent free of charge to all regular customers of Resistance Records and is published in a quarterly basis." "Unstoppable," *Resistance* no. 1 (Spring 1994): unpaginated 3.
135. Interview with Burdi.
136. The first issue of the magazine was published in January 1995 and sold music by bands including No Remorse, Svastika and Bound for Glory. *Nordland* no. 1 (Januari 1995): unpaginated 20. "Bart" was closely involved in Nordland, even receiving credit in the magazine.
137. William Luther Pierce, "Message from the Publisher," *Resistance* no. 10 (Winter 2000): 3.
138. Mark Cotterill, interviewed by Ryan Shaffer, audio recording, 14 October 2014. (Abbreviated as "Interview with Cotterill 2.")
139. William Pierce, "Message from the Publisher," *Resistance* no. 9 (Fall 1999): 3.
140. "Table of Contents," *Resistance* no. 9 (Fall 1999): 1. Interview with Cotterill 2.
141. "Hate Crime Scene," *Resistance* no. 9 (Fall 1999): 34, 36; Mark Cotterill, "Let the Revolution Begin," *Resistance* no. 9 (Fall 1999): 42.
142. Erich Gliebe, "Editorial," *Resistance* no. 10 (Winter 2000): 2.
143. Interview with Cotterill 1.
144. Ibid.
145. Ibid.
146. Ibid. Cotterill pointed out that contrary to public claims that he was "deported," he received an "exclusion order" for ten years from the country and was not officially deported.
147. "Editorial," *Heritage and Destiny* no. 10 (Winter 2003): 2; Peter Rushton, interviewed by Ryan Shaffer, audio recording, 16 October 2014.
148. "The England First Party Statement of Accounts for the Year Ended 31 December 2012." This document was filed with the Electoral Commission. Search "England First Party" at Electoral Commission, 2012; available online at https://pefonline.electoralcommission.org.uk/Search/SOASearch.aspx; accessed 1 July 2016; "Manifesto in Brief," England First Party, 2008; available online at https://web.

archive.org/web/20080305025225/http://www.efp.org.uk/brief-manifesto.html; accessed 1 July 2016.

149. David Bartlett, "England First Pair Quit Party," *Lancashire Telegraph*, 5 March 2007; available online at http://www.lancashiretelegraph.co.uk/news/1236399.england_first_pair_quit_party/; accessed 1 July 2016.
150. Matthew Taylor and Daniel Nasaw, "Suspect in US Holocaust museum guard killing has links to BNP," *The Guardian*, 11 June 2009; available online at http://www.theguardian.com/world/2009/jun/11/holocaust-museum-shooting-bnp-von-brunn/; accessed 1 July 2016.
151. Interview with Cotterill 2.
152. "Defending Who We Are," *Identity* no. 20 (May 2002): 19.
153. Michael Walker, *Nationalist Movements in Europe* (Marietta: American Renaissance, 1998) (DVD Recording).
154. *International European American Unity and Leadership Conference* (Mandeville: Free Speech Press, 2004) (DVD Recording). A text of the speech appeared in John Tyndall, "Whites' Choice: Fight or Die," *Spearhead* no. 425 (July 2004): 9–11.
155. Tyndall traveled to the United States in 1979, 1991 and 2004, not including his abortive attempt to enter the country in 1990. John Tyndall, "Tyndall in America," *Spearhead* no. 425 (July 2004): 8.
156. Edward Field, "The Duke Victory: How It Was Achieved," *Spearhead* no. 245 (July 1989): 13.
157. For example, Griffin met with American radicals in Britain. "Building the 'Nationalist International'," *Spearhead* no. 360 (February 1999): 9.
158. "America and Civil Liberty," *British Nationalist: Member's Bulletin* (June 2005): unpaginated 2; *European American Conference 2005* (Mandeville: The Duke Report, 2005) (DVD Recording)
159. Nick Griffin, *What is Left of Free Speech in Britain* (Marietta: American Renaissance, 2006) (DVD Recording).
160. "American Students Happy to Hear What the BNP Has to Say," *The Voice of Freedom* no. 90 (2007): 2.
161. "William Luther Pierce," *Identity* no. 23 (August 2002): 22.
162. John Tyndall, "Study of a White Titan," *Spearhead* no. 437 (July 2005): 18.
163. Nick Griffin, "How We Can Gain £1 Million Subsidy," *Identity* no. 33 (June 2003): 4.
164. "London Mayoral News," *Identity* no. 34 (July 2003): 13.
165. Nick Griffin, "Putting the Record Straight," *Identity* no. 39 (December 2003): 4.
166. "Euro Fund Appeal Update," *Identity* no. 41 (February 2004): 9.
167. "Euro 2004: Our Campaign in the North-West Has Begun," *The Voice of Freedom* no. 41 (August 2003): 4.

168. "Gravy Train Not for Us," *Identity* no. 42 (March 2004): unpaginated insert.
169. Cover of *Identity* no. 42 (March 2004).
170. "Now Let's Break All Records," *Identity* no. 43 (April 2004): 9.
171. "BNP Campaign News," *Identity* no. 42 (March 2004): unpaginated insert.
172. Ibid.
173. Cover of *Identity* no. 44 (May 2004).
174. Steve Blake, "Two Parties, One Passion," *Identity* no. 44 (May 2004): 6.
175. Ibid. See also: "A New Dawn for Britain?," *British Nationalist: Member's Bulletin* (May 2004): unpaginated 1.
176. "We Are Not Thugs & We Are Not Nazis," *Freedom from the €U* (n.d., circa 2004): unpaginated 8.
177. "What A Set of Results," *Identity* no. 45 (July 2004): 8; "800,000 Vote for Change," *British Nationalist: Member's Bulletin* (June 2004): unpaginated 1.
178. Ibid.
179. "British National Party 808,200," *The Voice of Freedom* no. 51 (July 2004): 1.
180. Nick Griffin, "Where Do We Go From Here," *Identity* no. 45 (July 2004): 4, 5.
181. "Richard Edmonds in Germany," *Spearhead* no. 411 (May 2003): 26; Tony Lecomber, "Red, White and Blue 2003," *Identity* no. 36 (September 2003): 10.
182. "Victory in Europe," *British Nationalist: Member's Bulletin* (June 2005): unpaginated 1; *Freedom, Security, Identity and Democracy* unnumbered (Welshpool: British National Party, May/June 2005) (DVD Recording).
183. "The Hand of Friendship from Across the Channel," *The Voice of Freedom* no. 61 (June 2005): 9.
184. "Invite to Paris Confirms BNP's Shift into the Political Premier League," *The Voice of Freedom* no. 66 (November 2005): 16.
185. Ibid.
186. *Red, White and Blue 2005* (Leeds: BNPTV, 2005) (Disc 2) (DVD Recording).
187. John Tyndall, "Wrong Priorities, Wrong Results," *Spearhead* no. 425 (July 2004): 7.
188. Ibid.; "Plus Four Concillors It Could Have Been," *Spearhead* no. 425 (July 2004): 26.
189. John Tyndall, "Non-Whites in the BNP," *Spearhead* no. 426 (August 2004): 6.
190. "Tyndall to Challenge for BNP Leadership," *Spearhead* no. 426 (August 2004): 15.

191. "Freedom for Europe Demonstration," *The Voice of Freedom* no. 12 (February 2001): 9.
192. Chris Beverley, "A Stunning Breakthrough in Germany," *Identity* no. 50 (December 2004): 18.
193. Chris Beverley, "A Saxon in Saxon," *Identity* no. 80 (July 2007): 15.
194. Ibid., 15, 16.
195. *Red, White and Blue 2005* (Leeds: BNPTV, 2005) (Disc 2) (DVD Recording).
196. Mike Bell, "BNP Aid Swedish Nationalists," *Identity* no. 72 (November 2006): 18.
197. "Red, White & Blue 2008," *Identity* no. 94 (September 2008): 15.
198. *Freedom, Security, Identity and Democracy* unnumbered (Welshpool: British National Party, August 2008) (DVD Recording).
199. "European Nationalists Rally Against Islam," *Identity* no. 97 (December 2008): 8, 9. Fiore's political party was featured that same year in a documentary showing ties with neo-Nazi skinheads. *Nazirock* (Milan: Feltrinelli, 2008) (DVD Recording).
200. "Divisions in the BNP: Let's Get It Straight Who Started Them," *Spearhead* no. 403 (September 2002): 4.
201. "A Night of the Long Knives?," *Spearhead* no. 403 (September 2002): 20; "Searchlight Mole Exposed," *British Nationalist: Member's Bulletin* (September 2002): unpaginated 4.
202. Interview with Rushton.
203. According to Axon, his suspension actually lasted three years and he returned in 2004, but was expelled in 2006 for asking about donations raised to cover costs in Sharon Ebank's legal fight with the Labour Party. Interview with Axon. See also: "Wolverhampton Group Formed," *Spearhead* no. 314 (April 1995): 22.
204. "Keith Axon: His Master's Voice," *BNP Organisers' Bulletin* (March 2002): unpaginated 2.
205. Simon Sheppard, interviewed by Ryan Shaffer, audio recording, 13 October 2014. He has also subsequently been convicted of similar charges and spent nearly a year detained in the United States while unsuccessfully seeking asylum.
206. Simon Sheppard, "Why Many White Women Prefer Non-White Males," *Spearhead* no. 405 (November 2002): 12.
207. Interview with Sheppard. According to him, this also included the Redwatch website.
208. "Identity Interviews Burnley Election Campaign Manager Martin Wingfield," *Identity* no. 20 (May 2002): 16.
209. "Suspended from Work for Not Being a BNP Candidate," *The Voice of Freedom* no. 62 (July 2005): 9.

210. See *Identity* no. 31 (April 2003): 2.
211. "Identity Interviews Long-Standing Nationalist Activist and Writer John Bean," *Identity* no. 26 (November 2002): 9. It is worth mentioning that Bean in this interview argued for "a confederation of the sovereign states of Europe," which is similar to what many Mosleyites desired. John Bean, "Nationalist Notebook," *Identity* no. 90 (May 2008): 23.
212. Graham Macklin, "Modernizing the Past for the Future," in *British National Party: Contemporary Perspectives* eds. Nigel Copsey and Graham Macklin (New York: Routledge, 2011), 36. Macklin argued that this actually had an ironic consequence by anchoring the BNP to the extremist views of 1960s British fascism.
213. "Dispatches: Making a giant leap of faith," *The Independent*, 19 May 2008; available online at http://www.independent.co.uk/news/media/dispatches-making-a-giant-leap-of-faith-830550.html; accessed 1 July 2016.
214. Kathy Brewis, "National Affront," *The Sunday Times Magazine*, 27 October 2002, 59.
215. "The Channel Four Fiasco," *Spearhead* no. 406 (December 2002): 4.
216. "Channel 4 and the YBNP," *British Nationalist: Member's Bulletin* (November 2002): unpaginated 2.
217. "BNP's Success 'Devastating'," *BBC*, 22 November 2002; available online at http://news.bbc.co.uk/2/hi/uk_news/england/2502759.stm; accessed 1 July 2016; Tom Moseley, "Blackburn BNP Candidate's Vile Racist Slurs," *Lancashire Telegraph*, 4 May 2011; available online at http://www.lancashiretelegraph.co.uk/news/9005214.Blackburn_BNP_candidate_s_vile_racist_slurs/; accessed 1 July 2016; "Victory At Blackburn," *Spearhead* no. 407 (January 2003): 26.
218. "And Then There Were Four," *The Voice of Freedom* no. 33 (December 2002): 1.
219. "The Real Face of the British National Party," *The Countrysider* (Autumn 2002): 8.
220. Paul Stokes, "Outspoken BNP councillor takes refuge in silence," *The Telegraph*, 25 January 2003; available online at http://www.telegraph.co.uk/news/uknews/1419972/Outspoken-BNP-councillor-takes-refuge-in-silence.html; accessed 1 July 2016.
221. Nick Griffin, "How Democracy Triumphed in Halifax," *Identity* no. 29 (February 2003): 4.
222. Nick Griffin, "Knowing Who We Are and Where We Have To Go," *Identity* no. 30 (March 2003): 4.
223. "It's A War About Oil and Israel," *The Voice of Freedom* no. 31 (October 2002): 1.

224. "British National Party Contests 224 Seats in Council Elections," *Identity* no. 31 (April 2003): 9; "BNP in Biggest Ever Local Election Push," *Spearhead* no. 411 (May 2003): 22.
225. "Biggest BNP Council Campaign Ever," *British Nationalist: Member's Bulletin* (March 2003): unpaginated 1.
226. "BNP Council Pledges: Our Twelve-Point Plan," *Identity* no. 31 (April 2003): 16, 17, 18; "Only BNP Councillors Will Put Pensioners Before Asylum Seekers," *The Voice of Freedom* no. 37 (April 2003): 1.
227. Zakia Yousaf, "Stop the BNP," *Asian Leader* no. 9 (April 19–May 2, 2003): 1.
228. Steven Smith, *How It Was Done: The Rise of the Burnley BNP: The Inside Story* (Burnley: Cliviger Press, 2004), 39.
229. Nick Griffin, interviewed by Ryan Shaffer, audio recording, 8 October 2014.
230. "BNP becomes Burnley's second party," BBC, 2 May 2003; available online at http://news.bbc.co.uk/2/hi/uk_news/england/lancashire/2994563.stm; accessed 1 July 2016.
231. Tony Lecomber, "Council Elections Results," *Identity* no. 32 (May 2003): 7, 9.
232. "BNP Steps Into the Mainstream," *The Voice of Freedom* no. 38 (May 2003): 1.
233. Benjamin Bowyer, "Local Context and Extreme Right Support in England: The British National Party in the 2002 and 2003 Local elections," *Electoral Studies* 27, no. 4 (December 2008): 611–620.
234. James Rhodes, "The Political Breakthrough of the BNP: The Case of Burnley," *British Politics* 4, no. 1 (April 2009): 44.
235. Tony Lecomber, "By-Election Results Analysis," *Identity* no. 38 (November 2003): 22, 23.
236. "First Council Defection to BNP," *British Nationalist: Member's Bulletin* (January 2004): unpaginated 1.
237. The members' bulletin reported that *Spearhead* and *Searchlight* were "banned" for "unity." "Disruptive Magazines Banned," *British Nationalist: Member's Bulletin* (January 2003): unpaginated 4; "Mr. Griffin Bans Spearhead," *Spearhead* no. 407 (January 2003): 22.
238. John Tyndall, "The Real Reasons Why We're Winning," *Spearhead* no. 411 (May 2003): 12.
239. Nick Griffin, "At The Crossroads," *Identity* no. 34 (July 2003): 4.
240. "Mr. Griffin's Latest Salvo," *Spearhead* no. 414 (August 2003): 28.
241. John Tyndall, "Stand By the BNP," *Spearhead* no. 414 (August 2003): 4.
242. "BNP Founder Reinstated," *Spearhead* no. 418 (December 2003): 27.

243. Martin Wingfield, "Comment," *The Voice of Freedom* no. 42 (September 2003): 8.
244. "BNP Founder Reinstated," *Spearhead* no. 418 (December 2003): 27.
245. Tony Lecomber, "Mapping Out A Winning Strategy," *Identity* no. 48 (October 2004): 24.
246. Ibid.
247. Copsey, *Contemporary British Fascism*, 165.
248. Steve Blake, "The Continuing Assaults on the British National Party," *Identity* no. 49 (November 2004): 18.
249. Eddy Butler, "The 200 Days Campaign," *Identity* no. 50 (December 2004): 13.
250. Nick Griffin, "New Target That's Going to Make it Special," *Identity* no. 52 (February 2005): 4.
251. Ibid.
252. Ibid., 5, 6.
253. Eddy Butler, "The 100 Seat Campaign," *Identity* no. 53 (March 2005): 16, 17.
254. "London Election Rally," *Spearhead* no. 435 (May 2005): 9.
255. *Rebuilding British Democracy: British National Party General Election 2005 Manifesto* (Welshpool: British National Party, 2005), 17.
256. John Tyndall, "The Party I Want," *Spearhead* no. 427 (September 2004): 6.
257. "Policy of Gagging Tyndall Still in Force," *Spearhead* no. 427 (September 2004): 4.
258. Ibid.; "Letters," *Spearhead* no. 426 (August 2004): 22.
259. *Spearhead Support Group Founding Meeting Leeds 2004* (Leeds: Far View Videos, 2015) (DVD Recording).
260. Ibid.
261. "Tyndall Throws Down Gauntlet to Griffin," *Nationalist Week* no. 7 (12 July 2004); available online at http://www.bpp.org.uk/nw7.html; accessed 1 July 2016.
262. John Tyndall, "The Party I Want," *Spearhead* no. 427 (September 2004): 6, 7.
263. John Tyndall, "Are These People Trying to Wreck the BNP," *Spearhead* no. 430 (December 2004): 9.
264. "Expelled—Yet Again," *Spearhead* no. 431 (January 2005): 4.
265. John Tyndall, "Enemy Finger in the Pie," *Spearhead* no. 431 (January 2005): 11; "Legal Fund," *Spearhead* no. 431 (January 2005): 26; John Tyndall, "New Party A Non-Starter," *Spearhead* no. 434 (April 2005): 6.
266. "Excellent Spearhead Group Rally," *Spearhead* no. 433 (March 2005): 27.

267. *Friends of Spearhead Dinner 2004* (Leeds: Far View Videos, 2015) (DVD Recording).
268. "BNP Men on 'Race Hatred' Charges," *Spearhead* no. 435 (May 2005): 27.
269. Ibid., 27. "The Secret Agent," *British Nationalist: Member's Bulletin* (July/August 2004): unpaginated 4.
270. Nick Griffin, "Attacks on the BNP," *Identity* no. 46 (August 2004): 8.
271. "BNP Rallies to Defend Freedom of Speech," *The Voice of Freedom* no. 61 (June 2005): 16; "Support at Court for Nick & Mark," *The Voice of Freedom* no. 62 (July 2005): 9.
272. "Emotional But Defiant," *The Voice of Freedom* no. 64 (September 2005): 12.
273. "May 5, 2005 General Election Results," ElectionResources.org, 2005; available online at http://www.electionresources.org/uk/house.php?election=2005; accessed 1 July 2016. See also the results printed in "General Election Results," *The Voice of Freedom* no. 61 (June 2005): 6–7, 10–11.
274. "'We've Already Won the Election'—Nick Griffin," *The Voice of Freedom* no. 60 (April 2005): 13.
275. Tony Lecomber, "General Election 2005," *Identity* no. 55 (June 2005): 8.
276. "General Election 2005," *The Voice of Freedom* no. 61 (June 2005): 1. See also: "BNP Moves Up To Fourth," *British Nationalist: Member's Bulletin* (May 2005): unpaginated 1.
277. Daniel Trilling, *Bloody Nasty People: The Rise of Britain's Far Right* (London: Verso, 2012), 127, 130.
278. John Tyndall, "Britain After May 5th," *Spearhead* no. 436 (June 2005): 8.
279. "The General Election," *Spearhead* no. 436 (June 2005): 4.
280. "Too Many Wrong Messages," *Spearhead* no. 436 (June 2005): 10.
281. Peter Rushmore, "Good But Could Have Been Better," *Spearhead* no. 436 (June 2005): 14.
282. "General Election 2005: The Final Review," *Identity* no. 56 (July 2005): 25.
283. "Race Charges: Case Adjourned," *Spearhead* no. 436 (June 2005): 28; "Sent For Trial," *Spearhead* no. 437 (July 2005): 27.
284. Richard Edmonds, "John Tyndall: A Titan Amongst Men," *Spearhead* no. 438 (August 2005): 2.
285. "Condolences on the Death of John Tyndall," *Spearhead* no. 438 (August 2005): 4–5; "John Tyndall's Funeral," *Spearhead* no. 438 (August 2005): 27.
286. "The Man Who Founded the BNP," *Identity* no. 57 (August 2005): 8.

287. John Bean, "John Bean Gives Some Personal Memories of 'A Great Patriot'," *Identity* no. 57 (August 2005): 9.
288. "Rudolf Hess March," *Highlander* no. 3 (n.d. circa 2003): unpaginated 3.
289. "Editorial," *Blood & Honour* no. 1 (Spring 1999): 2; "ISD Records," *Blood & Honour* no. 1 (Spring 1999): 27.
290. "Ian Stuart Memorial Concert England 2001," *Blood & Honour* no. 23 (2001): 16.
291. "Ian Stuart Donaldson Memorial 2002," *Blood & Honour* no. 26 (2002): 14.
292. "BNP Update," *Blood & Honour* no. 23 (2001): 21.
293. "British National Party Latest," *Blood & Honour* no. 26 (2002): 6.
294. Cover of *Blood & Honour Scandinavia* no. 1, 1 (Summer 1997).
295. See *Blood & Honour Danmark* no. 1, 1 (Oktober 1998).
296. See *Blood & Honour Division Espana* no. 1 (2000).
297. See *Vér & Becsület* unknown (2001).
298. For example, see *Blood & Honour Portugal* no. 4 (2007).
299. This is according to its own promotional materials. "Save Our Land Join CHS," Confederate Hammer Skins, n.d., circa, 1991. In possession. According to a founding member of the group, the Confederate Hammerskins originated with a group of skaters and sought to emulate the original British skinheads by copying their style from books. Anonymous 3, interviewed by Ryan Shaffer, audio recording, 6 April 2014.
300. Ryan Shaffer, "Bonded in Hate: The Violent Development of American Skinhead Culture," in *Global Lynching and Collective Violence*, Volume 2: *The Americas and Europe* ed. Michael J. Pfeifer (Champaign: University of Illinois Press, 2017).
301. "Hammerskin Press—Winter 1998," *Hammerskin Press* no. 2 (Winter 97–98): unpaginated 2.
302. "Hammerskin Nation," *Hammerskin News* no. 2 (n.d., circa 1999): unpaginated 16. This was published by the Calgary Area Hammerskins.
303. "Hammerfest 2001," *Blood & Honour* no. 23 (2001): 22, 23.
304. Ibid., 23.
305. "Hammerfest 2004," *Blood & Honour* no. 31 (2004): 22.
306. *Hammerfest, Atlanta 2005* (n.p.: White Aryan Resistance, 2005) (DVD Recording).
307. "Whitelaw," *Blood & Honour* no. 32 (2005): 34.
308. In fact, a *Blood & Honour* obituary called Tyndall "an inspirational figure." "John Tyndall," *Blood & Honour* no. 32 (2005): 35.
309. Tony Lecomber, "Red, White and Blue 2003," *Identity* no. 36 (September 2003): 10; "Stigger," *Viking* no. 4 (November 1995): 9.

310. Untitled, *Identity* no. 35 (August 2003): 23.
311. Interview with Griffin.
312. Radio White Europe, "Letters from Nick Griffin to W. Ashcroft," 1995–1998, Modern Records Centre, MSS.412/WA/3/1. Steve Cartwright wrote: "Griffin and I jointly produced a document called 'Radio White Europe' over a decade ago outlining plans to set up a pirate radio station for us in Eastern Europe." Steve Cartwright, "B&H Responds: Rock Against Griffinism," Final Conflict, available online at http://finalconflictblog.blogspot.com/2008/01/b-responds-rock-against-griffinism.html; accessed 1 July 2016.
313. "Great White Records," *Identity* no. 60 (November 2005): 19.
314. Ibid.
315. "Rule Britannia—Stirring Songs & Patriotic Music," *Identity* no. 56 (July 2005): 17.
316. Certificate of Incorporation of a Private Limited Company No. 56534 72, 14 December 2005. Search "Great White Records" at Companies House, 2015; available online at https://www.gov.uk/get-information-about-a-company; accessed 1 July 2016.
317. "'19 Years' and 'All Stand Together' Headline First 'Great White' CD," *The Voice of Freedom* no. 65 (October 2005): 9.
318. Ibid.
319. Richard Preston, "Various Artists, Time to Make a Stand: A Collection of British Folk Songs," *Resistance* no. 27 (Spring 2007): 38.
320. "Time to Make a Stand," *Identity* no. 59 (October 2005): 18.
321. John Milnes, "Music Critic, John Milnes Reviews Lee Hagan's Sensational Debut Album on Great White Records," *The Voice of Freedom* no. 66 (November 2005): 13.
322. Peter Ashford, "CD Review: Time to Make a Stand," *Identity* no. 60 (November 2005): 19.
323. *Nazi Hate Rock* (London: Five, 2009) (DVD Recording).
324. Stewart Maclean and Sue Blackhall, "Little Hitler: Vile BNP chief Griffin gets his 15-year-old daughter to make a hate-filled pop song for kids," *Sunday Mirror*, 5 February 2006; available online at http://www.highbeam.com/doc/1G1-141689500.html; accessed 1 July 2016.
325. "Great White Records," Great White Records, 2006; available online at https://web.archive.org/web/20060216052806/http://greatwhiterecords.com/; accessed 1 July 2016.
326. "Red, White and Blue 2005: Best of the Six," *Identity* no. 58 (September 2005): 12.
327. Ibid., 13.
328. Jackie Griffin, "Organisers' Conference 2005," *Identity* no. 52 (February 2005): 17.

329. "Fund-raising Barbecue for Arthur Redfearn," *The Voice of Freedom* no. 62 (July 2005): 8.
330. Ibid.
331. "100 At Bradford Meeting," *The Voice of Freedom* no. 63 (August 2005): 9.
332. "Our Delegates & Officials Have Their Say," *The Voice of Freedom* no. 79 (2006): 9.
333. Ian Dawson, "Summer School Success," *Identity* no. 68 (July 2008): 8.
334. Ibid.
335. Frank Brammah, "Red, White & Blue 2006," *Identity* no. 70 (September 2006): 13.
336. "Brightest and Best Prepared to Take BNP to New Heights," *The Voice of Freedom* no. 74 (2006): 8.
337. "Trafalgar Club Dinner 2006," *Identity* no. 72 (November 2006): 8.
338. Ibid., 9.
339. "Statement of Abbreviated Accounts Year Ended 31 December 2006," 2006. Search "Great White Records" at Companies House, 2015; available online at https://www.gov.uk/get-information-about-a-company; accessed 1 July 2016.
340. "Great White Records Releases Another Awaited Album," *The Voice of Freedom* no. 76 (2006): 11; "New Release from Great White Records," *Identity* no. 88 (March 2008): 28; *Red, White & Blue 2007 Live* (n.p.: Great White Records, 2007) (CD Recording).
341. "West Wind," *Identity* no. 77 (April 2007): 27.
342. Peter Ashford, "Album Review: West Wind," *Identity* no. 79 (June 2007): 12, 13.
343. Ibid., 12.
344. *West Wind* (n.p.: Great White Records, 2007) (CD Recording).
345. "Truth Hurts by Colin Auty," *The Voice of Freedom* no. 89 (2007): 9; Colin Auty, *Truth Hurts* (n.p.: Great White Records, 2007) (CD Recording).
346. "Racism row over BNP song," *Yorkshire Post*, 28 March 2007; available online at http://www.yorkshirepost.co.uk/news/main-topics/local-stories/racism-row-over-bnp-song-1-2443534; accessed 1 July 2016.
347. "Fury over BNP song: Savile Town attacked in 'deplorable' song lyrics," *Dewsbury Reporter*, 29 March 2007; available online at http://www.dewsburyreporter.co.uk/news/local/fury-over-bnp-song-savile-town-attacked-in-deplorable-song-lyrics-1-1343385; accessed 1 July 2016.
348. "Colin Auty's Controversial Song," Great White Records, 2007; available online at https://web.archive.org/web/20070512003443/http://www.greatwhiterecords.com/Colin_song.htm; accessed 1 July 2016.

349. "Auty's farewell beginning of the end for BNP," The Press, 11 July 2008; available online at http://www.thepressnews.co.uk/press-news/autys-farewell-beginning-of-the-end-for-bnp/; accessed 1 July 2016.
350. "Great White," *Identity* no. 86 (January 2008): 15.
351. "Merchandise," *Identity* no. 92 (July 2008): 21.
352. "Joey Smith Featured Artist," *Soundbites* no. 1 (Summer 2008): 4.
353. Ibid., 5.
354. Joey Smith, *Not Just About the Music* (n.p.: Great White Records, 2008) (CD Recording).
355. "Joey Smith Has the Opposition on the Run," *The Voice of Freedom* no. 99 (2008): 11.
356. Michaela Mackenzie, "A Warm Welcome to the British National's 2008 Summer School," *The Voice of Freedom* no. 97 (2008): 8.
357. "About Folk Against Fascism," Folk Against Fascism, 2015; available online at http://www.folkagainstfascism.com/about.html; accessed 1 July 2016. See also: "Musicians Fight to Keep Politics Out of Folk," BBC, 8 August 2009; available online at http://news.bbc.co.uk/2/hi/8191094.stm; accessed 1 July 2016.
358. Karl Spracklen, "Nazi punks folk off: Leisure, nationalism, cultural identity and the consumption of metal and folk music," in *Cultures of Post-War British Fascism* eds. Nigel Copsey and John Richardson (Abingdon: Routledge, 2015), 174.
359. Caroline Lucas, "The Imagined Folk of England: Whiteness, Folk Music and Fascism," *Critical Race and Whiteness Studies* 9, no. 1 (2013); available online at http://www.acrawsa.org.au/files/ejournalfiles/193Lucas20131.pdf; accessed 1 July 2016.
360. "Dissolved," 23 June 2009. Search "Great White Records" at Companies House, 2015; available online at https://www.gov.uk/get-information-about-a-company; accessed 1 July 2016.
361. Interview with Butler.
362. Patrick Harrington, interviewed by Ryan Shaffer, audio recording, 29 May 2010.
363. "Camp Excalibur 2004," *Identity* no. 48 (October 2004): 27. Early that year, the BNP reported that Jennifer was the "the youngest British nationalist ever to have a documentary about her shown on television." "Jennifer Presents the BNP to Wales and Does it in Welsh," *The Voice of Freedom* no. 47 (February 2004): 4.
364. "Camp Excalibur 2001," *The Voice of Freedom* no. 19 (September 2001): 12. See also: "Camp Excalibur 2001," *The Voice of Freedom* no. 20 (October 2001): 11.
365. "Two Excellent Events," *British Nationalist: Member's Bulletin* (October 2001): unpaginated 3.

366. "Excalibur," *Identity* no. 59 (October 2005): 27; "Celebrate Trafalgar with Excalibur Merchandise," *British Nationalist: Member's Bulletin* (October 2005): unpaginated 7; *England Expects* (Burnley: BNPTV, n.d., circa 2005) (DVD Recording). Bowden later was involved with Troy Southgate and the New Right. Troy Southgate, *Jonathan Bowden: The Speeches: A Collection of Talks Given at the London New Right* (London: Black Front Press, 2013).
367. Steve Blake, "England Expects—The New BNPTV DVD on Nelson," *The Voice of Freedom* no. 67 (2005): 9.
368. *East Ended: The Decline and Fall of the East End* (Burnley: BNPTV, n.d., circa 2005) (DVD Recording); A. Lecomber, "Historic 'East Ended' DVD," *British Nationalist: Member's Bulletin* (September 2005): unpaginated 5.

CHAPTER 7

The Fascist Peak and the Fascist Decline, 2005–2016

In 2005 the British National Party (BNP) received the highest number of fascist votes in any national election at that point and the party focused its resources in local areas, which led to a "breakthrough" in England. The party then used the ensuing media attention and momentum to win a seat on the London Assembly in 2008, and both Nick Griffin and Andrew Brons were elected to the European Parliament in 2009. Yet as the BNP reached new heights in terms of electoral success and party membership, the leadership started to fracture and the establishment of several breakaway groups diluted the BNP's influence. A mass exodus followed the 2010 general election as Griffin became more involved in international politics. He helped establish a transnational extremist alliance in the European Parliament and was a welcome guest in Syria during its civil war. While his international travel was widely reported in the press, the coverage did nothing to rehabilitate the BNP's declining local influence in Britain. Ultimately, Griffin resigned as chair but remained a member of the party until a public dispute with the new leadership led to his expulsion in 2014.

This chapter examines the British National Party in the later years of Griffin's leadership and explains how the party fractured just at the time when it was most electorally successful. Following the 2005 general election, Griffin faced criminal trials over racist comments, although this did not prevent the party from doubling its number of local seats in 2006 and later winning a seat in the London Assembly. The continued successes caught the attention of several former National Front

R. Shaffer, *Music, Youth and International Links in Post-War British Fascism*, Palgrave Studies in the History of Subcultures and Popular Music, DOI 10.1007/978-3-319-59668-6_7

(NF) leaders, influencing Brons to join the BNP and Patrick Harrington to serve as Griffin's advisor in the European Parliament. In many ways, the BNP mirrored the NF in the 1970s. Harrington along with key BNP organizers started a "nationalist" trade union for worker outreach, and the party received more votes than any other fascist party in British history, but tension within the BNP leadership boiled over. The focus on working-class voters reflected the party's base, as Robert Ford and Matthew Goodwin's survey data revealed that the BNP's supporters from 2004 to 2013 were mostly older working-class males.[1] Yet the splintering and infighting were the result of long-simmering personality conflicts and unrealistic expectations. Nigel Copsey wrote that "the BNP sustained a major—if not mortal—blow in 2010," which included local losses, broken momentum and activists defecting to other parties.[2]

Exploring these successes and failures, this chapter focuses on the BNP's outreach, campaigning and international contacts. Specifically, it shows how the BNP, unlike the NF, had members elected to positions of local power as it also focused on international affairs. By the end of Griffin's leadership it had become easier for the party to find sympathizers in foreign countries. Griffin was a founding member of the Alliance of European National Movements, which united extremist European political parties and hosted joint meetings. At the same time, Griffin continued his travels around Europe and also visited Syria and Russia, increasing the frequency of his trips following his 2014 expulsion from the BNP and involvement in the Alliance for Peace and Freedom. Though mocked by the press for the visits and his comments about world affairs, Griffin's travel and ideology demonstrated the completion of an ideological process started in the 1980s with the NF. British fascism was transformed into a transnational ideology wherein extreme British nationalism was attached to foreign ideas and radicals in the other countries. Nationalism, for the fascists, was no longer simply about the nation; rather, the nation was part of a network connected to other nations facing common struggles. Yet such ideology did not win the support of the electorate and the BNP's membership and resources were greatly diminished.

Local Breakthroughs

Immediately after the 2005 election, the BNP focused on "consolidating" its recruitment gains by gathering more resources for the next round of local elections.[3] In January 2006, Griffin explained that the party must establish roots in "core communities" and find ways to create income to make "such ventures possible."[4] However, he was also concerned about his upcoming trial alongside Mark Collett for inciting racial hatred. Griffin wrote to BNP members that "in historical terms, a lengthy prison sentence would be the best possible outcome" because going to prison for an anti-Muslim campaign would have "incalculable value."[5] The members' bulletin claimed that the July 7, 2005 terror attacks in London were "a tragic vindication of everything that the party has been saying," linking Griffin and Collett's upcoming trial to terrorism.[6] Griffin spoke to local party branches, making "demands" that the British government search minorities for bombs and ban Muslim women from wearing burqas.[7] Tens of thousands of leaflets expressing anti-Islamic sentiments were distributed weeks later stating that "diversity" was "death," and the BNP boasted about getting new members because of the issue.[8] However, in late 2005 the BNP leadership was accused of plotting its own terror campaign. Tony Lecomber contacted Joe Owens, who was part of Griffin's security team, about "direction action" to assassinate "members of the establishment who are aiding and abetting the coloured invasion of this country."[9] After Owens informed Griffin, the story was picked up in the press and Griffin announced that Lecomber had been told to resign so Griffin could focus on the court case.[10]

In February 2006, after a three-week trial, Griffin and Collett were found not guilty on half of the charges and the jury deadlocked on the other half, with a retrial planned for later in the year.[11] After the verdict, Griffin thanked the BNP's supporters and the BBC for generating the "largest block of donations we've ever had."[12] Collett became the BNP's head of publicity and *Identity* magazine claimed the trial outcome was "our greatest publicity coup ever."[13] The BNP's newspaper featured a photograph of Griffin gagged with the words "not guilty" and claimed supporters had demonstrated in Canada, Sweden and the United States for Griffin.[14] In November 2006, a jury found both men not guilty of the remaining charges, which the BNP claimed "unleashed a flood of unbelievably positive broadcast media coverage, with extensive live reports and interviews."[15] The BNP headline was "Justice is Done," and the party newspaper provided a daily account of the proceedings.[16] Griffin spoke outside the court to a crowd of supporters chanting "freedom" and said the verdict showed a "gulf" between the issues of "ordinary" people and the "fantasy" world of the government.[17] In a reflection on the events, Griffin told supporters that using non-threatening language, staying "positive," avoiding "insults," being "accurate" and assuming all comments were being recorded were lessons learned from the trial about how to avoid prosecution.[18]

In the midst of a trial over racist comments, the British National Party was still trying to shed the fascist label. When questioned in 2005 by Jonathan Bowden, during a mock press interview, about the BNP being a National Socialist party, Griffin replied, "the British National Party is not a fascist organization, it is an entirely democratic party from the top right through to the bottom … I changed the party, I moderated it to make it electable."[19] Griffin also sought to differentiate the groups within the "nationalist movement," writing that there were three sub-groups, including civic nationalists (such as the United Kingdom Independence Party, or UKIP), modern nationalists (including the BNP) and neo-fascists (such as the British People's Party).[20] Griffin described the BNP as rejecting the "neo-fascist" label and emphasized the need to distance the party from those "fixated" on "the nationalist totalitarianism of the 1930s" in order to remain a viable and broad party.[21]

Women were also a key element in Griffin's BNP and for shedding the neo-Nazi connotations. The party reported that "nearly half" of its members were women and sought to run a similar ratio in the 2006 election because "they render the Labour Party's anti-BNP literature, talking about Nazis and skinheads, irrelevant to voters."[22] When three more women agreed to contest local elections for the BNP, its newspaper celebrated their campaigns and highlighted "ladies in the frontline."[23] According to BNP activist Warren Glass, party members were routinely attacked and threatened by opponents, which caused him to discourage his wife from standing in elections or even officially joining the party.[24] His wife, Cheryl, became a member in 2004 following a series of local election victories as well as a move from London, where they felt safer.[25] Even as a non-member, she helped her husband's campaigns during the 1990s and gained experience with political issues so that just months after becoming a member, she was already prepared for her first of what became several local campaigns.[26]

The May 2006 local elections marked a new high point for the party, doubling its number of councilors.[27] Specifically, the BNP won eleven of the thirteen seats it contested in Barking and Dagenham, where it became the second party.[28] In total, the BNP had forty-six seats in England, with forty-nine city, borough and district councilors plus another four town councilors.[29] The party celebrated its win in the face of opponents who distributed hundreds of thousands of anti-BNP leaflets, as well as media criticism.[30] The BNP was jubilant, calling the elections a "breakthrough," with the "most dramatic West Midlands" contest being Sharon Ebanks's victory in Kingstanding, Birmingham, and even publishing a map of its council seats with town and councilor names in *Identity*.[31] Months later, Ebanks's election was overturned by a court, citing a vote counting error, but other BNP candidates increased their votes in the election.[32] Cheryl Glass, for instance, won 268 votes, more than her total of 203 in 2004, for a 32% increase, and Warren Glass's total grew to 243 compared with 183 in 2004.[33]

These gains were due in part to the party's increasingly effective campaign activities. The party launched Operation White Vote "to get every native Briton on their electoral register" because "your vote … could give your local council a British National Party councillor."[34] The leaflet told readers: "Gangs of anti-white thugs are turning more and more of our streets into 'No Go' areas for young Brits."[35] Eddy Butler, the BNP's national elections officer, credited the nature of local elections, where "the work you do locally can affect the result," and the media coverage showed "the party as a major force to be reckoned with."[36] He explained that Chris Beverley's victory in Morley was "the best approach" of a "broad front" where one can "hide the thrust a bit and to give credibility to the detailed local campaign."[37] Beverley credited his victory to selling the BNP newspaper door to door, where he received an "incredible response."[38] Butler also argued that improved branch management, such as coordination and supervision, would pave the way for better results.[39]

Aside from press coverage, the BNP councilors' influence on local government did not have any sustainable impact. Karin Bottom and Colin Copus wrote that claims the BNP "councillors are poor meeting attendees; do not take a full part when they do turn up; do not understand council procedures; are badly behaved; and are successfully isolated and ignored by other parties to such an extent that they can and do not achieve anything as councillors have been exaggerated, to some extent."[40] Nonetheless, councilors not part of a majority are hamstrung by definition, being unable to shape policy in council votes.[41] Moreover, the BNP's own reports about its political influence were limited to minor "victories," such as members voting with the majority in council motions and policy decisions.[42] Nevertheless, the BNP highlighted its councilors' local activities. Sharon Ebanks's council duties in Kingstanding, for example, were profiled in *The Voice of Freedom*, which described her taking constituent calls, not being allowed to ask questions at council meetings because they had to be submitted two weeks in advance and being invited to join one council committee.[43] Butler wrote about the pledge made by three BNP candidates who had won seats on Epping Council to address rising crime, asking the police to respond regarding the issues experienced by shop owners.[44] The police turned down this request citing political concerns, but Butler wrote that "some" police officers nonetheless worked with the BNP councilors to address the public's anxiety.[45] To improve councilors' effectiveness, the party hosted its first seminar in 2007 aimed at discussing ideas for the council chambers.[46] Local BNP branches also worked to give prospective and newly elected councilors an introduction to serving in local government by explaining responsibilities, expectations and functions.[47]

The British National Party proposed amending its constitution in 2007 at its annual conference. Though much of the event was devoted to projecting a "corporate image" and discussing how to a run a campaign, party publications focused on a new type of "membership."[48] Specifically, the party leadership created a "voting membership" tier that would allow people to propose and vote on policies at the annual conference, in addition to the standard membership that required an annual payment.[49] The "voting members" must have been party activists for two years and demonstrated commitment to the party through work authenticated by organizers.[50] While a new concept to the BNP, the policy was based on ideas gathered during a BNP delegate visit to the headquarters of the National Democrats in Sweden.[51] The voting membership "experiment" allowed policy proposals for June 2007 and an Advisory Council to consider the motions in the following months, which would then be voted on by the party in November.[52]

Plans for the May 2007 local elections began immediately after the 2006 victories, with high hopes that the party would continue its momentum.[53] However, this failed to occur and the 2007 results were summed up by Mark Collett as failing to provide "the breakthrough that many predicted and that we all wanted."[54] Though the party won several parish and town council seats, it blamed "postal vote fraud" and Prime Minister Tony Blair's resignation announcement for the BNP's failure to perform well.[55] Andy McBride also described how there was little contact between local organizers and the party leadership, leaving him to design his own literature and set up meetings in his area.[56] For campaigns and local organizing, success depended on the work done by activists, often without guidance.[57]

Despite the dashed hopes and organizational problems, the party was successful when compared with previous extremist movements. In summer 2007, the BNP had sixty-five councilors, making it the most successful British fascist party in history. Despite the party's success, Griffin faced internal criticism but overwhelmingly beat back a leadership challenge from Chris Jackson with 90.9% of the total vote.[58] Jackson, a North West regional organizer from 1995 to 2003, campaigned on establishing a "proper structure" for the party and argued that the BNP's methods for spending were "contrary to established, prudent practice."[59] In May 2007, the BNP ran a "record number" of candidates for the National Assembly for Wales with a goal of printing 1,200,000 leaflets and delivering them to every home in Wales.[60] However, the BNP failed to get any members elected, receiving 42,197 votes and celebrating becoming the "fifth party in Wales."[61] Meanwhile, that summer the party earned its best parliamentary by-election vote during July 2007 in Sedgefield with 2494 votes.[62]

The BNP blamed its failure to win more elections on opposition from anti-racist groups and scathing media reports about the party. In fact, Griffin described the BNP as "the most demonised party in modern British politics."[63] Moreover, Griffin pointedly accused *Searchlight* of recruiting people as "paid" informants to "subvert" the party.[64] In contrast, Eddy Butler's analysis was that the party was "out-organised" by opponents, including Hope Not Hate and Labour shifting its strategies, and the BNP needing to target more wards and "develop new deep community politics."[65] In fact, Nigel Copsey described the symbiotic relationship between the fascists and anti-fascists, arguing that "[w]hen the BNP turned to community politics, so the anti-fascist movement followed" to challenge their opponents.[66] Some BNP supporters also argued for collaboration with UKIP to unite against the left, but Griffin wrote: "we are forced to the conclusion that an alliance with UKIP would not in fact be desirable even if it were possible."[67] Instead, Griffin told supporters to turn their efforts to the 2008 Greater London Authority and the 2009 European Parliament elections.[68] The key to the next general election, Butler argued, was showing progress and growth in the smaller elections and targeting specific areas in the European elections.[69] Wingfield wrote that the BNP's modernization was "the main reason why the public is now so much more receptive to our message."[70] Likewise, the 2007 BNP summer school included a talk by Steve Blake on the history of "British nationalism," including Mosley's Union Movement and the National

Front, but mentioned there was no "change" until Griffin took over the leadership of the BNP.[71] The subsequent summer school in 2008 trained over two hundred people in using computer software to design leaflets that would be effective in local elections.[72]

The BNP's main focus was the 2008 Greater London Authority elections, which drew activists to London to campaign for mayoral candidate Richard Barnbrook and other London Assembly candidates.[73] For the monthly party DVD, Griffin interviewed dozens of party members from around England who leafleted in London and reported positive feedback from the public.[74] One of the party's main activities was spreading its brochure, *The Londoner*, in key areas, including giving out 100,000 copies in one weekend.[75] While *The Londoner* featured Muslim women wearing face veils, the inside highlighted Barnbrook's platform of improving traffic flow, making public transportation cheaper, lowering council taxes and stopping "health tourists" from abusing the health service.[76] Barnbrook participated in several local events, including marching with police who demanded higher wages.[77] During the campaign, the BNP reported that its website was receiving its highest ever levels of traffic, with 5000 to 7000 unique visitors daily, following the implementation of a new, "higher quality" design.[78] In addition, the British National Party released a "report" titled *Racism Cuts Both Ways* as well as an Internet campaign that Griffin described as proving "the silent epidemic of racist targeting of indigenous Britons for assault, robbery and murder by ethnic minority criminals."[79] With a foreword by Griffin, the controversial twelve-page publication listed three "case studies" and claimed "the English" were "relentlessly discriminated against and shamefully treated."[80] The xenophobic and racist literature led to more than a dozen BNP members being arrested under the Public Order Act for circulating the leaflet.[81] Likewise, rather than distancing itself from such accusations of racism, the BNP's publications praised the memory of Enoch Powell.[82] Griffin, for example, wrote that Powell was a "true prophet" who was "controversial, but broadly proven right."[83]

In May 2008, the British National Party helped Barnbrook get elected to the London Assembly and won several seats in other local elections. Barnbrook, who was leader of the opposition on the Barking and Dagenham Council, was selected as the BNP's top candidate after a "rigorous" decision process among ten BNP representative candidates.[84] The BNP celebrated the victory as being "against all the odds" and reported on other local victories, such as nine BNP councilors in Stoke, but remarked that Barnbrook's seat was "the most significant electoral victory."[85] As for the other elections, Collett wrote that the "handful of seats on town councils" marked "significant advances" despite the BNP's "national average" slightly declining.[86] According to Griffin, the party "allocate[d] our full £80,000 budget to the London Assembly elections" to win a seat "in one of the most powerful governmental bodies in the country."[87] Griffin commented that with 130,000 Londoners voting BNP to get Barnbrook elected, the party planned to save tax money and "roll back" the "social engineering" of the "far-left."[88] Indeed, the BNP's newspaper featured Barnbrook's first speech in the assembly, including asking Boris Johnson when retired Londoners would get "a 24 h travel freedom pass."[89] Basking in the party's success, during the BNP's late 2008 conference in Blackpool Griffin talked about the BNP overcoming criticism from the media and the major political parties, predicting that "our people [will] rise up" and "cleanse and heal this nation of ours for good."[90]

Beyond Campaigns

The British National Party credited its victories to spreading propaganda not only in campaign leaflets, but also in books. Writings and speeches by Arthur Kemp, a BNP activist originally from South Africa, promoted a "whites' history" of the world and opposed "a new, racially alien population" inhabiting Europe.[91] Kemp, who served as the head of voting member training, delivered speeches about history and race at large BNP events and smaller gatherings.[92] In late 2007, the BNP's Education and Training Department was started to "equip members with their own individual goals and the mechanisms to achieve those goals."[93] By 2008, Kemp was in charge of the BNP's merchandise shop, Excalibur, and the party described the position as paving the way for him "to concentrate more directly on politics and his role as part of our new Education & Training Department."[94] Kemp was already known as a writer in South Africa, including authoring a book about the Afrikaner Resistance Movement sold by the BNP, and was reportedly connected to the South African National Intelligence Service, allegedly supplying information connected to the 1993 assassination of Chris Hani, head of the South African Communist Party.[95] After moving to Britain and joining the BNP, he wrote anti-Muslim books, such as *Jihad: Islam's 1,300 Year War on Western Civilisation*, sold by the BNP's Excalibur.[96] Yet Kemp was not the only author publishing books that mirrored BNP policies and were sold by the party. Notably, the BNP promoted and offered to members *Neo-Conned*, an anti-Iraq War anthology that was edited and published by Derek Holland and John Sharpe.[97]

The party also engaged in other forms of outreach, including to organized labor. In 2005, Solidarity was started as a labor union and its 2006 government filing listed Patrick Harrington as general secretary, with BNP members John Walker, Lee Barnes and Kevin Scott holding leadership positions, while it had a membership of only forty-two people and £611 in assets.[98] Harrington developed the union after working on the railways and being expelled from the National Union of Rail, Maritime and Transport Workers (RMT) for his previous involvement in the NF.[99] Despite Harrington not being a BNP member, the union was closely associated with the party through BNP promotion and key BNP figures involved in it.[100] Harrington insisted that Solidarity was not a BNP union, but a union for "nationalists" and non-political workers, noting that out of about 150 cases he dealt with only about twenty were political.[101] Solidarity's newsletter, The *British Worker*, declared that it "oppose[s] discrimination on political and other grounds" and drew inspiration from socialist Robert Owen's "attempt to unite all the workers into one union."[102] It also borrowed from the 1970s National Party's publication of the same name, with Harrington using a style similar to that of the older publication.[103]

The BNP members in Solidarity positioned it as a BNP-friendly union that was in line with the party's philosophy. After a small start, the union grew each year, with 124 members in 2007, then 276 in 2008 and 400 in 2009.[104] In Solidarity's newsletter, president Adam Walker wrote "a personal message" to BNP union workers, describing leftist unions as attacking the BNP and calling for party members to join Solidarity, which it labeled "the independent Nationalist Trade Union Solidarity."[105] This language mirrored BNP thought and even Harrington was quoted in the BNP's newspaper calling for unions to cancel a conference that was opposed to "immigration controls."[106] Moreover, the union supported other workers who protested against the employment of foreign workers.[107] The union's second annual conference was covered by the BNP's newspaper, describing speeches by Walker and Harrington and noting that Griffin was in attendance.[108] Walker, a school teacher, faced pressure from community members who demanded his removal when it was discovered that he had used a school computer to post intolerant comments on a *Teesside Online* forum.[109] Harrington, acting on behalf of Solidarity, represented Walker at a hearing in front of the General Teaching Council.[110] Pessimistic about the hearing, the BNP reported he might be "thrown out of the teaching profession for good."[111] The BNP later claimed Walker was "cleared" by the council, with Harrington stating that Walker did not believe his posts were racist.[112] Walker, as union president, wrote that the union was open to workers from all backgrounds, opposed to discrimination and "won settlements in a number of cases involving members of the British National Party."[113] The group earned headlines in 2009 when Griffin donated £5000 to Solidarity, which was given to Griffin in an alleged "sting operation" by *The Times*.[114]

The party also promoted a religious image, despite Griffin being an agnostic.[115] Though the BNP had a secular orientation, many members were religious and the party pitched itself as welcoming Christians from "all denominations."[116] Furthermore, BNP publications described the party as "pro-life" and opposed to abortion.[117] The party even published an explanation of how Christians could "politely correct" church leaders who criticized the BNP.[118] It also argued that it was the "only" party that stood up for "our Christian faith," and the BNP's 2009 European election campaign featured an anti-Islam billboard with an image of Jesus and a Bible quote.[119] Griffin said simply that "Britain is a Christian nation" and even told the story of Jesus' birth during a 2005 internal BNP broadcast.[120] Andy McBride, a Christian, explained that Christianity did appeal to Griffin at times, but overall religion did not play much of a role in the party.[121] Nonetheless, Griffin wrote about Easter being an "important festival" because "indigenous Christian people of the British Isles have been celebrating Easter for centuries."[122] Not all Christians were supportive of the BNP, and vice versa. In fact, the party described the Church of England "banning" clergy from joining the BNP as "indicative of its moral decline."[123]

European Parliament

After several years of steady local success, the BNP targeted key seats in the 2009 European Parliament election. The party hoped to use its local support to generate more publicity and then receive the monetary benefits from elected positions in the European government. For the BNP, winning elections meant spreading the party message to as many people as possible. In April 2008, the BNP established a new quarterly magazine, *Hope & Glory*, for BNP members.[124] That year, Griffin announced a major push to get 500,000 copies of the BNP's European leaflet "into the hands of the public by Christmas."[125] Collett explained that BNP branches and groups "have already begun playing their part in the Euro Elections by producing local Patriot leaflets," and there was already demand for a new *Where We Stand* recruitment leaflet, with 50,000 copies purchased by organizers in the summer of 2008.[126] Similar leaflets, such as *British Jobs for British Workers*, promised to take the UK out of the European Union while denouncing the spending of taxpayer money and the EU allowing "immigrant labour to flood in and take British jobs."[127] Then it was announced that the 20,000 print run of *The Voice of Freedom* would be expanded, with a "printing [of] at least five times as many" to lower the cost per issue and use "marketing professionals" to circulate a "more positive" view of the party to the public.[128] By printing so many copies, it would drop the price by 20% and enable "a huge jump in the profitability" and make it possible to give away a large number of copies of the newspaper.[129]

Spreading literature and winning seats in the European Parliament was part of a larger strategy. Butler, as the national elections officer, explained, "our aim is to establish deep-seated local community support" through "intensive work" by regularly distributing literature, holding meetings, leafleting and targeting new areas.[130] Moreover, winning seats in the European Parliament would give the party "credibility," thereby helping to legitimize the party in the public eye.[131] Lawrence Rustem, a BNP councilor, wrote that joining resident associations, being welcoming to new members and building credibility were key to improving in elections.[132] After several years of public attention to the BNP's local victories, Griffin called 2009 a "crucial year" because the European election's new proportional representation system enabled the BNP to win seats.[133]

The British National Party appeared to be on the verge of winning seats after years of local gains, and the negative consequences of the 2008 economic recession threatened to shake up the political order. The BNP proclaimed that "British nationalism" was "the only way out of the global chaos," by nationalizing banks, being self-sufficient, leaving the European Union and taking businesses back from multinational companies.[134] Griffin wrote that the "collapse of the international financial system" and support for BNP policies meant "[t]he opportunities and the dangers are unprecedented."[135] The party published articles that accused the European Union of "assaulting" national sovereignty, linking it to the country's economic problems.[136] In early 2009, Griffin announced that June 4, the date of the European elections, was "our date with destiny" and would be a "springboard" to the 2010 general election.[137] By virtue of being in the European Parliament, members received a salary, paid staff and a €30,000 budget for publicity, which would help the BNP in its own national elections.[138] In addition to the "credibility" the European Parliamentary seats would give, the millions of leaflets distributed would expand membership and pave the way for more votes in future elections.[139] In fact, the BNP literature highlighted the European election's significance by calling it the "battle for Britain" and even organized a "multi-media" roadshow with speeches from Griffin in key constituencies.[140]

The British National Party's main focus was the European elections and the party targeted its Euroskeptic rival, the United Kingdom Independence Party. Griffin, for example, claimed UKIP was "coming off the rails" due to infighting and financial problems, while the BNP was "stronger."[141] The British National Party mobilized all of its resources for the election, including paying the £55,000 deposit and sending out 29 million glossy leaflets and taking advantage of free postage worth about 10 million pounds.[142] Using part of the hundreds of thousands of pounds raised, it also developed an automated system to send out information packs and set up a sales call center, an administrative office and a depot to send out supplies.[143] In addition to its Internet presence, the party also enabled supporters to receive updates via text message on their phones.[144] Highlighting the election's importance and drawing on history, posters were given out that called the election "the battle for Britain" and wrote that June 4, election date, "is our D-Day."[145] Griffin also appeared on television regularly, describing himself as being "vilified," which resonated with angry voters looking for alternatives and helped candidates win a proportional representation election.[146]

In June 2009, the British National Party won two seats in the European Parliament. The two victories were from among sixty-nine BNP European candidates who sought seats in eleven constituencies, which due to the proportional system, ranked the candidates with Griffin the first pick in the North West region and Andrew Brons, the former NF chair, as first for Yorkshire and the Humber.[147] Brons, who had remained with Ian Anderson's National Front, even into its transition to the National Democrats, explained that his previous political path had taken him "nowhere."[148] Seeing the BNP's successful campaigns, he joined the party in 2005 despite "misgivings" over Griffin's leadership, believing that with time Griffin had "matured."[149] *The Voice of Freedom* announced that the two successful elections and over one million votes proved the "BNP is now mainstream."[150] Griffin remarked it was a "great victory" that also saw three county councilors elected in the local elections.[151] In explaining how the European seats were won, fundraising was listed as "key" in supporting a professional campaign, but so was "tactical thinking" to capture the public's attention.[152] The party celebrated the two seat victories, reporting that Griffin received 132,094 votes and Brons earned 120,139 votes.[153] However, the party ran more than 450 candidates in the 2009 local elections, which received little attention in the party literature.[154] Out of hundreds of local campaigns, the results were a net gain of a mere three county seats.[155] Despite the BNP's good news in the European elections, there were signs of instability. Butler had expected the party to do much better in the European election, noting the party had grown and had better funding, but its gains were only a few hundred thousand votes.[156]

The British National Party's two seats in the European Parliament proved to be its peak success. Griffin and Brons attended the annual Red, White and Blue festival as triumphant elected representatives who would fight against European integration in Europe's transnational body. It was Brons's first appearance at the festival, and he used the event to meet with his staff to discuss "what was expected," believing opponents would be "scrutinizing our every move."[157] Brons was correct, but the BNP leadership would now need to focus simultaneously on domestic and international politics. In fact, as its leaders continued to make transnational connections through the European Parliament, the party began suffering from infighting at the local level, which was further exacerbated by the pressure of the 2010 general election.

True to the BNP's strategy, the Members of the European Parliament (MEPs) used staffing salaries and European Union money to spread the party's political message and improve its organization. Specifically, it hired staff so that BNP activists could conduct full-time political work on behalf of the party. The first appointments were Tina Wingfield, a former NF activist, as Griffin's office manager and Chris Beverley as Brons's office manager, while Martin Wingfield, a former NF chair, served as the campaign and communications officer for both representatives.[158] The British National Party also used its nearly €40,000 annual promotion fund to print newsletters and brochures "to spread the word."[159] The result was that the BNP had three former NF chairs, Brons, Griffin and Wingfield, being financed by the European Union who used the platform to spread their political message.

As the BNP celebrated its victories in the European election, the party was undergoing several changes as a result of the media attention it had received. In 2009, the Commission for Equality and Human Rights again threatened legal action against the BNP for refusing to let non-whites join the party. The BNP responded by claiming it was allowed this policy because the BNP "is an ethnic specific association."[160] Yet there were a few examples of minorities, notably Rajinder Singh, who supported BNP policies such as its anti-Muslim campaigns.[161] Singh had a regular column in *The Voice of Freedom* that condemned Islam and linked it to terrorism, despite not being allowed to join the party.[162] At the 2009 annual conference, the first topic on the agenda was the legal threat from the commission and the costs of fighting it, which was addressed by Simon Darby and Griffin.[163] During his speech, Griffin connected the legal challenge to "rewriting" other parts of the constitution, including protecting party officers from being held responsible for party debts and changing how party leadership elections were held.[164] The members debated and then voted at the conference in favor of holding an internal party election to change the constitution on those issues.[165] In February 2010, the BNP held an Extraordinary General Meeting (EGM) at a pub in Essex where the overwhelming majority voted to adopt a new constitution with the changes, including allowing "non-whites" to join.[166] Andy McBride served as the self-described "enforcer" for Griffin, and said the opportunity was used to push through other party changes that made it more difficult to challenge Griffin as leader.[167] Following the vote, the BNP newspaper reported that Singh became "the first ethnic member of the party" and was praised by Griffin for his criticism of Islam.[168]

Capitalizing on the BNP's seats in the European Parliament, the party highlighted Griffin's and Brons's European accomplishments to party members. *The Voice of Freedom*, for instance, published an article by Brons about helping a constituent who faced eviction.[169] The newspaper also reported that Griffin's first speech to the parliament "denounce[d] human rights violations against British National Party members."[170] Brons began writing a regular column in which he discussed his activities in the European Parliament as well as his views on political events.[171] For example, he wrote about topics in the transnational body and was critical of the European Union's immigration policies.[172] Similarly, Griffin's views and parliamentary speeches made news in the BNP's newspaper, such as his declaration that global warming was "a hoax."[173]

In light of the BNP's two seats in the European Parliament, in October 2009 Griffin was invited to be on *Question Time*, the BBC's popular political debate television program. The invitation was criticized by those, such as Member of Parliament Peter Hain, who did not want to legitimize Griffin and the BNP, but the interview went ahead nonetheless.[174] Griffin sat in front of a hostile audience and on a panel that openly opposed the BNP, recalling his past statements and even his trip to Libya. The publicity was overwhelmingly negative, to the point where Griffin said, "That was not a genuine *Question Time*; that was a lynch mob."[175] John Bean, mirroring comments from Griffin, wrote that the program would "go down as the event that cemented the BNP breakthrough" and reported 4000 new BNP member applications and 10,000 people requesting more information within 48 hours after the airing.[176] Equally as controversial was the May 2009 invitation that Richard Barnbrook, an assembly member, received to the Queen's Garden Party and Barnbrook's offer to bring Griffin along, which resulted in Griffin declining under heavy criticism.[177]

The May 2010 general election was the focus of serious campaigning by the BNP rank and file, but with its leader engaged in European Parliament activities, some of the party's energy was diluted. In early 2010, the party prepared for the general election by strategizing on leaflets and making campaign schedules.[178] The BNP's newspaper claimed the party was the "only" choice because it did not bow to a politically correct agenda and would protect Britain from the EU and immigration.[179] Local branches were heavily engaged, such as the BNP branch in Salford reporting that it disseminated 20,000 leaflets in two months and gave away 1000 copies of *The Voice of Freedom*.[180] The widely circulated manifesto, which was made available online in April 2010 as well, declared, among many other things, that the BNP would "take all steps necessary to halt and reverse" immigration.[181] In addition to issues of immigration and "over population," the party also highlighted its anti-war campaigns.[182] Specifically, the BNP remained opposed to the presence of British troops in Iraq and Afghanistan and wanted them withdrawn immediately.[183] The party criticized the Labour Party for its involvement in the wars, which had resulted in the loss of British lives in foreign lands, and claimed that "only" the BNP would stop the conflict.[184] Griffin argued that the way to "support our troops" was to "bring them home," which, he claimed, was the British majority's view.[185]

The party also changed its flagship magazine with hopes that it would reach a wider audience during the election. After one hundred issues of *Identity*, the party announced that the 101st issue would have more content, a new layout and be "available to all members as part of their membership."[186] John Bean, reflecting on BNP membership having grown by six times since *Identity*'s first issue, reported that the publication would become a quarterly magazine with its 101st issue and have a new design.[187] The magazine would also be expanded to sixty-four pages and be "perfect bound" to weigh less and increase its "educational and advertising reach by more than five-fold."[188] The reality turned out to be the opposite. Spring 2010 marked the last time *Identity* was published, as the party drifted into internal disputes and infighting following failures in the general election.

The 2010 general election brought about political change, with Labour being forced out when Conservative Party leader David Cameron won the majority in a coalition with the Liberal Democrats. As Nigel Copsey explained, anti-fascists made a serious and concentrated effort to defeat the BNP, including campaigns waged by Unite Against Fascism and Hope Not Hate against the party in Barking and Stoke-on-Trent.[189] The British National Party wrote that its 2010 vote tally was "three times" what it received in the previous election and it saved seventy-two deposits, which was "a record for a British nationalist party."[190] The party ran 338 candidates and received 564,321 votes, which a parliamentary report described as increasing its vote share, but did not come "close to winning a seat."[191] Indeed, the number broke the record by being the highest ever for a British fascist party, including far outpacing the NF's highpoint in 1979. Yet even the BNP's newspaper, which routinely made the best out of poor results, stated: "For the first time since 2002 the British National Party had a setback in the local council elections."[192] Though calling the local results "respectable," the party announced it would "be pulling out all the stops to get back on the winning trail again."[193] Another article in the paper described the BNP membership, details of which had not been released for decades, as being larger than that of UKIP, with a total of more than 14,000 BNP members.[194] Nevertheless, in the printed results of the elections, the paper admitted: "We lost some good councillors and the communities they served will be poorer for it."[195]

Infighting and Party Splits

The BNP's European Parliamentary seats made the party more involved in European Union policy and European extremism, but less involved in the local issues that initially increased BNP membership. Notably, *The Voice of Freedom* featured two pages, one for Griffin and another for Brons, about their activity "representing Britain" in the European legislature.[196] For example, the pages featured articles about Griffin's questions on the European Police Office (Europol) accessing private information and Brons speaking to a Hungarian delegation in front of the European Parliament.[197] In February 2010 Brons was part of a "fact-finding mission" to Rosarno, Italy to look into riots related to African immigration, and Brons wrote that he "did not hear much" from the immigrants and "ordinary population of Rosarno."[198] In March 2010, Brons was among a European Parliament delegation that traveled to Zagreb, Croatia for a dialog with Croatian officials, but used the opportunity to "warn" about the negative impact of joining the European Union.[199] Reflecting on his first year in office, Brons wrote that he "gained a deeper understanding of the institutions of the European Union" and attacked the EU's economic policies, which he believed undermined national sovereignty.[200]

The BNP leadership continued to develop an international outlook, but also attracted attention for its role in Europe. In July 2010, Griffin's invitation to the Queen's Garden Party was withdrawn, resulting in media attention, as Brons attended the event.[201] The BNP reported on Griffin being the "second best performing MEP representing the North West of England."[202] Griffin was also sought out by the foreign press for his views, which spread the BNP's ideas in major publications beyond British borders.[203] The BNP leadership, however, was not cohesive. Butler, who worked in Griffin's office, only spoke to Griffin about twice a month, as Butler ran the party while Griffin focused his energies on Europe.[204] Such issues did not quell disappointment in the 2010 election. Indeed, the 2010 summer school program had about seventy delegates, which was a large drop from the previous year.[205]

An editorial in *The Voice of Freedom* explained that the party "had a difficult aftermath" following the general election, but claimed its "Troops Home Now" campaign was "revitalising" the party.[206] Griffin explained, "the war actually threatens our people at home because the bombing of mosques and the killing of Muslims in Afghanistan only creates hostility amongst the Muslim communities living in Britain and make another London tube bombing a distinct possibility."[207] The BNP launched a nationwide petition drive, with about 120 branches circulating a petition in town centers, collecting an estimated 50,000 signatures.[208] Locally this message was spread by activists, including Adam Walker and several others campaigning in Durham to "bring our boys home."[209] The British National Party started new programs to promote the organization and recruit new members, including launching an online radio station.[210] Coordinated by John Walker, it aired interviews and daily news about national and international affairs through a live discussion format with Arthur Kemp.[211] In late 2010 the BNP attempted to restart its American Friends program, with Andy McBride serving as the overseas liaison officer, but this effort was quickly abandoned.[212] According to McBride, foreign contacts helped promote the party when Griffin's activities received no domestic coverage, but the new American Friends never had more than fifty members in its brief existence.[213] Meanwhile, the BNP also "rebranded" its image by unveiling a new logo with a heart-shaped Union Jack at its annual conference.[214]

Adam Walker and Patrick Harrington, who never joined the BNP, emerged as important figures in the party. Harrington became Griffin's advisor and researcher, while Harrington's American wife was also listed as a researcher and assistant.[215] Walker, a County Durham activist, received a series of promotions and much publicity, making him a rising BNP figure. In addition to being president of Solidarity, he was appointed BNP manager of staff and also became a paid member of Griffin's and Brons's staffs.[216] Indeed, Walker was not just known for his work in the BNP, but garnered public attention for posting intolerant comments that resulted in a hearing in front of the General Teaching Council.[217] Following his promotion to Griffin's staff in summer 2010, Walker attended a "nationalist conference" in Tokyo, Japan that also included Jean-Marie Le Pen and a controversial visit to the Yasukuni Shrine for deceased Japanese soldiers.[218] He then became the BNP national organizer and received 20.4% in the December 2010 town council by-election in Low Spennymoor and Tudhoe Grange Ward.[219] As the national organizer, he also participated in campaigns for seats in the National Assembly for Wales and the Scottish Parliament.[220]

At the 2010 annual party conference, Griffin proposed changes to the constitution, critiquing the BNP's "dictatorial" structure, as well as new initiatives to help the party rebound.[221] Specifically, he argued that the "burden" of leading the party was too much for one person and the BNP needed to adapt. Among the proposals was to have an Advisory Council of eight members elected by the party, which was denounced by Griffin's ally Arthur Kemp.[222] Rather, Kemp proposed having a committee executive led by a chair elected for a fixed term along with two regional representatives as well as three members selected by the chair.[223] The members voted on the proposal, which was then sent to be drafted for a ratification vote at the Extraordinary General Meeting. Andrew Brons supported the election of the Advisory Council and launched a blog with the text of the proposals.[224] Ultimately in 2011, the BNP's constitution was rewritten so that the chair was elected to a four-year term, an Administration Committee was appointed by the chair, and a National Executive mixed the chair with elected regional representatives.[225]

Following the 2010 general election failure, discontent with the party leadership boiled over and a significant number of members, having fallen out with Griffin and his allies, either left the party or were expelled. In fact, Nigel Copsey's analysis compared the aftermath of the 2010 election to the 1979 election, which led "to a period of internecine strife."[226] Already suffering from low morale, the British National Party had a "net loss" of eleven councilors in the May 2011 local elections and failed to win seats in the National Assembly for Wales.[227] The results were spun as "successes" with claims that its "tactics" were working, with ten BNP candidates standing as parish, town and community councilors.[228] Other BNP members, such as Alastair Lewis, believed Griffin was too focused on European affairs and did not devote enough time to domestic issues.[229] Griffin and Walker held meetings throughout England in an effort to quell the discontent, where the party leaders listened to officials and activists talk about what the party was doing right and wrong.[230] Griffin stated that the BNP was "like a family" with "disagreements, but within a spirit of loyalty to each other and the cause, that is perfectly acceptable."[231]

Yet they failed to convince some members. Former Tyndall loyalist Richard Edmonds, who earlier moved to Prussia for three years in disappointment over Griffin's chairmanship, announced his intention to challenge Griffin for party leader. Despite Edmonds's long tenure in the party and his activism since the BNP's founding, he was not able to rally enough support to win the leadership role. He withdrew his challenge in favor of the more popular Brons, who reluctantly decided to challenge Griffin and unite the warring factions.[232] Griffin's new opponents inside the BNP, including John Bean, launched a website, BNPIdeas.com, in support of Brons.[233] Bean, in a revised edition of his autobiography, had grown critical of Griffin and wrote: "I realise that Tyndall's honesty and reliability might have offset some of his political baggage—which turned out to be not much heavier than Griffin's."[234] The coalition against Griffin also included John Walker, who ran Radio Red, White and Blue and used the platform to support Brons.[235] In July 2011, the party membership voted and Griffin won re-election by nine votes—1157 to 1148—to serve a fixed term of four years as chair.[236] While some criticized the vote citing fraud, Edmonds attended the counting and believed there was no evidence of wrongdoing.[237] Likewise, Brons described some polling issues caused by inefficiency, but believed the final results "were probably pretty accurate."[238] Brons pledged to stay with the BNP despite the loss and bitter contest, believing unity was important for the party.[239] The party's internal bulletin proclaimed the leadership election was over, with "stability and certainty guaranteed for four years."[240]

The party election failed to resolve the internal disputes. Many of the problems predated the 2010 election, with members growing frustrated after a decade of Griffin's leadership and gaining no significant political power or influence. In April 2010, Griffin's former close ally, Mark Collett, was expelled from the party for allegedly saying he wanted to kill Griffin.[241] According to Butler, who was supposed to attend a meeting with Collett and David Hannam, Collett was set up by Hannam because Collett planned to initiate action over Griffin's use of BNP finances.[242] Following a police investigation, Collett was not charged with a crime, but announced he no longer had any connection to the party.[243] The press coverage of the BNP's internal troubles and a lower than expected election result caused further infighting.

Many people sought to move away from the transnational focus of the BNP, believing the leadership was too interested in foreign issues. In 2011, long-standing BNP activists Chris Beverley and Eddy Butler joined the English Democrats, even though Beverley continued to work in Brons's European Parliamentary office and Butler was credited with ushering in an electorally successful BNP.[244] Butler had grown critical of Griffin and was planning to challenge him as leader, but was expelled.[245] Beverley wrote that the BNP was a "thoroughly rotten organisation which can be best thought of as a cross between a criminal gang and a religious cult."[246] The English Democrats campaigned for an English parliament and hosted their annual conference in September 2011, where Beverley, then chair of the party's Leeds branch, gave a speech about "his previous political activities and told the delegation how he has moved on in [h]is life and looks forward to taking the English Democrats forward."[247] The BNP responded by calling the defectors a "little group of quarrelsome cranks, proven thieves, sacked incompetents and opposition plants" who were joining the "tiny" English Democrats in order to control it.[248] Moreover, the idea for an English parliament was not new among BNP circles and in fact was part of the BNP's 2005 manifesto.[249]

Beverley and Butler were not the only ones to split from the BNP that year. In summer 2011, former *Identity* editor Paul Golding, former fundraiser Jim Dowson and former BNP organizers Andy McBride and Kevin Edwards started Britain First as a holding name until it could launch the organization as a political party.[250] Golding described Britain First as "a modern, responsible patriotic campaigning organisation" that was opposed to "political correctness" and focused on helping local people, including Christians who "now regularly face discrimination and persecution in many areas."[251] Britain First was involved in several local initiatives, similar to the BNP, such as mobilizing supporters and lobbying representatives "to help highlight the silent majority of British race attack victims."[252] Likewise, Matthew Tait joined the BNP at age eighteen in 2004 after reading its website, but resigned during 2010 and then founded the Legion Martial Arts Club and the Western Spring website devoted to ethno-nationalism.[253] Demonstrating the transnational nature of British radical politics, Tait spoke in 2015 to an American audience about how he was part of a "global movement," which was exciting beyond "mundane" everyday existence.[254] Tait's website grew in popularity and noted that while it was British-based, the group's goal was in "representing the interests of White people everywhere, but in particular the interests of the White people indigenous to the British Isles."[255]

The BNP was hemorrhaging members in the aftermath of all the splits, diluting its already marginal appeal. These public defections painted a clear picture of a party in crisis, which was reflected in declining internal BNP membership numbers. Documents filed with the Electoral Commission by the BNP revealed that the party was suffering a severe decline in membership by 2011. In fact, the party lost around a third of its members that year, with 7681 having paid by 31 December 2011, compared with 10,256 on the same date in 2010.[256]

The records show that the BNP peaked in 2009 with 12,632 paid members (its mailing list had 40,000 individual names) and central account donation totals of £1,260,374, compared with 9801 members in 2008 with £662,271.[257]

Griffin hoped to put the party back on track following his narrow defeat of Brons in 2011. However, current and former associates began working with the BBC's *Panorama* on another episode about the party, but for the first time the documentary would not focus on the BNP's racism or fascism. In early October 2011, the television program, titled *BNP: The Fraud Exposed*, reported "new evidence of financial documents being falsified and fabricated in order to deceive the Electoral Commission."[258] Among the BBC's sources was Dave Hannam, then party treasurer and former Great White Records musician, who died shortly before the airing of the program.[259] Other figures who participated in the documentary included former Griffin allies, including Collett and John Walker. The BNP responded with many Internet articles and rebuttals to the broadcast as well as offering a free information pack and DVD.[260]

In 2011 the BNP held its annual conference near Liverpool on October 29–30, just a few weeks after the program aired. The conference began with a presentation by Clive Jefferson, national treasurer, which was described as "a full presentation of the 2010 accounts" with "a detailed explanation of current cash-flows and financial liabilities."[261] Other presentations were given by Young BNP activists and regional organizers, and debates were chaired by Simon Darby, including discussions about the 2012 London Assembly election.[262] Griffin's speech aimed to rally the party loyalists by denouncing the "lies" of critics and proclaimed the party was "united" from "external" differences.[263] He went on to say that the party was more popular than ever, people "still respect us," and the party has a "future."[264] Griffin's criticism turned to Labour for "blocking" the BNP's strategy in local elections, and he proposed adopting a "grassroots" method wherein BNP local councilors would serve for free.[265]

The BNP's decline did not curtail its international activities. Griffin, as a Member of the European Parliament, was an observer of Russia's December 2011 parliamentary elections.[266] He tweeted about his visit and experiences, concluding in an article on the BNP website that Russia's elections were "much fairer than Britain's."[267] His comments were criticized, as cases of voter fraud by Vladimir Putin's United Russia were clearly documented with video showing ballots being forged.[268] Nevertheless, *The Voice of Freedom* contrasted Russian and British elections, describing the "shame" of British democracy.[269]

Meanwhile, the BNP was active with like-minded groups in European Parliament. The Alliance of European National Movements (AENM) was established in September 2009 by right-wing parties in the European Parliament "devoted to preserving European civilisation."[270] A leaflet promoting the AENM told readers the group would fight the "undemocratic" European Union and encourage only "free sovereign nations who trade and cooperate."[271] The AENM consisted of nine extremist parties, with Bruno Gollnisch of France's Front National as president, Griffin as vice-president and Bleats Kovacs of Hungary's Jobbik as treasurer.[272] The group was formed based on common Euroskeptic ideas and sought the "preservation of the diversity of Europe that results from the variety of our identities, traditions, languages and indigenous cultures."[273] In 2012, the AENM was given €289,266 following its official recognition by the European Parliament. Griffin stated that "such funding should be stopped," but "while the present system stays in place, we will naturally seize every possible opportunity to level the playing field a bit."[274]

The BNP formulated its plans for the May 2012 local elections with a focus on familiar themes and areas, but lost the majority of its seats. With strained finances caused by membership decline, the party's strategy was to have standing literature orders for strong local funding and to concentrate its resources in specific areas with the best canvassers.[275] Meanwhile, activists campaigning in East London distributed "I love London" leaflets and other party literature.[276] The party focused on alleged cases of "race-hate" against whites and "no-go" zones.[277] At the February 2012 organizers' conference, Adam Walker discussed campaigning strategies while Clive Jefferson reported an "improved financial state" as the party planned to "win again" in the Greater London Authority election.[278] The party circulated *The Voice of the Londoner* in support of its London efforts, promoting BNP policies and Carlos Cortiglia as its mayoral candidate.[279] The voting results, however, demonstrated the party's decline as it lost seats in England and failed to win any council elections.[280] The BNP's analysis was that "voters wanted to punish the LibDems and teach the Tories a lesson" so they voted Labour, because when it is the opposition party "people unfortunately forget their misdeeds when in power."[281]

As the BNP struggled, the massive growth of the English Defence League (EDL) on the streets of England took what support the BNP had in the 1990s. The British National Party was critical of the EDL and described it as a "Zionist front" at an Alliance of European National Movements conference.[282] The conference, chaired by Griffin's wife Jackie, was significant because it was attended by delegates from all over Europe who listened to the BNP's reporting of events in England.[283] Griffin's ire was focused on the EDL's draining of the BNP's street support. Though the BNP was in favor of "the rank-and-file followers of the EDL," it claimed the EDL leadership "openly support the ethno-cultural genocide of the indigenous English through mass colonisation and multi-racialism."[284] The BNP released a "report" about the EDL, which Griffin summarized as: "These people are using legitimate concerns about Islam to whip up support for neo-con and Zionist wars that have nothing to do with Britain and the British people, and to try to split and distract the genuine nationalist movement."[285] In contrast to the mass EDL protests, the BNP reported that "the biggest BNP demo in years" saw about 250 local "residents" attend a protest against the building of a mosque in the Leicester area.[286] The number demonstrated a major drop in support, as the BNP organizers' conference in 2004 alone attracted two hundred activists.[287]

Implosion

Hoping to turn the tide, the BNP's 2012 annual conference was titled "Back to Winning" and focused on improving party recruitment.[288] In Griffin's closing speech, he said the party was "well underway" to "rebuilding," with thousands of leaflets distributed and activists being trained.[289] He described how the organization was becoming "a family again" and said the party wanted to win back the "good" activists who had been told "lies" and become "demoralized."[290] To rebuild the party, Griffin said, people must "get out there and build because there is not enough of us," and he told members to "use this new confidence" to bring in new people and welcome back former supporters.[291] Activists were told that treasurer Clive Jefferson had "transformed" the party's finances, submitting the accounts early to the Electoral Commission and passing an audit with "flying colours."[292] With the goal of recruiting new members and spreading its message, the BNP announced "the biggest range of leaflets ever" with several different themes, but also electronic sharing so they could be delivered "to friends via social networking."[293] The *Broken Britain* leaflet, for example, was posted online for download and alleged a "broken" social and economic system that caused millions of young and old Britons to live in poverty.[294] While the new BNP literature expressing local concerns, Griffin continued to forge international connections. That same month, Griffin was a monitor in the Ukrainian elections in October 2012 and though he reported that the Russian elections were better, he said both were "hugely superior to the undemocratic farce that would make Britain an international laughing stock if the reality was exposed."[295]

More than a year after challenging Griffin for leadership of the BNP, Brons announced he was resigning from the party. In a letter posted on his website, Brons complained about being marginalized and attacked by Griffin allies and said that "80 or 90% of the Party's membership, activists and former officials have left it and disappeared in several different directions. The current rump Chairman bears the heavy responsibility for having destroyed the Party of which he is still nominally head."[296] Brons later reflected that Griffin had "misused" his power in the party to force out dissenters, which in turn damaged party unity and morale.[297] In January 2013, Brons and several other former BNP members formed the British Democratic Party, which declared itself a "party of British identity," believing "[n]ationality is acquired by descent."[298] The party's constitution was adopted the following month, with policies reminiscent of the BNP.[299] At the party's first meeting, Brons, chair Kevin Scott and acting treasurer Adrian Davies discussed party administration, ideology and strategy.[300] The group also attracted former BNP councilors, such as James Lewthwaite, who led the BNP group on the Bradford Council.[301] Demonstrating the BNP's diminished position, while the British Democratic Party was critical of the Griffin-led BNP and most were former party members, its campaign material focused on its larger, anti-EU nemesis, UKIP.[302]

In early 2013, Griffin reflected on 2012, writing that the year "made it clear that the British National Party has already won the battle to re-establish itself on rock solid financial foundations."[303] He described the BNP as stronger than its "rivals" and condemned UKIP by describing it as "not nationalist."[304] Charlie Wythe reported to activists: "we've completely righted the financial crisis of 2009–2010" and "rebranded the BNP as 'the party with the heart'," but "still our actual votes suffer."[305] The party took pains to differentiate itself from UKIP by casting itself as for workers' rights, peace and public service in contrast to UKIP, which was "for war" and "for privatisation."[306] The BNP newspaper highlighted Griffin's campaigns in Europe, such as protecting British wildlife, while promoting the efforts of local councilors Richard Perry and Clive Jefferson.[307] The BNP began preparing for the local May elections along with its long-term goal to "expose the falsehood of the controlled media's claims that we've disappeared."[308] However, while the BNP ran ninety-nine candidates in the election, it failed to win a single campaign, leaving the party with a total of two county council seats.[309]

The BNP started several more initiatives to increase recruitment, including "free membership for redundant soldiers."[310] It hoped to revitalize interest by harnessing public concerns about race and immigration. The party mobilized supporters to "demand action" following the murder of Lee Rigby, a British soldier killed by two Muslim converts.[311] The BNP also launched an "online activist" initiative to spread the BNP message online, including connecting to people on Facebook.[312] However, such activities did not help overcome the loss of members. Throughout 2013 the party's membership continued to decline, with 4220 paid for by December 2013 compared with 4872 in 2012.[313]

In 2013, Griffin made his first of four trips to Syria in support of Bashar al-Assad as the country was engulfed in an increasingly sectarian civil war. In June 2013, Griffin traveled with a delegation from Belgium, Poland and Russia to Damascus via Lebanon, making live tweets and posting video online. According to Griffin, he was invited through Russian connections he had made while serving as an election observer.[314] The BNP described the trip as a "peace envoy" to stop the war against Syria, focusing heavily on Western intervention.[315] Griffin reported on his visit and claimed the media were not accurately representing the events in Syria, even confronting BBC journalists in Damascus.[316] Griffin's second visit to Syria in August 2013 followed an invitation to help the Syrian government write letters to the British Parliament about why Britain should not intervene.[317] Griffin met with Syrian leaders, including the prime minister and speaker to the parliament, to craft a letter to "humanize" the conflict.[318] Outspoken about Western intervention in the conflict, he claimed the visit "helped to reshape the political discussion."[319] Specifically, *The Voice of Freedom* claimed: "the BNP stopped the war on Syria" when seven MPs switched their votes to oppose an attack on Syria, which had used chemical weapons on civilians, because of a letter ostensibly from the speaker of Syria's

Parliament that was actually written by Griffin along with Clive Jefferson and Charlie Wythe.[320] Despite Griffin's claims, Brian Wheeler of the BBC reported: "It is not clear how much influence, if any, the Syrian letter had on MPs" because some did not even read the letter.[321] Griffin also used his position in the European Parliament to publicly express doubt that Assad's regime had used chemical weapons.[322]

The 2013 media attention did nothing to slow the decline of morale. In early 2014, Griffin personally was declared bankrupt after a legal battle with his solicitors, but he told members the ruling would not stop his political activism.[323] Meanwhile, Griffin was facing re-election in 2014 for his European seat, but with the party a fraction of its former size and lacking in funds to mount a large campaign, it was unlikely he would retain the seat. Even the BNP's 2014 EU manifesto reflected the diminished energy and resources, with a mere four pages that recycled earlier themes of anti-immigration and protecting "sovereignty."[324] Meanwhile Brons, who had defected from the BNP, declined to run for re-election. Brons continued to receive international invitations, including an opportunity to speak at the 2014 American Renaissance Conference, but did not make the trip after the US embassy in London "refused to commit itself to deal" with his visa application "quickly" over issues surrounding his 1983 conviction under the Public Order Act.[325] In commemoration of his time as an MEP, Brons issued a book containing his European speeches on topics ranging from anti-immigration to Euroskepticism, as well as statistics of attendance.[326]

Griffin maintained an active travel schedule as he campaigned for his seat, even speaking at the European Nationalist Youth Congress in Germany with youth from the Czech Republic, Belgium, France, Italy, Sweden and Switzerland.[327] Angus Matthys, BNP councilor and Griffin's son-in-law, had also engaged with continental extremists in a 2013 training seminar hosted by Jobbik in Budapest, Hungary.[328] In early March 2014, Griffin gave a speech at a "Europe Rises Again" conference in Rome, Italy along with Roberto Fiore of Forza Nuova, Antonios Gregos from Golden Dawn and Manuel Canduela of Spain's National Democracy.[329] Griffin said that Europe was facing a combined social, cultural and economic crisis due to "systematic" and "deliberate" destruction caused by Zionists, capitalists and neo-conservatives, but the "nationalist choice is very clear: we break the banks, we save our nations and we save our people."[330] However, domestic support for Griffin and the BNP was heavily eroded and Griffin lost re-election in May 2014, receiving 32,826 votes, which was less than 2%.[331] Griffin's position within the party was equally insecure, and he expected that members would push for a new leader.[332] Yet he still wanted to develop the party by continuing to work abroad and change how the party campaigned against Islam by making a distinction between the Shia and Sunni moderates and the hardline believers.[333] In July 2014 Griffin stepped down as chair, citing members blaming him for the "brutally hard" European election, and Adam Walker became acting chair.[334] A surprisingly selection, Walker made headlines the previous year when he was permanently banned from the teaching profession and was "given a suspended sentence for verbally abusing three boys and dangerous driving."[335] This was part of an agreement worked out by which Griffin pledged to remain with the BNP as honorary president, and some of the chair's powers would be devolved to the executive council.[336]

Behind the scenes there was a power struggle for BNP control centered on Griffin and the new leadership. In 2013, the BNP began a "will writing" and "executors service" for members interested in leaving a bequest to the party, telling members that two years earlier three timely bequests had literally saved the party.[337] In summer 2014, Griffin wrote a report to the BNP executive council outlining several "problems" in the party, ranging from website issues to oversight of the bequests.[338] The new leadership under Walker was supported by Jefferson, BNP treasurer involved in the estate planning, and Patrick Harrington. In early October Griffin was expelled from the BNP, with the official statement denouncing, among other issues, his "'report' which tells lies about key Party personnel and finances and approving the leak of these damaging and defamatory allegations onto the internet."[339] According to Griffin, the dispute was over money, with Jefferson overseeing about £10 million in people's estates, and Griffin believed the window for making change via elections was over while Jefferson still believed in elections.[340] After his expulsion, the attacks became more personalized and less about politics.

Despite no longer leading a party or having a seat in government, Griffin continued to play a role in marginal international politics. In November 2014 Griffin returned to Syria, appearing at conferences and on television and tweeting about "[n]ormal people enjoying normal peaceful lives."[341] Planning in "secret" during autumn 2014, Griffin, along with other European radicals such as Roberto Fiore and Udo Voigt, publicly announced the launch of the Alliance for Peace and Freedom (APF) in February 2015. The organization described itself as an international non-profit devoted to "a Europe of sovereign nations in which the independent states work together on a confederated basis to address the great challenges of our time and to protect, celebrate and promote our common Christian values and European cultural heritage."[342]

The Alliance for Peace and Freedom was an entirely pan-European organization that reached out to a variety of government officials and like-minded extremists. In March 2015, Griffin, Fiore and Voigt attended a small gathering at the International Russian Conservative Forum in Saint Petersburg, Russia.[343] Griffin spoke about Western Europe's loss of "sovereignty" and his support for "Russia's turn" as a "third Rome" to lead the world in order to stop a coming conflict of civilizations.[344] In early June 2015, Griffin retuned to Syria along with Fiore and Voigt in an eight-person APF "delegation," marking Griffin's fourth visit to the war-torn nation.[345] The men held meetings with ranking officials from the Baath Party and the Syrian Social Nationalist Party, but also with government officials such as Speaker of the People's Council Jihad al-Laham, Deputy Foreign Minister Faisal Mekdad and Information Minister Omran al-Zoubi.[346]

The Alliance for Peace and Freedom continued to gain financial support and members. In early 2016, the European Parliament awarded a €600,000 (£474,250) grant to the organization, which provoked an investigation, and later the 2017 funds were withheld.[347] Griffin continued his travels, visiting Belarus in April 2016 on behalf of the APF; he described the country as a "well-run east European nation" and claimed it was a "very successful" trip that would lead to "some really exciting pan-European nationalist progress in the future."[348] That same month the APF opened a headquarters in Brussels, naming it the Georgios and Manos Centre in memory of "two Greek Golden Dawn members who was brutally murdered in November 2013, outside of a Golden Dawn office in Athens."[349] Additionally, the Alliance for Peace and Freedom, represented by Fiore and Voigt, made another visit to Syria, while Griffin traveled to Serbia to speak at a conference organized by the Serbian National Party on the "threat" of immigration and Islamization.[350] In June Griffin made a three-day visit to Prague, where he met with members of the Workers' Party of Social Justice to discuss immigrants and the APF.[351] The organization also began publishing books, such as *Winds of Change*, which included Holland's *The Political Soldier: A Statement* (1984) and chapters from Fiore and Griffin.[352]

As Griffin made international connections, the British National Party continued to deteriorate, with Griffin loyalists leaving the organization and causing the membership numbers to further plummet. Records filed with the Electoral Commission showed the BNP membership for 2014 was 2992 and income was £480,602, with £25,199 left after expenditures.[353] Despite the BNP's diminished size and revenue, the party announced plans to contest seats in the May 2015 general election. A small, eight-page election manifesto listed key BNP policies, including animal welfare, banning the hijab and burqa, and stopping mass immigration.[354] Griffin, meanwhile, announced on social media that he would hold his "nose" and vote for UKIP in order to "help break up the Westminster system" as well as "hold Cameron's feet to [the] referendum fire."[355] The BNP ultimately ran eight candidates and received a total of 1667 votes throughout the country, which, compared with the Conservatives' winning vote of 11,334,576, demonstrated the extent of the BNP's implosion.[356] This did not mean that Euroskepticism and identity issues were absent from the election, because the Scottish National Party won fifty-six seats with 1,454,436 votes and UKIP received one seat with a total of 3,881,099 votes.[357] Nonetheless, BNP chair Adam Walker spun the devastating results as "mission accomplished," contrasting it with the 2010 election by writing that the BNP emerged from the 2015 election "debt free."[358] Some news outlets celebrated the BNP's failure, with *The Independent* stating: "BNP sees 99.7% drop in votes in 2015 general election, party all but wiped out."[359] Weeks later, the party failed to do any better in the local elections, running eight candidates, and Cathy Duffy, the BNP's only councilor facing re-election, all losing.[360] The party then turned to its own internal issues. In summer 2015 a BNP leadership contest was held, with Walker pushing back a challenge from Paul Hilliard by a vote of 523 to 145 with an alleged total membership turnout of 36%.[361]

Despite the loss of support and publicized problems, the BNP worked to rebrand itself and retain the members it had. In autumn 2015, the party relaunched *Identity* as a newspaper edited by Charlie Wythe, who wrote that it would offer "popularist and easy-to-read insight into the nationalist policies necessary to make Britain better."[362] The second issue focused on opposing immigration, describing Muslims from Asia and Africa as "threatening" British identity.[363] Meanwhile the BNP's November 2015 internal bulletin told readers: "With the difficult times behind us, our outstanding BNP Treasury team is forecasting the strongest financial position in the history of the BNP for the 2015/16 accounts."[364] Under Walker's leadership, the party condemned the Cameron government for housing

Syrian refugees instead of reforming the National Health Service and providing social welfare to Britons.[365] The BNP also continued to criticize Islam, writing: "Our precious and unique British culture is actively and stealthily being erased and replaced with Islam, and the treacherous Labour Party is actively conspiring with them."[366]

The 2016 elections proved significant for the direction of the country, but the BNP had even less influence than in the past. In the 2016 local elections, the BNP campaigned for the mayoral election in London on a variety of issues, including opposition to immigration, banning sharia law and "ensur[ing] that existing community buildings such as pubs and churches are not turned into mosques."[367] The results where humiliating, with the BNP's David Furness receiving 13,325 votes (0.5%), behind Britain First's Paul Golding who received 31,372 votes (1.2%), both of whom were dwarfed by the winning vote of 1,148,716 (44.2%) for Labour's Sadiq Khan, who became London's first Muslim mayor.[368] *Heritage and Destiny* described the 2016 elections as "a disaster of historic proportions for the British nationalist movement, forcing a serious rethink of our whole strategy and organisation," but the BNP did have one small victory, with a BNP-backed candidate winning a seat on the Heybridge Parish Council.[369] Moreover, decades of Euroskepticism culminated in the June 2016 EU referendum in which the BNP vocally supported the "leave" campaign, but the party's severely depleted membership and funds meant that it was not much of an influence.[370] The "leave" vote won and started the "Brexit" transition out of the European Union.[371] Griffin tweeted statements celebrating the fact that forty years of "rule" from Brussels had "ended," and saying that a man who had called him racist ten years earlier had apologized, telling Griffin he was "right all along."[372] The voting took place nearly a week after Labour MP Jo Cox was murdered while meeting with her constituents by Thomas Mair, who reportedly yelled "Britain First" and had a history of reading right-wing and neo-Nazi literature.[373] In August the BNP faced yet more controversy when police took Walker into custody and released him without charge concerning "election irregularities" in the May local elections.[374]

Conclusion

The final years of Griffin's leadership brought the BNP to new peaks and lows. The BNP more than doubled its number of local councilors, won a seat in the London Assembly and had two representatives elected to the European Parliament. In the face of increased expectations and the BNP leader becoming more involved with international affairs, members started leaving the party. Some of these people founded rival parties, while Griffin faced a serious leadership challenge from Brons. Many long-time British fascists were not accustomed to being in a party that won elections and had an international profile. Between the raised expectations and softening of the party image, some members expected more power and others longed for the days of hardline politics with no election victories. Internal pressure, compounded with a long list of disaffected and expelled members, pushed the party to a breaking point. With limited resources and receiving press that cast doubt on the BNP's future, the party's only member in the European Parliament lost re-election in 2014. Following continued internal disputes, including accusations of misuse of money and corruption, the BNP had imploded by late 2014. Subsequently, Griffin joined with fascists in other European countries to form a transnational political organization devoted to "European" culture. While British fascism faces an uncertain domestic electoral future, the radicals themselves remain transnational figures working in concert with extremists from other countries.

Notes

1. Robert Ford and Matthew J. Goodwin, *Revolt on the Right: Explaining Support for the Radical Right in Britain* (New York: Routledge, 2014), 153. See also: Robert Ford and Matthew J. Goodwin, "Angry White Men: Individual and Contextual Predictors of Support for the British National Party," *Political Studies* 58, no. 1 (February 2010): 1–25.
2. Nigel Copsey, "Sustaining a Mortal Blow?: The British National Party and the 2010 General and Local Elections," *Patterns of Prejudice* 46, no. 1 (2012): 38.
3. "Help Us Consolidate These Vital Gains," *The Voice of Freedom* no. 61 (June 2005): 5.
4. Nick Griffin, "The BNP Must Grow Community Roots," *Identity* no. 62 (January 2006): 5.
5. Ibid., 7.
6. "Does it Take A Bomb," *British Nationalist: Member's Bulletin* (July 2005): unpaginated 1.
7. *Freedom, Security, Identity and Democracy* unnumbered (Welshpool: British National Party, July 2005) (DVD Recording).
8. Ibid.

9. Joe Owens, *Action!: Race War to Door Wars* (Liverpool: Aryan Publishing Company, 2007), 278.
10. Ibid., 279, 280; Neil Mackay, "'Senior BNP Official Suggested Assassinating Prominent Politicians': Right-wing party in turmoil over sensational allegations," *The Herald*, 28 May 2006; available online at http://www.heraldscotland.com/sport/spl/aberdeen/senior-bnp-official-suggested-assassinating-prominent-politicians-right-wing-party-in-turmoil-over-sensational-allegations-1.19183; accessed 1 July 2016.
11. Martin Wainwright, "Retrial Ordered After Griffin Walks Free," *The Guardian*, 3 February 2006; available online at http://www.theguardian.com/politics/2006/feb/03/uk.race; accessed 1 July 2016.
12. *Freedom, Security, Identity and Democracy* unnumbered (Welshpool: British National Party, January 2006) (DVD Recording).
13. "Head of Publicity," *The Voice of Freedom* no. 71 (2006): 9; "Our Greatest Publicity Coup Ever," *Identity* no. 63 (February 2006): 4.
14. "BNP Support from Around the Globe," *The Voice of Freedom* no. 69 (2006): 3.
15. "How the Court Victory Was Won," *Identity* no. 73 (December 2006): 13. See also a brief mention in "Victory," *British Nationalist: Member's Bulletin* (December 2006): unpaginated 1.
16. "Free Speech Trial Revisited," *The Voice of Freedom* no. 78 (2006): 8.
17. *Freedom, Security, Identity and Democracy* unnumbered (Welshpool: British National Party, January/February 2007) (DVD Recording).
18. Nick Griffin, "Free Speech Under Attack," *Identity* no. 74 (January 2007): 4, 5, 6, 7.
19. *Red, White and Blue 2005* (Leeds: BNPTV, 2005) (Disc 1) (DVD Recording).
20. Nick Griffin, "Modern Nationalism: The New Force in Politics," *Identity* no. 66 (May 2006): 4.
21. Ibid., 8.
22. "Women of Britain: Your Country Needs You," *The Voice of Freedom* no. 69 (2006): 5.
23. "Women of Britain: Your Country Needs You," *The Voice of Freedom* no. 71 (2006): 5.
24. Warren Glass, interviewed by Ryan Shaffer, audio recording, 7 October 2014.
25. Cheryl Glass, interviewed by Ryan Shaffer, audio recording, 7 October 2014.
26. Ibid.
27. "BNP Doubles Number of Councillors," BBC, 5 May 2006; available online at http://news.bbc.co.uk/2/hi/uk_news/politics/4974870.stm; accessed 1 July 2016.

28. Ibid.
29. "34 BNP Victories Against All the Odds," *The Voice of Freedom* no. 72 (2006): 1.
30. Ibid.
31. "May '06 Election Breakthrough," *Identity* no. 66 (May 2006): 9; "BNP Council Map of England," *Identity* no. 66 (May 2006): 11.
32. "BNP's Sharon to Fight On," *Birmingham Post*, 28 July 2006; available online at http://www.birminghampost.co.uk/news/local-news/bnps-sharon-to-fight-on-3981809; accessed 1 July 2016. She started and led the New Nationalist Party, a BNP splinter group that existed from December 2006 to December 2007. Sharon Ebanks, "Statement by Sharon Ebanks," New Nationalist Party, 2007; available online at https://web-beta.archive.org/web/20080118084432/http://www.nnp.org.uk; accessed 1 July 2016.
33. Andrew Milford, "BNP Back for Grange By-Election," Get Hampshire, 4 July 2006; available online at http://www.gethampshire.co.uk/news/local-news/bnp-back-for-grange-by-election-5361022; accessed 1 July 2016.
34. "Operation White Vote," *The Voice of Freedom* no. 68 (2006): 6.
35. *Understanding the Power of Voting* (Welshpool: Young BNP, n.d., circa 2006): unpaginated.
36. Eddy Butler, "BNP Local Elections Success Gives Hope for the Future," *Identity* no. 67 (June 2006): 8.
37. Ibid., 9.
38. Chris Beverley, "How the BNP Overturned a 1038 Vote Majority," *The Voice of Freedom* no. 73 (2006): 16.
39. Eddy Butler, "We Are 'The Management'," *Identity* no. 68 (July 2008): 10.
40. Karin Bottom and Colin Copus, "The BNP in Local Government: Support for the Far Right or for Community Politics?," in *British National Party: Contemporary Perspectives* eds. Nigel Copsey and Graham Macklin (New York: Routledge, 2011), 159.
41. Trevor Maxfield, interviewed by Ryan Shaffer, audio recording, 10 October 2014.
42. "As BNP Votes Saves Local Council Payment Centres," *The Voice of Freedom* no. 46 (January 2004): 1; "Burnley BNP Wins 'Defend Our Democracy' Council Debate," *The Voice of Freedom* no. 46 (January 2004): 1.
43. "Seven Days in the Life of Councillor Sharon Ebanks," *The Voice of Freedom* no. 73 (2006): 3. She later resigned and was listed as "proscribed" by the BNP in 2007. "Proscription Notice—Sharon Ebanks," *British Nationalist: Member's Bulletin* (February 2007): unpaginated 7.

44. "BNP Councillors Restore Public Confidence in the Police in Epping," *The Voice of Freedom* no. 75 (2006): 13.
45. Ibid.
46. "BNP Councillors Meet in Stoke," *The Voice of Freedom* no. 82 (2007): 14.
47. For example, the Halifax BNP produced a twelve-page guide. Richard Mulhall and Geoffrey Wallace, *British National Party Councillors Handbook* (n.p.: unknown, n.d., circa 2004). Personal possession.
48. *2007 Annual Conference* (n.p.: British National Party, 2007), 8, 15.
49. Nick Griffin, "Voting Membership," *Identity* no. 75 (February 2007): 4.
50. Ibid.
51. Ibid., 5.
52. "Voting Membership Power," *Identity* no. 75 (February 2007): 9. "Voting Membership Criteria Approved," *British Nationalist: Member's Bulletin* (January 2007): 4.
53. Martin Wingfield, "Editorial," *The Voice of Freedom* no. 71 (2006): 12; "May 3rd 2007: The Campaign Starts Now," *The Voice of Freedom* no. 73 (2006): 5.
54. Mark Collett, "Council Election Analysis 2007," *Identity* no. 78 (May 2007): 8.
55. Ibid.
56. Andrew McBride, interviewed by Ryan Shaffer, audio recording, 19 September 2011.
57. Ibid.
58. "Securing the Future of the BNP," *The Voice of Freedom* no. 86 (2007): 1. The BNP printed the tally as Griffin with 3,363 votes and Jackson with 337. "Chairman Wins One Sided Contest," *British Nationalist: Member's Bulletin* (August 2007): unpaginated 5.
59. "British National Party Leadership Contest," *British Nationalist: Member's Bulletin* (July 2007): unpaginated 4.
60. "Welsh Regional Assembly Appeal," *Identity* no. 75 (February 2007): 26.
61. "42,197 Votes Makes the BNP the Fifth Party in Wales," *The Voice of Freedom* no. 84 (2007): 8.
62. "The BNP's Best Parliamentary By-Election Vote," *The Voice of Freedom* no. 86 (2007): 3.
63. Nick Griffin, "It's a Dirty Old Game," *Identity* no. 77 (April 2007): 4.
64. Nick Griffin, "A Tidal Wave of Anti-BNP Propaganda," *Identity* no. 82 (September 2007): 4; Nick Griffin, "Faction of the Fooled," *Identity* no. 86 (January 2008): 4.
65. Eddy Butler, "Lessons from the May Elections," *Identity* no. 79 (June 2007): 8, 9.
66. Nigel Copsey, "From Direct Action to Community Action: The Changing Dynamics of Anti-Fascist Opposition," in *British National*

Party: Contemporary Perspectives eds. Nigel Copsey and Graham Macklin (New York: Routledge, 2011), 137.

67. Nick Griffin, "The BNP & UKIP Won't Be Getting Married," *Identity* no. 79 (June 2007): 7.
68. Nick Griffin, "The Big Picture Behind Our Electoral Targets," *Identity* no. 83 (October 2007): 4.
69. Eddy Butler, "The BNP's Prime Electoral Targets," *Identity* no. 83 (October 2007): 8.
70. Martin Wingfield, "Modernisation Behind Our Success," *The Voice of Freedom* no. 84 (2007): 12.
71. *Summer School 2007* (n.p.: British National Party, 2007), 13; see also coverage in "Summer School 2007," *Identity* no. 83 (October 2007): 13; "Summer School a Big Hit Again," *British Nationalist: Member's Bulletin* (October 2007): unpaginated 2.
72. *Freedom, Security, Identity and Democracy* unnumbered (Welshpool: British National Party, June 2008) (DVD Recording).
73. "London 2008 Gets Off To A Flying Start," *Identity* no. 87 (February 2008): 14.
74. *Freedom, Security, Identity and Democracy* unnumbered (Welshpool: British National Party, February 2008) (DVD Recording).
75. "100,000 BNP Leaflets for London in Just One Weekend," *The Voice of Freedom* no. 92 (2008): 8.
76. *The Londoner* (Dagenham: British National Party, 2008): unpaginated 1, 3. *Freedom, Security, Identity and Democracy* unnumbered (Welshpool: British National Party, March 2008) (DVD Recording).
77. *Freedom, Security, Identity and Democracy* unnumbered (Welshpool: British National Party, January 2008) (DVD Recording).
78. "BNP Website is Breaking Records," *The Voice of Freedom* no. 92 (2008): 9.
79. Nick Griffin, "Racism Cuts Both Ways," *Identity* no. 88 (March 2008): 4.
80. *Racism Cuts Both Ways* (Worchester: British National Party, 2008), 2, 3.
81. "Liverpool 13 Demonstration," *Identity* no. 98 (January 2009): 17.
82. "Powell Lit the BNP's Torch for National Identity and Freedom," *The Voice of Freedom* no. 73 (2006): 10.
83. Nick Griffin, "The Last Days of 'Normal'," *Identity* no. 89 (April 2008): 4.
84. "Mayor of London and Greater London Assembly," *The Voice of Freedom* no. 93 (2008): 5; "Our London List," *The Voice of Freedom* no. 94 (2008): 8.
85. Cover of *The Voice of Freedom* no. 95 (2008); "Stoke Now Has Nine British National Party Councillors," *The Voice of Freedom* no. 95 (2008): 2; "A London Assembly Seat—BNP's Most Significant Electoral Victory," *The Voice of Freedom* no. 95 (2008): 2.

86. Mark Collett, "Election Review 2008," *Identity* no. 90 (May 2008): 12, 14.
87. Nick Griffin, "Update from the Chairman," *Hope & Glory* 1, no. 2 (July 2008): 3.
88. Nick Griffin, "London Victory," *Hope & Glory* 1, no. 2 (July 2008): 6, 7.
89. "BNP Make History," *The Voice of Freedom* no. 96 (2008): 1.
90. *Freedom, Security, Identity and Democracy* unnumbered (Welshpool: British National Party, December 2008) (DVD Recording).
91. "Britain Has the Right to be British," *Identity* no. 71 (October 2006): 13.
92. "Annual Conference 2007," *Identity* no. 85 (December 2007): 14; "Arthur Kemp Delivers in Shrewsbury," *The Voice of Freedom* no. 93 (2008): 14.
93. Steve Blake, "BNP E&T: An Introduction," *Identity* no. 84 (November 2007): 6.
94. "Building to Grow: The Results," *Identity* no. 87 (February 2008): 6.
95. Arthur Kemp, "Zimbabwe: A Warning For Us All," *Identity* no. 30 (March 2003): 12; "Victory or Violence," *Identity* no. 90 (May 2008): 7; Gavin Evans, "Camp and Cowardice," *Mail & Guardian*, 18 June 2004; available online at http://mg.co.za/article/2004-06-18-camp-and-cowardice; accessed 1 July 2016; Matthew Taylor, "BNP's attempt to gain first European seat aided by man linked to ANC leader's killer," *The Guardian*, 8 May 2009; available online at http://www.theguardian.com/politics/2009/may/08/bnp-nick-griffin-arthur-kemp; accessed 1 July 2016.
96. "Merchandise," *Identity* no. 91 (June 2008): 31; "Jihad: Islam's 1,300 Year War on Western Civilisation," *The Voice of Freedom* no. 97 (2008): 16; Arthur Kemp, *Jihad: Islam's 1,300 Year War on Western Civilisation* (Burlington: Ostara Publications, 2008).
97. "Neo-Conned and Neo-Conned Again," *Identity* no. 64 (March 2006): 9; D.L. O'Huallachain [Derek Holland] and J. Forrest Sharpe, *Neo-Conned! Just War Principles: A Condemnation of War in Iraq* (Vienna: Light in the Darkness Publications, 2005). O'Huallachain is Holland's Irish name and according to Virginia records, the IHS was chaired by John Sharpe and O'Huallachain was the vice-chair. "SCC Clerk's Information System," 2015; available online at https://cisiweb.scc.virginia.gov/z_container.aspx; accessed 1 July 2016.
98. "Form AR21," Solidarity, 2006. Search "Solidarity" and 2006 at Certification Office, 2015; available online at http://webarchive.nationalarchives.gov.uk/20140701201750/http://www.certoffice.org/Nav/Trade-Unions/Solidarity.aspx; accessed 1 July 2016.
99. Patrick Harrington, interviewed by Ryan Shaffer, audio recording, 29 May 2010.

100. "Solidarity," *The Voice of Freedom* no. 81 (2007): 6. Harrington also said, "I wouldn't vote for the BNP. I don't agree with the BNP on a whole range of issues." Interview with Harrington.
101. Interview with Harrington. He described how the newspapers and opponents were not interested in the cases he argued that dealt with issues such as smoking and vacation time.
102. "Solidarity," *The British Worker* no. 1 (n.d., circa 2006): 8.
103. According to Carl Booth, he sold copies of the National Party's *The British Worker* to Harrington and months later that same masthead and format appeared on Solidarity's newsletter, The British Worker. Carl Booth, interviewed by Ryan Shaffer, audio recording, 9 October 2014.
104. Search for specific years. "Solidarity," Certification Officer, 2015; available online at http://webarchive.nationalarchives.gov.uk/20140701201750/http://www.certoffice.org/Nav/Trade-Unions/Solidarity.aspx; accessed 1 July 2016.
105. Adam Walker, "Adam Walker Sends a Personal Message to BNP Trade Unionists," *The British Worker* no. 2 (July 2008): 4, 5.
106. "'Cancel This Conference' Urges Solidarity Union," *The Voice of Freedom* no. 92 (2008): 6.
107. "Solidarity Supports Aims of Wildcat Strikers," *The Voice of Freedom* no. 107 (2009): 4.
108. David Kerr, "Teamwork is the Hallmark of the Solidarity Trade Union," *The Voice of Freedom* no. 93 (2008): 9.
109. "BNP Teacher and School Stand Up to Labour Bullyboys," *The Voice of Freedom* no. 98 (2008): 3.
110. "Union Helps BNP Teacher Get a Fair Tribunal Panel," *The Voice of Freedom* no. 101 (2008): 14.
111. "Support Adam Walker," *The Voice of Freedom* no. 114 (2010): 7.
112. "Three Year Witch Hunt of BNP Teacher Ends in Failure," *The Voice of Freedom* no. 115 (2010): 3.
113. Adam Walker, "Solidarity: Promoting Nationalism and Freedom," *The Voice of Freedom* no. 121 (n.d., circa 2011): 9.
114. John Bean, "Smears, Stings and Solidarity," *Identity* no. 101 (2009): 10; "Solidarity: 'Our Members Call the Shots," Solidarity, 2009; available online at http://www.solidaritytradeunion.org/the-press/164-01062009-solidarity-our-members-call-the-shots.html; accessed 1 July 2016.
115. When asked about his religious beliefs, Griffin said he was agnostic. He rejected the atheist label as being "Marxist." Nick Griffin, interviewed by Ryan Shaffer, audio recording, 8 October 2014.
116. Tim Heydon, "Christianity & Nationalism," *Identity* no. 82 (September 2007): 11.

117. John Maddox, "Christianity in Britain: Self Harm or Suicide? Part 4," *Identity* no. 69 (August 2006): 27.
118. Andrew Vernon, "Answering Church Attacks Upon the BNP," *Identity* no. 72 (November 2006): 15.
119. "Only The BNP Stands Up For Our Christian Faith," *The Voice of Freedom* no. 104 (2009): 3.
120. "Nick Griffin on Britain & Europe," *Identity* no. 102 (2009): 40. *Freedom, Security, Identity and Democracy* unnumbered (Welshpool: British National Party, December 2005) (DVD Recording).
121. Interview with McBride.
122. Nick Griffin, "Celebrate Our Christian Heritage with Pride," *The Voice of Freedom* no. 105 (2009): 4.
123. "Church of England Discriminates Against the British National Party," *Hope & Glory* 2, no. 1 (March 2009): 10.
124. Nick Griffin, "Update from the Chairman," *Hope & Glory* 1, no. 1 (April 2008): 3.
125. Nick Griffin, "Party in the Streets," *Identity* no. 94 (September 2008): 5.
126. Mark Collett, "The 2009 Euro Campaign Starts Now," *Identity* no. 94 (September 2008): 18.
127. *British Jobs for British Workers* (London: British National Party, n.d., circa 2008): unpaginated.
128. Nick Griffin, "Surviving the Age of Scarcity," *Identity* no. 93 (August 2008): 6.
129. Nick Griffin, "Party in the Streets," *Identity* no. 94 (September 2008): 5.
130. Eddy Butler, "What is the BNP Doing," *Identity* no. 96 (November 2008): 12, 13.
131. Ibid., 15.
132. Lawrence Rustem, "Time to Improve Election Results," *Identity* no. 99 (February 2009): 8.
133. Nick Griffin, "2009—Looking Ahead to a Crucial Year," *Identity* no. 97 (December 2008): 5.
134. "British Nationalism," *The Voice of Freedom* no. 102 (2009): 1.
135. Nick Griffin, "Update from the Chairman," *Hope & Glory* 2, no. 1 (March 2009): 3.
136. Peter Strudwick, "EU's Assault by Stealth on National Sovereignty," *Identity* no. 98 (January 2009): 12.
137. Nick Griffin, "June 4th—Our Date with Destiny," *Identity* no. 98 (January 2009): 4.
138. Ibid.
139. Ibid., 5, 6.
140. "Battle for Britain," *Identity* no. 99 (February 2009): 17.

141. Nick Griffin, "A BNP Breakthrough—Hype & Reality," *Identity* no. 100 (March/April 2009): 6, 7.
142. "Your Money," *Hope & Glory* 2, no. 2 (June 2009): 6.
143. Ibid., 7.
144. "News Flash," *The Voice of Freedom* no. 104 (2009): 10.
145. *Help Us Win the Battle for Britain* (London: British National Party, n.d., circa 2009). In possession.
146. Interview with Griffin.
147. "Meet Our Candidates," *The Voice of Freedom* no. 105 (2009): 8.
148. Andrew Brons, interviewed by Ryan Shaffer, audio recording, 11 October 2014.
149. Ibid.
150. Cover of *The Voice of Freedom* no. 106 (2009).
151. Nick Griffin, "Update From the Chairman," *Hope & Glory* 2, no. 3 (August 2009): 3.
152. "How The Beachheads Were Won," *Hope & Glory* 2, no. 3 (August 2009): 9, 10.
153. "Victory in the North West," *The Voice of Freedom* no. 106 (2009): 2; "Victory in Yorkshire," *The Voice of Freedom* no. 106 (2009): 2.
154. "Spectacular Press Conference Launches Our Euro Campaign," *The Voice of Freedom* no. 106 (2009): 3.
155. "Local Elections 2009," *Parliamentary Research Briefing*, 2009; available online at http://www.parliament.uk/briefing-papers/RP09-54.pdf; accessed 1 July 2016.
156. Eddy Butler, interviewed by Ryan Shaffer, audio recording, 16 September 2011.
157. Andrew Brons, "Yorkshire & Humber MEP," *The Voice of Freedom* no. 108 (2009): 11.
158. "First Staff Appointments for Our MEPS," *The Voice of Freedom* no. 106 (2009): 11.
159. "MEP Newsletters and Newspaper Adverts Help to Spread the Word," *The Voice of Freedom* no. 112 (2010): 12.
160. "BNP's Reason for Its Membership Policy," *Identity* no. 101 (2009): 19.
161. "Sikh Spokesman at Northhampton Meeting," *The Voice of Freedom* no. 103 (2009): 8.
162. Rajinder Singh, "Raj on Britain," *The Voice of Freedom* no. 30 (September 2002): 4.
163. *British National Party Annual Conference 2009* (Burnley: BNPTV, 2009) (DVD Recording).
164. Ibid.
165. Ibid.

166. Chris Irvine, "BNP votes to allow non-white members into party," *The Telegraph*, 15 February 2010; available online at http://www.telegraph.co.uk/news/politics/bnp/7239396/BNP-votes-to-allow-non-white-members-into-party.html; accessed 1 July 2016; "Extraordinary General Meeting Passes New BNP Constitution with Overwhelming Vote," British National Party, February 2010; available online at http://bnp.org.uk/2010/02/extraordinary-general-meeting-passes-new-bnp-constitution-with-overwhelming-vote/; accessed 1 July 2016; See video of the vote here: "EGM Passes New BNP Constitution," British National Party, February 2010; available online at http://bnptv.org.uk/2010/02/egm-passes-new-bnp-constitution/; accessed 1 June 2012.
167. Interview with McBride.
168. "Only BNP Can Save Britain from Islamic Colonisation Says First Sikh Member," *The Voice of Freedom* no. 114 (2010): 6.
169. "Meet Andrew Brons—Britain's First Nationalist MEP," *The Voice of Freedom* no. 107 (2009): 7.
170. "British National Party MEPs Take their Seats in Brussels," *The Voice of Freedom* no. 107 (2009): 9.
171. For example: Andrew Brons, "Yorkshire & Humber MEP," *The Voice of Freedom* no. 109 (2009): 7.
172. Andrew Brons, "Yorkshire & Humber MEP," *The Voice of Freedom* no. 111 (2009): 7.
173. Nick Griffin, "Global Warming: A Hoax," *The Voice of Freedom* no. 111 (2009): 2.
174. "BBC to allow BNP on Question Time," BBC, 21 October 2009; available online at http://news.bbc.co.uk/2/hi/entertainment/8319136.stm; accessed 1 July 2016.
175. Hélène Mulholland, "Griffin: Unfair that Question Time was filmed in 'ethnically cleansed' London," *The Guardian*, 23 October 2009; available online at http://www.theguardian.com/politics/2009/oct/23/bnp-nick-griffin-question-time; accessed 1 July 2016.
176. John Bean, "Editorial," *Identity* no. 102 (2009): 5.
177. "London Assembly Member Richard Barnbrook Attends Palace Party," *Identity* no. 107 (2009): 9.
178. "General Election Planning Meeting in Cumbria," *The Voice of Freedom* no. 112 (2010): 12.
179. "Never Has There Been More Reasons to Vote BNP," *The Voice of Freedom* no. 114 (2010): 2.
180. "Salford BNP Distributes 20,000 Leaflets in 8 Weeks," *The Voice of Freedom* no. 114 (2010): 12.
181. "Manifesto," British National Party, 2010; available online at https://web-beta.archive.org/web/20100708142108/https://www.bnp.

org.uk/manifesto; accessed 1 July 2016; *Democracy, Freedom, Culture and Identity: British National Party General Election Manifesto 2010* (Welshpool: British National Party, 2010), 4.

182. Clive Wakley, "The Curse of Overpopulation," *Identity* no. 103 (Spring 2010): 57.
183. "Stop This War Now," *The Voice of Freedom* no. 107 (2009): 1; "Afghan Death Toll Rises," *The Voice of Freedom* no. 108 (2009): 3.
184. Nick Griffin, "Only the BNP Will Stop This War," *The Voice of Freedom* no. 107 (2009): 3.
185. Nick Griffin, "No Blood for Afghanistan," *The Voice of Freedom* no. 112 (2010): 2.
186. "Coming Soon," *Identity* no. 99 (February 2009): 30
187. John Bean, "Editorial," *Identity* no. 100 (March/April 2009): 3.
188. "Identity Magazine—Issue 100 and Beyond," *Identity* no. 100 (March/April 2009): 30.
189. Copsey, "Sustaining a Mortal Blow?," 31, 33.
190. Cover of *The Voice of Freedom* no. 115 (2010).
191. "General Election 2010," *House of Commons Library*, 2 February 2011; available online at http://www.parliament.uk/briefing-papers/RP10-36.pdf; accessed 1 July 2016.
192. "Our Verdict on Thursday 6th May," *The Voice of Freedom* no. 115 (2010): 2.
193. Ibid.
194. "14,000 Members: BNP Now Bigger than UKIP," *The Voice of Freedom* no. 115 (2010): 3.
195. "Local Elections Results Round Up," *The Voice of Freedom* no. 115 (2010): 18.
196. See *The Voice of Freedom* no. 116 (2010): 6, 7.
197. "MEP Gets Reassurance Over Europol," *The Voice of Freedom* no. 116 (2010): 6; "Understanding the Difference Between Nationality & Citizenship," *The Voice of Freedom* no. 116 (2010): 7.
198. "Andrew Brons Visits Rosarno," *Andrew Brons MEP, Annual Report 2009–2010* (Leeds: Andrew Brons MEP, 2010): 11.
199. Andrew Brons, "A Letter to the 'Telegraph'," *The Voice of Freedom* no. 115 (2010): 7; "Andrew Brons Visits Zagreb," *Andrew Brons MEP, Annual Report 2009–2010* (Leeds: Andrew Brons MEP, 2010): 12–13.
200. Andrew Brons, "Musing in My First Year as an MEP," *Andrew Brons MEP, Annual Report 2009–2010* (Leeds: Andrew Brons MEP, 2010): 4, 6.
201. "A Tale of Two MEPs," *The Voice of Freedom* no. 117 (2010): 5; Hélène Mulholland, "BNP leader Nick Griffin barred from Queen's garden party," *The Guardian*, 22 July 2010; available online at http://www.

theguardian.com/politics/2010/jul/22/bnp-nick-griffin-queen-party1; accessed 1 July 2016.

202. "Nick Griffin Second Top North West MEP," *The Voice of Freedom* no. 118 (2010): 6.
203. "Marianne Courts Nick," *The Voice of Freedom* no. 119 (2010): 6.
204. Interview with Butler.
205. "British National Party Summer School 2010," *The Voice of Freedom* no. 118 (2010): 5.
206. Steve Johnson, "Comment," *The Voice of Freedom* no. 119 (2010): 12.
207. *Bring Our Boys Home* (Welshpool: British National Party, n.d., circa 2010), 2.
208. "Support Our Troops, Bring Our Boys Home," *British Nationalist: Member's Bulletin* (November 2010): unpaginated 3.
209. "County Durham BNP Gathers Support for National 'Bring Our Boys' Home Campaign," *British National Party*, 2010; available online at http://www.bnp.org.uk/news/county-durham-bnp-gathers-support-national-bring-our-boys-home-campaign; accessed 1 July 2016.
210. "Radio RWB," *The Voice of Freedom* no. 116 (2010): 10. The website was at radiorwb.co.uk.
211. "More Radio RWB Programmes," *The Voice of Freedom* no. 117 (2010): 16; "Radio Red, White & Blue to Launch Daily Bulletins," *The Voice of Freedom* no. 121 (n.d., circa 2011): 9.
212. Interview with McBride; Nigel Morris, "BNP establishes 'social networking' branch in America," *The Independent*, 1 November 2010; available online at http://www.independent.co.uk/news/world/americas/bnp-establishes-social-networking-branch-in-america-2121847.html; accessed 1 July 2016.
213. Interview with McBride.
214. "Ushering in a New Era," *The Voice of Freedom* no. 120 (n.d., circa 2010): 1.
215. "Office and Staffing," NickGriffin.eu, 2011; available online at https://web.archive.org/web/20110709125059/http://www.nickgriffinmep.eu/content/office-staffing; accessed 1 July 2016.
216. "Adam Walker Appointed BNP's Staff Manager," *The Voice of Freedom* no. 116 (2010): 4.
217. Ibid.
218. "BNP Represented at Tokyo Conference," *The Voice of Freedom* no. 118 (2010): 8.
219. Stephen Palmer, "Spennymoor By-Election," *The Voice of Freedom* no. 120 (n.d., circa 2010): 9.
220. Adam Walker, "National Organiser's Call to Action," *The Voice of Freedom* no. 120 (n.d., circa 2010): 11.

221. *British National Party Annual Conference 2010* (Burnley: BNPTV, 2010) (Disc 1) (DVD Recording).
222. Ibid.
223. Ibid.
224. "British National Party Constitutional Consultation," Andrew Brons, 2010; available online at http://bnpconstitutionalconsultation.blogspot.com/; accessed 1 July 2016.
225. "The Constitution of the British National Party," British National Party, 15 July 2011; available online at http://www.bnp.org.uk/sites/default/files/constitution_12.3_with_candidate_contract.pdf; accessed 1 July 2016.
226. Copsey, "Sustaining a Mortal Blow?," 38.
227. "Vote 2011: BNP suffers council seat losses," BBC, 6 May 2011; available online at http://www.bbc.com/news/uk-politics-13313069; accessed 1 July 2016. The Welsh Assembly was a key target for the party. Brian Mahoney, "Welsh Assembly Elections 2011," *The Voice of Freedom* no. 115 (2010): 5.
228. "Successes on the Night," *British Nationalist: Member's Bulletin* (May 2011): unpaginated 3.
229. Alistair Lewis, interviewed by Ryan Shaffer, audio recording, 18 September 2011. (Abbreviated as "Interview with Lewis 2.")
230. "British National Party Activists Give Their Views," *The Voice of Freedom* no. 123 (n.d., circa 2011): 7.
231. Ibid.
232. Richard Edmonds, interviewed by Ryan Shaffer, audio recording, 15 September 2011; Interview with Brons.
233. John Bean, correspondence with Ryan Shaffer, 4 July 2011.
234. John Bean, *The Many Shades of Black: Inside Britain's Far-Right* 2nd ed. (Burlington: Ostara Publications, 2011), v.
235. "BNPIdeas Links to Radio Red, White and Blue," StormFront.com, 23 July 2011; available online at https://www.stormfront.org/forum/t818691/; accessed 1 July 2016.
236. "Party Leadership Election Result: Nick Griffin re-elected Party Chairman," British National Party, 2011; available online at http://www.bnp.org.uk/news/party-leadership-election-result-nick-griffin-re-elected-party-chairman; accessed 1 July 2016.
237. Interview with Edmonds.
238. Interview with Brons.
239. "Leadership Election Report on the Way," *The Voice of Freedom* no. 124 (n.d., circa 2011): 2.
240. "The Members Have Spoken," *British Nationalist: Member's Bulletin* (August 2011): unpaginated 4.

241. Adam Gabbatt and Matthew Taylor, "BNP official Mark Collett questioned over alleged threat to kill Nick Griffin," *The Guardian*, 4 April 2010; available online at http://www.theguardian.com/politics/2010/apr/04/bnp-mark-collett-nick-griffin; accessed 1 July 2016.
242. Interview with Butler.
243. "Police to take no further action over plot to kill head of BNP Nick Griffin," *Sunday Mercury*, 14 November 2010; available online at http://www.birminghammail.co.uk/news/local-news/police-to-take-no-further-action-250114; accessed 1 July 2016.
244. Ben Quinn, "English Democrats could become 'electorally credible' as BNP decline," *The Guardian*, 25 September 2011; available online at http://www.theguardian.com/politics/2011/sep/25/english-democrats-electorally-credible-bnp; accessed 1 July 2016.
245. Interview with Butler.
246. "'Why I Joined the English Democrats!': Testimony from Members," *England Awake* no. 2 (n.d., circa 2012): 6.
247. "Great Publicity Over English Democrats' 2011 Annual Conference," *England Awake* no. 1 (2011): 5.
248. "'Not real nationalists at all.' We expose the English Democrats and their new allies," British National Party, 2011; available online at http://www.bnp.org.uk/resource/%E2%80%98not-real-nationalists-all%E2%80%99-we-expose-english-democrats-and-their-new-allies; accessed 1 July 2016.
249. Nick Griffin, "The Need for An English Parliament," *Identity* no. 73 (December 2006): 4.
250. Interview with McBride. The group briefly used the name National People's Party.
251. Paul Golding, "Welcome to Britain First," *Sovereignty* no. 1 (June 2011): 2.
252. Paul Golding, "Campaign: Recognition for the British Victims of Racism," *Sovereignty* no. 3 (Spring 2012): 9.
253. Matt Tait, *Tragedy and Hope: Lessons from the Plight of British Nationalism* (Marietta: American Renaissance, 2015) (DVD Recording).
254. Ibid.
255. "About Us," Western Spring, 2015; available online at http://www.westernspring.co.uk/test-page/; accessed 1 July 2016.
256. "Statement of Accounts Year Ended 31st December 2011." This document was filed with the Electoral Commission. Search "British National Party" at Electoral Commission, 2016; available online at https://pefonline.electoralcommission.org.uk/Search/SOASearch.aspx; accessed 1 July 2016.

257. "Statement of Accounts Year Ended 31st December 2009." This document was filed with the Electoral Commission. Search "British National Party" at Electoral Commission, 2016; available online at https://pefonline.electoralcommission.org.uk/Search/SOASearch.aspx; accessed 1 July 2016.
258. "BNP: The Fraud Exposed," *Panorama*, 2011; available online at http://www.bbc.co.uk/programmes/b0161hqc; accessed 1 July 2016.
259. See BNP's response: "Open Letter from Simon Darby to the BBC concerning David Hannam," British National Party, 5 October 2011; available online at http://www.bnp.org.uk/news/national/open-letter-simon-darby-bbc-concerning-david-hannam; accessed 1 July 2016.
260. "Panorama—The Frauds Exposed," British National Party, 11 October 2011; available online at http://www.bnp.org.uk/news/national/panorama-%E2%80%93-frauds-exposed; accessed 1 July 2016.
261. "Annual Conference 2011," *The Voice of Freedom* no. 126 (2011): 4.
262. Ibid.
263. *Annual Conference 2011: Time for Action* (Burnley: BNPTV, 2011) (Disc 2) (DVD Recording).
264. Ibid.
265. Ibid.
266. "Nick Griffin in Russia," *The Voice of Freedom* no. 126 (2011): 5. This issue is incorrectly numbered as it is different from the previous 126th issue. See also: Anton Shekhovtsov, "Far-Right Election Observation Monitors in the Service of the Kremlin's Foreign Policy," *Eurasianism and the European Far Right: Reshaping the Europe–Russia Relationship* ed. Marlene Laruelle (Lanham, Maryland: Lexington Books, 2015), 223–239.
267. "Russian Elections 'Much Fairer than Britain's'—Initial Verdict from Nick Griffin," British National Party, 9 December 2011; available online at http://www.bnp.org.uk/news/national/russian-elections-%E2%80%9Cmuch-fairer-britain%E2%80%99s%E2%80%9D-%E2%80%93-initial-verdict-nick-griffin; accessed 1 July 2016.
268. Michael Schwirtz and David Herszenhorn, "Voters Watch Polls in Russia, and Fraud Is What They See," *New York Times*, 5 December 2011; available online at http://www.nytimes.com/2011/12/06/world/europe/russian-parliamentary-elections-criticized-by-west.html; accessed 1 July 2016; "Russian Democracy: Griffin Style," *Hope Not Hate*, 7 December 2011; available online at http://hopenothate.org.uk/blog/insider/russian-democracy-griffin-style-1506; accessed 1 July 2016.
269. "Elections—A Tale of Two Nations," *The Voice of Freedom* no. 126 (2011): 5.

270. "Alliance of European National Movements Expands to 9 Parties," British National Party, 2012; available online at https://www.bnp.org.uk/news/alliance-european-national-movements-expands-9-parties; accessed 1 July 2016.
271. *Tyranny in Europe Is Nothing New* (Matzenheim: Alliance of European National Movements, 2011).
272. "Alliance of European National Movements Expands to 9 Parties," British National Party, 2012; available online at https://www.bnp.org.uk/news/alliance-european-national-movements-expands-9-parties; accessed 1 July 2016.
273. "Political Declaration," Alliance of European National Movements, 2015; available online at http://aemn.info/political-declaration/; accessed 1 July 2016.
274. "Alliance of European Nationalist Movements Makes Euro Funding Breakthrough," *The Voice of Freedom* no. 127 (2012): 4.
275. "North East Plans for 2012," *The Voice of Freedom* no. 126 (2011): 10.
276. "Campaigning for Local Democracy in East London," *The Voice of Freedom* no. 126 (2011): 10.
277. "Shocking Reality of Race-Hate," *The Voice of Freedom* no. 127 (2012): 1.
278. "Organiser's Conference Report 2012," *The Voice of Freedom* no. 127 (2012): 6, 7.
279. *The Voice of the Londoner* (Enfield: British National Party, n.d., circa 2012).
280. "BNP fails to defend council seats," BBC, 5 May 2012; available online at http://www.bbc.com/news/uk-politics-17959612; accessed 1 July 2016.
281. "Elections 2012—An In Depth Analysis," *The Voice of Freedom* no. 128 (2012): 8.
282. "EDL Leadership—Zionist Front," *The Voice of Freedom* no. 129 (2012): 3.
283. "Allies in the Battle for the Free Nations of Europe," *The Voice of Freedom* no. 129 (2012): 4.
284. "What do we think of the EDL?," British National Party, 1 June 2013; available online at http://www.bnp.org.uk/news/national/what-do-we-think-edl; accessed 1 July 2016.
285. Nick Griffin, "What Lies Behind the English Defence League?," British National Party, 29 May 2013; available online at http://www.bnp.org.uk/sites/default/files/what_lies_behind_the_english_defence_league.r2.pdf; accessed 1 July 2016.
286. "Hundreds Attend Biggest BNP Demo in Years," *The Voice of Freedom* no. 130 (2012): 12.

287. "Tough Talking at the BNP Organisers' Conference," *The Voice of Freedom* no. 53 (September 2004): 12.
288. "BNP Annual Conference 2012," *The Voice of Freedom* no. 132 (2012): 4.
289. *Annual Conference 2012: Back to Winning* (Burnley: BNPTV, 2012) (Disc 2) (DVD Recording).
290. Ibid.
291. Ibid.
292. "New Precedent Set: 2012 Accounts Submitted in Advance," *British Nationalist: Member's Bulletin* (July 2012): unpaginated 2.
293. "Building the New Range," *The Voice of Freedom* no. 132 (2012): 3.
294. "Broken Britain," British National Party, 2013; available online at http://www.bnp.org.uk/resources/leaflet/broken-britain-a5; accessed 1 July 2016.
295. "Elections That Put Britain's to Shame," *The Voice of Freedom* no. 132 (2012): 10.
296. Andrew Brons, "Statement from Andrew Brons MEP," AndrewBrons.eu, 16 October 2012; available online at http://andrewbrons.eu/index.php?option=com_k2&view=item&id=628:statement-from-andrew-brons-mep; accessed 1 July 2016.
297. Interview with Brons.
298. *Policy Statement* (Newcastle upon Tyne: British Democratic Party, 2013): unpaginated 1. This document is the first version and is dated January 2013.
299. "Constitution of the British Democratic Party," British Democratic Party, February 2013; available online at http://britishdemocraticparty.org/constitution/; accessed 1 July 2016.
300. Andrew Brons, "The National Launch of the British Democratic Party," British Democratic Party, 2013; available online at http://britishdemocraticparty.org/the-national-launch-of-the-british-democratic-party/; accessed 1 July 2016. Electoral Commission records show the name was registered in 2011 with the party leader as Kevin Scott, nominating officer as Paul Newman and treasurer as Adrian Davies. Search "British Democratic Party" at Electoral Commission, 2011; available online at https://pefonline.electoralcommission.org.uk/Search/SOASearch.aspx; accessed 1 July 2016.
301. James Lewthwaite, "Letter From Bradford," *The Voice of Freedom* no. 55 (November 2004): 10.
302. *Vote UKIP for More and More Immigration* (Newcastle upon Tyne: British Democratic Party, n.d., circa 2014).
303. Nick Griffin, "View from the Top," *The Voice of Freedom* no. 133 (2013): 2.
304. Ibid.

305. Charlie Wythe, "Editor's Letter," *British Nationalist: Member's Bulletin* (February 2013): unpaginated 5.
306. "UKIP v BNP," *The Voice of Freedom* no. 135 (2013): 7.
307. "Saving Our Seals," *The Voice of Freedom* no. 133 (2013): 3; "Cllr Perry Talks to A Level Student," *The Voice of Freedom* no. 133 (2013): 8; "60s Interview," *The Voice of Freedom* no. 133 (2013): 8; "BNP Councillors Working for You," *The Voice of Freedom* no. 135 (2013): 11.
308. "BNP Officials' Conference 2013," *The Voice of Freedom* no. 134 (2013): 4.
309. Conal Urquhart, "BNP calls on members to breed more after elections disaster," *The Guardian*, 4 May 2013; available online at http://www.theguardian.com/politics/2013/may/04/bnp-members-breed-elections; accessed 1 July 2016.
310. Nick Griffin, "View from the Top," *The Voice of Freedom* no. 137 (2013): 2.
311. "BNP Demand Action," *The Voice of Freedom* no. 137 (2013): 3; "Real Justice for Lee Rigby," *British Nationalist: Member's Bulletin* (November 2013): unpaginated 1.
312. "BNP Online Activists Spread the Word," *British Nationalist: Member's Bulletin* (June 2013): unpaginated 3.
313. "Statement of Accounts Year Ended 31st December 2013." This document was filed with the Electoral Commission. Search "British National Party" at Electoral Commission, 2013; available online at https://pefonline.electoralcommission.org.uk/Search/SOASearch.aspx; accessed 1 July 2016.
314. Interview with Griffin.
315. "BNPeace Envoy," *British Nationalist: Member's Bulletin* (September 2013): unpaginated 1, 3.
316. Interview with Griffin; "Eye-witness Syria: Nick Griffin sees first-hand the brutal reality of the Islamist war on Syria," British National Party, 12 June 2013; available online at http://www.bnp.org.uk/news/national/eye-witness-syria-nick-griffin-sees-first-hand-brutal-reality-islamist-war-syria; accessed 1 July 2016; "Nick Griffin Visits Syria," YouTube, 22 June 2013; available online at https://www.youtube.com/watch?v=xtPpL7c8LTo; accessed 1 July 2016; Ian Black, "BNP leader Nick Griffin visits Syria," *The Guardian*, 11 June 2013; available online at http://www.theguardian.com/politics/2013/jun/11/bnp-nick-griffin-syria-assad; accessed 1 July 2016.
317. Interview with Griffin.
318. Ibid.
319. "The Road to Damascus," *The Voice of Freedom* no. 137 (2013): 5.

320. Interview with Griffin; "How the BNP Stopped the War on Syria," *The Voice of Freedom* no. 138 (2013): 5.
321. Brian Wheeler, "BNP's Nick Griffin claims he 'influenced' Syria vote," BBC, 4 September 2013; available online at http://www.bbc.com/news/uk-politics-23942041; accessed 1 July 2016.
322. "European Parliament—Syria," British National Party, 11 September 2013; available online at http://www.bnp.org.uk/news/national/european-parliament-syria; accessed 1 July 2016.
323. "BNP's Nick Griffin declared bankrupt," BBC, 3 January 2014; available online at http://www.bbc.com/news/uk-england-25590155; accessed 1 July 2016; "With You in Hard Times," *British Nationalist: Member's Bulletin* (January 2014): unpaginated 5.
324. "Out of the EU," British National Party, 2014; available online at http://www.bnp.org.uk/sites/default/files/bnp_eu-manifesto-2014_0.pdf; accessed 1 July 2016.
325. Andrew Brons, "Letters from Readers," *Heritage and Destiny* no. 61 (July/August 2014): 20.
326. Andrew Brons, *A Nationalist Perspective* (n.p.: 2014). This book, a paperback, reported he was ranked 101st out of 766 in number of speeches and 89th for plenary attendance. There are two versions of this publication compiled by Martin and Tina Wingfield, a paperback and a more comprehensive and indexed hardcover.
327. "Nick Griffin speaks to European Nationalist Youth Congress in Germany," British National Party, 25 March 2014; available online at http://www.bnp.org.uk/news/national/nick-griffin-speaks-european-nationalist-youth-congress-germany; accessed 1 July 2016.
328. "Training the Leaders of Tomorrow," *British Nationalist: Member's Bulletin* (October 2013): unpaginated 2.
329. "Forza Nuova e Alba Dorata in convegno a Roma: protesta contro il "raduno nazifascista'," Roma Today, 28 February 2014; available online at http://www.romatoday.it/cronaca/forza-nuova-alba-dorata-roma-1-marzo-2014.html; accessed 1 July 2016.
330. "Europe Rises Again," YouTube, 5 March 2014; available online at https://www.youtube.com/watch?v=kA4YHuZvaWc; accessed 1 July 2016.
331. Helen Pidd, "Nick Griffin concedes European parliament seat as BNP votes fall away," *The Guardian*, 25 May 2014; available online at http://www.theguardian.com/politics/2014/may/25/nick-griffin-concedes-mep-seat-european-elections; accessed 1 July 2016.
332. Interview with Griffin.
333. Ibid.

334. "BNP leadership—A personal statement by Nick Griffin," British National Party, 21 July 2014; available online at http://www.bnp.org.uk/news/national/bnp-leadership-%E2%80%93-personal-statement-nick-griffin; accessed 1 July 2016.
335. "BNP activist Adam Walker loses Michael Gove teaching ban challenge," BBC, 14 February 2014; available online at http://www.bbc.com/news/uk-england-tees-26191863; accessed 1 July 2016.
336. Interview with Griffin.
337. "Leave A Worthy Legacy," *British Nationalist: Member's Bulletin* (April 2013): 4.
338. Nick Griffin, *British National Party Problems For the New Leader, Problems For Us All and the Simple Solutions* (n.p.: NJG Report to Executive Council, 2014); available online at https://bnptruth.files.wordpress.com/2014/10/ec-report-final-draft.pdf; accessed 1 July 2016.
339. "Nick Griffin expelled from BNP membership," British National Party, 1 October 2014; available online at http://www.bnp.org.uk/news/national/nick-griffin-expelled-bnp-membership; accessed 1 July 2016.
340. "Where There's A Will There's A Way!," BNPTruth, 7 October 2014; available online at https://bnptruth.wordpress.com/2014/10/07/where-theres-a-will-theres-a-way/; accessed 1 July 2016.
341. Adam Taylor, "Life in Assad's Syria is great, tweets far-right British politician," *Washington Post*, 2 December 2014; available online at http://www.washingtonpost.com/blogs/worldviews/wp/2014/12/02/life-in-assads-syria-is-great-tweets-far-right-british-politician/; accessed 1 July 2016.
342. "Party Statutes," Alliance for Peace and Freedom, 2015; available online at https://alliancepeacefreedom.wordpress.com/party-statutes/; accessed 1 July 2016.
343. Courtney Weaver, "To Russia with love, from Europe's far-right fringe," FT.com, 22 March 2015; available online at http://www.ft.com/cms/s/0/556ed172-d0b9-11e4-982a-00144feab7de.html, accessed 1 July 2016.
344. "Nick Griffin speaks in St Petersburg," YouTube, 12 April 2015; available online at https://www.youtube.com/watch?v=zBgMWjtJJ4Q; accessed 1 July 2016.
345. Florian Stein, "European Nationalists in Top-Level Talks in Syria," Alliance for Peace and Freedom, 7 June 2015; available online at http://alliance-for-peace-and-freedom.com/2015/06/european-nationalists-in-top-level-talks-in-syria/; accessed 1 July 2016.
346. Ibid.; see also the video of the men talking about the visit: "European Nationalists in Top-Level Talks in Syria," Alliance for Peace and

Freedom, 7 July 2015; available online at https://www.youtube.com/watch?v=GhWKYSD_rsY; accessed 1 July 2016.

347. "MEPs Condemn €600,000 EU Grant for Far-right Bloc," BBC, 5 May 2016; available online at http://www.bbc.com/news/world-europe-36213156; accessed 1 July 2016; "Parliament launches investigation into compliance by Alliance for Peace and Freedom with EU founding principles," European Parliament, 12 May 2016; available online at http://www.europarl.europa.eu/news/en/news-room/20160512IPR27173/EP-to-check-Alliance-for-Peace-and-Freedom%E2%80%99s-compliance-with-EU-basic-principles; accessed 1 July 2016; "Help us to keep the APF-Headquarter," Alliance for Peace and Freedom, 18 March 2017; available online at https://apfeurope.com/apf-headquarter/; accessed 18 March 2017.

348. Nick Griffin, "Belarus: Report on APF Delegation to a Stronghold of Social Nationalism," Alliance for Peace and Freedom, 12 April 2016; available online at https://alliance-for-peace-and-freedom.com/2016/04/belarus-report-on-apf-delegation-to-a-stronghold-of-social-nationalism/; accessed 1 July 2016.

349. Stefan Jacobsson, "Grand opening of the Georgios and Manos Centre in Brussels," Alliance for Peace and Freedom, 25 April 2016; available online at http://apfeurope.com/2016/04/grand-opening-of-the-georgios-and-manos-centre-in-brussels/; accessed 1 July 2016.

350. Stefan Jacobsson, "APF-delegation in Syria," Alliance for Peace and Freedom, 25 April 2016; available online at https://apfeurope.com/2016/04/apf-delegation-in-syria/; accessed 1 May 2016; Nick Griffin, "Nick Griffin visits Serbia—more APF expansion on the way," Alliance for Peace and Freedom, 29 April 2016; available online at https://apfeurope.com/2016/04/1944/; accessed 1 May 2016. The Alliance for Peace and Freedom also hosted a meeting in the European Parliament under the slogan "Syria: tolerance or terrorism?" Stefan Jacobsson, "International Congress in the European Parliament: Syria: tolerance or terrorism?," Alliance for Peace and Freedom, 3 May 2016; available online at https://apfeurope.com/2016/05/international-congress-in-the-european-parliament-syria-tolerance-or-terrorism/; accessed 1 July 2016.

351. Nick Griffin, "Nick Griffin's visit to Prague Strengthens APF Links with Czech Partners," Alliance for Peace and Freedom, 3 June 2016; available online at https://apfeurope.com/2016/06/nick-griffins-visit-to-prague-strengthens-apf-links-with-czech-partners/; accessed 1 July 2016.

352. *Winds of Change: Notes for the Reconquista* (Belgium: Alliance for Peace and Freedom, 2016). Holland's biography states he currently lives in Ireland and "is heavily involved in a campaign to help families in debt."

353. "British National Party Regional Treasury Dept." This document was filed with the Electoral Commission. Search "British National Party" at Electoral Commission, 23 April 2015; available online at https://pefonline.electoralcommission.org.uk/Search/SOASearch.aspx; accessed 1 July 2016.
354. "Security Our British Future: British National Party Parliamentary Elections Manifesto 2015," British National Party, 2015; available online at http://www.bnp.org.uk/sites/default/files/bnp_manifesto-2015.pdf; accessed 1 July 2016.
355. "I will hold nose & vote Ukip because it will help break up the Westminster system. & hold Cameron's feet to referendum fire," NickGriffinBU, 29 November 2014; available online at https://twitter.com/NickGriffinBU/status/746414525117665280; accessed 1 July 2016.
356. "Election 2015," BBC, 2015; available online at http://www.bbc.com/news/election/2015/results; accessed 1 July 2016.
357. Ibid.
358. Adam Walker, "Official BNP 2015 Election Announcement," British National Party, 8 May 2015; available online at http://www.bnp.org.uk/news/national/official-bnp-2015-election-announcement; accessed 1 July 2016.
359. Christopher Hooton, "BNP Sees 99.7% Drop in Votes in 2015 General Election, Party All But Wiped Out," *The Independent*, 8 May 2015; available online at http://www.independent.co.uk/news/uk/politics/bnp-sees-997-drop-in-votes-party-all-but-wiped-out-10235624.html; accessed 1 July 2016.
360. Lee Marlow, "Parish and Ex-Borough Councillor Cathy Duffy: 'Why the BNP will be back in 2020'," *Leicester Mercury*, 27 May 2015; available online at http://www.leicestermercury.co.uk/8203-8203-Parish-ex-borough-councillor-Cathy/story-26580617-detail/story.html; accessed 1 July 2016.
361. "Candidates Announced for 2015 BNP Leadership Election," British National Party, 8 July 2015; available online at http://www.bnp.org.uk/news/national/candidates-announced-2015-bnp-leadership-election; accessed 1 July 2016; "BNP Leadership Election Results Are In," British National Party, 27 July 2015; available online at http://bnp.org.uk/news/national/bnp-leadership-election-results-are; accessed 1 July 2016.
362. Charlie Wythe, "Fighting for Our Britain," *Identity* no. 1 (2015): 2.
363. "Strangers in Our Homeland," *Identity* no. 2 (2015): 4.

364. "Spotless 2014/15 Accounts," *British Nationalist: Member's Bulletin* (November 2015): unpaginated 2.
365. *Cameron's Christmas* (Wigton: Heritage Content Management Limited, 2015).
366. "Defusing the Islamist Timebomb," *Identity* no. 3 (2016): 3. The cover featured an image of white British children above three women wearing burqas with the headline: "Clash of Cultures."
367. "Stop Immigration Now," British National Party, 2016; available online at http://www.bnp.org.uk/sites/default/files/bnp_london_manifesto_2016.pdf; accessed 1 July 2016.
368. "UK Election Results Tracker 2016," *The Guardian*, 6 May 2016; available online at http://www.theguardian.com/politics/ng-interactive/2016/may/05/uk-election-results-tracker-2016; accessed 1 July 2016.
369. "Election Results 2016," *Heritage and Destiny*, 5 May 2016; available online at http://efp.org.uk/election-results-2016/; accessed 1 July 2016; Katie Feehan, "Third BNP Member Elected to Heybridge Parish Council," *Essex Chronicle*, 12 May 2016; available online at http://www.essexchronicle.co.uk/BNP-member-elected-Heybridge-parish-Council/story-29252323-detail/story.html; accessed 1 July 2016.
370. For example: Martin Bell, "A Vote to Remain Is a Vote to Destroy Western Europe," British National Party, 2 June 2016; available online at http://www.bnp.org.uk/news/national/vote-remain-vote-destroy-western-europe; accessed 1 July 2016.
371. "UK Votes to LEAVE the EU—Initial Reaction," British National Party, 24 June 2016; available online at http://www.bnp.org.uk/news/national/uk-votes-leave-eu-initial-reaction; accessed 1 July 2016.
372. "Just woke up, having dreamt that 40 years of #Brussels rule had ended. Ridiculous, of course, but what a vision. 'Free! Free at last!'," NickGriffinBU, 24 June 2016; available online at https://twitter.com/NickGriffinBU/status/746348643532312576; accessed 1 July 2016; "Just had chap stop me in street & apologise profusely for calling me racist in a bank 10 years ago! 'You were right all along'. Shook hands," NickGriffinBU, 24 June 2016; available online at https://twitter.com/NickGriffinBU/status/746414525117665280; accessed 1 July 2016.
373. "Nazi regalia discovered at house of Jo Cox killing suspect," *The Guardian*, 17 June 2016; available online at https://www.theguardian.com/uk-news/2016/jun/17/jo-cox-suspect-thomas-mair-bought-gun-manuals-from-us-neo-nazis-group-claims; accessed 1 July 2016. See also: Mark Cotterill, "Will the real Thomas Mair please stand up?,"

Heritage and Destiny, 24 June 2016; available online at http://efp.org.uk/will-the-real-thomas-mair-please-stand-up/; accessed 1 July 2016;

374. "BNP Chairman arrested in Tory police scandal," British National Party, 14 August 2016; available online at https://www.bnp.org.uk/news/national/breaking-%E2%80%93-bnp-chairman-arrested-tory-police-scandal; accessed 1 October 2016.

CHAPTER 8

Conclusion

After the Second World War British fascism changed drastically, becoming transnational as it spread from London around the world. Under the National Front (NF) and British National Party (BNP), fascism never came close to any national breakthrough in Great Britain. Yet the radicals successfully spread their racism and anti-democratic politics to an international audience. The extremists found they had more in common with radicals in other countries than with mainstream society in their own nation. As a result, British fascism became increasingly transnational with an outlook beyond the nation, even as the radicals spoke about nationalism and patriotism. This stemmed from a search for new ideas and wider support. As Nick Griffin explained, "we were happy to take ideas from anywhere" to formulate ideology for a broader audience.[1] Reflected in music, such as songs about "white power for Britain," which were performed in countries and played on stereos throughout the world, British nationalistic rhetoric was not confined to Britain. Music helped pave the way for communication and closer collaboration between extremists in other countries. Specific individuals facilitated travel and promoted radical leaders in foreign countries, which was sometimes done for personal friendship or to demonstrate connections outside their own domestic marginality.

Post-war British fascism's image has come full circle. As Nigel Copsey has noted, under Griffin "the British National Party has undergone a transformation in both image and tactics," as the party has sought to divorce itself from the image of "skinhead thugs" and the use of

R. Shaffer, *Music, Youth and International Links in Post-War British Fascism*, Palgrave Studies in the History of Subcultures and Popular Music, DOI 10.1007/978-3-319-59668-6_8

"quasi-respectable language."[2] The irony in this was that Griffin was involved with the development of neo-Nazi skinhead images and culture as a member and later leader of the NF. Indeed, Griffin attended the first Rock Against Communism concert, organized White Noise festivals on his family's property and used the revenue from White Noise Records to further the NF's politics. The very subculture he would later chastise and ban members for adopting in the 2000s was a significant aspect of the organization he once led during the 1980s. This is also true of the wider fascist movement, as those who had once aligned themselves with radical, violent and hate-filled music later avoided association with those ideas and images in front of voters. There is a further contradiction as well, with self-described "nationalists" increasingly focusing on movements and individuals beyond their borders. For a variety of reasons, including social and financial, fascists have developed close working partnerships with foreigners, crossing borders together in order to condemn immigration. Yet their ideology and rhetoric remains rooted in the nation and opposition to changes in local communities.

As the image and ideology has shifted, the fascist movement in Britain has grown old. There are now fewer young white males with shaven heads in the audience at fascist gatherings. The main demographic consists of white middle-aged men who reflect on times past, when the ethnic composition of Britain was different. Robert Ford and Matthew Goodwin's data revealed that the BNP's base during its electorally successful years was mostly older, working-class men who lived in the North and Midlands regions where industry was declining.[3] This is not surprising given the BNP's ethno-nationalist view of the world, which is out of step with contemporary Britain, where multiculturalism is a fact of life and issues such as repatriation are not only dated but widely regarded as unfeasible. Not only did their political ideas become old over time, but fascist youth culture, such as neo-Nazi skinhead records from the 1980s, increasingly found itself out of step with contemporary music delivered through online platforms. For contemporary British fascism to attract youth, the fascists would have to adopt youthful ways and attach itself to current youth culture.

British fascism branched out in several directions, shaped by various NF initiatives in the 1980s, and this provoked changes in how authorities follow potential threats. In terms of neo-Nazi culture, Rock Against Communism and White Noise music found an international audience, which was further supported and developed as a transnational network under Blood & Honour. The international nature of violent skinhead crime required law enforcement to closely track individuals and websites that attempted to evade European authorities. Newly released Federal Bureau of Investigation (FBI) documents revealed international cooperation to monitor Blood & Honour activities. In May 2006, a man was targeted for an attack on Blood & Honour Poland and Polish Redwatch websites, which published a list of personal information about people who should be "eliminated from the earth."[4] He was stabbed outside his home in Poland by two attackers who punctured a lung and left an eight-inch wound. The suspects were captured and an international investigation ensued. Later that month, "the US Embassy received a formal Diplomatic Note from the Polish Government asking for help in shutting the websites down," which caused American authorities to closely examine Blood & Honour's activities as well.[5] By early June, several Polish men involved in the website had been arrested for inciting hatred, and American law enforcement helped locate the individuals connected to the organization and the websites.[6] In July, the Associated Press reported that American authorities had helped the Polish government close down the website and Polish police had arrested the webmaster in Poland.[7] This investigation is not the only example of foreign cooperation: documents point to other investigations and make numerous references to Blood & Honour/Combat 18's involvement in "international terrorism matters."

International skinhead-to-skinhead contact has not been the only development in British fascism to come out of the NF's activities in the 1980s. Parts of the Muslim world have turned to British radicals for political commentary and activism. In addition to Nick Griffin's visits to Syria and Libya as well as Derek Holland's and Colin Todd's travels to Iraq and the West Bank, other British radicals have established contacts in the Middle East. Peter Rushton, who spent more than a decade in the British National Party and edits *Heritage and Destiny*, accepted an invitation to travel to Tehran, Iran for a conference hosted by Iranian President Mahmoud Ahmadinejad.[8] Since then Rushton has been a guest on Press TV, which is an Iranian state-owned news service, commenting on Western foreign policy.[9] Indeed, Rushton has not been the only one to make contacts in Iran; for example, former Union Movement member and Muslim convert Robert Edwards was interviewed by Press TV and took part in Iran's International Holocaust Cartoon Competition.[10]

As Nick Griffin's leadership of the BNP brought electoral gains and internal party criticism, some extremists turned to memories of John Tyndall for inspiration and an alternative to the direction in which Griffin was taking the movement. After Tyndall's 2005 death, there was a revival of interest in his leadership and a re-imagining of his role in post-war radical politics. The first annual John Tyndall Memorial Meeting was hosted in Milton Keynes, and between 2010 and 2015 Mark Cotterill organized the event in Preston.[11] The yearly gathering is interesting because it brings people together to remember Tyndall's BNP leadership in a positive light, despite the party not having been nearly as electorally successful as it was under Griffin. Moreover, the event has proved increasingly important as it unites figures extending from skinheads to British Democratic Party leaders under one roof to discuss memories of Tyndall as well as the current state of radical politics. For example, in 2014 Andrew Brons, Richard Edmonds, Simon Sheppard and Benny Bullman, vocalist of Whitelaw, spoke to a crowd of about a hundred on topics ranging from immigration to Blood & Honour's history.[12] The tenth anniversary meeting in 2015 attracted even more people, with over one hundred and thirty attendees including visitors from Canada, Ireland, Italy and the United States, with speeches that were professionally recorded for a DVD release.[13]

While skinhead music was a fringe genre at its peak, in recent years interest in the music as well as its importance for fascism have diminished. According to the current operator of NS88 Videos and ISD Records, who lives in the United States, 99% of his customers are Europeans and about 80% of them are in Germany—despite efforts by customs officials to confiscate DVDs and CDs at the borders.[14] When asked about the total number of CDs sold by ISD Records in its history, he estimated about thirty releases with about 1500 copies of each pressed, which totals 45,000 copies of albums distributed.[15] He noted that as music trends have changed and Internet downloading has developed, his best-selling items are no longer music but Nazi propaganda films that are illegal to possess in several European countries.[16] In contrast, Pure Impact, a skinhead record label founded by Peter Swillen in 1996, closed down in 2014 due to declining interest and Swillen partly blamed the Internet for diminishing the culture, writing that "any clown can claim" to be a "skinhead, buy all the gear online and then pretend."[17]

Despite the fleeting role of rock music in fascism, the enduring legacy of the NF is its mark on the transformation of fascism in Britain. Fascism failed at the ballot box, but in terms of music and then international contact, it found new avenues and audiences through youth culture and the desire among like-minded radicals to cooperate. In many cases, extremists found it easier to gain support from similar groups in other countries rather than to change domestic minds. Though this strategy did not usher the NF or the BNP into power, it kept the groups going during periods of declining interest and dwindling election returns. In an increasingly global age, the extremists will no doubt continue to foster ties across borders. Indeed, continental extremists have done this successfully. Most notably, the Front National of France has close ties to Russia, which has provided the French party with financial loans while the Russian government received the party's vocal support after being marginalized by the European Union.[18]

Following his expulsion from the BNP, Griffin moved closer to continental extremists and traveled to Russia, praising the country's aggressive moves. Griffin's actions can be viewed cynically as a way to grab for any support he can get. While no doubt Griffin was seeking backing from new sources, his actions in the international arena follow decades of moving closer to high-profile actors in foreign movements. Extremists can boost morale, obtain financial help and get political ideas from international connections. Griffin was not alone in pursuing this path. British fascists, whether skinheads or campaign-oriented parties, regularly kept in contact with their fellow-travelers in other countries. First the NF and then the British National Party found a ready-made support group in fringe foreign populations. Even when radicals grow more marginalized in their own countries, they can and do find support and encouragement from people in other countries. Technology by way of blogging, social networking and video chatting has only made such links easier and will further transform how people see themselves and consequently alter their political approaches.

In the future British fascism is likely to maintain a strong transnational orientation despite its literature and campaigns having a narrowly nationalist focus. The Brexit vote will not change this or the fascists' efforts to build international alliances, but it will make it slightly more difficult for the fascists to fund staff and campaigns, and to network with Euroskeptic parties active in the European Parliament. Without European Union membership and the European elections, it will be harder to mobilize

British supporters for campaigns beyond local or national elections. Moreover, extremist parties have reaped benefits from the European Parliament, including salaries for political staff and financial support to print literature. Yet the fascists will continue to provoke ethno-nationalist sentiments in local elections as they use local ties and issues that more effectively resonate in smaller elections.

One of the differences between British fascists and other European fascists is their direct links with skinheads. It was the British fascists that fostered and developed the neo-Nazi skinhead scene, which stained the NF and BNP in the eyes of the British public. Though the British National Party worked to distance itself from the skinhead subculture, connections remained. Any effort to gain actual political legitimacy would require not just changing their image, but divorcing individuals, rhetoric, motivations and sympathies from crude forms of neo-Nazism, which proved difficult for the NF and BNP. The fascists' failure to embrace some of the benefits of modernity, along with their strong sympathies with foreign ideologies and foreigners completely outside the British mainstream, has made it difficult for them to recruit middle-class and wealthier supporters who could promote and fund the movement's growth.

While British fascism's history has been seen as a failure because no fascist party has succeeded in electing a single Member of Parliament, much less seized national power, it has left behind a powerful social and international legacy. Neo-Nazi skinhead music circulated around the world, introducing new forms of old ideas to youth in direct ways. It served as the soundtrack for some young men who committed murder and assault in the name of an ideology. Though this subculture no longer continues to play the large role it once did, post-war British fascism has left a mark on extremism throughout the world in ways that earlier British fascism under Oswald Mosley did not. Moreover, British fascism is nearly one hundred years old but has continually been resurrected during that time, and all the while opponents have predicted its downfall. While it appears unlikely that British fascism will pose a serious threat to the mainstream political parties, its stubborn existence continues to reflect the hopes and fears of a marginal portion of society that feels largely powerless in the face of change.

Notes

1. Nick Griffin, interviewed by Ryan Shaffer, audio recording, 8 October 2014.
2. Nigel Copsey, *Contemporary British Fascism: The British National Party and the Quest for Legitimacy* (Basingstoke: Palgrave Macmillan, 2008), 203, 204.
3. Robert Ford and Matthew J. Goodwin, "Angry White Men: Individual and Contextual Predictors of Support for the British National Party," *Political Studies* 58, no. 1 (February 2010): 2, 3.
4. "Blood & Honour," Federal Bureau of Investigation, Case no. 163C-WR-556, 14 June 2006, unpaginated 3. These documents were obtained from a Freedom of Information Request.
5. Ibid.
6. "Foreign Police Cooperation; Blood & Honour," Federal Bureau of Investigation, Case no. 163C-WR-556, 1 August 2006, 3–5.
7. "Polish police shut down neo-Nazi Web site, charge suspected administrator," Associated Press, 7 July 2006; available online at http://www.post-gazette.com/news/world/2006/07/07/Polish-police-shut-down-neo-Nazi-Web-site-charge-suspected-administrator/stories/200607070194; accessed 1 July 2016.
8. Peter Rushton, interviewed by Ryan Shaffer, audio recording, 16 October 2014.
9. For example, see: "US sanctions Iran over anti-Israel Stand," *Press TV*, 2015; available online at http://edition.presstv.ir/detail.fa/232655.html; accessed 1 July 2016; "No Peace in Yemen with Saleh in Power," *Press TV*, 2015; available online at http://edition.presstv.ir/detail.fa/182849.html; accessed 1 July 2016.
10. "Robert Edwards Interviews on Iran's Press TV," European Action, 2014; available online at http://www.europeanaction.com/id97.html; accessed 1 July 2016; "Book Review: Art of Controversy," European Action, 2014; available online at http://www.europeanaction.com/id81.html; accessed 1 July 2016.
11. "Far-Right Group to Hold Memorial Meeting in City," *Lancashire Evening Post*, 11 October 2014.
12. *John Tyndall Memorial Meeting 2014* (Preston: Heritage and Destiny, 2014) (DVD Recording).
13. "John Tyndall Memorial Meeting 2015," *Heritage and Destiny* no. 69 (November/December 2015): 18–19; *John Tyndall Memorial Meeting 10th Annual* (Preston: Heritage and Destiny, 2015) (DVD Recording). The video was filmed and edited by Tony Avery.

14. Anonymous 4 (identified as "Bart"), interviewed by Ryan Shaffer, audio recording, 7 April 2014. This person did not want his surname used.
15. Ibid. Some albums were pressed with 1000 copies and others had 2000 copies made.
16. Ibid.
17. Peter Swillen, correspondence with Ryan Shaffer, 5 December 2014.
18. Eleanor Beardsley and Corey Flintoff, "Europe's Far Right and Putin Get Cozy, with Benefits for Both," NPR, 26 December 2014; available online at http://www.npr.org/sections/parallels/2014/12/26/371670726/europes-far-right-and-putin-get-cozy-with-benefits-for-both; accessed 1 July 2016; David Chazan, "Russia 'Bought' Marine Le Pen's Support Over Crimea," *The Telegraph*, 4 April 2015; available online at http://www.telegraph.co.uk/news/worldnews/europe/france/11515835/Russia-bought-Marine-Le-Pens-support-over-Crimea.html; accessed 1 July 2016.

Erratum to: Youth Against Tradition, 1977–1983

Ryan Shaffer

Erratum to:
Chapter 3 in: R. Shaffer, Music, Youth and International Links in Post-War BritishFascism, https://doi.org/10.1007/978-3-319-59668-6_3

The original version of the book was inadvertently published with incorrect placement of footnote reference 145 in Chapter 3, which was corrected. The erratum chapter and the book have been updated with the change.

The updated online version of this chapter can be found at https://doi.org/10.1007/978-3-319-59668-6_3

R. Shaffer, *Music, Youth and International Links in Post-War British Fascism*, Palgrave Studies in the History of Subcultures and Popular Music, https://doi.org/10.1007/978-3-319-59668-6_9

Select Bibliography

Baker, David. "A.K. Chesterton, the Strasser Brothers, and the Politics of the National Front," *Patterns of Prejudice* 19, no. 3 (July 1985): 23–33.

———. *Ideology of Obsession: A.K. Chesterton and British Fascism* (New York: I.B. Tauris, 1996).

Balch, Robert W. "The Rise and Fall of Aryan Nations: A Resource Mobilization Perspective," *Journal of Political and Military Sociology* 34 (Summer 2006): 81–113.

Billig, Michael. *Fascists: A Social Psychological View of the National Front* (London: Academic Press, 1978).

Bowyer, Benjamin. "Local Context and Extreme Right Support in England: The British National Party in the 2002 and 2003 Local elections," *Electoral Studies* 27, no. 4 (December 2008): 611–620.

Brown, Timothy. "Subcultures, Pop Music and Politics: Skinheads and 'Nazi Rock' in England and Germany," *Journal of Social History* 38, no.1 (Fall 2004): 157–178.

Copsey, Nigel. *Anti-Fascism in Britain* (New York: Routledge, 2016).

———. "Changing Course or Changing Clothes?: Reflections on the Ideological Evolution of the British National Party 1999–2006," *Patterns of Prejudice* 41, no. 1 (February 2007): 61–82.

———. *Contemporary British Fascism: The British National Party and the Quest for Legitimacy* (Basingstoke: Palgrave Macmillan, 2008).

———. "Sustaining a Mortal Blow?: The British National Party and the 2010 General and Local Elections," *Patterns of Prejudice* 46, no. 1 (2012): 16–39.

Copsey, Nigel and Graham Macklin. *British National Party: Contemporary Perspectives* (New York: Routledge 2011).

R. Shaffer, *Music, Youth and International Links in Post-War British Fascism*, Palgrave Studies in the History of Subcultures and Popular Music, DOI 10.1007/978-3-319-59668-6

Cotter, John M. "Sounds of Hate: White Power Rock and Roll and the neo-Nazi Skinhead Subculture," *Terrorism and Political Violence* 11, no. 2 (Summer 1999): 111–140.

Dorril, Stephen. *Blackshirt: Sir Oswald Mosley and British Fascism* (New York: Penguin, 2007).

Eatwell, Roger. "Why are Fascism and Racism Reviving in Western Europe?," *The Political Quarterly* 65, no. 3 (July 1994): 313–325.

Eatwell, Roger and Matthew Goodwin. *The New Extremism in 21st Century Britain* (New York: Routledge, 2010).

Fielding, Nigel. *The National Front* (London: Routledge, 1981).

Ford, Robert. "Is Racial Prejudice Declining in Britain?," *The British Journal of Sociology* 59, no. 4 (December 2008): 609–636.

Ford, Robert and Matthew J. Goodwin. "Angry White Men: Individual and Contextual Predictors of Support for the British National Party," *Political Studies* 58, no. 1 (February 2010): 1–25.

———. *Revolt on the Right: Explaining Support for the Radical Right in Britain* (New York: Routledge, 2014).

Goodwin, Matthew J. "The Extreme Right in Britain: Still an 'Ugly Duckling' but for How Long?," *The Political Quarterly* 78, no. 2 (April–June 2007): 241–250.

———. *New British Fascism: Rise of the British National Party* (New York: Routledge, 2011).

Griffin, Roger. *Fascism* (Oxford: Oxford University Press, 1995).

———. *The Nature of Fascism* (New York: Routledge, 1993).

Hamm, Mark S. *American Skinheads: The Criminology and Control of Hate Crime* (Westport: Praeger, 1993).

Harrop, Martin, Judith England, and Christopher Husbands, "The Bases of National Front Support," *Political Studies* 28, no. 2 (1980): 271–283.

Husbands, Christopher. "The Decline of the National Front: The Elections of 3rd May 1979," *The Wiener Library Bulletin* 32, nos. 49/50 (1979): 60–66.

———. "Following the 'Continental Model'?: Implications of the Recent Electoral Performance of the British National Party," *Journal of Ethnic and Migration Studies* 20, no. 4 (1994): 563–579.

———. "The National Front Becalmed?," *The Wiener Library Bulletin* 30, nos. 43/44 (1977): 74–79.

———. *Racial Exclusionism and the City: The Urban Support of the National Front* (London: George Allen & Unwin, 1983).

———. "When the Bubble Burst: Transient and Persistent National Front Supporters, 1974–79," *British Journal of Political Science* 14, no. 2 (1984): 249–260.

Jackson, Paul and Gerry Gable. *Far-Right.com: Nationalist Extremism on the Internet* (Ilford: Searchlight, 2011).

Kaplan, Jeffrey and Leonard Weinberg. *The Emergence of a Euro-American Radical Right* (New Brunswick: Rutgers University Press, 1998).

Langer, Elinor. *A Hundred Little Hitlers: The Death of a Black Man, the Trial of a White Racist, and the Rise of the Neo-Nazi Movement in America* (New York: Metropolitan Books, 2003).

Linehan, Thomas P. *East London for Mosley: The British Union of Fascists in East London and South-West Essex* (London: Frank Cass, 1996).

Lowles, Nick. *Hope: The Story of the Campaign that Helped Defeat the BNP* (London: Hope Not Hate, 2014).

———. *White Riot: The Violent Story of Combat 18* (London: Milo Books, 2003).

———. *White Riot: The Violent Story of Combat 18* 2nd ed. (London: Milo Books, 2014).

Macklin, Graham. *Very Deeply Dyed in Black: Sir Oswald Mosley and the Resurrection of British Fascism After 1945* (New York: I.B.Tauris, 2007).

McLagan, Graeme and Nick Lowles. *Mr. Evil: The Secret Life of Racist Bomber and Killer David Copeland* (London: John Blake, 2000).

Pugh, Martin. *'Hurrah for the Blackshirts': Fascists and Fascism in Britain Between the Wars* (New York: Random House, 2005).

Renton, David. *When We Touched the Sky: The Anti-Nazi League 1977–1981* (London: New Clarion Press, 2006).

Renton, David and Nigel Copsey. *British Fascism, the Labour Movement and the State* (New York: Palgrave Macmillan, 2005).

Rhodes, James. "The Banal National Party: The Routine Nature of Legitimacy," *Patterns of Prejudice* 43, no. 2 (2009): 142–160.

———. "The Political Breakthrough of the BNP: The Case of Burnley," *British Politics* 4, no. 1 (April 2009): 22–46.

Shaffer, Ryan. "The Soundtrack of Neo-Fascism: Youth and Music in the National Front," *Patterns of Prejudice* 47, nos. 5/6 (2013): 458–482.

Skidelsky, Robert. *Oswald Mosley* (London: Papermac, 1981).

Sykes, Alan. *The Radical Right in Britain: Social Imperialism to the BNP* (Basingstoke: Palgrave Macmillan, 2005).

Taylor, Stan. *The National Front in English Politics* (London: Macmillan, 1982).

Thurlow, Richard. *Fascism in Britain: A History, 1918–1985* (New York: Basil Blackwell, 1987).

Trilling, Daniel. *Bloody Nasty People: The Rise of Britain's Far Right* (London: Verso, 2012).

Walker, Martin. *The National Front* (London: Fontana, 1978).

Ware, Vron and Les Back. *Out of Whiteness: Color, Politics, and Culture* (Chicago: University of Chicago Press, 2001).

Whiteley, Paul. "The National Front Vote in the 1977 GLC Elections: An Aggregate Data Analysis," *British Journal of Political Science* 9, no. 3 (July 1979): 370–380.

Index

R. Shaffer, *Music, Youth and International Links in Post-War British Fascism*, Palgrave Studies in the History of Subcultures and Popular Music, DOI 10.1007/978-3-319-59668-6

CPI Antony Rowe
Chippenham, UK
2017-12-01 23:27